HIGHLAND
LIONESS

The Highland Ballad Series
Book 5

Kristin Gleeson

An Tig
Beag
Press

Published by An Tig Beag Press
Text Copyright 2021 © Kristin Gleeson
Cover design by JD Smith Designs

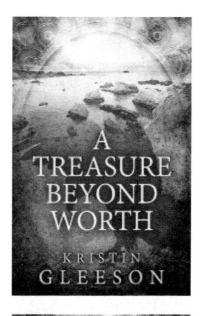

A TREASURE BEYOND WORTH

KRISTIN
GLEESON

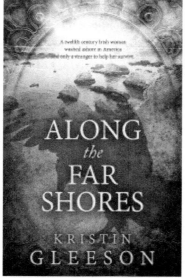

A twelfth century Irish woman
washed ashore in America
the only a stranger to help her survive.

ALONG
the
FAR
SHORES

KRISTIN
GLEESON

CHAPTER 1

*M*orag tugged at the wet neck of Iain's old leather jerkin that draped loose on her, and peered through the mist that hung heavy around her. She'd managed to adjust his old trews at least, so that she could move with ease in them. She peered again. Nothing. She shifted her highland pony cautiously for a better vantage, wincing at the sound of the hooves. Hopefully the mist would muffle the noise.

She called softly to her ghilly, "Rob."

A figure came up beside her. "Here, *cailín dhu*," he murmured.

"Are they there?"

"Aye. In the field below."

"Is there anyone attending?"

"At the far end."

"Davey and Calum, are they in place?"

"Aye."

She nodded. "How many can we manage in this mist? Five, six?"

"Less I'd say in this mist."

Morag gave a little snort. "Och, no. We'll go for six."

She heard the soft sigh. "Aye. Six it is." He moved away, swallowed by the mist.

She bit off a remark and wished yet again that it was Davey at her side and not Rob. Davey would have agreed with her sudden impulse to take six. Still, it was the point they were making and not the number. The Campbells would be furious that their prize cattle had once again been taken from under their very noses.

Morag started to urge her highland pony forward but a hand took her bridle. A familiar figure appeared out of the mist. Iain. She frowned and started to speak but he cut her off

"Signal them all to leave," he said in a low voice that left no room for anything but obedience.

She shook her head. She wouldn't obey him, no matter that he was her older brother and she had solemnly sworn to him three years ago she wouldn't go reiving again. That he hadn't caught her until now, she must count herself lucky and owe to the fact that he'd been living somewhere else for the most part, until events had allowed him and his wife to return to Glen Strae.

"I won't repeat myself," he said, tone razor edge sharp now.

Morag bit her lip, weighing the consequences against the beauty of this coup. To take the Campbells' prize cattle right under their noses. Who could resist such a challenge? And to the Campbells, who deserved every last humiliation that could be heaped upon them and more.

Iain clasped her wrist in a vice-like grip. "Will I have to take you away, lass?"

She knew what that meant and the mortification she would feel in front of the men who looked to her, whose respect she'd won over the years, was something he knew she wouldn't bear. She suppressed a fierce surge of rage and jerked her wrist from his hold.

"You no longer understand these matters, Iain. You've been gone too long."

He gave a snort. "I understand well enough and I'll not be moved. Will ye give the call or will I?"

His accent came thick and strong and she knew that he was very angry. She pulled in a frustrated breath and gave the faint bird call they used. Iain's posture eased and she glared at him.

"There. You can go now. It's done."

Iain frowned down at her. "We'll go. Together. Now. The rest can follow when they can." He reached over to take her reins but she pulled the pony aside before he could.

"No need for that. I'll come on my own."

Iain studied her and then relented. "Lead on."

She pursed her lips, and with a toss of her head and a few muttered words started the journey back to the castle.

THE MACGREGOR STOOD tall and imposing in the castle hall, despite the stick supporting him and the fur draped on his shoulders for extra warmth, as the fire was only embers at this time of the night. His grey hair hung loose around him, almost obscuring the deep scar to one side of his face. But his eyes were clear and full of fury.

Morag stood before her father and knew that this time there would be no softening, no words that would make him proud of her and her defence of the clan and its proud heritage that traced back to the first ruler of the Scots, MacAlpin. Beside her, Iain shifted his weight slightly, causing her father's attention to turn to him for a moment. But it was a moment only. His piercing eyes focused on her once again.

"So, you went against your pledge that Iain made you give." His tone was cold, a knife edge. He spoke in Gaelic, the language common here in the glen. He would want all in the household to know she was being reprimanded.

"I got to her before any harm was done, though," said Iain.

She glared at Iain, furious at him for betraying her to her father. How long had her father known about the pledge she gave to Iain three years ago? She straightened, determined not to let her father see her anxiety.

"It would have been six cattle at least, Father. Right under their noses." She made a disdainful noise. "They deserve it for the little care they take."

MacGregor brushed her comment aside with a wave of his hand. "I don't care for them, or what they do with their cattle. The point is you broke your pledge. And a MacGregor doesn't break his pledge. In all your eighteen years, did you not understand that much?"

She blanched under his stare, his words hitting home. "Nineteen years," she muttered and Iain gave a soft 'wheest' to hold her tongue.

"What did you say?" her father demanded.

She lifted her chin. "I said nineteen years. I am nineteen."

"Is it no wonder I mistake your age when you behave as though you're a babe?" He struck the heavy stick on the stone floor, the noise resounding in the hall. "You're my daughter and I expect you to behave like a MacGregor."

She bit her lip, fighting the tears. She wouldn't show him her distress. "I am sorry, Father, I did what I thought was best. The pledge to Iain I gave under duress." She gave her brother a dark look. "He didn't think I would hold to it, I'm sure."

Iain gave a nearly imperceptible shake of his head. She sniffed.

"It is clear you didn't understand my full meaning, daughter." He frowned and gave Iain a brief nod. "I've no choice, it seems. You're right, Iain. She must leave here and go to the court."

"What? No!" Morag said, shocked into the protest. "There's no need for that."

"There's every need," said MacGregor. "Since you clearly don't know how to behave as a lady of this castle, a daughter of MacGregor, we'll see if court can make a lady of you."

She couldn't leave her home, her Davey. Leave everything that meant anything to her. Morag cast her glance around the hall, noticing Abby, Iain's wife, seated in a chair by the table, her belly, swollen with child, only partially hidden by the large shawl she clasped around her shoulders. Next to her was crouched, Cú, the dog that had been Iain's but was clearly Abby's these days, loyal and protective, especially now. She'd been pregnant once before, but she'd lost that child before it was born, making this one even more special.

"Abby, please. Dinna let them send me away. Tell them I will mind them now. That I didn't mean to flout Iain. I will honour my pledge now. I promise."

Abby's eyes filled with sympathy. "Och, Morag, I know you couldn't help it."

Morag couldn't resist giving a small inward smile, despite the fact that she knew her cause was lost. After three years in Iain's company the faint trace of French accent that hinted Abby's years at the French court and her mother's heritage had disappeared, leaving a decided Scottish burr that gave her hesitant Gaelic a throaty sound that Iain loved. She'd grown to love and admire Iain's wife and was glad to have her as a sister, though her support was missing now. Morag turned back to her father and frowned.

She lifted her chin further. She wouldn't flinch or make any further fuss. "I am to go to court, then. When am I to go?"

"As soon as may be," said her father.

"And will Iain and Abby accompany me?"

She saw the unspoken communication between her father and Iain. Her heart sank further, knowing what was to come.

"Nay," said Iain. "Abby is too close to her time. It's not safe. And I won't leave her."

"Some of the ghillies will accompany you," said her father. "And a woman from the household."

Morag nodded, her face grim but taking care not to show the

anxiety that sprang up. She knew no one at court. She'd never had any desire to go there and practise all the courtly manners and skills to negotiate the turbulent waters of the Scottish court. Especially now with John Knox landed on the Scottish shores, stirring up unrest among the troublesome Protestant earls who sought to overthrow the Dowager Queen's authority as regent.

"What of Mister Knox and his ilk?" asked Morag. "Will it be safe for me there among such people?"

Her father frowned. "Don't think that using some clever angles will get you out of going, lassie."

"It will be safe enough," said Iain. "Better this than have you wreak havoc across the countryside and rouse the Campbells'ire further. Things are bad enough."

"Don't fret," said Abby. "I'll write to the Dowager Queen and ensure you a warm welcome."

Morag gave her curt nod. "That is kind of you, sister, but don't go to any trouble on my account."

Abby gave a wry smile. "It's no trouble, Morag. I'll do it."

Morag returned her smile with one that didn't reach her eyes. One letter would make no difference, she was certain. The time ahead would be something to endure. But first she must meet with Davey. Maybe he would have some idea to prevent this.

Iain came up beside her and grabbed her arm just as she was about to enter her chamber. Though she had height enough, he loomed over her and his piercing blue eyes looked into hers, a hint of frustration and anger present.

"You were lucky tonight, *a cailín*. And I know you think being sent to court is the worst thing that could happen to you, but it's for the best. Father could have been harsher in his punishment."

She snorted angrily. "Well, I don't know any harsher one."

He frowned. "And do you understand that if you'd killed one

of the Campbells, a punishment beyond what you could dream would come down on all of us? Campbell is not a man to be trifled with. Did you learn nothing from three years ago?" His voice had risen slightly, his words fierce and filled with anger.

She bit her lip, remembering when Iain was under the threatening shadow of banishment and the clan thrown into disgrace. It had only been by sheer luck and the wiles of Abby and Iain that they had managed to get his good name, and the clan's, restored.

"Yes, I did. And I'm sorry. But I've been careful. I would never kill any one of them. As much as they might deserve it."

Iain sighed and shook his head. "You could have had the clan put to the horn. We'd be disbanded and banished. Where would we be then? And our tenants?"

She shook herself from his hold, too ashamed, but unwilling to concede the point. "It wouldn't have happened," she muttered. "It didn't happen."

MORAG DREW up her pony outside the croft. The mountain was to her back and rose high behind her. The air was clear, but with a distinct bite from the late winter day. She drew her cloak around her as the wind caught it and lifted it from her skirts. After dismounting swiftly, she made her way through the gate to the door until she caught sight of a flash of colour in the stone shed to the right of the croft, across the small cobblestoned yard. It wasn't a large tenancy, but it provided enough for Davey and his widowed mother.

Morag turned away from the door and made her way to the shed, the penned ewes bleating as she passed. It would soon be lambing time and Davey had brought the ones at risk here, ready for his trusty and capable assistance. He came out of the shed as she approached and his brow furrowed in concern when he saw her. She admired the glint off his auburn hair, hanging in locks about his face. It was a face some might call pretty, with his long lashes, but she only could call it dear.

"Is something amiss, Mor—Mistress?" he asked in Gaelic

She bit her lip at the correction. He'd began to insist on calling her 'mistress' this past year or more, since Iain had reminded him after he'd overheard Davey's banter with Morag. She had scoffed at Iain's remark, saying Davey was a loyal clansman, a playmate of years and now her closest friend. Iain had just given her a look that spoke volumes.

"Morag, Davey. I've told you to call me Morag. Especially when we're alone."

Davey shifted on his feet and looked down as she came up beside him. He was little taller than her, with a wiry strength she admired. Perfect for these highland moors and crags. She put her hand on his arm. He blushed.

"Of course, mistress – and we shouldn't be alone. Ye know that it's wrong."

"It isn't for us, Davey. Never for us." She squeezed his arm. "Besides, it's important that we speak." She took his hand. "They're sending me away. To court."

Davey released her hand and stood back, his face full of surprise. "Nay. Why is that?"

"Because of what happened two nights ago. My father is determined that I should be taught a lesson for breaking my pledge to Iain."

"Pledge? You broke a pledge?"

She nodded. "Yes, well, not really. I mean, Iain never could imagine I would keep to it. He wanted me to give up reiving and taking action against the Campbells." She emphasised the last phrase, though she was certain he would know how important it was.

"You broke a pledge, though." His voice was filled with scorn. "To your family."

She looked into his hazel eyes and frowned to see the disappointment there. "But it was for a higher honour. The honour of the clan! You understand that, Davey, you must."

He nodded slowly, his eyes clearing. "Yes, for the honour of the clan. Yes, you have it right. As you always do."

She leaned over and kissed his cheek, relieved. He blushed again and looked down. "Mistress, you mustn't do that. It isn't seemly."

She placed a hand on his cheek. "It's me, Davey. Your playmate of years. Your companion in arms. And now won't you pledge to me?"

He looked up, startled. "I'm pledged to you already."

She frowned. "To my family. Nay, I mean pledge to *me*." It was her turn to look down, a small blush forming on her face. "Pledge your heart, Davey," she added softly. "For you have mine."

She leaned over and kissed him, a soft kiss, full on the lips. It was her first and she'd been long dreaming of how it would be and was glad to find it pleasant and warm. He kissed her back, but only for a moment, then pulled away with a gasp.

"I can't do this. It's madness. You're my lady, Morag."

She tugged him forward again. "Nay, Davey. I'm Morag and you are Davey." She took his hand. "And I am pledging myself to you, Davey."

He shook his head. "You don't mean it."

She smiled at him, her eyes twinkling. "I do of course and you must do as I say, for am I not your Lady Morag?"

He groaned. "How can I refuse you anything? You know I'll do whatever you ask of me."

"And I request we plight our troth. Here. Now. Before they send me away. So you know that it will always be you. And nothing they do will change that."

He gave her a puzzled look and then nodded. "Aye, I'll do it. But if at any time you wish to be released from it, I will do so."

"Of course. But that will never happen." She beamed at him and took his hands. "For you are such a grand companion and have always been in all the times we've had together. Better than any brother of mine."

He gave her a rueful look. "Only because you can bully me better than your own brothers."

She laughed. "Nay. That may be true, but I do care for you, Davey." She pressed a kiss on his lips again, fierce and long. Davey put a tentative arm around her. She sighed. Two kisses in one day. Her heart gave a leap. She was becoming a woman indeed. No courtier could gainsay her as a backwards highland lass.

She pulled away. "Now, we must say the words to each other. I'll go first and then you can repeat them back."

He bit his lip and then nodded. She took up his right arm and clasped it hard, then pulled out the bit of ribbon she had tucked in her kirtle and wrapped it around their clasped wrists.

"I Morag Elizabeth, daughter of Gregor MacGregor, descendant of MacAlpin, do pledge my troth to you, Davey of Glen Strae of clan Gregor until such time as we decide to release each other. Or," her eyes twinkled, "we bed each other as husband and wife, as custom dictates, and become truly wed."

Davey opened his mouth in surprise but closed it after a moment. He cleared his throat and at her nod he repeated the words.

"There," she said when he had finished. "It's done. We're pledged to each other." She released the ribbon and reached up to hug him tightly. His arms went tentatively around her waist. "I shall keep this ribbon with me always, Davey. So I know that no matter where I am, I will always have a part of us with me."

He nodded. "Of course. As you like." He released her and stepped back, shifting uncomfortably. "What's to do now?"

"Now we must create a secret code and manner in which we communicate while I am at court. So we'll know how we go on. And in case I might need you. For I don't intend to let them stop me from discovering a way we might revenge upon the Campbells."

"You still intend tae go reiving?"

"No, of course not. At least I don't think it could be managed so far away." She looked at him, a hopeful expression on her face. "Unless you have devised a manner in which it may be done?"

"What? Nothing of the sort. It seems more than impossible."

She sighed. "Yes, just so. But I won't give up. There might be some way, as I said. And I will tell you when I find it, so you can help me. You will help me, Davey?"

He smiled at her. "Yes, you know I will. Have I ever done anything but do as you wish?"

She grinned broadly. "Never. Is it any wonder I care for you so much?"

She hugged him again. "Now, I will have some of the ghillies with me. Rob, probably and a few others. I can send him to you with a note or something of that nature to tell you what I discover, or if I need you. My family will doubtless send me word from time to time and I will endeavour to send them messages for you in my replies."

He nodded slowly taking in her words. "Fine. I'll await your word."

She squeezed his arm. "Good. Now I must away. Someone is bound to be looking for me by now."

She put her arms around him and drew him closer once again. "Now give me a kiss again Davey," she said softly. "Forbye I don't know when I'll see you next and I want something to remember you by."

She pressed her lips to his and he returned the kiss hesitantly. She pressed tighter, wanting to feel as much as possible before she let him go. She felt him gasp, his mouth opening slightly and she pulled away, grinning. "Have you ever been kissed so well, Davey?"

He flushed deeply. "Never."

She gave him a smug smile. "Yes, well, be sure you remember that."

Morag drew away and headed towards her pony. She grasped the reins and pulled herself up on its back, blew him a kiss and trotted away. She'd done what she could to make experience at court bearable. She had her pledge with Davey and thoughts of revenge on the Campbells to help bolster her among the cruel and ruthless courtiers she was certain she would encounter.

CHAPTER 2

*M*orag tugged at her riding gown and damp cloak, shifting at the same time so that she might ride in a little more comfort than she had in the past four hours. The gown which draped across her legs and the horse in a manner that may have seemed proper and graceful, was in fact awkward and got in the way. The saddle, at least, allowed her to ride astride, a concession her father had made in return for the promise that she switch over to the lady's saddle and the mare on the final leg of her journey to Stirling Castle.

Behind her, she could hear her servant Bridie sniffling. She had the makings of a cold, which the light drizzle in which they travelled hadn't improved. She didn't know the thin, wiry girl that well, only that she was niece to Mistress MacNab, the castle housekeeper, and had been helping in the household for the past year. Morag held no opinion as to her suitability to be servant to her at Stirling, but only hoped that the young girl wasn't silly and could be relied upon to hold her tongue and be discreet.

Up ahead Rob led the way, his brown shaggy locks bouncing under his tan coloured bonnet, which was pulled low over his forehead. His stocky frame sat on his pony with ease and he seemed unbothered by the journey or the weather, his ballock dagger at his side, his targe tied to his saddle. But she would expect nothing less from him. He had joined her on many a night's reiving. By his side was his cousin, Mungo, a small man, who though quiet, could be relied upon in any skirmish.

They made for a small party travelling across the highlands and down to Stirling. Besides herself, Bridie, Rob, and Mungo, her horse and the baggage ponies, there were just two ghillies, Liam and Jemmy, who accompanied them on foot, their bare muscled legs scooting nimbly through the tufted hills, ever on the watch for any threat. She expected no trouble but still lamented that she wasn't allowed her own ballock and sword. Her small *sgian dhu* was strapped to her calf and she'd managed to conceal her ballock in her baggage, along with the leather jerkin and the trews, in case there was ever a need. She could only hope so, if her plan for Davey succeeded.

She'd questioned Iain and Abby before she left, to glean what information she could about who might be at court and what use they might be to uncover information about the Campbells. Something that could be employed for revenge. The Campbell himself was notoriously sly and always plotting to increase his influence and land, a bitter pill for the MacGregor clan who had seen their lands slowly whittled away by Campbell's machinations. But she would do her best to restore the MacGregor honour, if nothing else, as she had been doing these past four years. And perhaps, if the Campbells were made fools of often enough, the crown would see fit to restore some of their lands, if not all.

Rob slowed and waited for Morag to come up beside him. He looked around him and his eyes narrowed and he sighed, seemingly resigned. He turned to Mungo, who merely shrugged.

"Will you have a wee break now?" said Rob in Gaelic. "This place isn't so bad, and the best we've come across in a while."

She cast her glance around, eyeing the open area relieved only by a distant outcropping of trees. Around them, only a few large rocks provided any shelter. It wasn't the best for protection against the rain, but it would have to do.

"Yes," she said. "We'll stop here."

Morag dismounted from her pony with more agility than grace before Rob or either of the ghillies could assist her down. She stretched her back and began to ease out her cramped muscles. Her tension was not so much from riding, but from the destination. The journey took three days and they would spend the two nights at different clan member houses. The second night would be in Balquihidder Glen, newly acquired the previous year when the Maclaurin clan had lost it to the MacGregors after a clan struggle that had gone on for decades. She smiled, thinking that a small bit of restored honour and reputation for prowess might have been owed to her and her fellow reivers.

She sat on the small blanket that Bridie had lain out and picked up the heel of bread and a small chunk of cheese that sat on it. The men took seats on stones or squatted easily down, pulling up their plaids against the drizzle. They offered around a leather flagon of fiery *uisce*. Morag frowned when it failed to pass to her. On any raid it would have been offered without question. She held out her hand and glared at Rob, who was just about to stow the flagon. He paused before passing it over. Morag grabbed it from him and took a hefty swig, the liquid burning its way down her throat. She took a breath and took another swig, before handing it back, a look of defiance on her face. The burning continued and spread throughout her body, warming her considerably against the damp, chilly air.

Bridie sniffled and Morag glanced over at her. The poor girl looked truly miserable. Guilt seized her. She should have offered the flagon to Bridie, who needed it more than she did. For Morag it hadn't really been about warming her bones, she knew that.

She unwrapped the soft wool stole that was around her neck and held it out to Bridie.

"Here," Morag said. "Put this around you. You look half frozen."

Bridie looked up in surprise. "Och, nay mistress. I can't be taking your stole."

Morag pushed it on Bridie. "You can, of course. You should be abed. Not riding in this weather on a long journey."

Bridie gave her a weak smile, taking up the stole and wrapping it snugly around her neck, under her cloak. "My thanks to you."

Morag gave her an encouraging smile in return, trying her best to be friendly. She had little practice really, growing up in a family of men, her mother having died when Morag was very young. Until three years ago when Abby arrived, Mistress MacNab had been the only woman with whom she'd had other than a speaking acquaintance. It had taken her a little while to warm to Abby, distrusting her seemingly French origins, despite her Gordon name. But they were close enough now, though Morag still felt awkward around Abby's worldly experience of French and Scottish courts and all the required accomplishments of those places. Abby had tried her best, encouraging and building on Morag's singing abilities and making use of Morag's agility to a greater skill on the dance floor. She'd even taught her a bawdy song in French, one that Abby's father was known to have sung in private groups. That had made Morag grin and finally think that maybe she did have a kindred soul in her sister-in-law.

One of the ponies stirred and another gave a snort, shaking its head. The mare looked up, sniffing the air. The men kept talking, but their hands crept to the ballocks and swords at their sides. Liam stood up and wandered slowly over to the ponies, patting each pony and the mare, muttering words in Gaelic to them and carefully unhobbling the saddled mounts, all the while his eyes cast towards the horizon. Morag started to wrap up the food, her ears and eyes on alert. She handed over the bundle to Bridie who stowed it away among the leather bags she carried slung over her side. While it seemed unlikely there was any planned attack, it was best to take care and be prepared. A moment later, a group of riders appeared out of the trees.

Rob looked at Morag and she saw the message in his eyes and nodded. She rose and made her way to her pony and the others followed, their hands still on their blades. She heard a shout and then the thunder of hooves as the group of riders broke into a charge, brandishing swords. Rob and Mungo mounted their ponies quickly. The ghillies, along with the two mounted men, drew their weapons and slid their arms into their targes and took off. Morag rose to follow suit. She pulled Bridie up and mounted her on her pony, giving it a slap to send it on its way. Bridie grasped the reins, her eyes filled with fear.

"Head southeast," Morag shouted. "We'll keep them off."

Morag quickly mounted her pony, cursing her skirts, and urged it forward. There was no time to search her pack for her ballock. She would do what she could with her *sgian dhu* and her wits.

The two men reached the attackers and swung their swords and shouted wildly the MacGregor battle cry. The ghillies came up beside the two men a moment later and joined the fray. Morag stood back a little, scanned the group, assessing their strength and their identity. There were five of them and they fought fiercely. She urged her pony closer and caught a flash of red fiery hair. She frowned, hoping that her thoughts would prove wrong. But the red haired man looked over at her and she felt a flash of anger mixed with anxiety. Rory Campbell. It was as she feared. His surly and fierce expression was replaced by a predatory one and he gave a laugh, breaking from the group. She straightened and prepared herself.

He urged his horse towards her, his sword still brandished.

Rob, catching sight of him, tried to break from the man he was fighting, but his opponent blocked him with a slash and flick of his sword and Rob had to fight to keep his own sword from flying from his hand.

Morag tightened her reins, her face grim. She rode towards Rory, and just as he was upon her she swerved her pony to the left, causing him to halt suddenly. She swerved back again and galloped across his path, reaching out to shove him quickly. She'd done this manoeuvre in the past many times without any problem, but this was her first time in her skirts and she found that she couldn't grip her pony as well and use her knees in the usual manner to signal her intentions. The pony did his best, but he turned a little too late the second time and her intention to overset Rory served only to overset herself. She fell from her mount with a clunk that winded her. Rory laughed again as he dismounted quickly and went to her, his sword still drawn. She fought to catch her breath, but he was upon her, sheathing his sword. He pulled her up, drew his ballock dagger and, drawing her to him, held it against her neck.

"Not so prettily done," said Rory in Scots. "Surely a lady wouldna try such moves. But then I hear ye're hardly a lady. Especially when reiving."

She struggled against his hold, her breath hardly returned, but his grip was firm. He pulled her to his horse and shoved her up across its flanks, in front of the saddle, face down. He mounted up behind her. From her viewpoint, Morag had no idea as to the progress of the skirmish and tried to shout a warning, but her feeble voice came out as barely a squeak. Rory hit her with the flat of his dirk in retaliation.

"We'll have no sound out of ye," he said darkly.

Rory urged his horse forward and she bounced ungracefully against the horse as it quickly broke into a gallop. A short while later he drew up and dismounted. He pulled her down and threw her on the ground. She was surrounded by fir trees. She started to rise, but he was down upon her, shoving her back. Morag reached out to push him off, but he grabbed her arm with his free hand before she could. Her attempt to lift her knee was blocked by her own cursed skirts tangling. He brought the dagger to her throat again.

"Ah, ye willna foil me, hoor," he said, his eyes narrowing. "The only use your legs will get will be for parting."

Morag spat at him and it hit his cheek. He held the dagger closer and she could feel the cool press of steel against her throat. She lay still, her mind working furiously. Feeling her body slacken, he laid his dagger aside and caught up her arms and held them above her head with one hand while pulling up her skirts in the other. She rolled to one side and he fell off her, loosing his hold on her hands. She broke free and used the moment to pull her *sgian dhu* from its sheath strapped to her calf and hid it in her right hand.

Rory let out an angry growl and rolled back onto her, pinning her down with his weight.

"Ye willna escape me so easy," he said, his tone angry. He reached for her skirts again, shoving them higher. She made herself relax under him while he loosed his trews with his one hand, his other across her chest. She eased her right hand down her side as he began to grunt, his hand groping along her thighs. With a howling war cry she struck out with the *sgian dhu*, aiming for his back, shoving up under his ribs to his kidneys but he moved quickly and the knife fell short, sticking him in his side. She'd shoved with all her strength and was pleased to hear the cry and curse he emitted before falling away from her.

In an instant she was up and able to give him a good kick in the gut that she was certain would leave him breathless. She made her way to his horse without hesitation, and with energy she didn't know she possessed, vaulted herself along his back and threw her leg over. Her skirts nearly at her waist, she drew the reins in and kicked the horse into action. Behind her, curses and running footsteps sounded.

As she drew up alongside the still battling group, she was glad to note that her own men had bested their opponents for the most part. Three Campbells had already pulled away, disarmed and wounded. The other two still fought on, one on the ground, the other mounted. She had only to finish it off.

"Be gone, ye cursed Campbells, and take your injured halfling warlord with you!"

The men needed no other encouragement. With a shout and snarl they broke away, the dismounted one catching up his horse and was soon back astride with the help of his clansmen. They rode off towards Rory who shouted at them, his angry voice carrying far. Morag laughed and shouted the MacGregor war cry after them.

Rob came up beside her, his sweating, grimy face anxious. "Were you harmed, mistress?" he asked in Gaelic

She looked over at him and grinned. "Not I, Rob. But that Campbell twin didn't fare so well."

"You harmed Rory Campbell?"

"Yes. Not so badly as I might wish. But he'll suffer a sharp stab at his side for a day or two." She laughed. "Och, if you could have heard him when I mounted his horse and rode away, my *sgian dhu* sticking in his side."

Rob, looked at her and shook his head. "Aye, well, I'm glad it wasn't worse. The last thing we need is to have the Campbell down on our necks for harming his son."

Morag snorted. "No need to worry about that. He'll won't go bleating to his father that a mere *cailín* bested him with a knife."

One of the ghillies snickered and was soon joined by his companions. Mungo raised his brow. Rob gave the ghillies a dark look and they fell silent.

"Well that being well and good, we should still be on our way. The more distance we can put between us and their lands, the happier I'll be." He looked down to where the pack ponies stood, still hobbled in their original spot. "Where's Bridie?"

"I sent her ahead on her pony," said Morag. "I told her to ride south-easterly."

Rob opened his mouth but shut it again before he uttered a word. "Yes, well, all the more reason to ride on quickly."

Rob turned his pony and, with a nod, they moved off. One of the ghillies trotted over to Morag's pony that had found its way toward the group and grabbed up the reins. He followed the others, pulling the pony behind him until they reached the other ponies.

Rob eyed her mount. "Will you ride your own pony, now?"

She shook her head and patted the horse's neck. "Nay, I think I'll ride Rory's horse. He's a fine roan."

Rob cleared his throat and reddened. "Will you be wanting to adjust your skirts, mistress before we set out?"

She looked down. Her skirts had ridden halfway up her thighs, revealing her toned legs, clad in woollen hose and another *sgian dhu,* courtesy of Mungo. She sighed and tugged them hard, managing to cover most of her thighs. On the wider horse, it was more difficult to keep her skirts to her calves as she had before on her pony.

Morag gave Rob a haughty glare. "They will do for now." She urged her horse forward, pleased with his smooth response. She may have lost her *sgian dhu* but she had gained so much more in return. And the horse wasn't the best part of the bargain. Not by any means. She smiled to herself, her spirits the best they'd been since she'd left Glen Strae.

CHAPTER 3

*M*orag stared up at Stirling Castle, so visible from its high perch on the volcanic outcrop that commanded the upper Forth Valley. It was the most imposing thing she'd ever seen and all the nerves she had struggled to keep at bay rose up in force. The small triumph she'd felt only a few days ago at besting Rory Campbell seemed far away and trivial compared to what she faced now. The tense ride over the course of two days following the skirmish had worked to erode her good humour, as the unrest about the countryside became increasingly obvious. Knox and his cronies had made inroads into many of the communities they'd passed through and last night's stay at a distant kinsman's home had only reinforced that impression. Balquihidder aside, with the dark glances from Maclaurin kin and other clans with claims in the area, it was more a case of cautious obeisance and hospitality than any friendly journey among friends. The wind seemed to blow every which way between those who supported the Dowager Queen Marie and the supporters of the Earl of Arran, King James's illegitimate son who led the Protestant faction and the Congregation of Lords. These very politics that had seemed so distant and inconsequential to Morag when she lived at Glen Strae seemed very real after her journey to Stirling.

They made their way now on the gentle approach along the southeast slope that rose up to meet the first line of fortifications, in the form of a newly erected stone wall, following a farmer and his cart and some servants towing bundles at their side. The forework presented itself soon after, in the form of a curtained cross wall extending across the full width of the castle rock, the wall capped with a broadly crenelated parapet carried on a double-corbelled cornice. At each end was a rectangular tower.

Upon approaching each fortification her party were met with guards who, upon eyeing Morag, her riding gown freshly brushed, her hair caught under a modest hood and mounted in her lady's saddle, were quickly motioned onward. At the gate, the guards were little bothered by her appearance and merely gave everyone a nod and they proceeded through to the cobbled outer close which was busy with people either milling or walking purposefully, intent on their tasks. A few dogs weaved in and out of the legs of a group of noblemen over to the side, who were deep in discussion.

Rob brought them to a halt midway in the outer close and dismounted. He went to Morag and assisted her down from her mare. Liam and Jemmy brought up the pack ponies and Mungo drew up with Rory's roan in tow and alighted from his pony. After a glance around, Rob signalled to a small lad he spied running across the close carrying a large ewer. The lad halted uncertainly and after a few moments' indecision made his way to their group.

"Fetch the steward, if ye please, young lad. Tell him my lady of Glen Strae has arrived."

The lad stared at him, his brow knotted in incomprehension. Rob sighed and repeated himself, speaking slowly. The lad cocked his head and looked uncertainly up to Morag.

Morag grinned. "Tell the steward to come if he pleases, the

daughter of the MacGregor Chieftain has come," she said in her best and most distinct Scots. Clearly Rob's thick highland accent was beyond the lad, laden as it was with Gaelic inflections and manners of speech. Technically she wasn't the lady of Glen Strae, but it had been so long since the real lady had died that many referred to her in that manner. It would be Abby now, for she was married to the heir, and when her father died Abby would be the lady in truth.

Her words seemed to have penetrated for he was gone a moment later, headed towards the door to the main building – which she could only presume, based on Abby's description, was the palace. The wait allowed Morag an opportunity to look around and her eye was drawn to the group of noblemen at the far end. They were dressed in what she could only imagine was the latest fashion and lounged with an elegant ease that she found herself envying. One gentleman in particular caught her eye and in fact it was difficult not to have her attention caught, not just for his height, but for the colour and manner of his dress. Flamboyant was an understatement and Morag studied him in amazed fascination. He wore a light green velvet jerkin edged with gold, caught at the throat with a large gold filigree brooch. His sleeves were of a puce coloured satin that matched his slops, or pantaloons as they were sometimes called. The slops and sleeves sported many cuttes. The ones on his doublet revealed his white linen shirt underneath. Topping his head was a green velvet bonnet bearing a bright puce plume that waved in the breeze. He wore dark boots that seemed plain enough until the embroidered flowers that ran along the inside of each revealed themselves when he adjusted his stance and waved a large handkerchief gracefully with his long fingers.

The handkerchief had her mesmerised for a moment as she watched it flutter about in front of his captivated audience. A sardonic twist of his mouth was obvious underneath his small but beautifully styled beard. Despite the effeminate lean of his style she could say he cut a fine figure with his muscled legs, his broad shoulders and the bright sandy hair evident under his bonnet, except for the obvious large paunch that thickened his waist and ruined the perfect looks. Regardless of his paunch he was still not to her taste, being as far away from her beloved Highland men as he could get. He was no match for Davey.

She was just about to turn away when he caught sight of her gaze. She blushed and he cocked his head and made his way over to her, his lazy stroll showing an overt grace. His entourage remained behind at his bidding, but they looked on with interest and curiosity.

He drew up in front of her, swept off his bonnet, bowed and made a leg, fluttering his handkerchief for extra effect.

"Ye're a new arrival?" he said in Scots, his voice a high tenor. "Let me be the first tae greet ye. I'm Alexander Munro."

She swallowed a snicker and gave a curtsy to acknowledge his greeting. "My lord. I thank ye for such a greeting. I am Morag, daughter tae Gregor MacGregor, Chieftain of the clan."

"*Mais, vous êtes trés belle, mademoiselle,*" he said smoothly in French. "I believe I have a distant acquaintance with your family."

She'd blushed vividly at his initial remark, readily understanding him. Though she was no scholar, her father and her brothers had ensured she was conversant with French from childhood. With Abby joining the family, her grasp of French nuances had increased. His last remark, though, had made her smile inwardly. Everyone in the Highlands had a distant acquaintance with every family and if he was of the Highland Munro clan he would surely know that.

"I have some acquaintance with the Munros, but I am not certain of your specific relationship within the family," she answered in French.

He gave a titter and bowed slightly with another flourish of his handkerchief. "Ah, but don't trouble yourself over that, mademoiselle."

The steward, a tall dark man, approached them and bowed first to Munro. "My lord," he said in French. He turned to Morag and continued in French. "If you would like to follow me." She glanced over at Rob, uncertain if she should bid him follow. "Your men will be directed by one of the servants, as will your...attendant."

Morag swallowed a curt retort, disliking his haughty tone. She allowed herself a dark look instead. With a brief curtsy to Alexander Munro, who had an amused expression on his face, she followed the steward into the palace while Rob, Bridie and the others stayed behind to see to the baggage and horses.

They entered a long stone passageway and made their way along it, passing small antechambers. A servant passed them hastily and, jostling Morag, stopped to beg her pardon in French, before hastening onwards. They passed wordlessly along, until she found herself outside again in a small courtyard. From there, the steward turned into another door leading inside and they followed a shorter passageway before he led her up a set of stone stairs to the next level. They continued along a short panelled corridor with a door at the end and one to her right, another to her left. He stopped in front of the left door and opened it. Morag followed him inside, still silent. During her passage in this section of the palace they had encountered only a maidservant and a modestly dressed woman who might be one of the personal attendants to a noble lady, in Morag's estimation, but there had been no one else. From her journey, she had some idea that the steward had no great estimation of her status and the small antechamber he led her into did nothing to dispel that fact.

"Lady Erskine has charge of her majesty's young ladies," the steward said in a neutral tone. "But the daily supervision of said ladies falls under Madame Cunningham. She will be with you in a moment." He gave a short bow and left, closing the door behind him.

Morag blinked at the closed door, momentarily startled by his abrupt departure. She sighed. Well, this was far from the best beginning to make. She knew from Abby that it would be very French, but it was still different to what she expected. The fashions were outrageous, if the men in the outer close were anything to go by, especially Alexander Munro. Her first impression hadn't been good. She despised his effeminate mannerisms and his costume was the most extreme – and would be just short of ridiculous – if it weren't for his large frame and muscled legs. If that was an example of French fashion, Morag was certain she would never aspire to it.

But for all Munro's outrageous manner and costume, she couldn't help but feel he'd been mocking her the entire length of their encounter. As if he could sense her disdain and he found it amusing. Well, he could think what he liked.

She took a moment then to look around her. The room wasn't overly large, but it contained a large tester bed with dark brocade drapes, two linenfold chests, a table and two padded stools against the far wall, where a tapestry hung depicting a young maiden holding a ewer, surrounded by a field of flowers. Morag thought she was a rather insipid looking girl and wondered what she was doing in a garden holding a ewer on her shoulder.

The door opened and a woman came in, wearing a drab coloured but well-made kirtle and dark hood. "You are Morag MacGregor?" she asked in French that held a faint trace of her Scots origins.

Morag smiled inwardly at this thought and gave a brief curtsy. *"Oui, madame."*

She was uncertain of this lady's importance. Her clothes were unremarkable but of the finest cloth. Her face was plain, with a nose that was just short of hooked and a thin mouth. It was only her hands that held any amount of delicacy and bore no trace of reddening or soreness as might denote a seamstress or something of that nature.

The woman drew herself up, as though conscious of Morag's

thoughts. "I am Mistress Cunningham. I will be in charge of you during your stay here at Stirling. First, I must tell you that the Dowager Queen has strict rules governing the behaviour of her young attendants and it is my duty to ensure that you will comply with them."

Morag suppressed the urge to roll her eyes and curtsied more deeply this time. "Of course, madame."

A little mollified, Mistress Cunningham relaxed her stiff posture somewhat. "This is to be your chamber. You're sharing it with two other young ladies, Lady Barbara Sandilands and Lady Glenna Campbell. Perhaps you are acquainted with Lady Glenna? It was one reason I put you with her. That and she is close enough in age to you."

Morag's heart stopped at her roommate's names. Barbara Sandilands was unknown to her personally, but the Campbell girl she knew without a doubt. All the names of that hellish household.

"While I am not personally acquainted with her, I know her family. I believe she is sixteen or thereabouts," said Morag stiffly. "I am nineteen, madame."

"*Oui*," said Mistress Cunningham. "As I said. Now, as to your role here. You will attend the Dowager Queen when requested. She is particularly unwell at present, so the company of giddy young ladies may not always be desirous. In that situation you will go to the small sitting room with the others and work on your needlework."

Mistress Cunningham eyed her carefully, as if to detect some obvious fault she must identify and remedy. "In addition you will attend her at the evening meal with the rest of the court, if she requires it. But you will return to your chamber when the Dowager Queen retires. I will permit no late nights in...entertainment. And you will refrain from mingling with the male courtiers."

With that list of instructions and prohibitions completed, she looked at Morag expectantly.

Morag bowed her head after a moment and said, "Yes, Mistress Cunningham."

Satisfied, she gave her own nod. "I shall leave you now to get settled. Your baggage will be brought up shortly and your maid-servant. I'm not certain she will be fit for service here, though. But we'll see. Later, I'll have fresh water for a wash sent to you and the other girls before the meal tonight. They'll show you the way to the Great Hall."

Morag curtsied again, knowing her duty. "I thank you, Mistress Cunningham."

The woman gave a nod and turned, leaving the chamber with a thud of the door. Morag frowned and blew out a sigh, glad to be rid of the woman.

She removed her cloak and placed it on the bed. With a gentle tug she drew off her hood and loosened the pins from her hair until it tumbled down in dark curls to her waist. The pins had been digging into her head all morning and it felt good to be free of them. If only she could dispense with the rest of her restraining garments. She frowned at the busked and tight fitting kirtle that pushed up her breasts and pressed against her stomach. It was one of Abby's old outfits from France, and while they were the same height she was a little more endowed than Abby was at the time of its fashioning, a few years previously.

Morag went over to the window and looked out. She could see the countryside in the distance and since the day was fine and clear she could even glimpse, she thought, the distant mountains she knew were the Highlands. It made her homesick on the one hand, but she drew comfort from the sight as well, though she knew that the wind would likely blow a vicious gale through the room on stormy days.

The door opened, interrupting her musings and two young women entered noisily. Startled at the sight of Morag, they halted and stared.

The older of the two women was buxom and full lipped, with tendrils of brown hair peeping out from her pearl studded coif and hood that matched a pair of dark brown expressive eyes. She had a ready laugh that rang out in the room. The younger was a slim young woman with ginger hair visible through the beaded and jewelled snood that caught up her locks. Her blue eyes danced merrily until they caught sight of Morag, when they instantly turned cautious. And so she should be, thought Morag, cursed Campbell that she was.

"You must be the new Dowager Queen's attendant," said the buxom young lady in French. She gave a small curtsy. "Mistress Cunningham said you were arriving soon. I am Lady Barbara Sandilands and this is Lady Glenna Campbell. But you must call us Barbara and Glenna, of course."

Morag returned the curtsy and looked directly at Barbara. "I'm pleased to meet you. I am the lady Morag MacGregor, daughter to the MacGregor Chieftain."

Glenna began to open her mouth but shut it quickly. She made her own brief curtsy, her expression closed.

"We are to share the chamber, the three of us," said Barbara, her manner fulsome and expression open. She looked around. "Your baggage hasn't been brought up yet, I see. Never mind, it will come soon. In the meantime you're free to borrow anything of ours if you need it."

"You're most kind," Morag said coolly. "But I have no need for anything at present."

"But you'll want to change your gown before the evening meal," said Barbara reasonably. "You can borrow one of mine, though you're much taller than I am and not as rounded. But I'm certain we can manage something."

Morag stared down at her outfit, knowing it didn't compare with Barbara's for splendour or fashion. There was no adornment, no embroidery. It was a burgundy velvet, with a paler red underskirt, square cut at the neckline with a fine lawn partlet covering the neckline to the throat. The sleeves were wide and folded back, unlike the narrow sleeves she saw on the two who stood before her. Their skirts were narrower and the waist line lower cut, dropping to a vee in front. Not only was her outfit unfashionable, the skirts were somewhat crushed now and now she hoped that any trace of horse odour would be on her cloak rather than the gown. She'd chosen to wear it today, knowing it was one of the better gowns she possessed and she wanted to make a good impression. To do honour to the MacGregor name. She smoothed the skirt and drew herself up to her full height, tucking a lock of hair back behind her ear. She was taller than the two women; a full head taller than Barbara.

"I shall manage fine. But I thank you for your kind offer."

Barbara shrugged. "If you're certain. But we must all have a wash first. One of the servants is bringing some fresh water for us shortly."

Determined to change the focus of the conversation Morag asked, "Have you been with the Dowager Queen today?"

Barbara sighed and fell onto the bed, leaning back. "Aye," She said, lapsing into her Scots, "And it is very tiresome, ye ken? The Dowager Queen is old and sickly so it is all murmured conversation on politics or the health of some lord or other. Meanwhile, we are meant tae ply our needles or listen to dull old books in Greek or Latin, with only cheese, fruit and small ale to wet our thrapple throughout the day."

"But do ye no have meals with the Dowager Queen? Surely then there will be music and talk of interest?"

"Nay, there's nothing. The meals are simple, since the Dowager's constitution canna support anything much. The senior ladies can have the wine at least. It's only when she asks for someone tae play the lute or the clavichord that the tedium is relieved. There's nae conversation of interest, like who has taken the fancy of another courtier. We dinna usually see the men unless there is a formal feast, or she entertains the court in the receiving chamber. The senior ladies are allowed much more freedom than we are. They are there at the audiences and are able to mingle about the palace with the men."

"Nay," said Glenna softly. "It's no so bad as that. The music is fine, of the highest quality and ye do dance at the feasts and sometimes of an evening. There are plenty of courtiers who will lead ye out in branles and galliards."

It was the first Glenna had spoken since their introduction and Morag eyed her warily. She appeared on the shy side, even demure, but there was something about her that seemed to indicate a trace of stubbornness. She cast her mind back, trying to recall what Iain had said about Glenna. She'd been little more than a young girl when he had resided there, held as a hostage masquerading as a "guest" to ensure the MacGregor's good behaviour. Was Glenna the one who had assisted Iain's escape? Abby had told her with amusement that one of the Campbell girls had trailed after Iain like a puppy, clearly besotted with him. It must have been Glenna then, for the older sister was married now and too old to have been trailing after Iain like a puppy.

"The music is of the highest quality when ye're playing, Glenna," said Barbara and she giggled. "And the men do sigh after ye."

Glenna reddened and glanced at Morag. "They're only being courteous. They're courtiers. It isna serious."

"Aye, I'd heard ye play the lute," said Morag evenly. "My brother Iain remarked on it once. And his wife, another time I believe."

Glenna cast her glance down. "Did they? It is kind of them tae mention me."

Barbara sat up and glanced from one to the other. "Och, ye twa ken each other?" She let out a laugh. "Of course ye do. Ye're both Highlanders."

"I believe my mother is distant kin of her mother," said Glenna stiffly.

"Aye," said Morag, her tone icily polite. "She is. And does she fare well?"

Glenna gave a slight nod. "She does well enough. I thank ye for asking."

"Have ye heard word, Glenna? Your mother has recovered?" asked Barbara. "I'm glad for ye, forbye I ken that ye've been grieving that nae missive has come."

"Nay, there's been nae letter," Glenna said. "I spoke only in general terms."

"Hopeful words, then," said Barbara. "We'll join ye in that hope."

A knock sounded and the door opened, revealing a young servant boy with a large ewer of water. He bowed quickly.

"Your water miladies," he said in garbled French.

"Aye, laddie, ye can set it down on thon table," said Barbara, indicating the simple oak table set against the wall.

The lad did as he was told and then turned to regard Morag. "Mistress Cunningham bid me tell ye," he said lapsing into Scots with a relieved look, "that the maidservant ye had wi' ye willna do and will be sent home wi' the ghillies on the morrow. Ye're tae share the maid your chamber companions have."

Morag stared at the lad, too stunned to speak and watched him bow again and quit the room.

"Och, the old limmer," said Barbara disdainfully. "She's just trying to put ye out of kilter, so ye can be certain tae behave."

Morag gripped her skirts, willing herself to calm. She would deal with this later. Have a word with that woman. How dare she! She gave a sniff and looked over at Barbara.

"She may try to cow me, but I tell ye she willna succeed."

Barbara grinned at her. "Aye, of course. She doesna get her way. At least no where I am concerned. What she doesna ken she doesna grieve over."

And with those cryptic words Barbara rose and made her way to the table to begin her ablutions.

CHAPTER 4

*M*orag pulled herself up to her full height, took a deep breath and entered the Great Hall, refusing to smooth her travel stained gown one last time. She'd done her best to pin up her hair again and replace her hood but knew she'd make a poor show. Apparently this was one of the evenings the Dowager Queen had chosen to entertain the full court, since there were some visitors fresh from France in attendance. Such had been her luck, she thought, since arriving in this nest of vipers. Though she wouldn't class Barbara among the vipers, she was nonetheless a rattlebag of a lass as far as she could observe.

She followed Barbara and Glenna forward into the milling throng as they awaited the arrival of the Dowager Queen. The room was large, with panelled walls, tapestries and two long dining tables that stood in its centre. Above, there was a trumpet loft and a minstrel's gallery. She could hear the musicians tuning up their instruments there. Even in the limited light provided by the candles on the lit sconces on the wall, she could see the room was light and airy with a high hammer beamed ceiling and a pair of large projecting bay window lights in the east and west side of the dais. The main source of light was a series of paired rectangular windows set in the inner wall, undimmed by the few tapestries and dark paintings that hung along its walls. Underfoot was a highly polished wood floor, and a fire burned brightly in the stone hearth at the other end of the hall.

All of this she took in, weaving through the people, until Barbara and Glenna halted before Mistress Cummings. She was dressed in a dark velvet kirtle relieved only by the small pearl on a ribbon at her neck. Her iron grey hair was caught up in a matching hood. Barbara and Glenna curtsied low and a moment later Morag followed suit. She frowned down at them.

"So, you're all here." She turned and eyed Morag's mussed kirtle. "I hope in time you will prove worthy of your place at court and service to Her Majesty. It's a privilege that not every lady can hope to enjoy." She ran a glance over Morag again. "I suppose your hair is tidier and that I must draw comfort from. The clothes one can only hope will improve when your baggage is unpacked."

Morag stiffened and lifted her chin. "Madame, you will have no cause to doubt anything, I'm certain."

Beside her, Barbara tittered softly. Mistress Cunningham, unaware either of the titter or its cause, nodded a curt dismissal.

"Lady Barbara, you may show the others to their places. But remember, you must not seat yourselves until Her Majesty has arrived."

Barbara murmured something inaudible that seemed to satisfy Mistress Cummings. The three curtsied briefly and took their leave.

"That glaikit woman thinks I have nae sense at all," said Barbara disdainfully in Scots as she led them skilfully through the milling throng. She arrived near the end of the long table on the right and indicated to two seats. "There, that's where you'll be sitting, Morag. Next tae Glenna."

Morag eyed the seat with disinterest, though she suppressed a rise of anger that once again the fates seem determined to throw her in with a hated Campbell. She glanced at Glenna, who seemed no happier than she at the prospect.

The far door opened and a moment later the trumpeters up in their loft rose and sounded the announcement of the royal presence. A frail grey-haired woman advanced, supported on either side by women, each as elegantly attired as their companion. It was no doubt the Dowager Queen – and on cue, the whole of the inhabitants of the dining hall made their obeisance, the men bowing deeply and the ladies curtsying with equal depth.

The Dowager Queen made her way slowly to the head of the first table, the one opposite Morag's. Her kirtle was beautifully made of the finest silk, with an embroidery on the underskirt and along her narrow sleeves. A jewelled ruby pin surrounded by a ring of pearls that stood out against the deep purple silk was her only adornment. The woman to her left assisted her into her seat and murmured something in her ear.

"That's Lady Erskine," whispered Barbara to Morag. "She is one of the most senior of the ladies-in-waiting."

Morag examined the woman who was her titular supervisor. Lady Erskine was a tall, imposing lady, her fair hair caught in a jewelled coif that matched the richness of her jewel encrusted kirtle. Morag was surprised at the woman's youth, for she could be no more than a handful of years older than herself, but she had a command and bearing that marked her power and authority.

With the Dowager Queen seated, the rest of the company took their places at the table and sat.

With a small nod Barbara murmured, "I'll just be over on thon seat." She gave Morag's arm a squeeze and moved further along the table towards the centre.

"She is more senior than the two of us and her father has some influence at court," said Glenna in French, her tone formal.

Morag glanced over at Glenna, whose face remained carefully neutral. "I see."

She stared down at the empty seat before her and with a sigh took her place. Glenna followed suit wordlessly while around them servants emerged laden with dishes or carrying large ewers of wine and ale under the steward's watchful eye. Determinedly, Morag gazed around her, taking in the faces and dress. It was a colourful sight, everyone festooned in furs and jewels of myriad designs, colours and textures it almost made Morag dizzy and feel sorely the lack in her own attire. Judging from everyone else, her own clothes would compare very poorly. She could see only a handful of older women, like Mistress Cunningham, wore the square cut bodice and full sleeves folded back. Every other woman, especially the most affluent, wore gowns like Barbara and Glenna with narrow sleeves, though some were puffed at the shoulders. Her own clothes marked her for the old fashioned Highland girl she was. But there was nothing to be done about it.

Her eye was caught by a particularly colourful group assembled at the middle of the Dowager Queen's table. They were a flamboyant and lively gathering, already chattering and laughing and with one familiar figure in its middle. Alexander Munro. He'd changed his outfit for a vivid gold silk doublet with deep blue edging on its many cuttes that revealed the snowy linen beneath it. The sleeves were puffed at the top and sported cuttes there, in addition to the many that lined the rest of the doublet. It was the ruff around his neck that caught her attention and she was certain everyone else's. Its size and the deep blue flowers embroidered on it were remarkable. That was the most tasteful word Morag could formulate. She looked at his wrists and found the lace that peeked out from the doublet sleeves were indeed embroidered to match. A host of rings adorned his fingers, some of them jewelled. On the left side of his chest a large sapphire brooch was pinned. He wore no bonnet and Abby could see carefully oiled sandy-coloured locks gleaming in the candlelight. He held a lace edged handkerchief which at this moment he was gesturing down the table and speaking quite animatedly. It must have been a quip because it was met with loud laughter.

Morag shook her head at the scene. On anyone else, Munro's attire would be deemed ridiculous. Her brother would certainly have scoffed at it and his manner. But somehow Munro stopped just short of the ridiculous. She could see that those around attempted to ape some of his style, not quite succeeding with the panache that he managed. Still, he was not to her taste, so it mattered not.

"That man there is Alexander Munro," said Glenna, her manner studiously conversational. "He's a distant kinsman of Lady Erskine's. Though her mother is a Campbell," she added softly, her tone containing more than a little edge of warning to it.

"Oh?" said Morag. "So, is that how you managed to obtain a place at court? I have only my lineage, being a direct descendant of the original first king of Scotland."

"I'm sure they don't count that at all," said Glenna with false sweetness. "It must have been something else entirely. I do hear that the Dowager Queen is sympathetic to the plight of less fortunate, though."

So the little maid had teeth. With effort, Morag stilled her tongue. It would do no good to engage in battle with this Campbell girl. She must wait until she knew more about this court and her place in it before she made any moves to help her family. Besides, she had an inkling of an idea.

She steered her tone to be pleasant. "What is Lady Erskine like? Does she have much interaction with us?"

Glenna reached for one of the small partridges on the platter before her, placing it on her pewter plate. The task completed, she turned to Morag.

"She has little enough to do with us. Her primary concern is tending directly to the Dowager Queen. It's Mistress Cunningham who deals with us the most."

"Is Mistress Cunningham a relation of Lady Erskine's?"

"Of a sort, but it's very distant and through marriage only."

It was more or less what Morag had concluded. "She is married then?"

"Widowed."

"The thought of spending more time with his sour old wife probably sent him to his grave," Morag muttered to herself.

"Hmm, possibly," said Glenna in a low voice. "Though she will have him as a saintly human being incapable of anything but prayer."

Morag started for a moment at the remark. "Yes, but we don't know what he prayed for."

"Oh, I think we do," said Glenna, giving her a sidelong glance. Her face was expressionless.

Morag nodded sagely, her mouth quirking. "A saint indeed, or should I say, martyr."

A truce then. Morag was glad for it, really, because as much as she hated to admit it, she was finding her experience so far increasingly daunting. Each course that was brought to the table with its myriad dishes and continually flowing drink had left her struggling to contain her wide-eyed amazement. She was forced to rely on Glenna, either by surreptitious observation or outright instruction on the identity and content of many dishes and, on one occasion, the manner of eating it. She'd always been proud of her father's table, rich in abundance whenever they had guests, but she could see now that it was humble by comparison. She felt out of her depth and she struggled to suppress her feelings of inadequacy. She had much to learn, and she would strive to do it as much as she was able without calling attention to her lack of worldliness.

THE COURSES WERE COMPLETE, as far Morag could determine. People had risen and were starting to mill around and the musicians had progressed from more stately and subdued tunes with some accompanied singing to livelier dances that set feet tapping. Morag could see Barbara now. She was just rising, her cheeks flushed becomingly as she exchanged a flirtatious look with a young man nearby. With a small wink she turned and made her way towards Morag and Glenna.

"There now, there's nae need for ye tae remain seated," she said in a low voice in Scots. "The old limmer is engaged in toadying to Lady Erskine. There's enough of a squeeze here she willna notice if we have a wee bit of fun."

Morag looked a little uncertain for a moment, but after glancing around her and finding it was as Barbara said, she gave a small shrug and stood. Glenna was already at Barbara's side, a sparkle in her eye.

The three of them, with Barbara leading, made their way to a group of younger courtiers, mostly men. On seeing Barbara, the men turned and smiled at her appreciatively.

"If it isn't a young Venus come to grace us with her presence," said a dark haired young man in French. He was tall and slender, with a willowy grace as he executed a small bow. His doublet and slops were a fine light grey silk that set off his lively blue eyes.

"Ah, my lord, if I were to take you seriously my head would never fit through the door," said Barbara in fluent French. "And half the ladies would be in the same predicament because of your many compliments – and then who would you flirt with, because we'd all be confined to our rooms?"

He joined the laughter that accompanied Barbara's retort. "You will have it that none will take a word I say to heart, my lady."

Barbara laughed this time and she turned merrily to Morag. "You must have care with this one." She gestured to the rest of the group. "And his companions will spare no words if they think it will get them somewhere."

"And why would they think that, my lovely Lady Barbara if you haven't succumbed to my charms as yet?" said the man.

"And his charms are great and many," said a stocky, ruddy faced man. He turned to Morag. "Will you introduce us to your companion who is beside our dainty little Lady Glenna? I don't believe we're acquainted."

"Oh forgive me," said Lady Barbara hurriedly. "I meant to from the start, only Robert will say such outrageous things that it flew clear from my head." She gestured to Morag. "Thomas, please allow me to introduce you to the lady Morag MacGregor. Morag you have Thomas Maxwell and beside him with the flowery compliments is Robert Hay and the other gentleman is James Home and his charming companion is Margaret Ramsay, his cousin."

Morag found she liked Thomas Maxwell, whose good humour was so evident in his face and manner. James Home was fair-haired with a few faded pock marks, but no less handsome for it. Margaret Ramsey, though not in the first blush of youth, was comely, if only for her animated expression and dimpled cheeks. Her long, slender hands flashed with jewelled rings as she moved one hand to rest on the sleeve of Hay. She surveyed Morag's gown with a long, amused glance.

Each of the small group made their courtesies and Morag kept her face composed and expressionless, uncertain what to make of all of them except Maxwell. Beside her, Glenna had made her own curtsy and voiced a few pleasantries, but made little other comment.

Hay held out a hand to Morag, "Will you give me the pleasure of a dance, my lady? If only that I may have an opportunity to defend my honour after so scurrilous a dismissal of my efforts on compliments."

Barbara laughed. "Efforts to flatter them into your bed, you mean."

Morag was appalled to find herself blushing, and could only give a flustered nod and take his hand. Anything to escape the group, whose interactions and relationships seemed laden with pitfalls she had yet to fully discern.

Maxwell was close behind them with Barbara, and a moment later she saw James Home lead his cousin to join the set that was forming on the floor. Morag glanced around for Glenna, and eventually spotted her in the distance, talking to a young man she didn't know. A moment later they were joined by Alexander Munro, looking even more like a peacock in his gold hose and garters embroidered in deep blue. The signature handkerchief dangled from his wrist at the moment. She could see the young man with him also sported a handkerchief and he was waving it around. She stifled a laugh.

"You find something amusing? Oh, do tell me, that I might share it and discover what I may do to contrive your face to light up so appealingly."

She gave him a tight smile. "Only that young courtier and his handkerchief."

Hay turned to where she indicated. "Ah yes. That is David Montgomerie. He attempts to model himself after Lord Munro, but he doesn't quite appreciate what Munro is doing."

Morag raised her brow and Hay gave a lazy smile. "You see, it is all the rage in the English court, the handkerchief."

"And that is cause for Munro, I mean, David Montgomerie to imitate them? Surely the Dowager Queen and the rest of the court would find that offensive."

"But my lady, you misunderstand entirely. Munro is mocking them."

She turned and studied Munro, his slightly arched brow, the hint of amusement in the mouth as he listened attentively to the youth. Glenna touched Munro's arm, clearly interjecting a comment. Munro turned to her and his smile softened. Morag felt a flash of irritation. The two would be related, of course, albeit distantly, so they would naturally be in each other's company. She would have to watch herself.

As if feeling her attention, Munro lifted his eyes and caught hers. A twinkle appeared and with it she was certain the hint of a wink. She decided a moment later she was mistaken. But it left her unsettled. For what reason she didn't know at present, except there was something decidedly familiar about it, something she couldn't place.

The dance began and Morag set the puzzle aside in light of the need to concentrate. She wouldn't allow herself to exhibit any trace of hesitation or incompetence here. She was known to be a good dancer at home, and she was determined it would be no different at court. It was relief that she realised it was a stately allemande which would give her time to calm herself and become used to observe any new mannerisms. She progressed in the dance, aware of Hays' eyes on her, his amusement clear in his face. She gave him a stiff smile and became more determined to acquit herself with as much grace as possible.

Eventually, she was able to relax and by the end she managed to derive a little enjoyment from the dance. Hay was accomplished, which she appreciated, and though the dance was too sedate to allow much display of skill, it was enough that when the music finished and he bowed his thanks there was a small amount of appreciation replacing the amusement.

"Very charming, my lady."

She bowed slightly and murmured her thanks before he took her hand to escort her back to their small group that had reassembled, all except for Glenna. She glanced around but couldn't see her anywhere, until she heard some faint clapping that grew in intensity as all heads turned to the dais where a stool had been placed. A moment later, Munro stepped up on it, followed by Glenna, carrying a lute. She took the stool, propped the lute on her lap and began to pluck a few of the strings while adjusting a peg. Like Abby, and now Iain, she played with her fingers rather than the usual quill. Morag frowned, understanding suddenly why that would be.

Any further musings were interrupted by the sight of Munro taking a place beside her and leaning down for a moment to confer. Morag felt a twinge of irritation as Glenna nodded and struck up a tune. After a few bars Munro began to sing in a rich baritone that surprised her, given that his speaking voice suggested a tenor and a not very melodic one at that. She was unfamiliar with the song but listened intently to hear the words. It was in French with a pleasing melody.

She turned to Barbara and whispered, "Do you know the song?"

Barbara shrugged. "It's one the Dowager Queen has recently heard and likes. I can't remember the name."

Morag sighed, lamenting Barbara's disinterest. Iain and Abby would have known – and if not, would have discovered it quickly. She missed that shared interest and longed to be back at Glen Strae. She turned back to the performers, blinking back the sudden tears. It was no use mourning over what couldn't be changed. She remembered the thought that had struck her earlier. Perhaps she could change at least one thing.

The performers finished and the clapping was fulsome, led as it was by the Dowager Queen. Before Morag could lose her courage, she made her way forward, hoping that her next action wouldn't condemn her as an impudent ill-bred Highlander for the remainder of her time at court.

She found Lady Erskine not far from the Dowager Queen, turning away from a nobleman who had just taken his leave of her. Morag approached and gave her a swift curtsy.

"Lady Erskine. I am the lady Morag MacGregor, daughter of Gregor MacGregor of Glen Strae, Chieftain. I arrived today and wished to give you my greetings."

Lady Erskine frowned a little, eyeing Morag and, after a moment, inclined her head. "I trust you have settled in. Mistress Cunningham tells me that she's acquainted you with the manner in which we conduct ourselves here and all the other necessaries."

"*Oui, madame,* only there is one small thing I'm sorry to trouble you with."

Lady Erskine raised her brows. "And that is?"

"My maidservant, Bridie. I would wish to keep her with me. Mistress Cunningham felt her unsuitable and said she will send her home tomorrow. But Bridie is my distant cousin. Her mother and mine were milk sisters and I promised I would look after her when her mother died recently, because my mother has been dead a number of years and unable to do so. She's a good and capable maidservant, I promise."

Had she said too much? Overstretched her case? Morag waited tensely while Lady Erskine considered. After a few moments she gave a shrug. "Very well, I'll instruct Mistress Cunningham."

Morag curtsied deeply and expressed her thanks but Lady Erskine was already moving on towards the Dowager Queen, who was still seated at her table. Morag rose and smiled in satisfaction while Lady Erskine exchanged words with the Dowager Queen. When the exchange was completed, the Dowager Queen rose. Everyone else in the hall rose a moment later and made deep bows and curtsies as she processed to the door, supported on each side by Lady Erskine and another senior attendant. When all the attendants had disappeared everyone rose and it wasn't long before the chatter rose and the music struck up again.

Morag was still standing alone, the smile wide on her face when a young man approached her.

"Mademoiselle, you are alone and for one so beautiful that is a crime, though I know it will only be a moment before some young courtier claims your attention and asks you to dance. Will you let it be me?" He bowed low before her. "Allow me to introduce myself. I'm John Dunbar."

Surprised, Morag studied him a moment before executing a brief curtsy. He was without a doubt handsome with his startling hazel eyes and dark hair, and neatly trimmed beard. His clothes of black velvet and silver-coloured silk embroidered with dark thread were cut in the latest fashion and flattered his long, slim waist and shapely legs. The matching velvet cape draped on one shoulder and tied across his chest gave him a rakish look that she found she liked.

She smiled at him and introduced herself. He returned the smile, a smile that sported a dimple and surely designed to melt any heart, thought Morag. He offered his hand and led her to the dancing area as the sounds of a galliard struck up. She felt a thrill at the thought of dancing something so intimate and lovely with such a man. She moved into the steps with ease and excitement, delighting in her partner's firm, confident touch and practised skill.

They moved around the floor as the dance progressed and she laughed at the joy of it all and the feel of moving with the others as they all executed the steps. Her eye caught one of the dancers whose back was facing her and she allowed a moment to admire his skill and grace. She was startled when a moment later she discovered it was Munro. His partner, gathering herself to be lifted was flushed and her eyes sparkled. It was Margaret Ramsey, looking youthful and bewitching, her lips slightly parted. The hands at Morag's waist gripped her at that moment and lifted her above him. She looked down into his eyes and smiled as becomingly as she could. He let her down slowly, only just keeping with the music, his doublet brushing her bodice briefly.

The dance finished soon after and Lord John bowed over her

hand and for a brief moment held it to her lips. She stared down at his dark head and felt the tingle of his kiss.

"You must allow me to have the pleasure of another dance very soon, mademoiselle," he said. "With your skill and grace, I can find no other partner that would compare."

Morag blushed. "I should be thanking you, my lord, for your dancing is matchless."

"There you are," said Barbara coming up to her. "I've been looking for you. We must go before the gorgon discovers we're still here. She'll be back from attending Lady Erskine."

Dunbar bowed again. "You must both excuse me, then." He looked over at Morag and smiled. "Until the next dance, my lady," he said and took his leave.

"A conquest?" Barbara said in a teasing tone.

"A courtier," said Morag with a studied shrug.

"An attentive courtier, I would say. Taken with your charms by the way he was looking at you. Who was he?"

"You mean you don't know him? He introduced himself as John Dunbar."

Barbara shook her head. "Ah. I think I have heard his name. I believe he's only newly arrived, but that's all I know." She nudged Morag. "And that he is handsome and charming. What else is there to know?"

Morag smiled back. "He is indeed all you say." She turned and watched him stop and speak to an older gentleman. She sighed. She hoped it wouldn't be too long before the next opportunity to dance came. Or some other gathering where she might encounter him again.

CHAPTER 5

"We're milk cousins, Bridie," said Morag in Gaelic. "Don't forget it, if someone should ask."

Bridie gave a puzzled frown and looked up from her efforts smoothing out a creased kirtle she'd just withdrawn from the small kist at her feet. "Milk cousins?"

"Yes. Your mother and mine were nursed at your grandmother's breast," Morag said carefully.

Humour lit Bridie's face. "Of course we are. Why would I forget?"

Morag laughed. "Oh, you wouldn't."

Bridie's cold seemed to have benefited from a night's rest in the castle, wherever that may have been, thought Morag. She bustled around the room, smoothing and brushing out garments for Morag and laying them on the bed. Barbara and Glenna had left a while ago after their chambermaid had helped to dress them. Morag had politely refused the chambermaid's services and asked for her to send up Bridie as soon as possible. Bridie arrived just after Morag's baggage had been deposited in the room.

"These are in the best shape, milady," said Bridie in Scots. "I'll see tae the rest after I get ye dressed." She gave a shake of her head and a cluck. "I've had a look at some of the other young ladies' clothes and these dinna seem the thing. Though that ole scunner Mistress Cunningham wears this fashion."

Morag smiled at Bridie's words. This was the most life she'd seen out of the maidservant since they'd first been together. Perhaps her impulse to retain Bridie's services would have more benefit than just putting Mistress Cunningham's nose out of joint.

"Aye, ye're right, Bridie. My garments are of the old fashion. But there's little enough I can do about it."

Bridie cocked her head a little. "I might be able tae. Leave it tae me. With a bit of cutting, adjusting and some needlework I might contrive a gown or two that will pass." She gave a wicked smile. "There's a lad whose sister works as a needlewoman for the Dowager Queen's wardrobe mistress."

Morag laughed. "Och, Bridie ye sly thing." She sobered a moment. "But ye must have a care, at least for now. Mistress Cunningham willna take it lightly that I thwarted her wishes."

Bridie gave a sniff. "She's a sour old limmer. Do ye ken that she held back your baggage on purpose? I heard her telling one of the servants tae wait until morning tae put it in your room. And she told Rob and Mungo tae find a place in the stables tae sleep along wi' Jemmy and Liam."

"I can believe it. She wasna pleased that ye're staying. We should both steer clear of her for the present."

"Aye, it's best tae be careful. I overheard a few things that didna make me at ease. Too many rivalries and such."

Morag's frowned. She suspected as much, though she should hardly find it surprising, since this was the centre of power and the times were troubled.

Bridie patted her arm. "Dinna worry milady, I'll keep my eyes and ears open and pass on what I can tae help ye. Ye're no tae think ye're alone. And Rob has said tae tell ye that he'll bide a while, despite what the ole witch says. He's discovered his wife is kin tae one of the kitchen workers, who introduced him tae the head groom and he's a job for a while looking after the horses."

Morag felt a small burst of joy at Bridie's reassurances. She squeezed her hand. "I thank ye for such news,"

Bridie chuckled. "What else would a milk cousin do, aye?"

MORAG STABBED her needle into the fabric and winced as she caught the edge of her finger underneath. She drew her finger out from underneath and sucked it, hoping she hadn't got any blood on the cloth. Mistress Cunningham would be certain to catch it when she inspected each girl's work on the altar cloths at the day's finish and she would give Morag yet another lowering look that clearly said her upbringing as a backwards Highland girl was showing yet again. She had yet to forgive Morag for overriding her authority with Bridie and took every opportunity to give her a set down.

Morag was in the Dowager Queen's apartments, in the presence chamber, along with the other of the Dowager Queen's attendants. The Queen was in a chair while her senior attendants were ranged around her on cushions. The windows provided a vast amount of light, but some of the panes were ill fitting, making the fire and lit braziers welcome in the chill April wind.

The senior ladies-in-waiting, including Lady Erskine, conversed desultorily, discussing the books on their laps or the forthcoming hunt among themselves, while the Dowager Queen sat back in her chair, her eyes half closed. At her feet was the Dowager Queen's fool, Betsy Dunne.

The less senior ladies, along with Morag, Barbara and Glenna, were seated on cushions further back, under the beady eye of Mistress Cunningham, where seemingly more industrious work was undertaken. Beside Morag, Barbara plied her needle half-heartedly, one arm resting on the large cushion on which she sat, as she did every time they were called upon to work on the cloths. Her work was little better than Morag's, yet no words of scolding came her way or Glenna's. She looked over at Glenna who was scowling over her work, mouthing words as though she were reciting something. Morag leaned closer and she could hear the soft sounds of singing. In Gaelic. Morag repressed a snort and took up her needle again, her finger having ceased bleeding. Who was the backwards Highland girl now?

"What was it you heard about that troublesome Mister Knox?" said the Dowager Queen loudly across the circle to Lady Livingston, who sat on the far side.

"Only that he has been preaching again, sowing sedition and casting aspersions on Your Grace."

The Dowager Queen frowned. "You mean he is continuing to support this so-called 'Beggars' Summons' that threatens all good friars."

"The people have better sense than to support such an outrageous notion to hand over religious property to the poor," said Lady Livingston in a soothing tone.

There were murmurs of reassurance, though even Morag knew from the past few days at court that this was hardly the truth in the face of the wave of violence and disorder against religious houses that had broken out in the last year from Protestants.

The Queen sighed and cast her glance about until it fell on Glenna. She smiled a little and then leaned over and spoke to Lady Erskine, who nodded.

"Lady Glenna, we must praise you for your skilful lute playing. Perhaps you would play for us sometime in the privacy of our chambers."

Glenna rose, her face flushed, and curtsied. "You are too kind, Your Grace. I would be delighted to play for you."

The Dowager Queen acknowledged Glenna's reply with a nod. "Your father brought you up well, for to be so skilled."

Glenna stiffened slightly. "It is my mother who is musical, Your Grace."

"Ah, yes. Lady Erskine mentioned that your mother has been unwell, especially after the birth of her last child, so much so that the child was given to your older sister to raise with her husband."

"She is unwell, yes. I thank you for your concern."

"And the child, does it fare well?"

Glenna's face had turned to stone. "He does, Your Grace, as far as I am aware. I haven't seen him, or my sister, for some time."

"No, of course not," said the Dowager Queen. "Such a pity. But at least you're here and your music as well, which brightens us all with its charm."

Glenna curtsied again and the Dowager Queen nodded before turning her attention elsewhere while the senior ladies resumed their chatter. Glenna took her seat, her manner still stiff.

Barbara glanced sideways at Morag and smiled conspiratorially. "How's your needlework coming along, Glenna? I think mine has a life of its own."

Glenna took up the needlework but remained silent.

"Mine has no life at all," said Anne Scot, the pert young blonde on Barbara's other side. She gave a little giggle.

"I could do with some life, preferably of the male variety," said Jean Elphinston. She sighed. Plump faced, her steel corset only accentuated her round curves.

"Couldn't we all," said Barbara. She turned to Morag. "I know someone who would be very glad of your company in particular."

Morag threw her a puzzled look and gave a brief thought to John Dunbar. Barbara leered at her. "Robert Hay."

"Robert Hay?" asked Anne. She sighed. "He's so tall and wonderfully handsome."

Morag snorted incredulously. "I'm sure you're wrong."

"No, I promise you. Robert has expressed several times how taken he is with you. In fact he has asked me when you might be taking a turn in the garden so that he might chance upon you."

"Oooh, I wager he wants to do many things upon her," Jean said with a small titter.

Barbara snickered. "Indeed. But my preferences veer in Thomas Maxwell's direction. Height isn't the measure of a man." She gave a wicked grin. "For me, it's girth."

Gales of laughter followed that remark and earned them severe looks from Mistress Cunningham. For herself, Morag was glad that the focus of the discussion had turned away from her, though she wondered at Barbara's remark. She hadn't noticed Barbara paying extra attention to Thomas Maxwell.

When they had settled and Mistress Cunningham had taken up her conversation with one of the senior ladies-in-waiting, Jean spoke.

"You can speak to that as fact?" she asked Barbara, her eyes sparkling.

Barbara smiled slyly. "I might."

Morag turned to gauge the young woman. She was bold enough, certainly. "But surely, if you have…experienced his girth, doesn't that mean you'll have to marry him? I mean what if you should become…" she searched for the word in French…"with child?"

Jean gave her a condescending smile. "There are ways to deal with that, didn't you know? Measures you can take?"

Morag frowned at her. "Yes of course, but surely there is risk? And what of your, ah…maidenhead?"

Ann tittered. "Listen to the child."

Barbara patted her hand. "We have ways to deal with that as well. Men never know the difference between a phial of chicken blood and that from a woman's womb."

Morag blushed under the weight of the gaze of the three

women who regarded her, once again feeling ignorant and backwards.

"Some men wouldn't mind in any case," said Jean. "Especially if it's just an alliance between two families. They understand what court is like, after all. They appreciate a woman's experience, so that even the wedding night can be enjoyable for all."

Morag sat there speechless. Was this really how things were arranged here at court?

"Do all men and women have dalliances here?" she asked, finally. Though she knew the question would only reinforce their impression of her ignorance, she couldn't help it.

Barbara shrugged. "Many do."

Jean leaned forward. "Yes," she said, "but there is one man who is resisting every lady's efforts to get him to bed her. Do you know how much is being wagered against Lord Munro?"

"No. What is it now?" said Anne.

"Ten merks."

"That high?" asked Barbara. "For that amount he'll have all the women panting at his door night and day."

"He will," said Jean. "I wouldn't mind trying for it, despite his girth. He has a bonny look about him."

"Hmmm," said Anne. "He is handsome, though he is wide about the middle, but I think his airs venture too much into women's territory."

"That may be a good thing," said Barbara, considering. "He would possibly give due consideration to women's needs in the bedchamber."

The other two women gave assenting noises. "What do you think, Glenna?" said Jean.

Glenna looked up from her tightly gripped needlework. "I have no opinion on the matter."

Barbara glanced over at Morag. "And you, Morag. Do you have an opinion on the matter?"

"I'm afraid I hardly know the man to have an opinion."

"Oh, but you've seen him, in fact he's spoken to you, I heard, in the outer close when you arrived."

Morag bent her head over her needlework, trying to hide her expression of dismay. "I'm not certain I know what to think of the man, or his looks. But you may be safe in the knowledge that I won't be among the women panting at his door."

Barbara laughed softly and the other two women followed suit. "I'd say there are many women who can breathe a sigh of relief, now," she said.

Morag stiffened and gave her a weak smile, uncertain whether it was meant as an underhanded jab, but studying the friendly gaze she decided Barbara was just teasing.

"In any case, I'd much rather be with the Dark Ghost," said Anne.

Her remark was greeted with teeth sucking and sighs from Barbara and Jean.

"The Dark Ghost?" asked Morag.

"Aye, have ye no heard of the Dark Ghost?" asked Jean.

"No, who's he? Is he here at court?"

"Och, if only he was," said Barbara in Scots. "I'd certainly gi' him a warm welcome."

Morag looked at the three women and then over to Glenna, who refused to lift her head and concentrated on her needlework.

"Who is he?" she repeated.

"He's a legend," said Anne.

"A very large legend," said Barbara with a giggle.

"Large and dangerous," said Jean. She raised her brow. "My cousin said his sister met him once in the dead of night. Said he was extremely tall and carried a knife."

"Did he pierce her with his 'knife'?" said Barbara. Anne and Jean howled with laughter.

"Nay, it's truth, though," said Jean.

"What else did she say?" asked Barbara leaning forward. "Did she say where she met him?"

Jean shook her head. "That's all my cousin would say."

Barbara sat back with a frown. "That's no verra much."

"I've heard that he rides out at midnight on his dark horse and wreaks vengeance for little Queen Marie and her mother," said Anne. "And he has the darkest eyes, the broadest chest and he kissed a maiden until she fainted when she gave him a cup of wine when he was pursued by the Lords of the Congregation's men."

"He would have time to stop for a cup of wine?" asked Morag, puzzled.

The three women looked at her in disgust. "Ye ken nothing of his abilities," said Jean sternly.

Clearly she didn't. "And he's called 'The Dark Ghost?'" she asked sceptically.

"Well something of that nature. At least that's how they translate it from Gaelic."

Now they had her attention. "He has a Gaelic name?"

"Yes," said Anne. She paused a moment. "Was it 'drock sperod'?"

Did ye mean '*Droch Spiorad*'?" asked Morag

"Yes," said Anne. "That's it, I think. But how did ye ken?"

Morag shrugged.

"But of course," said Jean. "Ye speak the Gaelic, do ye no? Ye're a Highland lady. I'd forgotten for a moment."

"Ye speak French so well, it wouldna even occur to anyone ye might be from there," Anne said and eyed Morag up and down, "were it not for your clothes."

"She's a real innocent, too," said Jean, her tone smug.

Morag gave a weak smile and turned her attention to her needlework with renewed diligence. The digs faded somewhat while she pondered the recent conversation. Did these women really understand that his name in Gaelic meant something entirely different from 'Dark Ghost?' She gave a shudder. She wouldn't want to meet anyone who was called 'evil spirit', day or night.

"Will ye go hunting on the morrow?" Anne asked her.

"Hunting?" said Morag, dragging her mind away from her contemplation.

"Aye, did ye no hear? There's a short hunt and we're allowed tae go," said Jean. "Do ye have a proper mount?"

She'd heard about the hunt but hadn't known if Mistress Cunningham was giving them permission to go. It might be yet another in a line of petty revenges Mistress Cunningham had sought to dispel against her.

"I'm not certain I'll be allowed tae go," said Morag. "Mistress Cunningham hasna said a word tae me about it."

"It's only just been decided," said Barbara. "I'm sure they'll be nae problem."

She gave Barbara a sceptical look. "I wouldna be so certain."

Barbara raised her brow. "Is she still beating ye with that stick?"

"What stick?" said Anne quickly. "I demand tae be told."

Barbara leaned forward and recounted the details of Morag's clever manoeuvre against Mistress Cunningham over Bridie. When the tale was completed, the two other women regarded Morag with guarded approval.

"She has claws," said Jean.

Morag gave them an innocent smile. She did indeed, and she hoped they wouldn't forget it.

CHAPTER 6

*T*he outer close was alive with activity and excitement. Elegantly clad noblemen and noblewomen mingled, chatting amiably in the early morning, hot breaths punctuating the air. Footmen and pages weaved throughout carrying stirrup cups and plates of food, and footmen assisted the horses or helped riders to mount. Horses snorted and paced while in the distance the greyhounds and lymers, already set in relay stages along the hunting trail, barked, excited at the opportunity to have free rein on their energy in pursuit of prey.

Morag sat on Rory's roan courser, fighting to control him as he side stepped and turned. He was obviously uncomfortable with her mounted on a ladies' saddle. She was determined to ride him, even though an inner voice told her she was courting folly. It was just so irresistible to ask to have him saddled, knowing that his lines and quality were so much better than her own mare. Rory may be many things but he knew horse flesh. And could afford it. She just couldn't bear to be the object of more discussion and inference about her backwards Highland roots.

Her clothes at least wouldn't shame her. Bridie's skill with the needle and her deft negotiation had worked miracles and Morag was glad that for once she was supported by at least one genuine friend and well-wisher. She wore a skirt that was a slimmer version of the burgundy velvet she'd worn to the castle a scant ten days ago, and the once wide sleeves had been narrowed and a puff formed at the top. The waist of the bodice had been reshaped and lengthened with a bit of deft ingenuity and some clever inserts of gold brocade banding that accentuated and slimmed her waistline. That was no mean feat, as she had opted out of wearing the awful steel corset that Bridie had found someone to make for her and had presented to her a few days ago. Morag would leave that for more formal occasions. Though covered and padded, it was uncomfortable and she found it difficult to imagine anyone torturing themselves so, despite Bridie's protest that it would achieve wondrous things for her figure. She had no arguments about the bonnet she wore, though. She was thrilled at its clever confection. It was placed over the netted snood that kept her hair pulled back and matched her gown perfectly with its burgundy velvet brim and more gold brocade banding it on the brim. She wore it perched on her head at an angle

The roan paced and turned again and Morag tightened the reins. She glanced around her, looking for clues to signal the beginning of the hunt. She could see Barbara, Robert Hay, James Home and Margaret Ramsey talking together. Robert, a bow slung across his shoulders stood with Margaret, next to Barbara who was mounted on a sleek grey courser and looked a picture in her black and gold outfit. Mounted next to her was James Home.

"That a fine horse you have there," said a voice behind her.

Morag turned her horse with as much ease as she could muster and nodded to Glenna. Glenna grinned back at her, eyeing the roan.

"By the look of him I'd say he has a smart pace about him."

Morag studied Glenna, looking for a dig but was surprised to find that her eyes were twinkling.

"I think you may have the right of it," said Morag with a small smile.

"Oh, I think that my brother would know fine." She laughed and shook her head. "And I know that he would be most displeased to find you mounted on him, his finest horse."

Morag couldn't help but grin. "Yes, well he may now remember that even a MacGregor woman is best avoided."

Glenna laughed again. "That he would be so stupid. But his ego often overtakes his brain. And you, to give him a good thrashing in the bargain. He'll not live this down. Ever. And I feel I must thank you for it."

Morag looked at her curiously. "You're thanking me? And would you be sharing the roan's name with me as well as your thanks?"

"Of course. Though it does the Campbell name no good to have a MacGregor get the best of us, in this case I think on the behalf of womankind I must thank you."

"We've much to thank Lady Morag for," said Robert Hay who, now mounted, drew up on the other side of Morag.

"My lord," said Morag and bowed her head slightly in greeting.

Glenna murmured her own greeting and quickly excused herself and nodded to the roan. "Thunder," she said, and moved off.

"May I say how charming you look," said Hay. He lifted her free gloved hand and kissed the back of it.

"How very kind of you," Morag said, eyeing him cautiously.

"It has nothing to do with kindness, I assure you. I am merely stating fact."

Uncertain how she should handle this sudden attention, she looked around for Barbara or any of the others. She spied John Dunbar a short distance away and caught his gaze. He gave her a smile and began to amble his horse towards hers.

"A fine day for the hunt, is it not, my lady?" he said when he drew alongside. He nodded to Hay. "My lord."

Hay frowned at him and returned the nod. "Is this your first hunt at Stirling Castle?"

"It is."

"But you carry no bow, or fire arm."

"No, but I am content to watch."

"You are wise," said Morag. "It's my first as well and I too choose merely to ride and observe."

Hay looked at her in surprise. "You would shoot a bow?"

She gave him a brief look of disdain. "I would join the hunt at home and often take my bow."

"And I'm certain you made a very fine bowman," said Dunbar.

Hay made a polite noise of protest. "You must take care handling a bow," he said to her. "It's easy enough to become injured trying to use it and remain mounted. Even with the fine mount you have."

He eyed her and her horse with a sceptical look and Morag cursed inwardly that Thunder, if that was his name, chose that moment to fidget and then side step. She raised her chin slightly.

"It's different in the Highlands. The ground can be steep and uneven, so we use ponies specifically bred to the terrain. They are suited to a hunt in that situation and are easily managed."

"All the more reason for you to have a care today," said Hay. He reached out to pat her hand. "But I will be here to assist you should you need it."

"But I wouldn't want to keep you from the joy of going after the hart," said Morag.

"There's no need to worry," said Hay.

"No need to worry at all," said Dunbar. "I will be more than happy to accompany Lady Morag today, so you may pursue the hart with a free hand."

Hay swung the bow from across his shoulders, untied the quiver from his horse and handed them over to Dunbar. "Here, I insist you have my bow and quiver so that you may enjoy the hunt. I have been on many here and it is no great thing for me."

Dunbar took the bundle with an amused glance and a short bow. "You are too kind, my lord."

Horns sounded around them, calling everyone to make ready and head for the assembly point out in the fields beyond the castle. Dunbar hastily secured his quiver and slung the bow over his shoulder while Morag and Hay gathered up their reins and began to move out with the others.

The head huntsmen led the way and they were all soon cantering across the fields to the hunting grounds located previously by him and the lymer. Morag hung back at the rear of the group, reluctant to be caught should any sudden run be announced or a horn sound that would cause Thunder to move quickly before she had prepared. The horse was becoming more trouble than he was worth, she realised, what with the stupid skirt and her legs only on one side of the horse. She'd slipped away from Robert at the earliest opportunity, uneasy at his sudden attentiveness. She just wasn't used to courtly manners, she knew. It unnerved her, since Davey or her brothers had never treated her in that manner, or anyone else for that matter.

She reached the assembly point well at the tail end of the group so that the horn had already sounded and they were moving away, following the track the lead huntsmen had confirmed and established. She could hear the first set of lymers up ahead, barking in their pursuit of the quarry.

Morag followed easily, her horse gaining its stride and she felt that she might just manage this hunt and actually enjoy it. The countryside rolled by her, the gentle undulations giving away to trees. Up ahead she could hear more barking and another horn sounded. A mounted horseman in front of her drew up a little to avoid a branch and she checked her horse's stride. She slid on her saddle just a fraction and her leg moved. Before she knew it she was fighting to keep her seat and Thunder slowed and snorted. A moment later she could feel him check again and then slow, his stride uneven.

There were trees all around her now and she slowed to a stop so she could check on Thunder. Something was clearly wrong. When the horse halted, Morag unhooked her leg and slid carefully to the ground. Once there, she went to Thunder's right foreleg where she'd detected the problem. She stroked him first along his side, making soothing noises and whispering to him in Gaelic, then ran her hand along his foreleg, feeling for any sign of injury. There was nothing. She leaned against him, still speaking softly in Gaelic, and after a little nudge to his side, carefully lifted his forelock to examine his hoof. She leaned down closer to try and get a better view in the dim light of the trees. A small stone had found its way into the hoof and was caught against the shoe. She prised it out with a quick strong flick of her finger and it went flying. She let the hoof go and patted Thunder's side, praising him in Gaelic now. She made her way around to the other side and patted Thunder again so that she might gather herself to try and mount herself. It would be difficult, but she had done without a block or assistance before on her mare, albeit without skirts. She would at least try.

"Ah, a lady in distress."

Morag looked up and saw Robert Hay pulling up in front of her. He dismounted swiftly and came to her side.

"It's only a stone, nothing more," she said. "I've removed it and was just about to remount."

He gave her a lazy smile and put a hand over hers where it rested on the horse's side. "I'll help you mount then."

"That's very kind of you."

She gave him a wan smile and stood there, waiting for him to lean over and clasp his hands so she might place her foot in it, but instead he clasped his hands around her waist.

"Before I lift you up perhaps I might beg the favour of a kiss, a token by way of thanks for my assistance."

He leaned down, his eyes sultry, his mouth inviting. Morag's mouth opened in protest, her eyes wide and his lips bore down on hers as he pulled her into him. She gave him a shove and he released his hold, his face now filled with anger.

"Why so prim all of the sudden?" he said, his grip still firm on her.

Morag pulled away, dragging his hands from her, and moved back. "What do you mean?"

"I thought you enjoyed such encounters. That you wanted me to follow you here. The 'lame horse' being only a ruse so that I might come close, your dignity intact."

"What? This was no ruse, I assure you. It wasn't my intention to lure you or anyone else to my side for….an encounter. I don't know who gave you that idea, but they couldn't have been more wrong."

He released her and gave her a sour look. Before he could say anything more a group of horses trotted into view, their riders shouting with an obvious merriness born of high spirits of the liquid form.

"No, no, I'm certain I heard the dogs barking over here," said Munro, his cheeks ruddy and eyes sparkling. His fur lined cloak was a violent green with some brown stripes to suggest some type of plaid. Around him were equally flamboyantly dressed courtiers laughing and chatting.

"I wager it wasn't dogs barking but the birds screeching at the awful cut of Lord Home's cloak," said a thin nosed man with a loud guffaw.

"A cloak? Is that what you called it?" said a woman. "I wasn't certain if I should warn him he had a bear draped across his back, lest it be a testimony to his manly strength."

"That's no bear, my lady," said another man. "That's the rug from his bedside."

They pulled up at the sight of Morag and Hay. Morag flushed, knowing the sight of the two of them suggested anything but an innocent picture.

Munro gave small bow with a lazy smile. "My lady, have you lost your way like me? Can we be of assistance?"

"I thank you my lord. There's no need now. My horse managed to get a stone lodged in his shoe, but I've removed it now. My lord was kind enough to stop and assist me to mount once again."

"Ah, how fortunate Robert Hay happened upon you at your hour of need. But Lord Robert is always a man of courtesy, are you not my lord?"

Hay gave Munro a thin smile. "Of course, my lord."

"And being so chivalrous, would you mind if we all accompanied you back to the hunt? I am never good with stalking prey, as you can tell from my foolish straying so far away from the rest of the hunting party."

Hay nodded curtly and with a frown assisted Morag back up on her horse. Morag occupied herself with arranging her skirts carefully so that she wouldn't have to look at Munro, or anyone else of his party, her mortification was so great. She knew it was foolish to protest at the innocence of her actions, Munro's words had made that clear enough.

With no real effort, they found the hunting party and rejoined it amidst a cacophony of braying hounds and sounding horns. The prey had been sighted and the greyhounds had been loosed to chase the hart until it was too winded to run. Morag followed the chase half-heartedly, her mind playing over the scene that had just passed. How could it be that Hay had received the impression she was someone who'd welcome his attentions? She'd really given him no encouragement. She dare not approach him to ask. His anger was still evident. She'd seen the manner in which he'd sought John Dunbar out and persuaded him to return the bow and quiver. Only anger could have prompted him to behave in such an uncourtly way.

She hung back further, her taste for any type of exchange with the other participants evaporated under the cloud of her recent experience. Thunder slowed to a trot and then an amble. She was glad the scent of the chase held as little interest for him as it did for her.

"You would be better placed if you participated with a more joyful outlook," said Munro coming up beside her. He gave her an amused look. "Do you not hunt harts in your Highland home?"

She gave him a polite smile. "Och, we but we still manage tae take them wi' our speers, ye ken and nae hoonds tae run them doon," she said in the broadest Scots possible. "This hunt is for wee soft southrenners," she added rolling her 'r's' with as much force as she could muster.

Munro gave a hearty laugh. "Och weel, I ken ye dinna like the manner of the hunt, but ye shouldna let the gawked wee courtiers in thon group ken ye've anything tae be upset about."

She blinked and stared for a moment, then found she was grinning a little. "Aye," she said. "I ken ye may be right."

She stiffened her back and nudged her horse into a trot that shortly became a canter. She sensed Munro close behind her, and on impulse she broke into a gallop, crossing the long field where shortly before the hunting party had travelled. Munro met her stride for stride, and for a moment she felt a thrill of the ride. A sense of freedom she hadn't experienced since her arrival at court.

She pulled up when she came near the hunting part and turned back a moment to flash a smile of victory to Munro, only to find he was right beside her. He grinned back and pulled out ahead of her. She laughed good humouredly and glanced ahead at the slowing hunting party. It seemed the hart had been cornered and it was only a matter of time before the bowmen took their shot. It was then she glimpsed the back of a familiar figure and froze. At that moment the mounted figure turned and spotted her and her worst fear was confirmed. Rory Campbell here at court. How? When?

He gave her a furious look and, turning his horse, made his way over to her. Coming alongside he leaned over and whispered angrily in her ear, "I will have my horse back," he said in Scots.

"You mean Thunder?" she said with a forced blandness. "The horse I'm riding at this very moment? The horse I took from ye after ye attacked me and my escort while I was on my way tae court? On the way tae *serve the Dowager Queen.*"

He flushed and Morag felt a small sense of triumph. "I think not, my lord, but I will remember the courteousness with which ye made the request."

She turned her horse aside and trotted away to join another part of the assembled hunting party and made a valiant effort to stifle her fury.

CHAPTER 7

*M*orag headed over towards the long rug laid carefully on the ground and laden with the latest fare to feed the hungry hunters now the chase was over. The hart had been slain and all those who'd participated in the hunt were assembled back at the starting point for their reward.

Morag tried to halt the anger still coursing through her. She'd given Thunder over to a groom with strict instructions that she and only she was the one to collect him. Nevertheless she keep a wary eye on Thunder.

"Feeling protective toward your horse? He should be fine after the stone," said Munro, drawing up next to her. He held a plate and was picking at the small quail on it with a delicacy that Morag suddenly found amusing.

"I'm sure he'll be fine, but I can't help but worry."

He raised a brow. "A bit more than a stone's worth of worry?"

She flushed. "Perhaps."

He looked at her in amusement. "I think you might be overestimating your foe."

She gave him a startled glance.

"Calm yourself, my lady. You can rest assured that there is no one else here who knows how that lovely horse came to be yours, besides the man himself. Well, perhaps Lady Glenna. And may I say I take my metaphoric hat off to you and offer you a metaphoric bow? I would do so in earnest except that I would fail to do it justice while holding a plateful of food."

She stared at him, too astonished for anything more for a moment. "How do you know?" she said finally.

"Let's just say a bit of observation and I chanced to hear some whiny mutterings."

She looked away, uncertain what to say. "He could likely cause me trouble now, of that I have no doubt."

"I think you are more than capable of telling him the folly of that. And if I'm not mistaken you already have."

She studied him carefully, suddenly aware she really had little idea of the man. He gave her a mock smile and took another bite of his quail and winced.

"I do find the spicing a bit strong for such subtle tasting bird. And it just seems so inappropriate to have something as delicate as quail after pursuit of a large virile animal. It's as though we do the hart dishonour to eat fowl. But I suppose then we would then have to do something like drink its blood or roast it on the spot." He gave a shudder. "Well, that's my appetite done for." He smiled at Morag. "If you'll excuse me, I shall find something to drink."

He gave a small bow and moved off, his mincing movements nevertheless carrying him quickly away, only to be intercepted by two of his friends. Morag shook her head, not knowing what to make of him.

"What has caused you to shake your head?" said a voice.

Morag turned and found Barbara at her shoulder. She gave her a wan smile. "Oh, Lord Munro. He's a puzzle."

"You mean whether he likes the men or ladies?" said Barbara with a twinkle in her eye.

Morag gave her a shocked look. "Is that why he's had no woman succeed in getting him to bed her?"

Barbara laughed. "Or no lady who would tell. Perhaps he's paid her to keep their mouth shut. Or man."

Morag laughed at that. "You really think he likes men?"

Barbara gave her a small nudge. "Are you going to have a go at him yourself?"

"No, none of that. Especially after this morning's experience."

Barbara's eyes lit up with interest. "Why, did he flirt with you?"

"Lord Munro? No, not at all. No. It was Robert Hay."

"Robert Hay flirted with you? Oh, tell me!"

Morag felt herself redden. "Well it was more than a flirt. He... he wanted us to go further than that. In the woods, no less."

Barbara gave a delighted laugh. "But you never turned him down, did you?"

"Of course I did," Morag said, indignation in her tone.

"Oh you Highland goose, you should have just fobbed him off with a promise for later. A more convenient location, a more convenient time, so to speak."

"But I don't want to meet him at a later time, or a more convenient location. There is no convenient location," she said firmly. She frowned "And I don't understand how he might have been given the impression there was!"

Barbara sniffed. "Well, I didn't want to say anything earlier, but now I can see you arena pleased, but I must tell you I did see Lady Glenna talking to him earlier this morning at the assembly and she was gesturing in your direction. I would guess she may have had something to do with it."

"Lady Glenna?" For a brief moment she let outrage fill her before she tamped it down. "And why would she do that?" she said, in what surprised her as a calm voice.

"Oh, I suppose it might have something to do with the fact that she has a real fancy for Lord Munro and he's paid you particular attention on a few occasions."

"Munro?" The disbelief in her voice rang loud. "But that's

ridiculous. He cares nothing for me. We've barely spoken ten words." She faltered. "Well maybe a few more than ten, but it was purely the merest courtesies he would give to anyone."

Barbara shrugged. "I don't know for sure, but that would be my guess on the matter."

John Dunbar approached, two goblets in his hand. "May I offer you ladies both a cup of spiced wine?" he said.

"Oh, *merci beaucoup*," said Barbara. She gave him an appealing smile, her eyes wider. "You are a true courtier."

Morag, watching the display, repressed a snort.

"Did you enjoy the hunt, mesdemoiselles?" he asked.

"Oh, but who could not?" said Barbara. "And such display of prowess. I thought I would positively faint when Thomas Maxwell dismounted his horse and let loose his bow in one move.

"Did you see that Lady Morag? It was quite the most daring display I've seen." She turned her head coquettishly and looked up at Dunbar. "But then you must have much experience doing such displays yourself, my lord."

Morag observed Barbara with fascination and wondered how Maxwell's swift dismount was an act of prowess, especially when the hart was trapped and hardly going anywhere amid baying dogs and a circle of people around him. Displays of prowess she'd seen were bloodier and sweatier.

Dunbar, ever the courtier, bowed and said, "You're too kind, Lady Barbara."

"Lady Barbara is always kind," said Margaret Ramsey in a sweet tone. She drew Barbara's hand through her arm. "And I'm hoping she'll be kind enough to give me a moment of her time. And I must hear more about Lord Thomas's prowess. I'm afraid I missed that."

"You were otherwise engaged?" said Morag, her tone equally as sweet. She'd caught sight of Margaret slinking off with someone that looked remarkably like Robert Hay as everyone was dismounting in preparation for the kill.

Margaret forced a smile. "I'm afraid I was unable to obtain a clear view of that moment."

Morag nodded. "It would be difficult from certain vantage points."

"You must excuse us both, then," said Margaret.

She gave a brief nod and took off with Barbara in tow. Morag watched them go, uncertain whether to be amused or disgusted. She watched as they passed a couple exchanging words in earnest and she frowned, recognising Glenna and Rory.

"Is something troubling you, my lady?" said Dunbar.

She turned to him, assembling a pleasant expression on her face. "No, I'm sorry. Just a thought crossing my mind."

He glanced over at the direction of her gaze before. "Ah, Lady Glenna and I believe that's her brother?"

"Yes."

He looked and studied her. "You know them well? I think they might be neighbours of yours?"

She gave something that approached more of a rictus than a smile. "Yes. You might say they are neighbours."

"It's not easy sometimes living with one's neighbours. They are those type, I take it?"

She gave a small laugh. "They are rather like that."

"Ah. And this goes back years?"

"Centuries might be more accurate."

"So there is little love lost between the families."

"I wouldn't couple love in the same sentence as Campbell."

"My sympathies, my lady. I too have such neighbours," he said and then grinned. "But then this is Scotland, is it not?"

She looked up into his twinkling hazel eyes and smiled in response. "Yes. And I thank you for your words."

He took her hand and kissed the back of it. "Not at all.

Anything I can do to please you, you have only to say. I wouldn't allow anyone as charming and beautiful as you to be unhappy."

She blushed and lowered her eyes, unused to such words that seemed more than just courtly manners.

"You're too kind, my lord," she murmured.

"Now, I must see if I can tempt you to something from the fine repast laid on for us after such astonishing prowess."

Morag giggled and allowed him to lead her to the large array of food, thinking for the first time that she might find some things to enjoy about her time at court.

THE ROOM SEEMED overcrowded with bodies and clothes, though if Morag was honest she knew it had nothing to do with those two elements that made the air stifling. It was the tension of being in the bedchamber in the presence of Glenna. Despite the fact that their maidservant was dressing first Glenna and Barbara and her own Bridie was adjusting her underclothes in preparation for her outer garments or that the conversation flowed, Morag could feel unspoken words between herself and Glenna hanging in the air.

"You seem troubled," said Bridie in Gaelic, keeping her voice low.

"It's Glenna, *an diabhal*," said Morag murmured. "She played an infamous trick on me this morning."

Bridie glanced over at Glenna, who was conversing intently with the maidservant about the small tear in her seam. "Did she? What happened?"

"She told Robert Hay that I would be happy to have him…" Morag thought how she might best phrase it in Gaelic and not shock Bridie.

"Sample your goods?" said Bridie, her eyes twinkling.

Morag stifled a giggle. "Yes, that's one way of putting it."

"And did he? He's a fine looking man."

Morag gave her a mock outraged look. "What? No, of course not. It was insulting to think he felt he could though."

"Perhaps it was a misunderstanding."

"I doubt it. Remember who we're talking about here."

"Hmm. Maybe. Though she doesn't seem like the others, if I may say so."

Morag glanced over at Glenna again and this time, caught her eye. The look Glenna gave her was wary. Morag turned her eyes away and gazed out the window. She felt the corset tighten up around her, like a manacle.

"Why would she be any different? It's in her blood and that blood is evil and tainted."

"Your brother didn't think so, from what I understand."

"My brother can be wrong."

"Aye, he can," said Bride, switching to Scots. "Now hold your hair up if ye would, my lady while I put the kirtle over your head."

Mostly the two kept up a formal front, that was in keeping with the notion of milk sisters and the court's more strict rules of hierarchy but when they were alone Bridie would allow the formalities to drop and address her frankly and honestly, and now Morag recognised the wisdom of such a practice. That Bridie would appear only as something as inconsequential when seen as her maid and not a friend or someone from her home.

Bridie lifted the kirtle and carefully slipped it over Morag's head. It was a new creation, made from lengths of cloth Bridie had somehow bartered for with the redoubtable wardrobe mistress. It was made of watchet, a colour and shade that ill-suited the Dowager Queen and the silk not of the first quality since it contained a few slubs that marked it as European silk and not Chinese. But Morag thought it was wondrous, the colour like the changing sea and Bridie said it matched her eyes.

"There, now," said Bridie, adjusting the low drop waist over the farthingale frame. "Ye look a perfect picture."

Bridie plucked at the matching sleeves that were fashionably puffed at the top and narrowed as they dropped along the arm. Morag looked down at the dress and marvelled once again that she could be so fortunate to have its like.

"You look lovely," said Barbara. "You'll be catching Robert Hay's eye again, there's no doubt about it. And every other courtier."

"Yes," said Glenna. "It's a fine kirtle indeed. Your maid is skilful with a needle."

Barbara came closer and studied her. "It's a perfect gown for what I had in mind for us tonight. As a reward for the painful and interminable dinner we shall have in the Dowager Queen's apartments."

Morag gave her a curious look. "What is it?"

Barbara gave a conspiratorial wink. "You must keep it to yourself, but I heard that Lord Elphinstone is hosting an entertainment in his apartments."

"You want to take us to one of Lord Elphinstone's entertainments?" asked Glenna. "But they are known for their gaming and wild behaviour. Surely Mistress Cunningham would know if we went there."

"How will she know?" said Barbara. "No one would dare tell her we were there, for then it would admit tae their own appearance. And none of the regulars would bother to mention it to her, for they wouldn't give her the time of day."

Glenna considered it a moment while the maidservant began pinning her hair up. "Yes, you're probably right." She smiled at Barbara, a challenge in her eyes. "And will they admit us? They are usually very selective to who they allow entrance into the entertainment, from what I understand. Don't tell me that you've been to them yourself?"

Barbara raised her brows. "But of course. Would you think otherwise?"

Morag watched the exchange, a bit of unease rising inside her. "What kinds of entertainment?"

Barbara laughed. "Ah my little innocent. Don't worry yourself. You'll be fine. It's just a bit of gaming, conversation, and perhaps ...a bit of instrument playing." She started to fall into fits of giggles. "That's if you're lucky," she concluded.

Morag nodded, unwilling to say anything more that might bring on another wave of mockery. With a barely repressed sigh she took a seat as Bridie began to dress her hair. She tried to conceal the growing dread of the evening to come. In some ways she wished the evening meal would go on forever, for that would mean she wouldn't have to face Hay again and endure the possibility of rude remarks at best or even more unwanted attentions. She looked over at Glenna and frowned. If she could find a way to get Glenna sent home from court she would be delighted. Or better still, to have both Campbells sent away. Permanently, if possible. And while she was wishing, she might was well have it that the Campbells were disgraced, put to the horn and forever banished from the lands they currently occupied.

CHAPTER 8

*W*hen Morag entered the apartment behind Barbara and Glenna a few hours later, she was immediately assailed by the noise of conversation and the unmistakeable odours of heated bodies in close quarters and spilled wine, overlaid with a clash of the perfumes of jasmine, musk, ambergris and tuberose. The drapes were closed over the windows and a fire burned in the fireplace which, combined with the press of people, made the room nearly too warm. Candles lit the chamber in clustered areas, especially the table where several people were gathered and playing cards. Morag immediately recognised Alexander Munro among them, his flamboyant manner and clothes too striking to miss.

Tonight Munro seemed to have outdone himself in dress. He wore a doublet of verdigris silk with canary yellow trim at the large cuttes. His ruff was high and the lace at his cuffs very long, his customary handkerchief hanging out of his left hand. It was his discard hand, so whenever he took a card from the stack or placed one on the table, his handkerchief flounced about in an alarming manner. But never did he knock over any card on the table or cause any other mishap. It held Morag's fascination for several moments. It was only when he looked up and caught her eye, raising a brow, that she made herself look away and survey the rest of the room.

Barbara was already chattering away to some man that Morag didn't know to the left of the chamber and Glenna had headed toward a small group of people listening to someone playing the lute. Other corners of the room were less well-lit and she could only see huddled figures on benches and chairs. One lady sat with an older man and appeared to be consulting a large book and exchanging intense looks and conversation in low tones.

There were several people standing around talking to one another, their amusement and laughter very plain. Some held cups of wine that the two servants present had clearly provided from ewers they carried around the room. One servant approached and offered to provide her with a cup of wine and something to eat if she so desired. She declined the food but accepted the wine, for lack of anything else to do.

Morag was about to join the cluster around the musician when she saw Margaret Ramsey approach Munro and speak to him.

"You are in luck tonight, my lord?" she asked.

He flashed a smile, waved his handkerchief around. "I am indeed, my lady." He winked. "Am I about to have my luck increased?"

She giggled and gave him a flirtatious look. "Ah, if I might in any way help you increase your luck I would be happy to do so." She ran a finger along his neck.

"Is my ruff gone awry, my lady?" he said in mock devastation. "If so, please adjust it at once, for I would never have it said that any garment on my person should be anything but perfect."

"Of course, my lord. I am happy to help you with your garments, on or off your person, whenever you should wish."

His eyes twinkled and he took up her hand and kissed the back of it. "Your attentions are always pleasing, my lady. But I am in the midst of the most entertaining play at this table and I dare not risk my attention elsewhere just for now." He gave a sly smile. "Perhaps later."

Margaret Ramsey gave him an uncertain smile, murmured "of course" and "later would suit her well as she had her own attentions requested in a few moments elsewhere..." and retreated with as much dignity as she could muster.

"Another one's hopes for winning the bet dashed."

Morag turned to see John Dunbar at her side. He was grinning, his hazel eyes twinkling with humour. He offered her another cup of wine and she took it gratefully, her first empty already.

She smiled in return. "My lord. You think it won't come to pass?"

"What? That she will win the bet? Or someone else?"

"Either. There seem to be many determined women," she said as another lady sidled boldly up to Munro. She was much younger and giggled more than anything, her dishevelled hair and glittering eyes telling the true foundation of her courage.

"I don't think Margaret Ramsey has any hope, quite frankly. Now or in the future," he said, wry amusement in his voice. "But whether some other young lady will entice him is another thing."

"Why not Margaret?"

"She is not his type, I fear. He seems not to care for those who have...experience, though he mixes quite frequently with them, playing cards, dancing and riding, among other things. They are safe interactions, not tempting for him."

"You seem to have studied him quite a bit for all your short time at court."

He turned to look at her. "I've studied many things since my arrival at court. Some more attractive than others. I have, for example, noticed that you are an excellent dancer. And I would desire to know more about your other accomplishments. Do you play an instrument? The lute perhaps?"

She felt a blush creep up. She wasn't used to such compliments and found it difficult to assign it to courtly manners once again. Especially in one so handsome who had beautiful address.

"I play the lute only indifferently when compared to my brother or his wife, but I do sing well enough."

"I should count it fortunate if I might hear you sing. Would you do so here? There is someone playing the lute over there."

She turned to see a young man plucking out a tune on the lute and recognised him after a moment as David Montgomerie, the man who modelled himself after Munro. Next to him was Glenna and her brother. He finished his piece and after a quiet discussion handed the lute to her. She smiled at him prettily and hesitated a moment before taking the lute from him. He rose and offered her his seat and she sat down gracefully. Morag was forced to admit she looked very lovely with her fair colouring and hair that looked red-gold in the candle light. Rory was scowling down at her, his words clearly curt, but she seemed to ignore him and struck up a tune on the lute.

"Shall I ask the young lady if she would permit you to sing with her?" asked Dunbar.

She pursed her mouth. "No, thank you, but I would prefer not to."

"Don't you know the young lady?"

"I do. She is Glenna Campbell."

"Ah, yes, of course," he said in a smooth voice. "I remember now. The Campbells are not at all to your liking."

"Not particularly."

"And rightly so. I now recall your clan particulars," his tone edged. "I too, have a similar situation. My family wouldn't be very well disposed to that clan either."

She turned to study him with new interest. "You have no liking for the Campbells?"

"Let's just say that my family have come up against them at

certain points and would be heartily glad if they were removed from every sphere of influence in political circles."

"Yes, that would my sentiments. And those of my family. I would do anything to see them banned or exiled to some far corner of the country on a patch of land so small it would hardly keep a few cattle."

He laughed and squeezed her hand before lifting it to his hand for a kiss. "You, my lady, are enchanting and I can see that we have much in common." He gazed into her eyes and she saw them twinkle again. "If you'll excuse me for a moment?"

She murmured her permission as he made a short bow and took his leave. While a servant refilled her wine cup, she watched as he made his way over to Glenna, who by now had a small little group circling her. Her piece was an allemande, lively to a degree, but if Morag were to pass opinion, too stodgy for a gathering such as this. Dunbar joined the small circle and listened politely while she played. When she'd finished he bowed to her and murmured something that caused her to look at him in puzzled amusement. He had a playful look and his mouth was quirked on one side. She nodded and handed him the lute, exchanging places with him. He sat down with a flourish and with a wicked arch of his brow began to play the lute.

It took Morag a few moments to realise he was playing the same allemande, but with flourishes that were almost outrageous. He said a few words and the small audience laughed. He played some more phrases, this time slowed to an almost erotic pace and she heard him intone some words. The response from the group was laughter that was even more animated.

Morag stood drinking her wine for a while, but in the end she couldn't resist. The implied humour and wit drew her towards the group and she arrived just in time to hear the end of the next phrase, played at a fast clip and the words that accompanied it. …"and she told him there was no hurry, he could dance on her floor all night."

She smiled, though she had little comprehension of the words except that it seemed suggestive and lewd. The group tittered and giggled. She looked at Glenna, hoping for distress that her stately piece was now the subject of satire, but she only saw a blushing face and a suppressed smile.

Dunbar carried on with the rest of the piece, interjecting verses, changing tempo as the story of a lover's encounter continued, its meaning and words just on the wrong side of what might be considered permissible. But his delivery, his use of the lute at just the right moment allowed all who listened to forgive him and take great pleasure in it. In fact he drew several more to the group, attracted by the noise of laughter and the music. His playing slowed, his tempo and phrasing once again erotic and smooth.

One couple stood to the right of Morag, the young man brushing his fingers along the bare neck of the fair-haired young lady with him. She gave him a coquettish look and he bent down and whispered something in her ear. A moment later he quickly licked and nipped her ear and she shivered in response.

Morag took a deep draught of her wine, unable to refrain from staring at them. She'd seen loving attention between Iain and Abby, but this seemed something more, a desire that she could almost envy. She had no illusion that these two were betrothed, or in any way heading towards matrimony and in some ways it disturbed her. She'd never experienced that kind of desire, and here she was watching two people in the throes of it and finding it was affecting her. Even Davey had done little to arouse anything approaching what she was witnessing. She took another long draught of her wine in an effort to suppress the uncertainty that unsettled her.

"Enticing, isn't it?" said a voice quietly in her ear.

Startled out of her reverie, she turned and looked at James Home who stood behind her, his face in shadow, his eyes dark and smoky.

"My lord?"

"The young couple. The music has affected them both, has it not?"

She nodded slowly, uncertain if he meant the music was enticing or the young couple.

"It's a heady thing, and watching them one can but hope for some part of it for oneself, *n'cest pas?*" he said with an emphasis so perfectly French and smooth, it was as if it was a word of caress.

She felt herself nod, unable to speak or do anything more. He placed his hand on her shoulder and it moved slowly down her arm until he reached her hand and grasped it.

"Come, I let me show you something I think you will find amusing and may help you understand what I am trying to say."

Home led her away, weaving through the clustered groups, past the gaming tables, stopping only so that a servant might fill her cup and his, until he reached the other side of the room. There were a few couples there, on chairs and benches. He led her to a free seat and sat her down. There was a small sconce of lit candles on the wall a short distance away and she took comfort from that. The draped window was to her back.

"Just sit there and I will only be a moment."

She nodded dumbly, and sipped away at her wine, too nervous now to be able to utter a word. Out of the corner of her eye she could see a couple in a darkened corner locked in an embrace and found herself once again watching. The man kissed the woman's mouth, his hand cupping her face and then stroked her jaw lightly. She gave a low moan. The man lifted his lips and began kissing her ear, moving along to her neck as his hand caressed the top of her bodice.

"Now, I wasn't wrong, was I?" said Home.

She looked over at him, her mind fuzzy and filled with what she'd just witnessed. She licked her lips and tried to focus as he sat beside her and pulled her in close to him. He pulled a book onto their laps and opened it, draping his arm around her. He leaned towards her and spoke softly.

"What delights you'll see here, my lady."

His hand caressed her neck again and she shivered under his touch. She took a drink from her wine cup, hoping to clear the feeling. He gave a soft chuckle, his fingers drifting along her neck.

"Cast your eyes at this, my lady," he said in a low voice.

She looked down at the page and she saw it was filled with a drawing depicting two naked bodies, one a woman, the other a man. The drawing was explicitly erotic and it stunned her at first with its open sexuality. She blinked, trying to focus, searching her mind for what she should do with this image that lay on her lap. In one sense it was horribly fascinating. She took another drink of her wine and felt the fingers moving further and further along her neck and down along her breastbone. A moment later there was a light kiss placed on her ear and the book laid aside, the free hand placed on her knee.

She was speechless, unable to utter a word, at once both filled with the desire she'd longed for a minute ago and enraged that such liberties be taken of her. It was when the kisses trailed along her neck, downward to her breasts and the hand on her knee beginning to lift her skirts that Morag found her power to move. She rose unsteadily, spilling the wine on her sleeve, and moved away, stuttering apologies.

She stumbled across the room, pausing only to refill her cup and found herself coming up against Rory Campbell.

"Liking the wine a little too much, my lady?" he asked, his voice filled with sarcasm.

"That is one thing I like about this evening," she said, in a forced attempt to pull herself together.

"What, not gaming? I would have thought you would be at the table the whole of the night, such is your luck."

"Are you implying that I acquired your horse by luck?"

He shrugged. "That's the best description."

"Only by someone with no eyes in their head."

He scowled at her and she moved on, her gait somewhat difficult. She concentrated on her direction, looking toward the small bench near the gaming table. It seemed the safest place for her and she could watch the gaming for amusement.

She settled herself eventually, once she'd gotten her feet untangled and realised it was best to be seated before one crossed ones ankles. How was it that she hadn't understood how complicated it was before now? She took a deep restorative drink of her wine, licking her lips. This was truly delicious.

She glanced over at the table. Munro was still there, flicking his cards with a flourish on every discard and waving his handkerchief around. She followed the piece of white linen, fascinated once again, studying how it sometimes gracefully flew through the air like a white dove. She began to look forward to his discards so that she might experience the flying dove. She leaned a little closer and realised she could make out Munro's cards. She leaned a little further, so that she might see them more clearly and predict what he might discard and then see the dove flying around. Before she knew it she was falling forward and she reached out to try and catch herself and grabbed for the nearest thing to steady her, which happened to be Munro's arm. Unfortunately that arm contained the hand that was holding the cards and with her hard tug it was no surprise that the hand loosed the cards and they went tumbling on the table, his lap and even the floor.

She looked up at him with dismay. "I am so sorry, my lord. You see I found myself in peril of falling and grabbed onto your arm so that I might steady myself."

He arched a brow at her, his face unreadable. "A likely story."

She made an effort to stand up, but realised that might be too ambitious as she wasn't at this point certain if her legs would hold. She muttered a curse in Gaelic and grabbed hold of the back of Munro's chair and with that support found she could manage to maintain an erect posture filled with all the dignity she could muster.

"No, I am telling you the truth. I would not for the world have interrupted your play." She looked down at the card. "Indeed, my lord, you should be thanking me – for you had a foul hand and you may count yourself fortunate that you will have to start with a fresh hand and not lose your shirt as you seemed inclined towards, given that pile of coins piled for the bet."

A roar of laughter went up around the table and Morag gazed around at them in puzzlement. She looked once again at Munro and found him staring at her, a hint of amusement in his eyes.

"My lady, you are right, of course, and I owe you a thousand thanks." He bowed his head briefly.

She beamed at him, glad that he had seen her point and not taken offence. She had no idea she could argue a point so well. She must tell Iain this. He had little appreciation for the finer points of her arguments and discussions at home. Home. Suddenly, she found herself wishing to see Iain at that very moment. And Abby too, so that she might ask her all the questions she had about court and matters of desire and romantic encounters. She knew that she was woefully ignorant. She felt tears well up and lifted her cup to take another drink, but found that a hand restrained it. She looked down to see that it was Munro, his face showing a hint of concern.

He stood and took her hand, taking the cup from it and setting it on the table. "I think that you might want a bite to eat, my lady. Why not enhance the taste of the excellent wine with some capon to go with it?"

"Capon?" she asked. "There is capon?"

"Yes, and dressed beautifully if I may say so."

"Really? I don't think I have ever had beautifully dressed capon."

"We must remedy that at once."

He bowed to the other gamers, taking his leave and led Morag to the small table filled with a variety of fowl and pastries, slaking the edge from any appetite that might arise throughout the night. He placed a small capon on a free plate and handed it to her. She looked at it and then up at him, uncertain how to manage it. With a sigh he took up the capon and tore a small portion of it off the bone and offered it to her. She took it gratefully and popped it in her mouth. She chewed it slowly and savoured the peppery taste that mixed with the lovely marinade and sauce.

Eventually she looked up at Lord Munro delightedly. "You're right, my lord. It is beautifully dressed. Will you give me another piece?"

He gave a small snort and picked off another morsel, this time feeding it directly to her mouth. She took it gratefully and ate it quickly. He pulled apart the small wing and gave her the rest of the pieces one by one, and as she took it her face lit up with enjoyment.

"It's just as though you are feeding a bird." she said when he was nearly done and the thought struck her. "Like your dove!" She was proud of her analogy. Alisdair should hear of this. She was certain he would be impressed with her philosophical turn of mind for once.

"My dove?" he said quizzically.

She motioned to his handkerchief. "The way it waves around, it's just like a dove."

He gave her a quizzical look of amusement. "Just so," he said.

She swallowed the last bite and smacked her lips and licked them. "Oooh that was so good. The Dowager Queen never has anything so lovely at her meals. And the wine. That is just as lovely." She looked around. "Where did I leave my cup? I have more left, I'm sure of it and it would be a shame to waste it."

She made a move towards the gaming table but found herself a bit unsteady. Munro put a supportive hand under her arm and suddenly the room stopped tilting so much and she found her feet.

"I think perhaps it's time we got you back to your chamber." He scanned the room quickly. "It seems that the ladies who share it with you are gone. Is there another lady who would escort you back?"

She shook her head slowly and then stopped, disliking the spinning sensation that seized her once again.

She blinked and straightened. "You must not worry, my lord. I'm certain I can make my own way back to my chamber."

He gave her a wry look. "Well there's no need for that. Come."

He took her arm firmly and directed her through the dwindling group to the door and out into the corridor.

"It would probably not go amiss if we went through the inner close to your chamber. You could do with some fresh air."

She giggled. "Fresssaiirr. Fresser," she said in Scots. "Sounds nearly like Fraser when ye say it in Scots, does it no?" She repeated it again for him, certain he would see it if only she repeated it often enough for him.

"Aye, I do see it," he said with a soft chuckle.

They were outside in the inner close now, the stars shining overhead, a rare clear sky that graced an occasional early spring night. Morag looked up and was amazed at the twinkling dance overhead.

She squinted, studying it carefully and grabbed his arm. "Oh, look, my lord, there's a shooting star. Quick! Make a wish."

He looked up where she indicated and eventually shook his head. "I'm afraid I didna see a shooting star. But the sky is bright tonight."

"Never mind. I made a wish for both of us." She smiled brightly at him.

He laughed. "And how does that work, if I may ask?"

"I asked that we both might get our dearest wish. Is that no clever?"

"Aye, verra clever indeed. Now, my poppet, let's get you tae your bed."

He began to direct her forward and she leaned her head against his arm, so that he put his arm around her shoulder and drew her into his side for better support.

She sighed. "Only my mother and Iain ever called me poppet. But my mother is dead and Iain wouldna do that, for he kens that I would object."

"Is that so?"

"Hmm," she said, nodding agreeably. "But ye may. In this instance."

"I thank ye humbly, my lady," he said.

"Of course," she said, dreamily.

The fresh air had made her feel better but now she was feeling sleepy, and it only got worse once they were inside again. He led her along the short corridor to the stairs and steadied her as she ascended them, catching her when her foot slipped. It was when they neared her chamber that she stopped, a sudden thought occurring to her.

"There was one other person who called me 'poppet'. I just remembered." She placed a finger to her mouth. "But ye mustna tell."

He grinned at her. "Your secret is safe with me."

"Sandy. He called me 'poppet'."

"Sandy?"

"Aye. My brother's friend. He came to visit when Iain was about twelve. I was only five at the time. But he was lovely." She picked at his sleeve. "So lovely…" she said dreamily. "I've only just remembered. I told him I was going to marry him when I grew up."

She heard his soft laugh. "And what did he say?" he asked.

"He said we would indeed. And I was only tae let him know when I was ready for the marriage. I said it would be a few years yet, since I wanted tae spend time teaching my pony some tricks." She giggled and looked up at him. "I was a silly little thing."

"Nay," said Munro. "Ye were charming, I have nae doubt."

He reached her door and knocked softly. A few moments later it opened and Bridie stood there, stifling a yawn.

"Och mistress, I was fretting myself here, thinking something might have happened. Where have ye been? The other ladies have long since returned."

"She just got caught up watching the card play. And taken in a wee bit too much wine, I fear." He handed her over to Bridie. "She just needs tucking up now. In the morning she might be a little worse for wear, though."

Bridie nodded her head. "Aye, my lord. I'll see tae it. And thank ye."

Morag turned to Lord Munro and gave him a little wave. "Thank ye, my lord. Ye've been verra entertaining and kind. I'll no forget it."

He nodded and bade her goodnight with a smile. "I wonder if ye'll remember much come the morning."

With that remark he took himself away and Bridie shut the door, leading Morag to the chair so that she might undress her and get her into bed. Morag allowed herself to be undressed while she dreamily mused on shooting stars and Sandy, the golden haired youth who'd been so kind. Where was he now, she wondered?

CHAPTER 9

*M*orag blinked against the blinding light that shone through the window as Bridie proceeded to dress her hair for the day. She felt as though a herd of cattle had stomped on her head in the night and then taken up residence in her mouth for a time. Her stomach was another matter. Even the small amount of bread she managed to get down her was now threatening to come back up. Bridie had clucked over her and taken away the plate that she'd brought to tempt her.

She glanced at Barbara and Glenna resentfully. They seemed no worse for the outing the night before as they stood there, Barbara primping the lace at her cuff and Glenna submitting to the maid's ministrations on her hair. Morag knew her own face was most likely pasty and her eyes dull. But she could hardly care when her first priority was to refrain from spilling all the contents of her stomach at this very moment.

"Will you be well enough to go tae the Dowager Queen's apartments?" Bridie asked softly in Gaelic. "Shall I tell Mistress Cummings that you've taken ill?"

"Nay, Bridie. She'll only come and drag me out of bed." Morag sighed. "I'll just have to make the best of it and take a seat near the door so that I may excuse myself quickly if I should need the guarderobe."

"If you're sure," said Bridie, her face filled with concern.

A knock sounded at the door and a servant opened it and bowed. "Mistress Cunningham says ye're tae meet her in the inner gardens. The Dowager Queen wishes tae take the air this morning as the weather is so fine."

Barbara gave him a regal nod and thanked him. Morag felt a smile tug at her mouth and glanced at Glenna on impulse and saw the humour in her own face. Their eyes met for a brief moment, sharing the joke before Morag caught herself and hastily looked elsewhere.

Soon after they were all ready and they made their way down the stairs and out to the knot work garden which contained yew topiary and some feeble shoots of plants and flowers struggling to pop up in the early spring sunshine. Some courtiers and ladies-in-waiting were already assembled on benches around the Dowager Queen, who sat in a carved wooden chair. More active courtiers stood in small groups or walked the paths created by the topiary hedges and flower beds.

Morag spied Mistress Cunningham heading toward towards them and winced. The strong light was bad enough on her head, but the strident tones of Mistress Cunningham would probably be too much for her. Mistress Cunningham stopped and waited for them to reach her. She eyed Morag and frowned.

"You look as though you're sickening for something. If that's the case, it's best you keep your distance from her Highness." She studied Barbara and Glenna. "It seems you haven't contracted it yet, but it's best to be safe and have all three of you at a distance. If I could, I would send you back to your chamber, but I prefer not to have Lady Erskine hear that you shirked your duty, or that you would find yourselves sick." She glanced around. "I would think if you kept away from the outer circle you should be fine. But don't approach Lady Erskine, and if any of the other senior ladies-in-waiting should come near, for pity's sake excuse yourselves quickly."

The three of them nodded meekly and Mistress Cunningham gave a curt nod back with a deep frown and took her leave.

After Mistress Cunningham had achieved a sufficient distance, Barbara began to giggle. The giggle turned to full on laughter that she suppressed as much as was possible behind her hand.

"Oh, that's just too much," she said, her eyes alight. "I guess she didn't consider the possibility that she might get sick after coming in contact with us and take it back to Lady Erskine or, heaven forbid, Her Highness."

"I imagine she knows that no illness would dare enter her body," said Glenna dryly.

Morag gave a faint smile. The air was doing her head some good, she was glad to say. She looked over at a shaded area longingly. She would appreciate a refuge from the strong sunlight, though.

"If you don't mind, I'm going over there where it's shady. The sun is a bit too much for me at the moment." She moved away from the two of them.

"Ah," said Barbara with a giggle, trailing after her, "I take it your particular illness has something to do with last night?"

Morag kept walking in the hope that Barbara would lose interest and go somewhere else, but that hope was quickly dashed. Barbara slipped her hand through Morag's arm in a companionable manner.

"Now tell me, please," she said, her tone conspiratorial. "I've been anxious to know. What was it like?"

Morag gave her a puzzled look. "What was it like?"

Barbara gave her a little shove. "Don't play coy with me, Morag. How was it with him? Was it good? Tell me all."

"Who are you talking about?"

"Lord Munro, of course. Who else? No, don't tell me, you had James Home as well!"

Morag blushed scarlet. Home? Munro? She rubbed her forehead trying to piece together the muddy memory of the night before. She vaguely recalled meeting Home and talking to him.

"There's nothing to disclose, I assure you," said Morag. She struggled hard to recollect exactly what had transpired and hoped she could bluff her way through. "What you might have seen was certainly jumping to conclusions."

"Oh, it wasn't me, so much as others. Glenna was the one that said you had gone off with James Home. And had a very intimate conversation with him…." She arched her brow in a suggestive manner. "Rory was the one who told me about Lord Munro."

Morag looked around her, fighting the confusion and her aching head. How had she heard this so soon? Had Rory spoken with his sister before they had left the chamber? It seemed impossible. But perhaps Rory had seen Glenna the evening before and told Glenna, who had then seen fit to pass it on. She rubbed her head again and tried to think.

"I assure you nothing happened between myself and John Home or Lord Munro," she said in the firmest voice she could muster.

"You can't deny you left Lord Elphinstone's chambers last night with Lord Munro, for I have that on good authority."

"Whose authority?"

"Well, Rory of course, for he left the same time as you and watched you go with Munro down the corridor, heading towards his rooms." She looked at her smugly. "And the maidservant, Annie. She saw you in the courtyard with him and said the two of you were embracing."

Morag opened her mouth to object and then had a vague recollection of looking up into the night sky with someone's hand on her shoulder. She shut her mouth and swallowed hard.

"Come now, you must tell me, for everyone will be talking

about it soon enough and want to know if you will collect the bet. I'll help you, since you must keep it quiet, if you can, from Mistress Cunningham. She's sure to send you packing if she gets wind of this." She gave her a speculative look. "But only imagine. You, newly arrived at court and getting the famous Lord Munro to bed you. Why he chose you, now that's the real puzzle."

Morag looked at her in horror. "But he didn't," she protested weakly. She was certain it couldn't have happened. Surely she'd remember if it had? She searched her mind again, trying to recall all the details, but all she knew was that her head was aching badly again.

Barbara's eyes flashed with something unreadable. "You've become a legend overnight."

"But, who else knows? I mean there's nothing to know so there is nothing to discuss."

"I imagine that there are few among Munro's circle that don't know, for they were the ones who put the largest wagers on. But I don't think anyone had put you forward as the likely candidate."

Morag took a deep breath and gathered all her wits and strength. "Barbara, I would appreciate it if you would do your best to suppress any of these rumours, for that is all they are. I did not get Lord Munro to bed me, nor James Home. Lord Munro merely escorted me back to my chamber – since neither you, nor Glenna, saw fit to seek me out when you decided to return."

She turned on her heel and walked away, down towards the farthest line of topiary in the garden. The shade there was even deeper and by the time she reached it she was calm enough.

"My lady, you seem distressed."

Morag turned to see John Dunbar in front of her, his face filled with concern. She gave him a weak smile and shook her head.

"I assure you I'm fine, now. Just a bit too much sun after a long night."

He pulled a wry face. "Yes, I can imagine."

She stiffened. "You've heard something about me?"

He looked puzzled. "No, should I have? I assure you I only meant that I felt the same, having had one too many cups of wine last night and staying much later than was good for me."

She relaxed a little. "Yes, the wine was strong and I drank far too much of it."

"I fear there were a few things that may have provoked you to over indulge," he said. "Lady Glenna? I tried to allay your feelings somewhat when I asked if I might have the lute from her." His eyes softened. "And I had hoped that you might have joined me there and sung with me."

She grimaced. "I am sorry. I'm afraid I was drawn away by James Home. He insisted that I come with him."

Morag reddened at a sudden flash of memory of him leading her to a bench and placing a book in front of her. She cursed silently as the memory fleshed out. She pressed her lips to refrain from saying the number of expletives that came to her.

"I saw him draw you away," said John. "And I was sorry for it. I hope he didn't do anything…upsetting."

She drew herself up. "No, why would you say that? Did Lady Glenna mention anything to you?" Her face darkened. "Or her brother?"

"If Lady Glenna said anything, I can assure you I disregarded it. And I would do the same of anything her brother said," he said in a firm voice. He took her hand and bowed over it. "Please believe I hold you in the highest esteem and would countenance nothing that alters that. Besides, I have little liking for anyone of Campbell blood."

"And Rory has told you nothing of Munro and the wager?" she said, bracing for the answer.

"The wager? You mean the wager that some woman will get him to bed her?" He looked a little flustered. "I believe I heard Campbell say something about it."

"About me?" she asked querulously.

"Uh, I didn't hear your name mentioned specifically." He took her hand again and clasped it tightly. "I feel I must state again how much I hold you in esteem and wouldn't believe anything ill of you."

Morag put a hand to her mouth to stop herself from crying out in dismay. It was as she feared. Everyone was discussing her supposed tryst with Munro. All because of the Campbells and their wicked tongues. She clutched her hands at her sides with rising fury.

She looked at John and took a deep breath. "The Campbells I fear, are attempting to get me dismissed. And they will stop at nothing to bring it about. Even circulating bold faced lies."

"Such behaviour is intolerable," he said, his own anger lighting his face.

He turned and looked at the group clustered at the other end of the garden where Glenna, Barbara and the other junior ladies-in-waiting gathered at the periphery of the circle around the Dowager Queen. It seems they weren't concerned with Mistress Cunningham's instructions any more. She could see Lord Munro approach them, making a flourishing bow. His gesture was met with simpers, curtsies and much giggling and laughter. She supposed that he was only egging them on. Would he confirm the liaison and put a stop to all the jests and flirting that he'd been exposed to since the wager was initiated? She tried to remember exactly what had happened, but her mind was still too fogged. How would she have done such a thing anyway? She hardly thought of him in that manner. His large stomach was off putting at the very least. Surely she would have remembered encountering that monstrosity. How would he ever manage bedding a woman? She gave a snort of satisfaction, certain there could be no basis of truth. But for now, she had only to convince everyone else. Hopefully word wouldn't get back to Mistress Cunningham before she did.

She frowned. Her eyes rose up to his face, the deep blue eyes, the generous mouth, until she caught herself. He was nothing like Davey. Davey. She must send him a message at the first opportunity. She thought of the green ribbon from their handfasting she'd tucked lovingly in her kist back in Glen Strae. Where had that gone? Had Bridie unpacked it and put it among her hair ribbons?

She must put these thoughts out of her mind and deal with the matters at hand. She scanned the group again, trying to locate Rory so that she might accost him and demand that he stop spreading the rumour. She would tackle Glenna later. Rory was the one spreading the gossip about Munro. But Morag could see no trace of him.

"We will make a plan," said John Dunbar, pulling Morag's attention back to him.

"A plan?"

"Yes. We'll discover a way to get them both banished from court. I'm certain if we put our heads together we can contrive to make it come about."

She looked at him thoughtfully. "It does sound promising. To find some way for it to happen." She smiled. "Yes. I'll see what I can discover. Perhaps Barbara knows some scandal concerning either one of them that might be sufficient to ensure that if it comes to Mistress Cunningham's ears they will be dismissed. Or better yet, Lady Erskine's ears directly, for it is she who will decide such things."

"Lady Erskine. Yes, indeed. And her husband would certainly look less favourably on the whole of the Campbell clan." He clasped her hand again. "We shall make a promise on it. We'll both do our best to discover something to bring this all about."

"We will indeed," she said, smiling. Already she felt better. She would put a stop to the rumour and then find something to hold over one or both of them.

He offered her his arm. "May I escort you on a small turn about the garden? Your colour seems to have returned."

She smiled at him and agreed. He led her slowly around the perimeters of the garden, along the castle wall and then up near the gate that led out to the outer close. As she passed by the gate, now slightly ajar to allow for passage of servants bringing some light refreshments, she caught sight of a figure on horseback. She recognised the horse at once as Thunder and the mounted rider as Rory Campbell. A Gaelic expletive emerged from her mouth.

"What is it? Something upsets you?"

She stared as Rory cantered his way into the yard, headed towards the stable and then forced herself to turn to John. She plastered a smile on her face.

"It is nothing, my lord. Only that I believe I stepped on a stone and it caused a pain in my foot. It's gone now."

He looked down at the foot that peeped from her gown and back up at her.

"I am glad to hear it's nothing serious."

"You're too kind, my lord – and as you say, it most assuredly is nothing serious."

She looked over at the empty yard and smiled to herself. Rory thought he would attempt to retrieve his horse. Well, he would be in for a big surprise.

CHAPTER 10

She finally managed to get hold of Bridie just before they were to return to the Dowager Queen's apartments. Morag had made an excuse to go to her chamber and found Bridie there, returning some mended underclothes to Morag's kist.

"There you are Bridie. I am that glad to see you," Morag said in Gaelic as she entered the chamber. She glanced around to check for the other maidservant and, finding her absent, grinned at Bridie.

"You'll never imagine."

"What is it? You look very flushed."

"Rory Campbell, may the devil seize him, had the gall to take Thunder out for a ride."

"And that causes you happiness?" she asked, puzzled.

"Nay, it doesn't. It vexes me to the extreme, but I've now thought how I may trump him for good on that account." Morag gave a hearty laugh. "I just wish I could be present when he discovers it."

"What do you mean to do?" Bridie's eyes were alight. "I wager it can't be as bad as he deserves."

"Well, it will certainly bring him into a rage, and that's something to savour. If I can bring it about." She moved to Bride and put her hands on her shoulders. "Come, you must go to Rob and tell him to meet me outside the stables at dusk."

Bridie gave Morag a dismayed look. "Oh, Morag, I'm so sorry. Rob left this morning. He told me to tell you when I next saw you that he will go on to Dundoon, where Liam and Lemmy are. They said they had no more work for him now that the Frenchie visitors have gone."

"Oh, dinna say so! Of all the things." Morag said, switching to Scots. She frowned. "I will have my revenge. I must do. Especially after spreading the outrageous tales with his swick and claiking to all manner of people."

"Aye, it was terrible of him," said Bridie. "He deserves tae be sent off with a clout tae his head and backside."

"Ye heard it as well?" said Morag with a small wail. "Is there nae person who hasna heard this malicious tale? I suppose it's only a matter of time before Mistress Cunningham takes me aside and bids me on my way."

"Nay, nay, ye mustna fash yourself. It is all but over and done now. Why in the same breath I was told of the tale, the absolute denial of its truth was voiced. Apparently Lord Munro has said so himself, and with a great amount of sorrow that it wasna true. Verra pretty speech, but firm as well, from what they say."

"Munro denied it?" said Morag doubtfully. On the one hand she was appalled that it had come to his ears so quickly and on the other hand she was filled with gratitude that he had gone to her aid.

"He did also say that the wager had reached such proportions that if ye had done as it was said, ye would have gone straight off tae collect the wager this morning. That ye hadna done so was proof enough it wasna true."

Morag smiled, picturing him saying the very words, his eyes twinkling. She pushed the thought aside.

"He's a very courteous man," she said.

"Aye, he is that, from what I've heard. Though his clothes certainly are more fitting for a jester than any Highland lord."

"Highland lord?" asked Morag. "I thought he was a relative of Lady Erskine's."

Bridie shrugged. "I dinna ken. I just heard one of the old servants call him that. But they were perhaps mistaken."

"Aye," said Morag. "I expect they were." She frowned as her current dilemma returned to her mind. "Now, since Rob isna here tae help me, it seems I'll have tae take matters in tae my own hands."

Bridie frowned. "What do ye mean, take matters in tae your hands?"

Morag stared out the window, lost in thought. Would she dare? She thought of Thunder and decided she would dare.

"Bridie, I want ye tae take out my trews, shirt, doublet and bonnet and find somewhere tae hide them downstairs near the door. I know, the small store room off from the Steward's office. Do ye ken? They must be there ready for me by dusk. I'll make an excuse of a headache to avoid the meal and this evening's entertainment. If the ladies should come tae the chamber before I return, just say that I've gone tae seek out my horse, for I was worried having just heard he is unwell."

Bridie gave her a dubious look. "Aye, I'll do as ye say. But what do ye mean tae do?"

Morag grinned again. "I, my dear Bridie, am going tae take Thunder out from Rory's reach."

It was past dusk by the time Morag managed to steal down the stone stairs to the floor below and to the small store room. Once there, she retrieved the clothes stored in a small covered wicker basket and exchanged them for the simple kirtle she had on. She bundled up the shucked garments and put them in the basket. With a deft movement she scooped up her already braided hair and stuffed it in the bonnet, pulling the brim down as much as possible to obscure her face.

She made her way outside and headed towards the stables. Once there, she was greeted by a young groomsman.

"My master says ye're tae saddle Thunder, the roan horse he rode this day," she said, keeping the pitch of her voice as low as possible.

"T'is a bit late tae be going riding," said the groomsman in cheeky tone.

"Aye, but it's nae business but his own why he wants it saddled," she said in a firm tone.

He gave a snort. "Whatever his lordship wishes."

He moved inside and Morag waited impatiently, praying no one else would come and ask what she was doing. Eventually, she could hear the clop of Thunder's hooves on the cobblestone and she breathed a sigh of relief.

She took the reins from the groomsman, who looked around. "Where's your master? He isna here yet?"

She frowned and gave him the most disdainful look she could muster. "He has bid me tae take his horse tae a kinsmen, so that he can be taken on from there tae his home. Though why ye should question his wishes, I dinna ken. So if ye'll excuse me, I'll go."

Without waiting for a reply Morag led the horse over to the mounting block, her nerves tight. She didn't think he would prevent her, but she couldn't be certain and she hoped no one more senior than he would emerge and question her. She realised then it would be less easy to make her way through the gates.

Once mounted, she urged the horse to the gatehouse, where she knew at least one guard would be posted. She was soon proved right. It was not just one, but three of them standing around talking. She nearly cursed aloud at her poor luck and heaved a sigh of resignation. She would have to brazen it out.

She drew up at the guard house and nodded to the three guards. They eyed her with amusement.

"Bit late tae be goin' a ridin' laddie," said the stout older man.

"Aye, and I would rather be in my bed this night, but my master will have it otherwise."

"Your master? And who would that be?" asked the bearded guard. He began to walk around her, examining the horse first, and then her. She pulled her bonnet down a little and tried to appear relaxed.

"Lord Rory Campbell. He bid me take his horse on tae Balquihidder where a kinsmen lives. He has nae need to stable two here now and would rather he be there, with the kinsman."

The third man, young and with no trace of facial hair, sniggered. "Aye, he has plenty tae ride here, from what I heard."

Morag grinned. An interesting piece of knowledge to tuck away. "Exactly, why trouble tae bring your own, when ye have new horse flesh to select from here?"

"Flesh is what it is, fresh and otherwise. But then he's nae different from all the others of his ilk," said the bearded man. "Highlanders." He turned and spat. "They're all the same. Cowked creepers the lot of them. They are always scrabbling and scrapping for nought but a muckle's worth of land and some crabbit old coos."

Morag gave them a tight smile. "Och, weel, I wouldna ken that much, having only been in Lord Rory's employ since he came tae the castle and being from near Bannockburn."

The three of them chuckled, sharing some joke. "Is it nae as I said?" the man with beard chirped. "Nae coin tae their name, for all they may shriek and howl their war cries. And never would I count on them in any battle. Sure tae go lepping back up tae their precious hills in a fright."

Morag was ready to climb down from the horse and take the

small *sgian dhu* she had tucked in her doublet and shove it right up into his breast bone. But before her building rage overcame her, the stout older man spoke.

"Wheest, Jack, ye're full of bluster and more. Let the laddie get on his way and save your havering for those who care tae listen."

The young man began to move back, sniggering as he did so and soon the others followed suit. Morag forced herself to nod and moved forward, so taken up in her anger that she felt little relief at being allowed to pass through. Once free of the castle outer walls she broke into a slow trot, still brooding over the brazen soldier's remarks, vowing that she would find a way to repay him for his words.

She was so caught up in her thoughts that she nearly fell off the horse when a mounted man came alongside her and grabbed her reins and brought Thunder to an abrupt halt. She struggled a moment to regain her balance, before fear and anger rose up and she faced the man who'd waylaid her.

For a moment she thought it might have been Rory, but one glance at the stranger told her it was not, if only by his size. There was little else to make out though, because of the growing gloom and his dark garb. A large bonnet pulled down low obscured his face and prevented any clue to his identity to be found there. Still, he brandished no weapon and did nothing more than hold her reins firmly while her horse settled himself.

"Why do ye detain me, my lord?" Morag said, forcing her voice to a lower range, despite her growing anger.

"Are ye gone mad?" said the man, the deep timbre of his voice resonating. She didn't recognise it, though he seemed overly familiar in his manner.

"What are ye doing sauntering out so at night, on your own?" the man said darkly. "Do ye no ken that it isna safe? That there are men intent on destruction and harm, especially for those who serve the royal household?"

"I'm no going far," she said in a haughty manner. "Ye need no concern yourself, sir."

"Near or far, it doesna matter. The upstarts and rabble are everywhere."

"I'm perfectly able to outride or defend myself, should the need arise," she said.

He snorted. "Ye'd be a pretty sight after a mob of them decided tae show ye different. I had little enough trouble in stopping ye. What makes ye think ye'd fare any better with them?"

"That was different," said Morag defensively. She was glad he couldn't see the flush on her face. "Besides, what business is it of yours? Who are ye tae tell me where and when I should go about my master's business?"

"Your master's business?" he said, his tone sceptical. "What master asks his servant tae take a journey at this time of the evening?"

"Though it's none of your affair, I was asked tae take his horse tae his kinsmen this evening, so that it may then be ridden on tae his home for safe keeping."

The man paused, eyeing the horse and then its rider. "And thon horse belongs tae your master? And who might that master be?"

She took a deep breath and was about tae answer when he leaned across his horse and placed a hand on her arm. "Dinna bother lying, lass. I ken the horse you're riding and I think I may have an idea why ye're taking him."

He released her arm, sat back in his saddle and sighed. Morag remained silent, her thoughts racing in bewilderment. How the devil did he recognise the horse?

"Who are ye, my lord, that ye ken the horse I'm riding?" her voice wavered a little on the last few words. She cursed her weakness and took a deep breath, steeling herself. "It really is nae concern of yours, I assure ye. And if that's all, I'll be on my way."

She tried to retrieve her reins from him, but he held on tight.

"If ye please, may I have my reins?"

"Nay," he said. "I dinna say ye could go. And I willna let ye go. How the devil did ye think ye would get back here by dawn?"

"I'm no going far, only tae Dundoon."

"And then what? Were ye going tae walk back?"

"Nay, of course I'm no going tae walk back," she said disdainfully. "I'm going tae exchange horses with another."

"Ah, I see."

Morag could have been mistaken but she thought she detected a hint of amusement in the last words. She gave a frustrated sigh.

"Now that ye ken my plan, may I have my reins?"

"I said I willna let ye go on and I meant it. Nay, I'll take your horse on for ye to your man, if you're that set on the plan, but first I'll see ye back tae the castle."

"What? Nay. I'll no have ye do that," she said, shocked, her voice higher than before. She caught herself and continued in a lower pitch, "I dinna ken who ye may be but ye have nae business in this affair, my lord."

"Och, wheest, lassie. We've nae time to chitter over this, if I'm tae do all that I must this night."

He kicked his horse forward, leading hers behind and left the road, weaving among some of the trees. Eventually he halted and dismounted, tied his horse to a low limb and then came over to her. Before she knew what he was about, he grasped her waist and took her down from the horse. In the dark she could hardly make out his shape, but his hands were strong and firm and the arms she placed her hands on, firmly muscled. She knew there was no denying now that she was a lass, with her womanly curves so fully in his grip. She backed away and he released his hold.

"Now, I'll leave the horses here for safe keeping, take ye back and then return tae them and be on my way."

"How can I trust ye? How will I tell that ye have done as ye promised?"

"I'll have word brought tae ye from your man saying that he received the horse, will that suffice?" There it was again, that trace of amusement.

"And how is it that ye ken my man? Or his whereabouts?"

"Och, because ye'll tell me now, will ye no?"

She nearly laughed and was glad that he couldn't see the grin on her face. "Aye, fine I will tell ye." She folded her arms. "I didna lie about the destination. And ye'll take him tae a man named Rob MacTavish of Glen Strae. He shouldna be verra difficult tae find. Ye can tell him if he will tae take him home. And if ye please tae say to him, *thoir breab math don asal seo.*" She gave him a smug look, for all that he couldn't see it in the dark. "He'll ken what tae say back and if ye send his words back tae me I'll ken that ye were true tae your word."

"But will I be able tae after a good kick?" he said, laughter in his voice.

"What?" she said, the breath gone from her. Did he understand Gaelic?

"Well did ye no have me tell him tae give me, or should I say, 'this ass' a good kick?" he said.

"I-I...ye ken the Gaelic?"

"Ye have tae ask?" he said. He laughed softly now, deep and resonate. "Can I suggest a different message so that I may be free tae return unharmed? Or Rob? For I canna promise that I won't do him the greater harm, should he try tae give me a good kick."

She gave a resigned sigh. There was no choice – it seemed she had to trust the man, whoever he may be. That she had no clue to his identity made it all the more frustrating and it was clear he wouldn't tell her, no matter how much she insisted. She muttered a curse in Gaelic softly and it was met with another chuckle.

"My apologies," she said. "I suppose if ye just leave it up tae Rob, he'll give ye the word and ye can see that I hear of it."

She moved forward and tied the reins of her horse on the same limb as his own. That task complete, she turned.

"Lead on, my lord."

He took her hand and escorted her through the trees until they came to the road. Quickly, he led her forward, his stride long and purposeful. She worked hard to keep up with him, glad for the boots she wore. His gloved hand was firm on her bare hand and on occasion he kept her from stumbling as she attempted to match his pace.

"How will I get back in the castle?" she asked suddenly. "The guards willna have changed from when I rode out and they willna believe that I have returned from my journey already."

"Dinna fash yourself about that," he said. "It's all in hand."

They drew near the castle's outer walls and as they approached the gate the man drew up by the walls, placing her behind him. He made his way carefully to the entrance and slipped inside, towing her in his wake. They crept their way along the wall and then crossed the small grassed area to the next wall. He drew her along the wall for some time, until they came to a small gate. There he stopped and released her hand. With a swift movement he withdrew his gloves, tucked them away and withdrew a small purse. He opened the purse and took out a key which he placed into the gate's lock. A low click sounded and after a little push the gate swung open silently. He slipped inside and a moment later took up Morag's hand and drew her in with him.

She met this process with an amazed and puzzled silence, tucking away everything for later consideration, when her mind was less in a whirl. She heard a clank and froze. A moment later the man had his hand across her mouth and had embraced her in his cloak, her back to his chest and up against the darkness of the wall. Startled by the moves, she instinctively put her hand up along his to remove it, but stopped once she realised that he was only protecting them from any unwanted sound she might make.

His hand felt firm and strong against hers. She could feel a ridge of scars along the fingers and another at his wrist. An experienced fighter. A man who crossed swords and admitted he could better Rob in a fight without any trace of bragging. A man who spoke Gaelic. A Highlander without a doubt.

She heard voices now and stilled her mind as well as her body, willing the people approaching to pass without remark. She heard his soft breath above her, but nothing more, for she dare not even breathe. The voices passed and faded into the distance and she breathed out. The hand released her mouth and he drew back from her.

Without any word, he took up her hand and drew her along the perimeter of the wall until he came to another, smaller gate.

"This leads in tae the gardens. Ye ken how tae go from there, do ye no?"

"Aye," she whispered.

"Now, go directly tae your rooms, no side trips or wanderings, promise?"

She laughed inwardly. This was all so fantastical. "Aye, I promise, but who am I tae promise, for ye still havena told me your name."

He laughed softly. "Och, ye ken who I am. Just think on it a wee bit, *mo ghaol.*"

"But I dinna ken," she said, protesting.

Before she could say any more he leaned down, kissed her cheek and was gone.

CHAPTER 11

The memory of the night before lingered with Morag throughout the next day, as she sat through a tiresome reading of someone's dry account of the Lenten observances in France while sewing away at an altar cloth in the Dowager Queen's apartments. It was his final words that puzzled her most. It wasn't until Barbara began a whispered conversation near her that her attention was caught.

"Did you hear that John Knox is stirring the rabble again?" Barbara whispered to Jean.

"Oh, that's not news," she said.

"No, but this time he's joining that rabble that are determined on destruction. I hear they are now intending to gather and march here, to Stirling!"

"That can't be true, surely? They wouldn't dare." Jean's eyes were round and anxious.

"And why would they not dare? When already they have done more than anyone would have thought possible," said Barbara.

"It's that wretched 'Beggars' Summons'. They are trying to show her that they won't obey her commands, I'll warrant," said Jean.

"And now we're to receive the brunt of their disobedience," said Barbara, her tone full of drama. "When they murder us in our beds!"

"Surely the Dark Ghost will warn us and protect us," Jean said, with a visible effort at calm.

Morag started to open her mouth to cast doubt on the so-called Dark Ghost's ability to defeat a mob on his own, but she shut it. They wouldn't appreciate her contribution.

"If he but knew, it might be so," said Barbara. She sniffed. "I've not heard a tale of him for some time. Perhaps..." she leaned over meaningfully..."they have killed him already."

Jean gasped. "No, I can't believe it. He's too clever and skilled by half to be killed by a raggedy bunch of villeins."

"We can only hope so, but I for one intend to have a ballock dagger ready by my side at all times."

Jean scoffed at her. "Where would ye get a dagger? I can't see that any of your kin here would allow it."

Barbara sniffed. "I'm sure Robert Hay, James Home, Thomas Maxwell, or any number of my companions would be willing to provide me with one."

Morag suppressed a smile at the thought of Barbara wielding a ballock dagger, waving the long blade at some threat. She would more than likely get it caught in her kirtle instead of wounding anyone. She looked up and briefly caught an amused look on Glenna's face and it made her smile more until she caught herself.

She turned her thoughts once more to her own dilemma. She may not have succeeded in coming up with a plan that would result in Glenna and Rory's banishment from court, yet, but at least she had bested Rory in the matter of Thunder. That is, if the dark stranger who wasn't a stranger kept his promise. She puzzled again over his identity. He certainly seemed to under-stand the dangers abroad last night and had warned her against it. She frowned, a notion starting to dawn on her. It couldn't be that he was the Dark Ghost? Or the *Droch Spiorad* in Gaelic as he called himself. For this stranger had Gaelic and was dressed exactly as the others had described him. Suddenly, she knew it was so.

THE EVENING MEAL was nearly finished. It was in the Great Hall this evening with the full court in attendance and musicians in the gallery. Though not so formal a meal as the one when the French dignitaries had attended, it was still an elaborate enough affair, with many courses. Morag felt a great deal more confident than she had on the last occasion, not the least because the state of her clothes had been much improved. This time she wore her gown of watchet silk, the colour she knew offset her eyes and suited her dark hair which she had twisted and braided and caught up in a pearled netted snood. The snood was Bridie's latest triumph, contrived by herself with some seed pearls retrieved from an old gown and some clever twisting with cast off silken threads. Morag wore matching pearls at her ears and a small pearl brooch that had been her mother's.

She sat in the same seat, Glenna next to her and Barbara further along. But this time she recognised the other young ladies-in-waiting, and some of the men as well. Munro and his group were at the other table as before, his dress no less flamboyant as any other time. His colour of choice was murrey and a yellow which accented his corn coloured hair and his blue eyes, she was certain, except for the fact that a large plume in his bonnet hung low and nearly obscured the whole upper half of his face.

Morag caught herself studying him. His mouth was now pursed in thought as he listened to his companion, some over-flirtatious woman with too much cleavage. The lips curved sensuously and seemed to promise much. She looked away, then a few moments later back again, trying to compare him in a dispassionate way to the *Droch Spiorad*. Just before she'd entered the chamber, she'd had conveyed to her a brief note stating the safe delivery of her horse, giving her satisfaction, except that his identity remained a mystery. There was nothing dark or ghost-like about Munro's great fat figure. She could hardly picture him stealing into the castle with her.

As if to reaffirm her musings Munro waved his handkerchief to make a point, his own long lace cuffs fluttering along with the gesture. He was such a peacock, she told herself, trying not to watch his hands and marvel at their grace. She must find a moment alone with him after the meal, though, so that she might thank him for his efforts to quell the rumours about her. She owed him that.

She glanced down the other end of her table and saw Rory Campbell there, staring at her, his eyes full of anger. The woman on his other side drew his attention and Morag was able to observe Rory a while as the woman attempted to flirt with him. She drew a little satisfaction that his anger was such that the woman couldn't succeed in distracting him fully.

Beyond him, she caught sight of John Dunbar and he gave her a wry smile. She nodded slightly back, feeling even lighter now. He raised his cup to her. She grinned. He had heard. She supposed Rory had made it known around the castle that she'd taken his horse. But she didn't care, in fact she was glad, for it showed him up to be the whining scoundrel he was. The fact that she'd shown up with the roan spoke volumes and if he was too pathetic to understand it, well she couldn't help that.

It was a short time later that the last course was removed and the courtiers rose from the table and began milling around, chatting and flirting. A few ministers were clustered together on the other side of the room, their faces serious and full of concentration, with an occasional sidelong glance at the Dowager Queen, who looked tired and distracted.

"Her Majesty is worried."

Morag turned, smiled at John Dunbar and nodded. "I think you're right. She has many cares, so it's no surprise."

Morag caught sight of Munro talking to David Montgomerie and Margaret Ramsey. Though she had little liking for his company, she knew she couldn't delay her obligation any longer.

"I'm sorry, my lord, but could you excuse me? I must speak with Lord Munro."

Dunbar nodded his assent, a little bemused. She moved away from him and headed towards Munro, arriving just as Margaret Ramsey gave a peal of laughter that was nearly ear piercing at such close range. Morag tried to suppress a wince, but was only partially successful. She caught Munro's eye and saw a hint of amusement there. Those eyes, now visible since he'd removed the plumed bonnet, were a blue that she now realised were more like the colour of the sea when it was summer bright. And large, with a thick fringe of lash. He gazed beyond her and his expression darkened. Before she could speak, Munro placed a hand on her arm.

"But Lady Morag, you are just the person. Did you know I was looking for you? I wanted to ask you about something Lady Glenna mentioned. You both play the lute, is that correct?"

Startled, she blinked. "I-I play the lute, but only indifferently. I mainly sing."

"Of course, that's what she meant. Come now, we'll seek her out this instance before the dancing commences." He nodded to the other two with a wide smile and a dip of the leg. "You will excuse us? We cannot refuse a beckoning lute."

Before Morag knew what was happening, he was ushering her away from the two others, and out of the corner of her eyes she saw Rory heading her way, until Munro steered her away from that direction.

"I-I'm sorry, my lord... I don't think this is a notion that will have a happy outcome," she said stiffly after a moment. She refused to be lost in the warm gaze he directed towards her.

"Nay," he said in a low voice in Scots. "Ye're doing me a favour."

"A favour?" she asked, bewildered. Forgetting her resolve, she looked into his eyes, and there they were again wide and that summer bright blue. She made herself lower her gaze.

"Aye. If ye will indulge me and ask nae questions."

"Of course," she said without thinking, too concerned with her desire to avert her eyes. She caught herself, realising what she just agreed to and sighed. "Aye, I do owe ye a debt and it was that I came tae speak tae ye about. I wanted tae thank ye for quashing the rumours about me."

He looked down at her, and batted his eyes like a girl. "Och, lass, do ye think they believed it of ye?" He patted his stomach.. "It'd take someone of more stamina than ye, I think." He tittered and waved his handkerchief. "Nay, ye have nought tae thank me for."

She nodded dumbly, looking over his shoulder and tried to keep the titter in her head. "Well, I'm grateful nevertheless."

He nodded and ushered her along, weaving through the various groups, until he came to stop before a small group that contained Margaret Ramsey, a fair-haired young woman named Jane Hamilton that Morag recognised as part of Munro's set, Glenna and another man, William Fergusson, who could nearly be said to be as flamboyantly dressed as Munro, except he was older and shorter and somehow didn't show his flair so well. The group nodded to Munro and then Morag. Munro introduced her to the two she hadn't formally met and they exchanged pleas-antries in French. Jane Hamilton gave an almost imperceptible sniff and smiled thinly at Morag, while William Fergusson planted a wet kiss on the back of her hand.

"Lady Glenna," said Munro. "I've yet to inquire after your

mother, please forgive me. Last we spoke you said she was taken ill and couldn't leave her bed. Has she improved?"

Glenna reddened and she blinked several times, struggling with her emotions. She looked down at her hands and took a deep breath. "I'm afraid I've heard nothing still, my lord."

Munro put a hand on her shoulder and gave it a brief, almost intimate squeeze. Morag studied his face, wondering at their relationship. Was he attracted to Glenna? Surely not. He was…what was he? Too old? She bit her lip and acknowledged that it wasn't really the case. Though his girth might be something you would find on a much older man, he couldn't more than five and thirty. If that. She studied his face, losing herself, despite all her efforts

"I'm sorry," Munro said, his expression full of compassion. "I hope you hear good news soon. Your brother has received no word from your father at all?"

Glenna raised her head and stiffened. "I've had no word from my father directly. And I'm not aware if my brother has had any word either. If he has, he hasn't said anything to me about it."

"But that is such a pity," said Jane. She lay a commiserating hand on Glenna's arm. "We can only hope that it won't be long before you hear something. And I'm certain it will be good news."

Morag eyed Jane sceptically. The woman was as sincere as a cold draught on a winter's day. Currying favour with Munro? She had no doubt. She glanced at Lord Munro, who regarded Jane with a bland look, then, catching Morag's eye, arched a brow. Morag flushed.

She gave a reassuring smile. She'd nothing against Glenna's mother and wouldn't wish the lady any harm. She would show Munro she could be gracious, unlike the harridan, Jane. "Yes, I'm certain your mother will recover. My brother Iain spoke very highly of her. She was most talented on the lute, I think. Well, he used to play for her, as I understand it. Is that where you get your talent?" Morag realised she was babbling and made herself stop.

"She must do, for Glenna plays beautifully," said Lord Munro.

Jane's eyes tightened at this remark. Oh, that was a spoke in her wheel, thought Morag, smiling inwardly. This was more amusing than she'd thought it would be, though it was Glenna who was the object of Munro's attention. Well, it was no concern of hers if he chose to dangle after Glenna.

"And you," said Munro, regarding Morag. "You play as well. And I think the Dowager Queen would be delighted if the two of you could perform."

"No, no," said Morag, instantly flustered. "No, I'm an indifferent player, really."

"Ah, yes, you did say that, though I think you're being modest," said Munro.

William Fergusson bowed slightly to Glenna first and then Morag. "It would be a veritable treat to have you both perform."

"Oh, yes, we'd love to hear you both play," said Jane, her smile just a crease across her face.

"If you insist," said Glenna. "I would most certainly hate to disappoint you. Since I know you have great appreciation for music."

Morag glanced at Jane, certain the remark was far from the truth. Any doubt over its barb was immediately dispelled when she saw the brief flash of anger in Jane's face, hastily replaced by a benign smile.

"I'm afraid it will just be Glenna who will provide the performance," said Morag. "I'm really not being modest when I say that I am an indifferent player. Both of my brothers would tell you so."

"Ah, brothers, they're not the best judge of these things," said Munro, his eyes filled with amusement. "Isn't that so, Lady Glenna?"

Glenna looked at him and then gave a genuine smile, a little twinkle in her eyes. Yes, those two certainly had some kind of connection. Barbara was no doubt right in this matter at least.

"No, indeed," said Glenna. "My brothers certainly cannot be counted upon to be the best judge of many things."

"Ah, of course," said Munro. He placed a hand on Morag's arm briefly. "I will take you at your word, my lady, so may I ask instead that you and I sing together, with Lady Glenna accompanying us?"

Surprised, she didn't reply at once, caught by his eyes that at this moment were an indecipherable darker, deeper blue.

"Of course," she said. Had she just agreed to sing? Why would he want her to sing? And with him? "What piece would you have us sing?" she asked.

"Do you know any French chansons?"

She thought of the few that Abby had taught her. The first two were about love. Lusty love and unrequited love. She needed one without love. So important not to feature love, lusty or otherwise. For so many reasons. It wouldn't do just after Lord Munro had quashed the rumours to sing with him about love. That was the primary reason. Most definitely. She made herself look at his large paunch and calculate how much he must eat to maintain its roundness. Finally, she thought of a suitable one. "*Quand Je Bois du Vin Clairet*?" she said uncertainly.

"Ah, *mais oui, c'est perfait*," he said with an exaggerated accent. He looked at Glenna, a brow raised. She nodded.

"Good," he said with a nod and turned to William Fergusson and Jane Hamilton. "Now if you excuse us, my lady, my lord, we'll depart on our mission to bring some cheer to Her Majesty."

Before Morag could collect herself, Munro had her and Glenna before the Dowager Queen presenting his suggestion. The Dowager Queen smiled in delight and clapped her hands declaring it was an old favourite. Morag felt a rising dread. She only hoped she remembered all the words. She'd only sung it with Abby a few times.

As if sensing her unease, Munro lay a reassuring hand along her back and guided her towards the dais, where she stood a few moments next to Munro and Glenna while a stool and a lute were fetched. Morag tried not to think of the reassuring warmth of his hand on her back and refrained from leaning into it.

When Glenna was comfortably seated, lute in place on her lap and the tuning complete, the audience hushed. The Dowager Queen spoke, her reedy voice rising to fill the hall. She introduced the song and announced her pleasure at such a delight.

Glenna played a few bars of the opening verse and then paused a little. Morag's nerves suddenly seized up, until Munro's heavily beringed hand took hers and gave it a little squeeze as they stood next to each other behind Glenna. Munro began to sing the first verse, his wonderfully rich baritone voice giving a fullness to the song. The words started to come to Morag and by the beginning of the second verse she was able to take over at his nod and smile. She sang with increasing confidence, and by the third he was joining her, adding harmonies where possible. It filled her head and she blended her own voice with his, feeling the perfect tone. They repeated the first verse again, playing with harmonies, providing little flourishes all the while watching him, drawing on the laughter and enjoyment that danced in his eyes and letting it feed her own.

By the song's conclusion, Morag briefly wished that they might have another to sing, so that these shared moments wouldn't end so quickly and that she still might hold his hand a little longer. She was surprised to find his skin rough and calloused, not at all what she expected.

The last words were sung and Glenna's playing came to an end. Morag sighed softly missing his hand when he released hers. She turned to face the audience and forced a neutral smile for the Dowager Queen. Her Majesty showed her own appreciation with great enthusiasm, clapping hard but briefly, her worn eyes alight with joy.

Munro took Morag's hand again and led her out from behind Glenna and she curtsied and he bowed, Morag clutched his hand hard, reluctant to let him go again. Munro indicated Glenna, who rose and joined them, her lute in one hand. The audience continued to clap with polite appreciation. Morag saw Rory glare at his sister and she smiled inwardly at the sight. There were some benefits to putting aside her dislike of Glenna.

Glenna handed off the lute to one of the musicians. Munro ushered Glenna and Morag from the dais and onto the floor. Conversation resumed and the musicians began to tune up for the dancing. The small group had hardly progressed far when Rory came up to Glenna.

"What were you doing, consorting like that with a MacGregor?" he hissed.

"It's no affair of yours," said Glenna, her face reddening with anger.

"It is, if you're making the Campbells look like fools," said Rory.

"I fear you do that without my help," said Glenna.

Rory looked at Morag. "As for you, if you think you can get away with your little trick with Thunder you're very much mistaken."

Morag gave him an innocent look. "I'm afraid I don't know what you're talking about."

"You know exactly what I mean."

"Oh, cease your bluster," said Glenna. "We all know she made a fool of you. Twice, if I'm not mistaken."

Rory gave her a murderous look. "She acted with no honour or grace, but that's not surprising since she's nothing but a MacGregor."

"Now, my lord," said Munro. "I wouldn't like to have you sent home. Or is that what you're hoping for? But then I think your father would take it amiss to know that his son was dismissed from court for childish and unseemly behaviour towards women."

Rory looked at Munro, his face ablaze. "My lord, this is a family matter and no concern of yours."

"I would say it is a concern of mine, especially if you're preventing me from my partner in this opening dance." He turned to Morag, and with a small bow proffered his hand. "My lady? You did say it would be mine to claim."

Surprised, Morag took his hand and allowed him to lead her away. She glanced around the room, hoping that no one over-heard the exchange with Rory, and Munro's words to her. Just when she thought she knew this man, he could unsettle her in a dozen different ways. They took their place on the floor with the dozen or so other couples. He released her hand and gave a flour-ishing bow which she acknowledged with a brief, slightly embar-rassed curtsy. The musicians struck the opening bars of a branle. She took his hand again tentatively and he led her through the opening steps. His fingers, so gentle, yet firm felt warm against hers.

She didn't know what to expect, his girth, notwithstanding, she knew only that he'd been graceful in the few dances she'd seen him execute. But as they danced the steps, his hands firm on her waist at the lifts, his footwork sure, she knew that she would dance with him all night if she could. His hands on her, his gaze when they came together were all most too much and she was glad it was a vigorous dance that only allowed him to lift her on occasion and break away to take the arms of other dancers for a brief time. The joy of it didn't escape her and the energy of it stirred her blood. There was only one intimate moment when he pulled her close and she gazed into his eyes, which were so dark in the candlelight that they seemed almost black. For a moment, she thought they contained desire, but it was gone so quickly she wondered if she'd just imagined it, as she was imagining too much, lately.

The dance finished and Munro bowed to her elaborately, waving his handkerchief, but hardly out of breath.

"You dance very well, my lord," she said. She dared a glance and saw only amusement in his face.

"You mean I dance well for my size?" he said, his eyes mocking.

She blushed. "No, I-I meant you have a real grace and I thank you very much for such an enjoyable experience."

He laughed. "Despite my wide girth?"

Morag bit her lip and looked at him, the blue eyes intent on her. She allowed herself a grin. "Yes," she said with a mischievous tone. "Despite your size."

"If I may claim the next dance, my lady?" said John Dunbar coming up to them. "It sounds to me that it will be an allemande."

She turned to him and smiled warmly. "Of course, my lord. It would be my honour." She curtsied to Munro and murmured further thanks. He bowed an acknowledgement and left the two of them.

"An odd fellow," said Dunbar. "It is to be wondered why this wager exists and all the women clamouring for his attention, for he is hardly the picture of courtly looks. His dress is outrageous and well, one cannot deny that he is quite fat. And to think they linked him with you. It's outrageous. "

Morag opened her mouth to deny his words and shut them. What could she say? It was not wise to draw attention to any kind of praise of Munro's kindness or his other attributes. She wouldn't list them even to herself. It was too unsettling. She pasted another smile on her face and took his proffered hand. The dance began and she moved into the steps, trying to focus on Dunbar and not his previous comments.

"I know it must have been difficult to have shared the dais with Lady Glenna just now. You were admirable. Not only did you appear unruffled by the occasion but you sang beautifully."

"Thank you, that's very kind of you," said Morag.

"It is only the truth, my lady. You have the voice of an angel."

He gave her a warm look, his manner so charming, eyes filled with admiration.

She blushed under his gaze and lowered her eyes. He possessed very courtly manners and it was difficult not to succumb to them. They pulled apart in the course of the dance and came together again and his hand grasped hers, giving it a meaningful squeeze. She looked at him and he smiled at her delightedly.

"I think I may have hit on a plan," he said.

"A plan?" she said, bewildered.

"For the Campbells."

"Oh," she said. She'd nearly forgotten their agreement with all that had happened. "Yes, of course. What plan have you devised?"

He shook his head. "I can't speak of it here, and I'm not yet certain of it. But I will let you know in a day or two."

"I see. Of course. That's too good of you," she said, trying to sound grateful. She didn't know what she felt about him seizing the idea and forming it himself without consulting her beforehand.

The dance concluded and he kissed the back of her hand, bowing. "Be certain I will not lose time in contacting you when everything is in place." He held her hand a moment, caressing the back of it with his thumb. "Trust me," he said. "I have only your best interests at heart."

CHAPTER 12

*G*lenna glanced at Morag again in a sidelong way as, with Barbara, they made their way to the Dowager Queen's apartments. The smile of amusement seemed sincere and shared with Morag instead of directed at her, but Morag couldn't be sure.

"Your singing was lovely last night," said Glenna. "I had no chance to say it to you before now."

"Oh, yes, Morag, very nice indeed," said Barbara. She beamed a smile at Morag. "Especially after your nerves settled down. My Lord Munro was so very courteous and helpful about that. But then he often is like that, or so I've found. He can be a bit extreme with his clothes choices and," she waved her hand in a flutter, "his manner a trifle too womanly, but you cannot deny his kind heart."

Morag's face turned as red as Glenna's kirtle. She opened her mouth to speak but Glenna got there before her.

"Oh, Barbara, you know nothing of music, that is obvious. That wasn't nerves at all and Lord Munro was right to open with the first verse. We had no time to confer, the three of us, and so we none of us certain who should open. Lord Munro being courteous, of course, thought that Morag might, and Morag, being no less courteous thought he would, so since he was more familiar with the Dowager Queen's taste, Lord Munro took the lead when it was clear Morag was deferring to him."

Surprised, Barbara turned to study Morag who hastily put a neutral expression on her face and shrugged. "It is as Glenna says. It's a matter of taste who begins that song, but since it's about drinking, Lord Munro was right to start it off."

"Besides," said Glenna, "it was a good musical decision to begin with the deeper tones and introduce the higher tones later, once the melody has been firmly established. Is that not right, Morag?"

"Yes," said Morag, fighting the tug of amusement at her mouth. "Exactly so. I must compliment you on your own playing last night. You're very deft. I especially enjoyed the way you rolled the chords just before the last few phrases of each verse. Gave a real emphasis on the words."

Barbara looked between the two of them, a puzzled frown on her face. "Well," she said. "That all may be clear to the two of you but you can't expect any ordinary person to understand, or be interested in that much detail. Let's just leave it that it was a very pretty piece."

She moved off from them and approached the door to the Dowager Queen's apartments. She knocked a few times, then opened it and entered. Glenna and Morag followed, not before exchanging glances of real amusement. Morag was just about to go into the apartment when a young footman approached.

"My lady Morag?"

Morag smiled at him in a friendly manner. "Yes, did ye seek me?"

"Aye," he said. "I was telt tae give ye this." He handed her a small folded parchment with a plain seal on it.

Puzzled, she took it and thanked the footman.

Glenna gave it a curious look. "A tryst?" she said, her tone teasing.

Morag laughed, the absurdity of it so strong. "Nay, more like a summons from Mistress Cunningham, or some such."

She broke the seal, unfolded the paper and scanned the contents. She read it again, to be certain that she understood it correctly.

Meet me in the gardens just after noon, I have news to give you. JD

John Dunbar? There could be no other person in the castle that she could imagine would have sent her this note. What would he want with her that needed a private conversation in the garden?

"Is it Mistress Cunningham?" said Glenna.

"Pardon?" she asked still caught up in her musings. "No." She coloured.

Glenna arched a brow. "An admirer?"

Morag was startled at the thought. Was he? And more to the point, what did she think of that? "Ah, perhaps. No, I don't think so."

"Is it John Dunbar?" Glenna asked.

Morag nearly jumped. "What makes you say his name?"

"Don't look so surprised. Anyone would say that he's paid you some attention since you arrived at court." Glenna smiled and leaned forward. "I think he is a very handsome and gallant man. I'd be pleased to have his attentions. And it wouldn't be Lord Munro, for all the rumours that have been circulated. I know that you think of him as no more than a courteous older man."

"He's not that old," said Morag without thinking. "What I mean to say is that I regard Lord Munro as courteous and kind, just as I regard John Dunbar in the same manner." Munro came to her mind without bidding. His twinkling eyes. She pushed the image aside. Davey's my man. Davey, who she still hadn't written to. She felt a hand on her arm.

"Are ye well?" said Glenna, her face full of concern. "You've gone very pale."

"No, no, I'm well. Just a bit of a headache all of the sudden." She folded the note and forced a smile. "The note is nothing, a mere trifle from Dunbar saying he admired my gown last night, but never found the opportunity to tell me."

Glenna smiled widely. "Ah, so I was right, then. It was John Dunbar and he does favour you with his attention. Well you couldn't have picked a more handsome man. His eyes are a wonderful colour and when they look at you, well, I can see it would melt a heart."

Morag nodded absently and entered the room with Glenna, trying to recall exactly what colour John Dunbar's eyes were. She had a feeling they weren't the deep blue of Munro's.

MORAG ENTERED the Dowager Queen's knot garden tentatively. It was cooler than she had thought it would be and the thin cloak she'd put on couldn't block the chill of the wind that was blowing strands of hair loose from her snood. She glanced around, but couldn't see any sign of Dunbar or anyone else. Well at least she wasn't going to be spied meeting with him by any passing courtier. She glanced behind her and up to the sole window that she could see, but no figure stood there or was passing by. She lifted her eyes up further to try and look through the other windows in the higher levels but the light refracting off them prevented her.

She made her way over to a cluster of topiary and a tree that would block her from anyone's view and give her some shelter from the wind. She stood there for a while, fiddling with the clasp on her cloak where she realised she'd managed to catch a loose strand of hair that had blown from the snood. She was so intent on her task that she didn't hear anyone approach.

"Having some trouble?"

Morag looked up to see Lord Munro before her. Surprised and a little breathless at his appearance, she attempted a deep breath and gathered her thoughts.

"It seems as though my hair is caught in the clasp and I was attempting to free it," she finally managed to say.

"Let me assist. It will probably be easier and quicker."

His tone was even, though his mouth gave a hint of a smile. She found herself flushing and looked away.

"Lady Morag?"

"Oh, yes," she said, chastising herself mentally. "If you would be so kind."

The minute she'd said the words she instantly regretted it. No, it wasn't a good notion at all to allow him closer. He unnerved her and she didn't like it. She looked down at his fingers, gently working the strand of hair out from where it had become wound around the brooch clasp. Despite the many rings that cluttered the fingers, she could see they were long and slender, though there was a strength about them. She stared at them in fascination, watching them work. She sighed and caught herself with a yelp.

"Did I hurt you?" he asked and raised concerned eyes to hers. "I beg your pardon if I did."

"Nay, nay, it was a slight tug that caught me by surprise," she managed to say, her voice a whispering rasp.

He studied her a moment and resumed his task, this time biting his lip in concentration. Morag stared at him, mesmerised once again. What was it about him that unnerved her? She shivered.

"You're cold? Just a moment, more. There. I think I have freed you now."

He tucked the offending strand back into her snood and his finger brushed her ear in the process. Her skin came alive there and she edged away.

"You were waiting here for John Dunbar, I think?" he said.

"John Dunbar?" she said, puzzled for a moment. Her eyes flew open wide. "Oh, that is, I was thinking to take the air," she added, struggling to collect herself yet again. She took a deep breath and looked at him directly. She would concentrate on the matter at hand. "Did he tell you that he was meeting me here?"

"In a manner of speaking. But he has to attend to another matter, it seems, so he won't be meeting you."

"Oh," she said, frowning. Why would Dunbar have told Munro he was meeting her here?

"It's just as well," said Munro. "You know you shouldn't be meeting a young, unattached man here in the garden. It wouldn't do for you, one of the Dowager Queen's ladies-in-waiting."

Stung by the fact he had reprimanded her as if she were a child, she remarked, "I know what is proper, my lord. It wasn't a tryst, if that's what you're thinking." She'd pronounced "tryst" with a disdainful tone. "It was about a matter of importance. A private matter. Besides, is it not just as improper for you to be with me here?"

He chuckled. "Possibly. But the Dowager Queen knows me well enough to realise that I wouldn't dally after a young lass such as yourself."

His words cut deeper than any insult she could imagine. She pressed her lips together and straightened.

"Nay, lass," he said, switching to Scots. "Dinna get yourself in a taking. I meant nae harm in my words. I was only thinking of your reputation and what Mistress Cunningham might conclude if she should get wind of it."

He put a hand on her shoulder. No doubt with fatherly intent. She sniffed.

"Aye, my lord. Of course. I appreciate your kindness," she said with as much aloof coolness as she could muster. "Now, I must return."

She gave him a brief curtsy, avoiding any direct glance and

left him, making her way back into the castle in the stateliest manner she could contrive. Davey would never have treated her in such a manner. He was noble in his own right. Well built. Were Davey's eyes blue? Most certainly they were blue. Or perhaps they were brown. Yes, she seemed to recall that they were, for his mother had brown eyes, didn't she? Next time she saw him she would check. In the meantime she would write that letter.

CHAPTER 13

*N*o Protestant would ransack a church with this altar cloth, Morag thought, struggling with another snarl in the thread. They would surely mistake it for one of their own churches. Perhaps that was a good thing and Mistress Cunningham would praise her for it. She nearly snorted at the thought and glanced over at her, chatting in low voice to one of the senior ladies-in-waiting.

"Do you like my handiwork?" said Morag to Glenna in a low voice. "I call it the 'Protestant Disguise' example. Dull and ugly."

Glenna looked up from her own stitching and cocked her head. "Hmm. You have a real eye for design, I can see. I'm sure the cardinal would see it as a divine gift."

She grinned at Morag and Morag responded in kind. It was nice to share this humour, especially with her thoughts and emotions so much at odds. Morag had surprised herself by choosing to sit near Glenna after the Dowager Queen had finished her rest following the midday meal and they had all assembled once again. Her own excuse of a visit to the stables to check on her mare and pony had given no cause for questioning. Not even from Barbara, who generally quizzed her on most everything she did lately. At the moment Barbara sat next to Jean, the two of them whispering almost conspiratorially.

"What do you imagine those two are gossiping about?" said Morag.

"Something stupid, I have no doubt."

"Shall we wager on it?"

Glenna looked at her, her eyes alight. "Yes. What will you wager? Asking a dance with a courtier?" She raised her brow. "With John Dunbar perhaps?"

Morag blushed. "Hmm. Are you interested in him? If not, it isn't much of a wager. How about Lord Munro."

"Lord Munro?" Glenna said quizzically.

"Yes, you're interested in him, are ye no? Or perhaps..." she widened her eyes, "it's the wager?" Morag had no idea why the words were tumbling out of her mouth and if she had any control or sense in her addled mind she would have clapped her hand over her mouth and kept it there until nightfall.

Glenna looked at her in amazement and then laughed. She laughed harder, struggling to suppress it so much that she ended up hiccupping.

"Do you need to excuse yourself, Lady Glenna?" Mistress Cunningham said severely in French.

"Oh, *mais non*, Mistress Cunningham," said Glenna, laughter now suppressed. "I'm sorry, but I seem to have had something catch in my throat. I'm better now, though."

Mistress Cunningham pressed her lips together and nodded, though her look said in no uncertain terms that she wasn't to let such interruptions occur again. Morag saw the look, then exchanged laughing glances with Glenna and fought her own urge to give into hysterical giggles.

"What was so funny?" asked Barbara, leaning over towards them.

Morag looked at Glenna and pursed her mouth together, fighting the urge to succumb again to giggles.

"Well, if you must ask, it was you who started it. What were the two of you talking about? Jean's eyes had gone round as two plates!"

Barbara's eyes flashed. "The wager."

"The wager?" asked Morag.

"Yes. Jean and I are decided. I shall go after the wager. With Lord Munro."

"You're going to get Lord Munro to bed you?" asked Morag, stunned and irritated at once.

What made Barbara think she could manage it? She examined Barbara, with her curvaceous figure that no amount of corseting could make anything else and her inviting lips and manner. Yes, she could see.

"You want Lord Munro to bed you?" asked Glenna. "But why?"

"For the wager," said Barbara, impatiently. "And for interest."

"Interest?" said Morag.

"Yes. Because... well you understand he is so..." Barbara waved her hand airily.

"Nice? Kind?" said Glenna in a bland voice.

"No, you fool. His manners, well they suggest he may not be interested in women. I mean to find out if it is so." Her eyes twinkled with mischief. "I mean to see what exactly he keeps in his codpiece." She giggled loudly.

"And you think you could do it?" said Glenna.

Barbara leaned back and tilted her head coquettishly. "Aye, of course. If I set my mind to it."

Glenna looked over at Morag, smiling. "Maybe we should put a wager on that. What do you think, Morag?"

Morag gave a weak smile and nodded. "Yes, of course."

Glenna didn't seem to be upset at the thought of Barbara, with her flirtatious manners and well-formed figure, setting her sights on Munro. And Barbara certainly didn't seem worried about flaunting her intentions in front of the very person who had confided of her liking for Munro. Morag studied Glenna in wonder. She certainly would dislike it intensely if Barbara would do that to someone she professed to be interested in. In fact, she was indignant on Glenna's behalf.

"You can't think that Lord Munro would like such a mercenary play for his attentions?" she said, forcing a neutral tone. "Or that he wouldn't see through them for what they were? You may as well try to bed the 'Dark Ghost'."

"The 'Dark Ghost'?" said Barbara. "Hmm, now there would be a man lusty enough for me. I'd give much to enjoy what he has in his codpiece."

"Oh, of course you would," said Glenna, stitching mindlessly at her needlework.

"Yes, and I wouldn't mind having a look at your brother's either," said Barbara.

Glenna's eyes flew up, an incredulous look on her face. "My brother?"

"Aye, he's a sonsy fine fellow," said Barbara switching to Scots with a gleam in her eye.

Morag gave a shudder. "Nay, he is not."

"Morag is right. There's nothing sonsy about my brothers. Either of them. Ye'd be more accurate if ye said it about Morag's brother," Glenna added with a half-smile. "He is worthy of consideration."

"Iain?" said Morag. "Aye, I suppose, except he wouldna appreciate it now. He's much taken with his wife."

Glenna sighed. "Aye, I ken that well enough. What's your other brother like?"

"Aye," said Barbara. "What your other brother like? Is he sonsy, like Glenna says Iain is?"

Morag twisted her mouth. "Weel, I wouldna call him sonsy myself. He's a younger brother, ye ken. And though I find Iain tiresome sometimes, Alisdair is most tiresome all the time."

Glenna laughed. "Aye, ye've summed up my brothers entirely. And most of my family."

Morag gave her a sympathetic smile. "I'm afraid ye have nae arguments from me on that account. But I think ye would find Alisdair kind and fearfully learned."

"Och, but is he fair of countenance, does he cut a good figure?" asked Barbara.

Morag paused. "I dinna ken. I suppose. He isna inclined toward the sword. He is more one for the books."

"Books?" Barbara said with a scoff. "That will get ye nought but squinty eyes."

Glenna exchanged amused glances with Morag and shook her head. "There's much tae be said for squinty eyes in some cases."

Morag paused to look out the window into the garden. The days were drawing out and the light was just fading. She could still see a few streaks of red across the sky from the setting sun. She half wished she might be in the garden now to enjoy the view and inhale the scents of the evening. She sighed, longing for the freedom to roam among the Highland gorse that would be in full and vibrant bloom.

She drew herself away from the window and began her descent down the stairs, vowing she would catch up Glenna, Barbara and the rest of the young ladies-in-waiting freshly dismissed from the Dowager Queen's attendance. Before she could begin, a hand gripped her arm and pulled her back into the corridor.

"My lady," said John Dunbar courteously. "Would you grant me a moment to have a word with you?"

She glanced around, and seeing no one, nodded. She saw he wore discreetly coloured doublet and slops. He drew her further towards a dark corner and all she could see for a moment was the glitter of his eyes.

"Have I done anything to offend you, my lady? I assure you I didn't mean to, for I've only tried to serve you in any way possible."

She gave him a puzzled look. "I don't understand. Of course you've done nothing to offend me. Why would you think so?"

"But I must have, since you wouldn't meet me in the garden."

"I wouldn't meet you? No, you're mistaken. I said no such thing. In fact I waited for some time in the garden."

"I was given to understand from Lord Munro that you had decided not to meet with me. I did find it odd that he would give me the message from you, in fact I told him so, but he said it wasn't you directly but your maidservant, who'd passed the message to him so that he might inform me."

Surprised, Morag said nothing for a moment. Obviously, Munro felt he could take it upon himself to arrange her matters. She felt a burst of irritation at his effrontery. With some effort she set it aside and turned her thoughts to the matter at hand.

"Well there was obviously some misunderstanding," she said. "For I had every intention of meeting you."

He took her hand and kissed it, first on the outside and then in the palm of her hand. "I'm glad of it. I would hate to know you thought ill of me."

"Indeed no," said Morag, slightly flustered. She withdrew her hand carefully, a bud of anxiety arising.

"There, I knew my faith in you wasn't misplaced. That I wasn't mistaken in your kind regard for me."

"You're not mistaken, no," she said faintly. She collected herself. "What was it you wanted to say to me in the garden?"

He leaned down closer, his mouth almost to her ear. "It is of the utmost importance that you keep this secret, but I can now tell you that I have discovered a way that we may discredit the Glenorchy Campbells."

"You have?" Her attention was caught now and she hardly noticed that he took up her hand again, holding it this time while he kissed the back of her fingers.

"Yes. I'm told that Campbell is intending to join the Lords of the Congregation and will be helping to support the rabble who are intending to march here for the Dowager Queen's summons soon."

"Really?" said Morag, indignant. "But that is traitorous!"

"It is indeed, my little hornet." He kissed her fingers again, making soothing sounds. "And, I am also reliably informed that his son Rory is here to discover as much as he can about the Dowager Queen's intentions and convey that information to his father."

"But that is terrible. We must tell the Dowager Queen at once!"

"Ah, but that is the issue you see. We must have proof. All we have now is hearsay."

"Surely the Dowager Queen's ministers would unearth the proof?"

"Alas, but we can't be certain of that, for we don't know who might else be secretly in allegiance with the Protestant lords. I even heard that Lord Erskine is considering it. Especially since Châtelherault's wavering loyalties are becoming more evident. He is fiercely jealous of the Dowager Queen, you know and feels that he should be Regent, as he was before, being the late king's son, albeit illegitimate."

"Yes, of course. I've heard something of that nature," she said, considering. "But how does this fit in with Rory and his perfidy?"

"That's the best part, my beauty." He kissed her palm several times and rubbed his finger along her thumb. "The Campbell boy has been seen in conversation with Lord Erskine and one would conclude is interested in an alliance with his father. In light of this, it's obvious that there would be proof among his papers."

"Obvious? But how? Have you knowledge that he has written of his involvement with the Protestant lords to Campbell?" He was there at her fingers again, distracting Morag, so that her train of thought tapered off.

"I have in fact come to hear that, my sweet," he said. "Only think, if we could get hold of those letters we could show the Dowager Queen and expose two heinous traitors."

"How do you propose to do that?" she asked doubtfully.

He lifted his other hand and stroked the side of her face. "There is no need to worry. It won't be more than a moment's work, hardly any time at all, for I know exactly where his important documents are kept."

She was conscious of his finger tracing under her chin and then along the top of her collar bone. "What do you mean?" she said faintly. She didn't know how she allowed such liberty, but for some reason she found herself powerless to move. It was as if she weren't fully present, that he'd somehow mesmerised her and she was no longer in full possession of her body.

He planted a small kiss on her jaw before he answered. "I mean that you, as one of the ladies-in-waiting to the Dowager Queen, could easily slip into his chamber when he isn't there and take the documents from the casket. He wouldn't even know until it was too late."

"No," she whispered. "I couldn't possibly do that."

He kissed her nose. "But of course you could. You are my dear fierce Highland lady, are you not?"

She licked her lips, staring at his eyes. "I-I don't think it would be possible. I would be challenged. They would find it strange that I would access Lord Erskine's chambers."

"Of course you could," he said, running his finger along her mouth. "You need only say that you're in search of Lady Erskine, if someone should challenge you, which I doubt they will." He kissed one cheek and then the other. "You've the courage of a lion and you're clever. I have every faith in you." He brushed his mouth across hers. "You do want to have that troublesome Campbell boy banished, don't you?"

Morag blinked, her thoughts confused, her emotions all over the place. "I will consider it," she said finally, stalling.

"I know you will," he said softly. "And when you do, you'll see it for the perfect plan that it is. I have every confidence in you." He lowered his lips on her again and gave her another kiss, deeper this time and accompanied by a sigh. She parted her lips slightly and he took advantage, slipping in a probing tongue. The sensation was strangely stirring, sending her mind in a tumble. He moved his hand down, grazed his fingers along the top of her breast and she felt a tingle.

"My darling beauty," he said when he lifted his lips, "don't wait too long before you do it. We don't want to miss this opportunity."

He straightened and lifted her hand up again, giving it a long lingering kiss. "Until we meet again, my sweet." He started to move away. "Oh, one more thing. Have a care in Munro's company. I have reason to suspect he might be in league with the Protestant lords. I should hate for such an affiliation to bring you to grief in any way. I care for you too much to allow that."

Morag watched him take his leave, staring after his retreating back. She was at a loss as to what to make of this encounter. His revelations, the plan and his manner left her in a fog of apprehension and tumult.

CHAPTER 14

*M*orag stared at Mistress Cunningham's hooked nose and imagined a bird perched on top of it. A rook, a small one, granted, but still, it should fit.

"Did you hear what I said?" asked Mistress Cunningham.

"I'm certain everyone did," said Morag, her nostrils flaring slightly.

Behind Mistress Cunningham, Barbara tittered.

Morag suppressed a sigh. She'd only just finished dressing when Mistress Cunningham had entered the room and began her diatribe, but not before sending Bridie and the other chamber maid out. Glenna and Barbara had remained, in response to Mistress Cunningham's eloquent glance when they had tried to excuse themselves. Apparently the two were to bear witness to her scolding.

"Didn't I make myself clear when you arrived that you were to behave beyond reproach?"

"You did indeed, Mistress Cunningham."

"Then why have you chosen to act in a manner that would be considered wanton? Are you addled in your head, or did you think that I didn't mean what I'd said?"

"No, of course not, Mistress Cunningham," said Morag.

She sighed inwardly as she was subjected to yet another round of the very same words and scolding that she'd endured the first time. No amount of explanation or argument of any kind made a difference, so she decided not to bother.

"Yet despite professing to understand all my strictures, you insist on acting like a woman with loose morals! With Lord Munro, of all people! What will the Dowager Queen think when she hears? Let alone Lady Erskine? You know of his reputation. What were you thinking? I won't have my girls in his company unchaperoned. Or even chaperoned. I would go as far as to say with a whole room full of people in the Great Hall. It's bad enough you had to dance with him, but to…cavort with him in the garden. That is just too much."

Cavort? That was new this time round. Was it possible she was getting more worked up? Morag strove for calm. "I wasn't cavorting with him, Mistress Cunningham, I assure you."

"Indeed? Then what would you call it when you two were seen standing there, close as you please, deep in conversation?"

"I beg your pardon, Mistress Cunningham," said Glenna. "But it was on my behalf that Morag was there, for you see I asked her to seek out Lord Munro and give him a message for me. The Dowager Queen had expressed an interest in a particular song and I thought to ask him if he might sing it while I accompany him on the lute. I couldn't manage it myself, being taken up with a task Lady Erskine set me, and I knew that Lady Morag would be in a position to discuss the merits of the song with him. I told her that the refrain must be played in a different mode, as Purcell was occasionally wont to do, but he might not contrive to sing both modes comfortably. If not, I would set it as a two-part song."

She finished, her face a picture of innocence. It was all Morag could do to match the innocence with her own. Mistress Cunningham, halted in the middle of her diatribe, looked completely off balance. She blinked, opened her mouth and closed it twice. Finally, she seemed to find her voice.

"Yes, well. Of course, dear Glenna, you are always so thoughtful in your attentions to Lady Erskine and Her Majesty." She looked over at Morag and her expression darkened. "I see, perhaps the meeting was something else entirely than what was reported. But you can understand how such terrible conclusions are so easily reached here at court and why I insist my charges are beyond reproach. My rules are there for a reason and I expect you to follow them, or I shall have to insist to Lady Erskine that you be dismissed."

The three young women curtsied and murmured their understanding. Her point made, Mistress Cunningham sniffed and made her exit.

When the door had closed behind her, Barbara broke into a fit of the giggles. Morag stared at her, too rattled to say a word.

"Oh, but her face," said Barbara, when her giggles had subsided. "She clearly didn't understand a word you said about the music, Glenna, and I must say I didn't either. But then I make no pretensions to such things. Was there anything to what you spoke?"

Glenna narrowed her eyes, her expression dark. "Of course there was. Why would I say otherwise?"

Barbara shrugged and looked over at Morag. "I would hate to think that Lord Munro would contradict what you said. Can you be sure that she won't ask him?"

"She won't ask him because, unlike you, she hasn't any reason to distrust what I say," said Glenna.

Morag schooled her expression to remain neutral. "There isn't any reason to doubt any of it, because that is what has occurred. And I thank you Glenna for explaining it to her. I didn't want to involve you at first and I thought she would have her say and be done with it, but apparently she thinks if she repeats herself several times, and at increasing volume, I shall finally understand what I am too sheep brained to understand at the first two tellings."

"Yes, that would be enough to paralyse anyone," said Glenna with a wry smile.

"Oh, the woman is a positive cake," said Barbara. "Only fancy thinking that Lord Munro would be interested in you, when only yesterday he told me I had fine eyes."

"He told you that you had fine eyes?" said Glenna sceptically.

"Yes, he did. And I know that you have your own sweet spot for him, but I'm speaking the truth, and you may as well get used to it. I'm going to win that wager."

Glenna looked at Morag and arched a brow. "I would dearly love to be there when he leads you away for a bedding. Otherwise you could just as easily say you've bedded the Dark Ghost, for all we would know."

Morag's pulse quickened at the mention of the Dark Ghost. She'd heard nothing more from him or about him, really. Unconsciously she placed a finger on her cheek where he'd kissed her that night, as if to summon him.

"Well, if you must be there, I'd be more than happy to oblige you," said Barbara, her eyes agleam with recklessness.

Distracted from her musings, Morag studied her carefully, imagining Barbara playing the seductress with Munro and realised it was an image she found uncomfortable and surprising. She pushed the thought away. "Has he given you a reason to make you think he would do such a thing?"

"Well, maybe. It's only a matter of time."

"And you have no fear of dismissal?" asked Glenna.

"Well I am no pea brain that I would do it in front of Mistress Cunningham, Lady Erskine, or anyone like that. Nay, it shall be at a private entertainment and I'll ensure that you'll be there." She gave Morag a smug look. "Both of you. And you'll know that it is me who has won the wager."

"And how will we know that you haven't just asked him to go

into the corridor to look at the bunion on your foot?" said Glenna.

Barbara drew herself up. "You'll be left in no doubt why we are leaving the room. When we do."

"You may have the appearance you may be about to be bedded," said Morag, forcing herself to enter the spirit of Glenna's taunting strategy. "But you could just as easily have a small kiss and cuddle and leave it at that. You'll have to provide proof. Otherwise the wager isn't won."

"I think I'd rather bed the Dark Ghost," said Glenna, her eyes twinkling. "It would be easier. I mean, you can't easily sit on Lord Munro's lap, and if you get close enough, you'd be in danger of that handkerchief swatting you on the face, or landing in your eye while he waved it about."

"Or one of his feathers," said Morag, determined to go along with it.

"The Dark Ghost?" Barbara gave a scornful laugh. "If I wished it I could, but it wouldn't serve a purpose. And he would gladly leave his exploits for the Dowager Queen for it."

"Exploits for Her Majesty?" asked Morag. She thought of her meeting with him outside the castle several days ago.

"Yes," said Barbara dismissively, "Surely you know of that he is trying to help her quell the unrest. He's her *Chevalier d'intrigue.*"

"Her *Chevalier d'intrigue?*" Morag repeated. "What do you mean by that?"

She was rewarded with a look that implied she possessed all the stupidity Barbara had claimed before. "Did I not say that he does her bidding? Well, that's what he does."

"And how is it you know this, now?" asked Morag.

Barbara shrugged. "That's what is being said."

"By whom?" asked Glenna.

"Oh, I don't know. Perhaps I heard it from Robert Hay or James Home. Or maybe it was Margaret Ramsey. She is forever ferreting out secrets. Yes, I think she said it. But she told me that her cousin had said it to her. Or maybe it was Robert Hay. Or someone else. Does it matter?"

"Margaret Ramsey," said Glenna. "Well that's no surprise. She imagines all sorts, including imagining that Lord Munro would bed her, I think." She narrowed her eyes at Barbara. "Is that why you think you'll get Lord Munro to bed you? You think you'll best her?"

Barbara gave her an airy glance. "Why would ye imagine I care what Lady Margaret thinks?" She tittered. "Or that Lord Munro was seized by his bowels and had to excuse himself to the guarderobe when she offered herself to him like a guinea fowl on a plate?"

Morag couldn't suppress the grin at her last statement, but then shook her head. Glenna sniggered and caught herself.

"I wish you the best of luck with your own play," she said, forcing any emotion from her mind. Let be, she thought. Let be.

MORAG PLACED her hand on Glenna's arm as they made their way into the dining area of the Dowager Queen's apartments. It was the first opportunity she'd had to have some sort of private conversation all day. Barbara and Jean hadn't left their side since they'd arrived at the apartments that morning and it was only now, as they made their way to the evening meal that she seized a few moments.

Glenna gave her an inquiring look and paused. Morag drew her aside into an alcove near the curtains.

"I wanted to thank you for what you said to Mistress Cunningham," Morag said in a low voice. "Ye didn't have to take my part. And in such a manner. I am in your debt."

"Oh, it wasn't a debt-worthy gesture," said Glenna. She grinned. "And I enjoyed it far too much to even be owed thanks."

Morag smiled at her words. "It was so well done, though. You are clever." She gave Glenna a direct look and surprised herself by adding, "and a good friend."

Glenna flushed, a shy smile appearing on her face. "Thanks. I am proud that Iain's sister would call me such." She took Morag's hand and pressed it.

Morag warmed at her response. "Iain is discerning in his friends and he counted you as such, I'm sure, so I am grateful you would be mine."

"As for Lord Munro, even if that she were to ask him, he would never willingly betray us over the music conversation. But you may need to warn him about it, so he would know what was said." Glenna gave Morag a speculative look. "He has a care for me, being a distant cousin, and, I think, maybe, a care for you."

"I don't think so," Morag said hastily. "He met me there merely to pass on a message from John Dunbar to say he couldn't meet with me."

"John Dunbar? Why were you meeting with him?"

Morag reddened. She couldn't possibly say the real reason to Glenna. She took a deep breath. "Well, he asked me to. I don't know exactly what he wanted."

Glenna raised her brows. "A tryst?" She paused and covered her mouth as a fit of laughter overtook her. "So it really was a lover's meeting. Only Mistress Cunningham imagined the wrong person. Oh, Morag, that's the funniest thing I've heard in an age."

Morag gave her a weak smile and said faintly. "It is indeed."

Glenna gripped her arm. "Well? Are you to meet him another time then? Has he made an arrangement?"

"We…met in the evening," she said slowly. "He approached me outside the Dowager Queen's apartments."

Glenna's eyes widened eagerly. "What did he say? Or, better yet," she glanced around her for any approaching figure, "what did he do? Were there any kisses involved?"

Morag opened her mouth but no words came out. How had she got herself in this situation? She couldn't tell her the whole truth. But what was the whole truth? John Dunbar had in fact taken liberties. Kissed her in a manner that was far from courtly.

Glenna squeezed her arm. "He did!" she said in a breathless whisper. "What was it like? He is very handsome and has lovely address. Were his kisses as good as I would imagine them to be?"

Morag searched her mind for words to express what she felt. "I...don't know," she said finally. "His lips were soft. But it was so brief, it...it didn't make a definite impression, really. He spent most of the time on my fingers."

"Your fingers?"

She bit her lip. "And my hand."

Glenna blinked. "Oh. But of course, that must have felt so... sensual." She looked at Morag's face and laughed. "No, don't regard me as if I were a woman of easy virtue. I'm just curious. I haven't been kissed at all."

"I don't know what to say. It was nice, I suppose. I mean, I didn't object to it."

Glenna frowned. "Nice? Is that all? How disappointing."

Morag gave a little laugh. "Yes, well, it was hardly anything."

"Was it your first kiss?" Glenna asked curiously.

She thought of the kiss she'd had with Davey. It seemed as though it were years ago when she'd done that. "No, it wasn't my first kiss. But I haven't had many."

"What were they like, the other kisses?"

Morag gave her a wry look. "Nice?" She pushed away the memory of that kiss on her cheek. That was brief, but so much more than nice. But it would do no good to call attention to it.

Glenna snorted. "That again. If they are only nice, why would you bother?"

"Well, there was a little tingle," she admitted. "Perhaps with some practice, they might be more."

"Yes," said Glenna, considering. "That's probably the reason."

Morag looked up and saw John Dunbar approaching. Glenna's eyes followed the direction of her glance and smiled back at

Morag. "I'll just go now and leave you to your man with the 'nice' kiss."

She was off a moment later, heading into the dining chamber, leaving Morag to face John Dunbar who paused by her and bowed, taking her hand up for a kiss. His lips lingered on her hand, his eyes raised in warm regard.

"My lady," he said in French. "You look enchanting."

"Thank you," she said.

"Will you allow me to escort you through to the chamber and to your seat?"

She glanced around for any other ladies-in-waiting. "That would be kind of you," she said, trying to keep her voice calm.

He clasped her hand firmly, rested it on his arm and made his way into the chamber.

"If there is an opportunity after the meal, I would beg a word with you," he said.

"Of course," she said. "If there is an opportunity." She frowned inwardly. What was she to say? She was no longer certain she wanted to bring down the whole of the Campbell family. Or if it mattered now that Rory was here. Could she hurt Glenna in such a manner? For there was no doubt it would hurt her if her family were disgraced in the Dowager Queen's eyes. She was certain to be dismissed. And Morag found that she couldn't bear the thought of losing Glenna's company now.

CHAPTER 15

*M*orag found herself wishing that they were eating in the Great Hall with its never ending courses, multitude of dishes and large numbers of people, rather than the relative intimacy of the Dowager Queen's dining hall and minimal amount of courses. Here she couldn't fail to know exactly where John Dunbar was at all times, without even looking in his direction. No amount of light and witty banter could distract her from the thought of the conversation she was to have with him afterwards.

All too soon, the meal came to an end. The musician, only one this time, continued playing, but nothing suggestive of dancing. It wouldn't be long before the Dowager Queen would retire. In fact, Morag wished the moment was now. But luck was not with her in this case. She looked over at Glenna and was about to go to her and ask that she not leave her side, but Jane Maxwell approached Glenna instead. An unusual sight, since as one of the faster women of Munro's crowd, Jane would be more inclined to find a flirtatious target than spend time with Glenna. But Glenna received her with an unsurprised expression.

Morag felt a presence at her side and with some hesitation she turned to see John Dunbar, his expression as warm as it had been before. He took her hand and pressed it to his lips. She forced a smile.

"My lord," she said and carefully withdrew her hand.

"I've sought you out, as I promised," he said.

"Yes," she said. "I'm very flattered."

"It's not flattery when there is true beauty involved," he said.

"My lady Morag," said Lord Munro in a loud voice, appearing at her side.

He gave a flourishing bow and took up her hand and kissed it. The kiss was soft and light. She could feel the kiss lingering there, though he'd let her hand go. She looked up at him blankly and tried to read his face, but to no avail. He scrutinised her a brief moment before nodding to Dunbar.

"My lord," he said. "You'll pardon my intrusion but there is a pressing matter concerning a song." He waved his handkerchief. "It involves a dreadful decision regarding modalities that we have yet to conclude. I tried to make Mistress Cunningham under-stand the matter just a moment ago, but it was useless." He gave a great sigh and pursed his lips. "The woman is a Philistine. Don't you agree, my lord?"

"I am afraid I have no opinion," said Dunbar, stiffly.

"Really?" said Munro. "That is a great pity. Such an affliction to have, not to be able to render any kind of judgement. How could one live one's life without an opinion? To be unable to decide whether it is better to wear the puce and gold doublet with the green hose and embroidered gloves or the silver and red doublet with the double cuttes and a ruby brooch, when it is obvious that neither is suitable for the occasion and only the black and gold will do."

Morag tried but failed to keep the smile from her face, but the laughter that welled up she hid behind a discreet cough.

Munro looked at her with obvious mock seriousness. "I hope,

my lady, that you have opinions, so that we may decide about this song. I need to know at once, I insist upon it."

A little bemused, Morag gave Dunbar an apologetic look and tried to suppress her relief.

"You will excuse me," she said to Dunbar.

He frowned at Munro but bowed to Morag. "Of course, my lady. I look forward to resuming our discussion at another time."

A few moments after they watched Dunbar leave, Munro spoke. "Imagine, having no opinion."

Morag gave a little laugh. "That was very wrong of you."

He gave her a look of mock horror. "But I protest. I didn't ask him to offer up his wisdom on the nature of free will, or if there is to be plague this year. Just if he agreed with me on one small point."

She pretended to consider. "Perhaps he has no understanding of music either and couldn't judge Mistress Cunningham's lack of knowledge."

Munro nodded slowly. "Yes, yes. I see. Of course, that must be it. My lady, you're a sage. I salute you."

"No, you are painting me too richly. I am nothing of the sort."

She smiled at him, fighting the mirth, but also puzzled. His manner was so mercurial, sometimes. At one moment he seemed the epitome of a fop, the next moment full of wit and insight.

"If anyone is the sage, it's you," she said. "Or at least quick witted. I meant to warn you beforehand that Mistress Cunningham might approach you about our meeting, but I had no chance. I can only apologise and thank you at the same time. You see, she was told about our meeting and concluded that I was behaving, in her words, as 'a woman of loose morals'. But Lady Glenna stepped in and fabricated this story that we were discussing a song."

"So I gathered," said Munro, amusement filling his eyes. He switched to Scots, his voice lowered. "I imagine we will have tae conjure a *chanson* tae perform for the Dowager Queen. Do ye have another we could sing?"

Her eyes widened. "Is it really necessary?"

"Maybe no, but there's little tae fear. Your voice is charming."

She grimaced. "Charming is what is said tae a wee lassie showing her needlework for the first time."

"I meant it in quite a different way," he said, even more quietly. "You've nae cause tae feel your voice isna worthy of performing in front of the Dowager Queen, because I assure ye it is."

"My thanks," she said. "But in regard tae the *chansons*, I'm afraid I'm sadly lacking. I ken only the few that my brother's wife taught me. She spent much time at the French court."

"Aye, I'd heard that. I heard also that she's a musician, so ye've been taught well, I'm sure."

"The teacher might have been good, but the pupil is another thing entirely."

He gave her a puzzled look. "Why are ye so modest? This isna the woman who bested the Campbell lad more than once."

Her eyes flew to his. "Ye've heard about that?"

He gave a soft laugh. "Ye think it's a secret?"

"Nay," she said, trying to cover her confusion. "But I didna think it would be common knowledge."

"I dinna think it's common knowledge," he said. "Thon Campbell lad made it known when he first arrived that he thought ye a thief. But when I pressed him as tae the details of the theft, he turned very taciturn. After that he was less free with his words. It was Glenna that told me the whole when I asked her."

"Aye, I suppose she would ken the whole of it." She glanced at him and saw laughter in his eyes. She looked away so that she wouldn't be caught up in them. "He deserved it. He's a sniftering gomeril who has more bluster than a winter wind and nothing else. He ought tae be ashamed tae call himself a Highlander. There is nothing honourable about him."

"Aye, that may be so. But ye must be careful how ye anger him, quean, for he could do ye a grave damage if he chose."

She looked up sharply, suddenly wary. Did he know something of her talk with John Dunbar? She studied his face but there was nothing she could detect.

"I appreciate your kind words on all points, my lord," she said, her tone more formal than before.

He regarded her silently for a moment. "I hope ye do more than appreciate them." He glanced over her shoulder. He switched to French. "*Bien sur,* I think your Mistress Cunningham is signalling the young ladies-in-waiting to leave. The Dowager Queen is about to retire. I'll escort you to Mistress Cunningham."

She looked around and saw he was right. Wordlessly she allowed him to guide her to the retreating group of junior ladies-in-waiting, relieved she wouldn't be able to speak to John Dunbar just yet. She needed to think about her discussion with Munro. It had been unsettling on so many levels, especially the last words that echoed in her head. And why it was that he called her "quean", the endearment that Iain used on occasion for her, one that made her feel special and loved, should now be the one thing she focused on most?

By the morning she was ready to face John Dunbar, at least she felt she'd convinced herself of that fact by the time she was making her way to the Dowager Queen's apartments with Barbara and Glenna. Barbara was unusually pensive, so much so that Glenna gave her wary glances. Once inside, Morag was relieved to find that she didn't have to work on the interminable altar cloth, whose progress was slower and more clumsy she was certain than any other lady in waiting that ever served. She would probably be grey by the time it was completed. Or, she thought, smiling, someone else would be destined to succeed her to its grand work. Today, the work was to be set aside and some travelling musicians would entertain them for a while.

"Do you suppose Barbara is sickening for something?" remarked Glenna while the musicians were tuning up.

Morag looked over at her. "Never. No, I think it's something else."

Glenna frowned. "Yes, I think you're right. Something's happened, or she's planning tae do something."

"Sow some more untruths?" said Morag. She'd no doubt now that it was Barbara behind the so-called misunderstanding with Robert Hay when she was tending her horse – and she wouldn't be surprised if Barbara was behind Mistress Cunningham taking her task about Munro.

"Do you think Lord Munro has bedded her?" Glenna studied Barbara. "Or perhaps she's planning to try to do it this evening. Is someone entertaining in their apartments tonight?"

"I don't know. Ask her. If anyone would know, it would be her." Morag made an effort to look unconcerned. "You think she's going to do it this evening?"

"Oh, who knows, but I'd dearly love to witness her attempt."

Glenna rose, moved over to Barbara and spoke to her in a low tone. Morag tried to decipher the conversation, but it proved useless. Barbara's expression was studied nonchalance and to Morag it indicated everything and nothing that she feared. It wasn't long before Glenna returned and took her seat next to Morag, who composed herself and gave Glenna an inquiring look.

Glenna shrugged. "She says there's something on tomorrow night in Sir William Kirkaldy's chambers. 'An intimate gathering' as she put it. But though Lord Munro will be there, she claims tomorrow night won't suit her for the grand seduction. But I canna believe her."

"I don't know. Maybe she means it," said Morag hesitantly.

"Nay, I doubt it. We'll go and see. I canna wait to see Lord Munro's face when she tries."

Morag smiled weakly. She could imagine the scene, as much as she'd prefer not to.

"Has he been long at court then? He seems very used to its ways."

"Yes, well, I suppose he's used to them because he was at the French court. At least that's what I've heard. He's been here less than a year. But ye wouldn't guess for all the fuss the Dowager Queen and everyone makes of him."

"The French court? How long was he there? I wonder if I met my brother's wife."

"You can ask him. Though I'm certain he would have said, don't you think?"

"Yes, he would have," said Morag thoughtfully. She tried to think of a way that she could ask more about him, his background, his history. "Do you know his family?" she said finally. "I think you said he was a Highlander?"

Glenna looked at her carefully. "I don't know his family, in truth. I'm not exactly sure where he's from."

"But is he not distant kin?"

Glenna laughed. "Very distant. No, we joke about it only. I am acquainted with him because of the music, and that's all. He was very kind to me when I first came to court and I appreciated it."

Morag nodded. She was at once both relieved and disappointed, though she refused to explore the reason for either and labelled it all curiosity. She would rather know nothing that would lower her opinion of him on the one hand, and on the other hand she would like to know more. And that was all.

She was still thinking about it and full of speculation on what else she might have heard about Munro when she was sent on an errand for Lady Erskine to relay a message to the Dowager Queen's chamberlain. Reaching the bottom of the staircase, she was surprised when she encountered John Dunbar leaning up against the wall. He straightened when he saw her, his face lighting up.

"My lady," he said, approaching her and bowing slightly. "The sight of you has made my day brighter."

He took up her hand and kissed it, keeping it at his breast.

"My lord," she said. "You've startled me. I wasn't expecting to see you here."

"I pine for the sight of you, my darling beauty. Any chance I may have to see you in the day I must seize."

He kissed her hand again and drew her closer. Flustered, she made a small effort to draw back, but he held her firmly up against him.

"Shh," he whispered up against her ear. "There's nothing to fear. How can I help but admire your beauty?" He kissed her behind her ear. "I am only stealing a few moments with you, my little bird."

He brushed his finger along her chin and then her lips. He leaned down and kissed her softly at first, then deepened the kiss. His lips were warm against hers and they pushed her own open, and the tip of his tongue slid in, meeting hers. It surprised her and felt strange, but he was there for only a moment before he ended the kiss and moved his lips to her neck while his fingers brushed the skin by the top of her bodice. She felt a flutter in her stomach, a mixture of apprehension, wonder and uncertainty.

"You are exquisite, my sweet innocent," he murmured between kisses, while his fingers continued to caress along her breastbone.

"I-I must complete my errand," she said when she could get her breath.

"Of course," he said, still continuing his journey with his fingers and his kisses. "I just wanted a few stolen moments to see if you had decided on my proposal." He looked up at her, his eyes dark and full of desire. "And of course so that I might have yet another sample of your delightful charms."

She opened her mouth to speak, but all the breath was gone from her. Words had vanished from her head. His actions confused her too much. His kisses, his touch, left her unsettled, out of sorts. Was this desire? Did her inability to pull away signal lust? She trembled a moment and his eyes lit again as he leaned down to kiss her mouth, this time his lips were more insistent. She responded tentatively until he broke away and looked at her.

"Do I take that as a yes? We will go ahead with the plan, my darling little bird?"

She looked into his glittering eyes and took a deep breath. "I'm not sure that I can," she finally managed to say. "The risks are great and I have thought what it might mean for Glenna."

He ran kisses along her breastbone and back to her mouth once more. Eventually he lifted his head and smiled. "Your reticence does you credit. You're wise to consider this carefully and it makes me admire you all the more. But let me assure you it will be fine. There's little chance that you will be discovered, and if you are, you have a perfectly good reason to be there as one of the Dowager Queen's ladies-in-waiting. As for Glenna Campbell, she will be married soon enough and any damage to her family will be of little consequence to her."

She looked at him a little incredulously. "But it will surely affect her chances of contracting a good marriage."

"Nay, she's already contracted to marry someone."

Morag could hardly contain her surprise. "She's said nothing to me about it."

"Well perhaps she doesn't feel too favourably towards the marriage."

Morag was bewildered. "But how is you know this?"

"Because the man is a Cameron and a distant relation to my mother."

"A Cameron?" Morag felt confused again. It was possible, she supposed. And she shouldn't feel back-footed just because Glenna had chosen not to tell her about it. She could ask her, but she wasn't even certain she could bring herself to question Glenna about it. Perhaps they hadn't become the friends she'd thought they had.

John pulled her in to an embrace and kissed her again. "Don't fret, my sweet one. All will be well, trust me. I'll let you know what evening we'll do this and we'll fix a detailed plan." He gave her a final kiss on the lips and then her hand and was gone.

CHAPTER 16

*B*ridie's eyes were wide with meaning when she greeted Morag the next morning. The night had given Morag no rest or respite from the thoughts that crowded her mind, so she was slow to understand Bridie's unspoken message. Morag left her bed reluctantly, even though Barbara and Glenna were already donning the first layer of their clothes, chatting with the maidservant, eating bits of bread and drinking cups of small beer.

Morag moved slowly over to her kist, where Bridie stood laying out her clothes. On the floor beside it, out of sight, Bridie had placed a small tray of food and a sealed letter. At the sight of the letter Morag stopped and raised her eyes to Bridie. This was the first she'd received since arriving at the castle. She glanced over at the others, but they were still engaged in their morning routines.

Bridie leaned over and picked up the letter and handed it to her. "It's from Glen Strae," she said softly in Gaelic. "Came this morning with a carter. I happened tae be in the yard when he arrived and could take it from him."

Morag stared down at Iain's familiar writing and her heart leaped. Finally, word from home. Suddenly she longed to hear what had passed there. Perhaps her father would allow her to return. She wanted to tear into it now, but refrained. She would save it for later, when she could read it in private. Then she could savour every word and not be afraid of any tears of homesickness it would surely give rise to.

She set the letter back on the tray. When she was dressed she would secrete it in her kirtle. After murmured instructions from Morag, Bridie began to help her dress slowly, taking time over each article to ensure it was thoroughly brushed, any wrinkles smoothed, she'd even insisted something on the corset was faulty and removed it for a few moments while she fiddled around with some of the ties. Morag watched her, putting a dispassionate expression on her face.

"You're as slow as a turtle this morning," said Barbara sniffing. "And you were restless as a cat in heat in bed. I was awake half the night. If you think I'm waiting for you, after all that, you're mistaken. I promised Jean I would see her before the others arrive, so I'm leaving now."

"I'll wait for you, if you like, Morag," said Glenna, hesitating by the door.

"No," said Morag. "It's fine. You can go without me. I won't be long."

Glenna studied her a moment and then nodded. She turned and followed Barbara and the maidservant out of the door. When it had closed, Morag breathed a sigh of relief. She picked up the letter and went to perch on the edge of the bed while Bridie quietly tidied up. Morag broke the seal and unfolded the letter carefully and scanned the contents eagerly. It wasn't long, barely covered the whole page, but still she had to read its contents twice, before she looked up at Bridie in horror.

"What is it?" asked Bridie in Gaelic, a tremor in her voice. "Is it the laird? Is he ill? Has something happened to Iain's wife?"

Morag blinked at her and shook her head. "All is well on that count."

Bridie crossed herself. *"Buidheachas do dhia."*

Morag stood up, clutching the letter in her right fist, anger building. "Don't be too hasty thanking God. It's Rob. He's been badly wounded. Rory Campbell, *an gorach pios de cac*, had some ghillies ambush Rob on the way to Glen Strae with Thunder and they wounded him badly and took the horse." She spat and muttered, *"bod ceann."*

Bridie's face filled with shock. "Is he all right? Will he live?"

Morag shrugged. "They hope so. If the wound doesn't fester. My brother spends the rest of the letter berating me for creating this situation. As if it's my fault that Rory can't behave in a proper Highland manner and accept that I got Thunder in a fair fight."

Bridie lifted her brows but said nothing. "Is your brother going to do anything about it? To the Campbells, I mean?"

Morag shook her head, her anger starting to run away with her. "He says not, since it was I who stirred the trouble in the first place. What kind of man is he? I did nothing that they haven't already done to us and countless worse. I haven't stolen their land, their heritage. I haven't tried to get their clan put to the horn! They deserve retaliation of some kind, or they will see us as weak and take advantage of us."

"Rory is a man without honour, there's no doubting that," said Bridie. "He's had half the chamber maids whether they will or no. I've no doubt he's preying on the young noblewomen as well, the ones who are willing."

Morag frowned. "His honour is non-existent. He's a toad. But never fear. I'm not beaten yet. I will see that he receives the punishment due to him. *Tolla thon."*

Bridie laughed. "Well you've called him everything a man has and does with it except the best part, so I've no fear that you'll find a fit punishment."

Morag forced a smile. "It will be a fitting one, you can be sure of that.

～

THIS TIME, she was glad to see John Dunbar in the door of the Dowager Queen's dining hall when they were gathering for the evening meal. She had seethed all day, first in the Dowager Queen's apartments and then walking in the chilly gardens with the other attendants, speaking the bare minimum to both Glenna and Barbara. Barbara was happy to leave her to her own company, though Morag couldn't help but notice that Barbara's own behaviour was a mixture of giddy flirtatiousness and anxiety. Glenna had commented on it and added that she thought it proved her point that Barbara was determined to make an effort to win the wager this night. Morag had forced aside any irritation at the thought of it and focused instead on the need to see John Dunbar and put into action the first steps for punishing Rory Campbell.

Now, she moved towards Dunbar eagerly and was pleased when he saw her and his face lit with pleasure. There was time enough to have a few words before she had to take her seat.

"My lady," he said, when she arrived at his side. He sketched a bow and kissed her hand, his lips lingering a few seconds. "What a joy it is to see you. You've had a good day? I understand the Dowager Queen was well enough to enjoy the gardens this afternoon."

She made a brief curtsy. "Thank you, yes. A good day. The gardens are looking finer now the weather is becoming milder. And it is a fair, sunny day."

He regarded her warmly. "And how could it not be fine with such a beautiful flower as yourself to grace it?"

She laughed and realised she was becoming a little giddy. She took a deep breath to calm herself. "Really, you exaggerate too much, my lord. But I thank you anyway."

He placed a hand at his heart. "I'm wounded that you would

think so. I am a poet, and as such I recognise beauty and must speak of it."

She suppressed a frown, suddenly impatient to move on and get to the point. She wanted this settled before she sat down. "Yes, well it's nice of you to say it. But I did want to speak to you on the matter we discussed the other day. I wanted let you know that I've decided to agree to it."

He smiled, his eyes filled with delight. He leaned down and whispered into her ear. "Oh, my sweet, you won't regret it, I assure you."

She nearly jumped at his mouth to her ear. "Can we arrange something, then?"

He took up her hand and kissed it briefly. "It would best to do it in the next few days, if possible, while he's away," he said in a low voice.

She stared at him, deciphering what he'd just said. Lord Erskine was away? Yes, of course he was. She recalled over-hearing one of the Dowager Queen's senior attendants briefly discussing it with Lady Erskine.

"Tonight," she said on impulse. And why not? Best to get it done quickly.

He looked at her quizzically. "Tonight?"

"Yes. I'll do it tonight." The thought settled. Yes, while so many were at Sir John Kirkaldy's entertainment.

He broke into a big smile. "My lady you are perfect. Did you know that?" He took up her hand and kissed it once again. "Such decisiveness. Such spirit. I adore you."

She smiled back up at him and watched him hold her hand that little bit longer. He was right, she was fierce. And Rory Campbell would soon know how fierce she was.

~

MORAG HADN'T REALISED Munro was beside her until he spoke. She'd been gazing in the direction of Lady Erskine, pondering on the night to come and completely unaware of her surroundings.

"You're deep in thought," he said in a low voice in Scots. "Thinking of home?"

She looked at him sharply. "Why would you say that?"

"You look a little unsettled. Have you heard anything from your family yet?"

She studied his face. In the candlelight his eyes were a deep, dark blue and largely unreadable, but nevertheless they hypnotised her, until she forced herself look away.

"Yes, I had a letter today," she said finally, keeping her tone even.

"And is all well with everyone? Is Iain's wife well? Didn't you say she was due to deliver a child soon?"

Had she said? She glanced over at him again, unable to recall. Not daring to look at his eyes, she noticed that how dark his beard looked when groomed with oil.

"Is it bad news?" he said, patiently.

She gave herself a mental shake. "No. That is to say, Abby hasn't had the child yet. But the news wasn't good. Well, it concerned a clansman of ours. It seems he was badly wounded."

He placed a hand on her arm. "I'm truly sorry to hear such news. He will recover?"

"They don't know."

"And you were close kin? I mean that your family would write to you about him."

"Yes, close enough." She sighed. "He accompanied me here and it was when he was returning to Glen Strae that he was wounded."

She dared to steal another glance and saw that he was studying her carefully. She recognised the moment he understood, but it was suppressed in a flash. She looked away.

"Thunder?"

She nodded mutely. Then anger rose again and she nursed it. "Rory Campbell, may he rot in hell."

"Oh, the fool," Lord Munro murmured. "I'm sorry for it, Morag. That it's come to this grief. Your man didn't deserve that."

She clenched her teeth. "No, he didn't deserve it. Rob is a decent and kind man. And a canny Highlander, but when you're outnumbered as he was, there was nothing for it but to let the horse go."

"The horse wasna worth it, lass," said Lord Munro softly in Scots.

She glared up at him. "Do ye think I dinna ken that? Nay, Rob is a grand man. And whether he lives or no, I'll make Rory pay for this, ye can be sure."

Lord Munro squeezed her arm. "Wheest, lass. Dinna take on so. I ken ye're upset and ye've every right tae be, but have a care. I wouldna want ye tae get in a spleiter." He smiled at her, his eyes sparkling with humour.

She attempted to rein herself in, charmed in some degree by his attempt to joke her out of her temper.

"The best action, sometimes is inaction," he said. "Wait and see if the Earl of Argyll hears of this and what he thinks about it. Ye may be surprised tae find that Rory may have tae account for his deed."

She gave a snort. "I doubt that. They would likely see it as a great triumph and proof of the Campbell's power, especially now, since Iain says he willna retaliate for it."

Lord Munro gave her an inquiring look. "Oh, aye?"

She reddened and looked down at her hands. "He says since it was my deed that brought this all about, there isna cause tae retaliate." She knew her words sounded sulky and she kept her eyes down.

He chuckled and she looked up at him. Was he laughing at her? She drew herself up.

"Nay, dinna get your hackles up, quean. I meant nothing in

the laugh but appreciation. Ye're a little firebird, are ye no? But ye ken that already."

There he was again. Unsettling her. She felt the flush rise again and fought against it and the tears that suddenly pricked her eyes. She studied her hands again to cover her confusion.

"Aye, well," she said finally. "It was verra kind of ye tae offer your counsel. I will think on it."

He took her hand out of sight of everyone and squeezed it. "Lass," he said in a low insistent voice. "Ye maun take care. There is real danger here, for ye and for your family and clan. There are some who would see ye fail. And your family."

He released her hand when he finished and she moved away, again fighting tears and the sense of confusion he left her with. At the moment she didn't know what to think.

CHAPTER 17

Morag drifted around the crowded room, aimlessly sipping her cup of wine, her eyes scanning the people gathered there, but not really taking note of their presence. She was dressed in dark colours which she thought ironically matched her dark mood. And apparently darkness appealed to many of the courtiers here. At least the ones not gaming or presently engaged in pursuits in the shadows. She'd been here only above an hour and already she'd been approached by the likes of Robert Hay and a few other men she only vaguely knew.

At least Lord Munro hadn't decided to come and pry out the reason for her behaviour and was sitting at the gaming table deftly dealing cards, waving his arms and tossing witty remarks around the intent group. She stared at him, unable to help herself in her current mood, marvelling at the way he mesmerised them. His outrageously colourful clothes, that would appear foolish on so many, did nothing to detract from his appeal. His stomach was barely visible, and she thought that might be it, as she followed his graceful long fingers pick up his wine cup and replace it after he'd taken a drink. His other hand held the cards, managing them with ease, despite the numerous rings he wore. He caught her eyes and for a moment she imagined a spark of light there, but he was in that instant obscured from her by Barbara who chose that moment to lean over Munro in an exaggerated pretence to look at his cards and pass a witty remark.

The action made Morag blink and look away, but something made her look again. Barbara was perched on the arm of Lord Munro's chair, in a manner that was ensured to display her busty charms to best advantage. With one hand she ran a finger through his blond curls, twirling and playing with them. Lord Munro gave her an amused look and murmured something, and Barbara laughed, a long tinkly affair that Morag thought couldn't sound more fake.

She watched in horrified fascination as Barbara ran her other hand along his arm, stopping occasionally to finger the cloth, rubbing it slowly. Why hadn't he sent Barbara on her way, she wondered bitterly? She took a deep draught of her wine. There would be no living with Barbara now if she won that wager. She made herself turn away and spied James Home coming towards her, eyeing her speculatively. She groaned inwardly. It was too late to head in another direction.

"My lady."

He bowed, took her hand and kissed it a bit too long. She withdrew it from his grasp before he finished and refrained from pulling a face. She'd hoped that of all people she wouldn't have to contend with him tonight, but it seemed as though her hopes weren't going to be met in this case either.

"May I say that you're looking particularly striking, this evening?"

It was all she could do not to sigh and answer in the negative, but she forced a smile and thanked him.

"Would you like to sit down? I've been watching you walk around for a while here and you seem in need of direction. A seat in a quiet corner might just give you what you need."

She gave him a faint smile. "I've really no desire to sit, I assure you. I'm perfectly content here, observing the gaming."

He grinned. "Yes, there is quite a game going on there. I don't blame you for wanting to watch." He licked his lips. "It can be very…inspiring."

She had no doubt as to his meaning. "Any inspiration I might have found was lost a little while ago. There is no sport in the game going on there now. It's more of a feeble farce."

"Yes, but it is surely interesting to note the strategy employed," he arched a brow and looked at her chest, "and perhaps note a good tactic that, employed by the right person, against a proper opponent, might reap some handsome rewards."

Morag swallowed the laughter that rose up, understanding that it was triggered in part by hysteria. "I'm afraid I find it more tedious than noteworthy," she finally managed.

She took another deep drink and glanced around, noticing Rory Campbell for the first time. He caught her eye and gave a self-satisfied grin. She looked away, sudden anger quashing the hysteria. She looked over at James Home, already tired of his suggestive banter. If anything was tedious, it was this conversation.

"If you'll excuse me, I see someone over there I have to speak with," she said, and gave him a brief nod.

She headed off, not waiting to see how he received her rudeness. She didn't care and felt nothing but relief that she was rid of his wearisome company. She would rather be alone. Her wish was not to be granted though, because no sooner had she moved to the other side of the room, Rory came up and planted himself in front of her.

She turned to look somewhere else, but he grasped her arm, leaned over and said in a low voice. "What troubles you, my lady?" he said. "You aren't afraid of me, are you?"

His French accent was awful and she took a spiteful comfort in that. "No, I assure you, I'm not afraid of a coward."

A momentary flash of anger crossed his face, but then he

smiled again. "I suppose that's the best you can manage. Words. Now that Thunder is back safely at Glenorchy, there's nothing you can do. You thought you could outwit me, but you were too stupid to understand a Campbell would not let a wrong such as that go unpunished."

The flash of anger she'd felt before lowered to a slow but fierce burn. "There was no 'wrong' involved. It was a clear case of honour on my part and cowardice on yours. How many of your men did it take to get Thunder back? And from one man? A man who had to be wounded severely before the deed was accomplished? You couldn't even manage the deed yourself, because you know you would have been beaten. Again."

She hurled the last word at him in a low angry voice filled with all the venom that now burned inside her.

"My lady?"

It took a few moments for the words to penetrate Morag's mind before she turned away from Rory, his face now blazing with his own anger, and looked at the man beside her. It took her a short while to recognise him as David Montgomerie, one of Munro's flamboyant companions.

"Yes?" she uttered. She gave herself a mental shake and tried to concentrate on his words.

He executed an elaborate flourishing bow that took several moments before it was completed and then spoke. "That chanson you sang for Her Highness. I have been meaning to ask you about it. Would you have the time now to discuss it?"

She looked at him blankly. His face was full of patient inquiry, a look difficult enough to achieve, since it was surrounded by a ruff the size of a platter, embroidered with tiny stars. He was her height so that she felt as though the ruff might swallow her if she wasn't careful. Suddenly his dark eyes and tiny mouth appearing almost fishlike only seemed to emphasise the platter effect. All of the sudden she wanted to giggle, but she collected herself in time.

"Of course," she said and smiled at him briefly before turning to Rory. "I'm certain you would find your own lack of musical ability and knowledge would make this conversation extremely boring for you, so we'll take our leave of you."

Before Rory could say anything more, she placed her arm through David Montgomerie's and led him a safe distance away before she stopped and spoke.

"Are you a singer yourself, my lord?"

"I sing a little, but not as well as you," he said. "But I was most interested to hear how you came to know it and who wrote it. It was very amusing, but also seemed to suggest more than a simple song."

She nodded, caught by the subject and began to explain what little she knew about it and her thoughts about its meaning. He listened to her with deep absorption and made a few comments that warmed her to the subject further. It wasn't until Glenna came alongside of her that she realised some time had passed since the conversation had begun.

"You two are deep in discussion," said Glenna, smiling.

"Yes," said Montgomerie. "We've been discussing the chanson the three of you performed before Her Highness. Very enlightening. My lady was kind enough to explain its meaning and origin."

"Oh, Morag is quite knowledgeable about music. Her brother too." She raised her brow slightly at Morag, her eyes twinkling.

Morag protested but Glenna interrupted. "You're too modest. You have a lovely voice and understood the chanson fully."

"There's no need to tell me she is knowledgeable. That was clear from the discussion." He smiled at Morag. "Now if you ladies will excuse me, I must take my leave. After such a noble pursuit of a virtue, I'm compelled to follow a vice. The gaming table calls me."

He took his leave and Glenna smiled after him.

"Well that was a surprise," said Morag. "I'm not really acquainted with him. He's never sought me out before. But I fear I have misjudged him. He seems very kind and nice."

"You mean despite his mistaken sense of fashion?" said Glenna, her voice filled with humour.

Morag gave a light laugh and nodded. "Yes," she said. "I'm going to have to learn to not judge people so quickly." She looked at Glenna and realised that it wasn't just David Montgomerie she was talking about. And the fact that Glenna hadn't said anything about her betrothal could be no more reason than it was a topic she liked to forget.

Glenna, as if sensing her meaning, squeezed her arm and smiled. "Yes, I know that I have the same task for myself." She frowned a moment. "I wanted to tell you that I am more than sorry to hear about your man and the awful manner in which he was wounded. My brother is a sniftering swick," she said, lapsing into Scots. "And I told him so. A real *gorach pios de cac*," she added under her breath.

Morag, whose good humour had started to fade at Glenna's words, now rose again at her uttered comment about Rory. They'd echoed her own earlier words about him so perfectly. He was a piece of shite. Morag guffawed and put a hand to her mouth, her eyes dancing merrily.

"Sorry," she said. "But I canna help but agree. In fact I called him the very same thing."

"Tae his face?" said Glenna hopefully. "Och, I hope so. He's an awful man, and I'd sooner no be related tae him."

Morag squeezed her hand. "Nay," she said softly. "I dinna blame ye for it. I've learned that much at least."

Glenna looked at her, tears glittering in her eyes. "I'm glad. For ye must ken that I like ye verra well, Morag, and I should hate tae lose ye as a friend."

Morag nodded and found herself saying. "Aye, I feel the same, *mo cara.*"

Glenna nodded and after a moment her eyes lit up and she grinned. "Did ye no see Barbara there, flinging her paps about thon Lord Munro?"

Morag's smile faltered. "Aye, I saw, the wee hoor."

"Och, but it was pure fun! The sight of her. And Lord Munro as cool as ye please."

"She was murmuring in his ear and her hands pawing him all over," Morag said sourly.

"Aye. And the more she pawed, the more he just sat there bantering away, discarding his cards, even when she leaned over and was clearly issuing her invitation."

Morag frowned, "I think I missed that. James Home decided to pester me."

"Och, him? Aye there's a pest if ever one could be called so."

Morag steeled herself for her question. She dared not look behind her over to the gaming table. "Well? Did he accept the invitation?"

"Lord Munro? Och, I doubt it. He's still playing cards, though our hoor has slinked off somewhere, nae doubt hoping he'll join her soon. I'd say she has a long wait."

Morag dared then to turn around and look at the gaming table. Lord Munro was still there, cards in his one hand, the other poised over top of it, considering the discard.

"Aye, I see he's still there," she said softly.

"Of course he is," said Glenna. She looked over Morag's shoulder. "Och, there's Jean. I'll just go ask her the tale."

Morag nodded and let her go off. She looked down at her cup and saw that it was empty. She gave a brief thought to getting it refilled when she realised she should think about her task tonight. Would one more give her courage? She gave the cup a dismal look. Somehow, it didn't seem something she could do to Glenna, no matter how much Rory deserved it.

A hand gripped her elbow. "Ah, my sweet," said John Dunbar, taking her hand and kissing it. "I'm so sorry I was delayed. I know you must be anxious to put everything in motion as soon as possible."

He kissed her hand again and led her to a darkened corner of the room. "There now, we can talk unobserved." He reached up and brushed a stray strand of hair back from her face. "You look beautiful tonight. Like an enchanting avenging angel."

"I'm not sure an avenging angel could look enchanting," she said, a caustic edge to her voice. She felt unsettled, uncertain what she would say to him, or what course of action she would take, now that the time was upon her.

"You manage it, though no one else could," he said, his voice soft. He put an arm around her. "Take heart, my dove. I saw Rory talking to you earlier and I could tell that he upset you. Comfort yourself that soon he will be gone, and in such disgrace he'll never return."

She thought of Rory's spiteful words and his cowardly behaviour and frowned. "It would be a great relief to know that was certain."

He squeezed her shoulder. "It is certain. Come now. Let me fill your cup and then we'll be off so that first step can be taken." He took her goblet and went to a nearby table containing a flagon. After filling her cup with its contents he returned and handed it to her. She'd watched him, trying to keep the thought of Rory to the forefront of her mind, noticing little about her surroundings or John's actions, so that when he handed her the cup she took it without a word and drank from it.

"Now," he said after she'd taken a few sips. "We'll go."

He took the cup from her again and placed it on the nearest surface. He grabbed her hand and, after a brief kiss to her knuckles, escorted her through the groups of people to the door, his hand on her elbow. She felt detached, noticing nothing except the feel of his hand on her elbow.

Once outside the chamber, John halted and withdrew a candle from his doublet. He took it over to the torch on the wall, lit the candle from its flame and handed it to her.

"Now," he whispered, "there will be a small casket of letters there. Probably on his desk. Just bring the letters you find in the casket. The key should be in the small pot on the shelf against the wall."

She gave him a quizzical look. "How is it you know this?"

He smiled and kissed her forehead. "I am of some use in this court. Did you think I just languished after a beautiful woman all day?"

"Oh." She looked at the candle she held and suddenly wanted to give it back to him.

"Come, now," he said gently. "It's not far."

He led her down the corridor to Lord Erskine's chamber. When they were at the door, he kissed her on the lips and smoothed her hair.

"I'll leave you now," he said. "I'll get the letters from you tomorrow, as you make your way to the Dowager Queen's apartments. Lag behind the others so we can be alone."

"You're not waiting here?"

"No, my sweet. It would look suspicious if I was waiting outside Lord Erskine's chamber."

After a final squeeze of her arm he left her, walking swiftly back down the corridor and disappeared into Sir John Kirkaldy's room.

Morag took a deep breath and steeled herself. She tried to open the door, but it wouldn't budge. It was locked. John had known so much about the location of the casket and its key, why hadn't he known the chamber would be locked?

She cursed and looked around her, trying to come up with some method that would help her open it. There was nothing. For a moment she thought about abandoning the idea altogether, until she remember her *sgian dhu* strapped at her calf. She'd decided to wear it lately because she'd didn't trust Rory not to accost her at some point or do something else equally underhanded. Now, she would see if she could shift the lock with it.

She retrieved the *sgian dhu* while holding the candle as best as she could. Carefully, she put the knife into the lock and jiggled it around. It took a little while, and during that time Morag glanced constantly up and down the corridor, praying no one would come along, but finally she heard the lock give. She gave a relieved sigh and after a turn of the latch, the door swung open and she was able to slip inside.

It was dark after the torchlit corridor, the feeble light of the candle barely able to guide her. Morag stood there for a moment until her eyes adjusted. When she was finally able to discern more than vague shapes, she moved forward to the desk that she could now see at the right side of the room. It was covered with pieces of paper and parchment, some rolled and tied with ribbon. There were a few books, some quills and an inkpot. But no casket. She scanned the table behind the desk at the side and saw two caskets. She was just moving around the desk towards the table when she heard the door open and close softly.

She turned and saw a large figure coming towards her. Horrified, she dropped the candle.

"What in God's name are ye doing here?" The figure said in a rough whisper.

He was right upon her now and she recognised him. "Lord Munro?"

"Aye. Now tell me what's going on." His voice was low and firm and he gripped her arms so that she was unable to move.

"I-I…" she faltered, uncertain what to say.

Suddenly, he placed a finger on her mouth and looked up, listening. He leaned over her and said softly, "say nothing."

Before she could blink he had shoved her over the table and was her kissing her deeply, his body covering hers. Startled, she laid there stiffly, feeling his weight on hers, the hard belly pushing against her, his lips pressed against hers, firm and insistent, then soft and probing and gentle. He cupped his hand at the back of her head while his other hand stroked her jaw and then along her neck. She felt herself relax under his touch, her lips coming alive under his, her ears roaring with the blood that raced along her body.

The door burst open and light filled the doorway. Morag started to rise, but Lord Munro held her in place, his kisses and caresses continuing as though nothing had happened. She began to tremble, her fear and desire creating a tumult of emotions.

"Did I no tell ye Robert?" said Rory, his speech slurred with drink. "He's bedding her! Ye can pay up now."

"Och, he's no bedded her yet," said Robert Hay.

"It willna be long, they're halfway there," said Rory.

"Nay, nay. I'll no pay until the deed is done," said Hay.

Lord Munro lifted his lips from hers. "Laddies," he said. "I care nought for your wager, but if ye continue tae keek like little boys, instead of leaving me tae get on wi' it, there'll no be a wager won."

There was shuffling and mutterings, but after a few moments the door closed and the room fell into darkness. Lord Munro waited a few moments, his head still raised, his body pressed along hers. Eventually, he lifted himself off of her. She lay there, unable to move, paralysed in body and mind from what had just transpired. Then she started to tremble again, her breaths coming in short gasps. She attempted to get up but found her legs giving way until Lord Munro caught her up and folded her into his arms.

"Wheest, lass. Calm yourself, now. It's all over."

She made an effort to calm her breathing and slow her racing heart, as he smoothed her hair and rubbed her back. She found after a while she was able to breathe easier and stand of her own accord. It was then the enormity of what had just passed hit her. She had failed miserably in obtaining the letters and now she was to be labelled as the woman who had won the wager. Rory would see to that and ensure that she would be banished from court.

CHAPTER 18

"*N*ow, tell me what that was all about," said Lord Munro.

He looked at Morag sternly, his arms crossed, while she sat on the stool he'd found for her. He'd been solicitous up to that point, ushering her cautiously from Lord Erskine's chamber, careful that no one saw them, and then on to his own chamber. He'd done that with reluctance but, he told her once they were inside, there was no other place to speak frankly. Once she was seated on the stool, his tone had become clipped and hard.

She bit her lip, still feeling shaky and remained silent.

He gave an impatient sigh. "What made you go to Lord Erskine's chamber? Don't you understand that much could be made of it if you'd been discovered there alone?"

She looked up at him, anger starting to rise inside her. "As opposed to being caught with you? By Rory Campbell, who is certain to blacken my name from here to the Highlands and ensure I'll be labelled a whore and banished from court."

She blinked back the sudden tears that filled her eyes. It was all so unfair. Her emotions were in turmoil. The failure, the certain disgrace and then, the kiss. The kiss that made her feel much more than she should, much more than she wanted to. The sensation of his lips on hers that she could feel, even now, was still there. She closed her eyes a moment, before looking back up at him, determined to be firm and distant.

His eyes softened. He rested a hand briefly on her head. "Och, lass dinna fash yourself about that," he said, switching to Scots. "He dinna see it was ye. It was so he wouldna ken it was ye that I pressed on the desk and lay on top of ye. Combined with the darkness, there's nae doubt they would have only seen me and nothing of ye or your clothes."

"How would he no guess, though? He saw me leave and then ye followed me. He's been watching me like a hawk all evening, taunting and looking for any opportunity tae injure me further than he has done already. He even told me so."

"Och, ye're no the one who was throwing out lures tae me all evening, though were ye? It wasna only ye that he was watching all night."

She stared at him, unbelieving. "Barbara? Ye think he believes it was Barbara ye had spread on the desk kissing?"

He grinned briefly. "Aye. Of course."

She gave him a sceptical look. "But Barbara will tell him it wasna the case and then it will be only a matter of time before he realises it was me."

"Nay, Barbara will say nothing. Do ye no ken she would rather have it known that she was the person who finally succeeded in getting me tae bed and win the wager, than admit she failed?"

She thought about it for a moment and had to concede that he was probably right. She looked up at him. "I owe ye my thanks," she said meekly.

He nodded and then his eyes darkened to a deep blue, like the waves on a stormy day. "Ye can show your gratitude by telling me what ye were doing there."

She paused, considering what she should say. It seemed a

muddle in her thoughts, the reasoning behind her decision to retrieve the casket.

"I was looking for evidence against Rory Campbell," she finally said in a low voice, her head lowered.

"Evidence? What do ye mean evidence?"

She took a deep breath. "Some letters. In a casket that would show Rory tae be a traitor."

"Ye thought Lord Erskine would have letters that showed Rory Campbell tae be a traitor?" His voice was filled with disbelief.

She nodded her head, unable to say anything more.

He gave a frustrated sigh. "Lass, there are nae letters of that nature in any casket, I can assure ye."

"And how do ye ken there are none?" she said, a slight belligerence creeping into her tone.

"Lord Erskine wouldna waste time on a jumped up snotty lad who fancies he is a Highland warrior if he steals a few cattle. There are far more important matters that take up his attention."

She bit her lip. "But I understood that there was a locked casket with letters that showed it," she said stubbornly.

"Well ye were misled. Any casket, especially if it were locked, contained matters tae do with this present crisis of the Lords of Congregation and most likely delicate negotiations with France." He pressed his lips together. "Who told ye about the casket?"

She looked at him, taking in his words and trying to deny what was slowly dawning on her. She opened her mouth and closed it, unable to utter a word, her horror growing.

"Was this John Dunbar's idea?"

She looked up sharply her eyes widening. "John Dunbar?"

"Aye, John Dunbar. He's been dangling after ye for the last while. I canna imagine who else would have put such a notion in tae your head."

She looked away and nodded. He sighed.

"He's a sympathiser with the Lords of the Congregation and

most likely in correspondence with the English, lass. But of course ye dinna ken that."

She shook her head, her mortification too overwhelming for words.

"Nay, of course ye dinna ken. Not many do, so dinna feel so badly." He knelt down and turned her head tae face him. "Ye were verra foolish, do ye ken? If ye'd been discovered there, even without the casket, ye could have been taken as a traitor. A traitor who wouldna meet a pretty end." He frowned at her, his eyes serious and hard. "Ye must take care here at court. There are so many people ready tae use ye for their own ends."

She looked at him, full of confusion and shame at her gullibility as well as irritation at his gentle scolding. "But ye have nae wish tae?"

He gave her a puzzled look. "Nay, of course I dinna want tae use ye for my own ends."

He got up and went over to the window. Dawn was beginning to break and light was streaking in through the window, playing with the sharp planes on his face. She looked down at her hands, trying to sort through her emotions. Munro had so many different sides and it was this sincere caring side that contained no trace of mockery, flattery or elaborate gestures that affected her most. And to put a kiss and an embrace on top of that. An action he'd done purely to protect her honour. What on earth was she supposed to feel about that?

She sighed and looked up at him, trying to gather her thoughts so that she could depart. She needed to return to her chamber soon, if she was to have any chance of creating a believable tale that would cause few questions.

Munro looked down at her then, as if sensing she was about to speak. The light shone behind him, casting his golden curls into a halo that surrounded his head and his face. He looked younger in that light, and the way he smiled at her sent her mind reeling back to a memory long ago. Her little girl self, looking up at a smiling lad of sixteen years, his blond curls blowing in the wind, appearing so braw and bonny on his horse, the tartan fluttering in the wind. She blinked, unable to believe it.

He turned back to look out the window again. "We need tae get ye back tae your chamber. It's beyond time."

"Sandy?" she said softly.

He turned his head sharply and stared at her.

"It is ye, is it no?" she whispered. "My Sandy, who came tae visit Iain all those years ago." The Sandy she pledged to marry as a silly young girl. The Sandy who promised one day he would marry her. It was a foolish promise made to indulge a precocious child, but one she'd felt was true for years after.

He gave her a gentle smile. "Aye, poppet. It's Sandy."

She got up from the stool and took his hand. "But why did ye no say?"

He sighed and squeezed her hand. "It was a long time ago and many things have passed since I saw ye as a wee lass of five. Besides, ye didna even ken who I was until just now. And why should ye? Ye're a bonny lass who has so much life and all the world tae interest ye. Ye'd have little enough time for a fat old cuddy like me."

She gave him a hurt puzzled look. "Nay, I wouldna think that. And ye're no old! Why ye canna be but a few years older than Iain."

"Old enough lass, in experience and many other ways," he said.

She frowned. "But can we no be friends at least?"

"I thought we were already friends," he said with a teasing tone.

"Aye, of course," she said. "Of a sort. But I mean more"...she searched for words that would convey what she needed from him, what she wanted from him.

"Like a brother?" he said playfully. "Of course I'll be a brother tae ye, though ye mustna tell Iain I kissed ye, even if it was tae protect your honour. I'd doubt if he would distinguish the difference."

Her heart fell, but she forced a nod. "Aye, like a brother. If that's what ye think."

He gave her a peck on her forehead and released her hand. "Now, we must get ye back to your chamber. The household will be stirring soon. But before we go, though, I want ye tae promise me that ye'll stay away from John Dunbar."

"But he'll want tae hear if I succeeded," she said.

"Leave that tae me. I'll speak with him."

"But he'll still will seek me out at the first opportunity. I ken him well enough tae predict that."

He held up a warning finger. "Ye must leave it tae me. I'll ensure he doesna bother ye, I promise. Now, do I have your word?"

She gave him a reluctant nod. "But if he does accost me, what will I say?"

"Say nothing. But if ye must say anything, tell him that ye have had second thoughts and have nae intention of doing anything more for him."

She sighed. "As ye say. I'll tell him that."

He held out a hand for her and she took it, fruitlessly searching his face for something, though she had no idea what it was. Or if it had passed too long ago.

MORAG FELT GLENNA stirring beside her and rolled over, determined to resist the pull to consciousness. She would rather ignore the need to rise and delay her duties for the day for as long as possible, in the hope that if she did so long enough she might just wake up and find herself back in Glen Strae. The aftermath of realising what she had narrowly avoided came home to her once she had slipped into bed beside Glenna who, along with Barbara, was thankfully asleep at the time. She'd lain there shaking, while anger fought with the tears of relief. And then her thoughts had turned to Munro. Sandy. In the light of her discovery, she'd felt compelled to review every conversation and meeting they had. She marvelled that she'd never detected that it was him before this, despite the young age she'd been when she'd seen him last, but now that she remembered their encounters, the different sides to him, the rare time she caught the spark and light in his eyes, she marvelled that she hadn't known it before. Even from the first, when he'd swept off his bonnet and made an elaborate bow to her, his eyes filled with amusement. The eyes, of course she should have known them.

"Come, you lazy beast," said Glenna. "You must rise. Your maidservant is here already for you."

Morag pulled the covers over her head and moaned. "No," she said, her voice croaky. "I can't."

Barbara snorted. "Yes, I know that it was a late night for you. And just what were you doing that it kept you out until all hours, hmm?" she added suggestively.

Under the covers Morag pursed her lips and took a breath, willing herself to say the lie that Sandy had suggested. "Ugh, nothing pleasurable, I assure you. I spent most of the night in the guarderobe."

"Oh, Morag, are you still ill?" said Glenna, concern in her voice. "Are you sickening for something?"

"No, it's nothing more serious than something I ate, I think. Though I will stay abed in case it becomes something worse."

"Is there anything I can get ye?" asked Bridie in Scots. "A bit of weak beer? Some broth?"

Morag pulled back the covers and looked at her. "If ye can get me some weak beer and a bit of bread, I would appreciate it. I'm not certain I can keep it down, but I think I should try."

"Aye, I will. And when I return I'll give your face and hands a wash. That will help ye, ye'll see."

KRISTIN GLEESON

Bridie left and Morag watched the other maidservant attend Glenna. Barbara was sluggish enough and had made no move to shed her nightgown, but was instead nibbling on a small chunk of cheese from the plate of food the chamber maid had brought.

"You're a fair bit draggy yourself," Glenna said to Barbara, a teasing grin on her face. "And you weren't in bed much before Morag. I don't suppose you were in the guarderobe half the night too?"

"What would you have me say?" said Barbara. "Though I can assure you it wasn't the guarderobe where I spent my time."

Glenna eyes widened. "You did the deed?"

Barbara gave her a coquettish look. "There were deeds done, rest assured."

Glenna looked over at Morag, her eyes twinkling. "No! You don't mean it. All that come thither, crawling into his lap and it worked? You got Lord Munro to bed you?"

Barbara raised her brows suggestively. "Did you think I would fail?"

Glenna laughed. "Well, I must say I wasn't certain anyone could. The wager has been going a while."

Barbara wandered over to where her clothes were laid out. "I'm disappointed you don't have more faith in me. You should know that I'm a woman of many charms."

"As many a man can testify?" said Glenna, a trace of sarcasm. "Well, we'll see what Lord Munro has to say to all this."

Barbara sniffed, but said nothing more. There were few words exchanged after that and for the respite Morag was glad. She lay back in the bed, the covers up around her and reflected on Barbara and Glenna's words. She should be glad that Barbara was already making it easy for the rumours to confirm it was her in Sandy's arms, but she wasn't. Though it would ease her mind and remove a serious threat to her place here at court, she found herself irritated by Barbara's lie and the inference that Sandy would have found her irresistible, unlike every other woman who tried to tempt him to bed. It was silly and irrational, but Sandy was hers and no one else's as far as she was concerned. The thought made her want to frown and laugh at the same time.

She forced herself to put all that aside and think on John Dunbar's actions. The deliberate manipulation, which she now recognised his attentions for exactly that. It left her more annoyed with herself that she'd allowed it, hadn't realised it, than she was distressed that his attentions involved no real feelings for her. For that part of it, she found she cared nothing. Her annoyance gave way to anger again, as she remembered all the falsehoods he'd told her and how he pressed her to act. And such action would have easily seen her branded as a traitor, if she'd been discovered. The man was the worst sort of coward and coarse ole swick that she would dearly love to throttle at this moment. She drew a slow breath, willing her thoughts to calm. She would deal with him. She would find a way and he would think again about using her in such a manner. She had a day in bed to think about it.

Barbara and Glenna's toilet complete, they made their way to the door after bidding Morag farewell. The chamber door opened and Bridie entered, a tray in her hand, her face flushed.

"I'm so sorry, mistress, for the delay, but I was waylaid and told tae give ye a message," she said. "It's your brother. He's here."

"My brother?" said Morag. "What on earth is Iain doing here?"

She thought of the baby and hoped something hadn't happened to Abby or the unborn child that caused him to come to court to fetch her.

"Nay, my lady," said Bridie. "It isna Iain. It's Alisdair."

"Alisdair?" she stared at Bridie in disbelief. "Why would Alisdair come here?"

Bride shrugged. "I dinna ken. I was only told tae inform ye of his arrival and ask if ye were well enough tae receive him."

Morag glanced over at Barbara and Glenna. Glenna gave her a sympathetic look and Barbara merely looked amused.

Morag sighed. "Leave the tray here, if ye would, Bridie, and tell my brother if he can take his ease for a few hours, I'll be well enough then and I can receive him in the small chamber next tae the Steward's office. I think Mistress Cunningham would have nae objection tae that."

Bridie placed the tray on the small table, curtsied and left the three women.

Glenna came over to the bed and placed a hand on Morag's shoulder. "If ye need me ye ken where tae find me. I can be there with ye when ye receive your brother if ye fear it willna be pleasant news."

Morag gave her a weak smile. "Aye, thank ye for the offer. I dinna think it will be anything serious. Perhaps he has decided tae come for a visit, since he is only in Edinburgh."

She said the words to reassure Glenna but also to reassure herself, though it failed miserably. She knew there could only be something serious to draw Alisdair away from his studies to come to her.

CHAPTER 19

*S*he entered the small chamber, trying to suppress her anxiety about the cause of Alisdair's visit, and saw a tall figure facing away from her. She realised then he was no longer the little younger brother that somehow she still recalled, but a man, topping her by a head and broadened considerably in shoulder. He turned and the pale blue eyes were his, but now, with the height and breadth along with the mouth and nose he looked so much like Iain, if it were not for the fair hair. His expression was filled with concern as she moved to him and they embraced. He gave her a few awkward pats and then pulled back. She gestured to the bench and they sat.

"Are you certain you're well enough to talk?" said Alisdair in Gaelic. "You look very pale, *mo cridhe.*"

She smiled and nodded. "Oh, I'm fine, Alisdair. It was no more than a bit of something I ate that didn't agree with me."

His face eased and he nodded. "I'm glad to hear it." He continued to examine her closely.

"Is the family well?" asked Morag. "I had a brief letter from Iain a few days back and he mentioned Rob's injury. Has something more happened? Is that why you're here? Not that I'm no glad to see you, Alisdair, for it's been a fair while, so much so that I hardly recognised you. The size on you. It's fair grown you are now." She realised she was babbling and made herself stop.

He flushed at words, his fair colouring always the giveaway to his emotions. Only now Morag had no idea whether it was anger, embarrassment or something else entirely.

"I heard about Rob's injury from Iain," he said, frowning. "And the cause of it. Do you have no sense at all Morag?"

Morag blinked, unwilling to credit that her younger brother was taking her to task. She bristled. "Yes, I have sense. And if you heard the full story you'd see that it wasn't my doing but Rory Campbell's."

"But you provoked him," he said sternly, his expression filled with disapproval. "And you didn't stop at wild acts of provocation but you must behave as the wanton as well."

She drew back, stunned. "What! I haven't done anything of the sort." She fought for calm, her temper flaring, trying to get the better of her. "Who told you that? Surely it wasn't Iain." she added stiffly.

"Don't you know that I am in Edinburgh, which covets court gossip? It's there I heard. Tales of the Highland lass newly arrived at court causing a stir, flirting with courtiers in gardens. I knew that it was you, for who else could it be?"

She was speechless with anger, now. She took deep breaths, fighting for control. After last night, this was nearly too much. "And of course you chose to believe the worst of your sister!" she snapped.

"What was I to think?"

"That I'm your sister, who you profess to know well enough, so that you would realise it was no more than malicious gossip."

"I don't know one way or the other, for court is a veritable nest of vipers and you are easy prey, as well as wild and always filled with some mischief or other, with no understanding to its consequences," he retorted sharply.

Tears filled her eyes suddenly. Was that how he really saw her? A silly, mischievous child filled with pranks? She blinked back the tears. She would prove to him that she wasn't the child he saw.

She drew herself up. "It was malicious gossip. In truth, it was a discussion with Sandy about a song we were to perform before the Dowager Queen. About differing modal keys. It was Mistress Cunningham who saw us and he explained the misunderstanding to her."

"Sandy, is it then?" he said tersely. "You're very familiar with his name."

She flushed and hoped it wasn't too tell-tale. "I know Lord Munro well, of course I do. You'd have been too young to remember, but Sandy spent a summer visiting Iain, many years ago." She'd adopted the patronising older sister tone, glad to find some way to gain the upper hand.

Alisdair gave her a sceptical look. "Years ago, was it? And just how many years ago?"

"When I was young, and you were a babe in arms," she said.

"And if I wrote to Iain and asked him about this Alexander Munro, he'd know who I meant?"

"Of course," she said sharply. "If you have so many doubts, why don't you ask Sandy about his time at Glen Strae? I'm certain he would ease your mind. Since I canna seem to," she added, a tinge of a sour note in her voice.

"I will," he said, stubbornness apparent in his expression.

She sighed inwardly. "Is there any other news you have? Or did you just come to test the truth of the gossip you heard."

He frowned again. "I came because you're my sister and I care for your well-being, even if you don't care yourself."

"Well you can see you came for nought."

"No, I came mostly to tell you that I don't care for the situation that's brewing with Mister Knox and the Protestants. It's very serious, Morag, and could easily spell danger for you and the rest of the court. The populace are angered and there's been gatherings where many have incited the rabble to act. And act they have done. Damaging property and injuring people. Gravely."

She gave him an anxious look. "But surely Lord Erskine must know all of this, and if there was any serious danger, he would remove the Dowager Queen to safety."

Alisdair shook his head. "That may be so to a degree, but dangerous situations can flare up quickly and in places you might least expect it. No, I think you must let me take you back to Glen Strae."

She looked at him in astonishment. A month ago she would have welcomed this statement with all eagerness, but now, she realised she wouldn't consider it for a moment. She couldn't leave, not now. She had friends, now. And she had unfinished business with John Dunbar. And Rory, if she thought about it. And Sandy. She couldn't leave him, not now. Because, she told herself, she needed to be certain that he would be untroubled by Barbara and by John Dunbar. And, she acknowledged, there were so many unanswered questions about him and his behaviour. Questions to which she needed answers.

"No," she said quietly. "There is no need. I would be glad of your company here, if you've a mind to stay, but I won't go home to Glen Strae just now."

"But why? There is nought to keep you here."

"But you forget. There is my duty to the Dowager Queen. I can't quit court without her leave, for a start."

"But you can secure her permission, surely, once you explain the reasons for it."

"No. Surely you see that if I do ask, I am stating that I don't trust her ministers, her soldiers, to keep me safe, and I have no care that she may be at risk."

He looked at her sceptically, but eventually he nodded. "Very well. I'll bide here for the time, though."

She repressed a smile. He was so stuffy, with his Edinburgh ways. Nothing like a Highlander. But perhaps that's what he wanted. "What of your studies?"

He shrugged. "You're more important."

She raised her brows. Now, that did surprise her. "I appreciate that," she said softly. Perhaps there was more of the Highlander and less of the scholar than she thought.

THE STEWARD SECURED HIM A CHAMBER, and though shared with another courtier, he was near enough Alisdair's age. Morag was glad to hear it when he told her later that day, in the garden attending the Dowager Queen. He'd been presented to Her Majesty and she'd been delighted to receive him, the finer weather improving her constitution. Alisdair, reddening under her scrutiny, had nevertheless managed to speak to her with an informed air and fluent French that reflected more of his facility for languages than Abby's coaching. The Dowager Queen was charmed and Morag was relieved and even a little proud.

It wasn't until the later, when they'd finished the evening meal, that things began to go a little awry. Alisdair had been placed next to her as a courtesy and she chatted with him about his Edinburgh experiences. He was filled with enthusiasm for his tutors and some of his fellow scholars.

"But some are quite taken up with the Protestant cause," he said, shaking his head. They'd been speaking in French, but for this comment he spoke low, in Gaelic. "And I like it not, for they seek out those nonconformists and stir up the rabble."

"So you think it will become serious?" she asked.

"It is serious, as I told you," he said. "In just over a week's time it's the deadline for the so-called 'Beggars' Summons'. And there is harm to come in that, you can be sure."

"But haven't Lord Erskine and the other ministers advised the Dowager Queen about how it must be dealt with?"

Alisdair shrugged. "I hope so."

Glenna approached at that moment, taking Morag's hand, her eyes twinkling. "Come, you must hear Barbara talk about the wager. Jean is just quizzing her now."

Alisdair rose and Morag followed a moment later. "Glenna, let me introduce my brother, Alisdair," she said, switching to French.

Alisdair gave a short bow and briefly kissed Glenna's hand, murmuring a greeting.

Glenna smiled at him, her face flushing with pleasure. "Alisdair, yes. I saw you with the Dowager Queen in the gardens. I'm very glad to meet you. Your sister has told me so much about you."

Alisdair gave a wry grin. "Most probably about a pesky younger brother, no doubt."

"Not at all, I assure you," said Glenna. "She spoke highly of you, in fact."

"I told her that she would like you much better than some of the dolts that are here," said Morag.

Alisdair laughed. "Why that's high praise indeed. And praise I feel under obligation to attempt to fulfil. Perhaps you could honour me with a dance, if there is any to be had tonight?"

Morag marvelled at her bookish brother suddenly filled with charm and address. Perhaps Edinburgh had done more than just filled his mind. She glanced over at the few musicians gathered near the dais. They hadn't struck up any dance music yet. And there was a small amount of room for about six couples, so it might be possible.

"If there is dancing, I would be happy to accept," said Glenna, lowering her eyes.

"Until then, I'll introduce you to a few others, Alisdair," said Morag, adopting a teasing tone. "So you can see I am not living among a dubious and immoral rabble."

He looked around, gave her a sideways glance and shook his head. "Already I have my doubts."

"Doubts?" said Morag.

"That you could find anyone besides this young lady here who could meet that challenge."

Morag laughed. "We'll see. There's nothing I like more than a challenge."

They moved through the groups of people and Morag caught sight of Sandy. Her heart gave a little jump of pleasure and she smiled, heading towards him, but Alisdair held her back, so that Glenna sailed ahead, oblivious that the other two had fallen behind.

"Who is she?" he said in a low voice. "You said only that her name was Glenna."

Morag blinked at him. "But I thought you knew. She's Glenna Campbell."

He blanched. "Campbell?" he hissed in Gaelic. "Surely not a Campbell of Glenorchy."

"Yes," she said, her tone containing a hint of defiance. She could see the change in his expression and she felt annoyance and anger stir.

"What in God's name are you doing with a Glenorchy Campbell?"

"She's my friend."

"Friend?" His tone was incredulous, his eyes narrowing. "You, a friend of a Campbell? What is it you're really doing?"

"Nought," she said icily. "We share a chamber, became acquainted and then friends. She isn't like her family. Certainly not like Rory."

He looked at her sceptically. "Well, I don't care if she isn't like her family or just like the devil Campbell himself, but it isn't seemly to be so friendly. What would Father say? What would Iain say, for that matter? Ye don't want to cause trouble."

"Iain?" she said, her voice rising. She took a deep breath and fought for control. "Iain would be glad, for did he not praise her after he returned from Glenorchy?"

Alisdair snorted. "That was some time ago. We don't know what she may be like now, or that she may not take advantage of any weakness of yours and exploit it."

"She wouldn't. She is genuine. You even liked her before you found out who she was, so don't deny it."

"I'll not deny a thing. But understand this. I've warned you and I expect you to have a care."

She frowned at him. "You expect me to obey you on that. Well you can remember then that I'm older than you and I know that I am able to judge a person just as well as you, in fact better."

"You may be older by a few years, but you have less common sense," he said sternly.

The stuffy Edinburgh lad had returned. She bit her tongue to cut off any further retort. It was useless. She would do what she thought best anyway.

"Come, then. I'll introduce you to others. So ye don't have to feel compelled to speak to Glenna as much."

She turned and led him back through the groups of people gathered around, searching for Sandy once more. She finally spotted him, chatting with someone. He looked up, caught her glance, smiled and took in the two of them, her hand in Alisdair's, leading. She smiled, but he gave her a puzzled frown just as Barbara came up beside him and touched his arm. He turned to her, his face alight with interest. Barbara leaned up and spoke in his ear, her hand slipping through his arm. He smiled at her, an engaging twinkle in his eyes. Morag watched, her smile fading, as Sandy led Barbara away with him and exited the hall.

WITH HER BROTHER BESIDE HER, Morag focused on Jean's mouth, knowing she was speaking, but the words remained unheard.

Anne was there too, and along with Alisdair, they made contributions to the conversation, though Morag had no idea what it concerned. Her mind was still locked on the image of Sandy leaving with Barbara. Was he going to put truth to Barbara's claim that they had bedded? She'd heard the statement repeated often enough and it was beginning to sicken her rather than give her the immense relief it should. Had the news about Barbara reached the Dowager Queen's ears? Would she be dismissed? The speculation was great, but the general consensus seemed to favour that she wouldn't be dismissed, given her family's rank and status. That rankled with Morag, and she tried to convince herself that it was merely principle that caused such feelings and not because it wasn't her name linked with Sandy's.

"My lady."

Morag started at the sound of John Dunbar's voice. She turned her head, pasted a smile on her face and greeted him.

"Might I have a quiet word with you?" he said pleasantly. "Just for a moment, as I see you're engaged."

"Of course," she said.

She glanced at her brother who gave her a puzzled look, halting his comment. She made a brief introduction. "I'll only be a moment. It's just an inquiry to do with a song I sang before," she murmured.

She moved away from the group, Dunbar following her. As soon as they were an acceptable distance he stopped.

"Well, did you have success?" he asked in a low voice.

She arranged her face into a disappointed expression. "I'm afraid not. I went to the door but was unable to enter," she said. "I didn't want to linger in the hallway too long. I will try again soon, but the next time I will come prepared for the locked door."

He studied her face for a moment, some doubt in his expression, until finally it cleared and he nodded. "Well, there's nothing to be done about last night now. As you say, we'll just have to try again. As soon as possible," he added firmly.

She gave an inward snort, noting how he was quick to say "we", when it was she who would be taking all the risks. In theory. She had yet to come up with a plan, but she was determined she would best him at the very least. It was just payment for how he'd used her.

CHAPTER 20

*S*he knew it was risky, she knew it was foolish. She knew without any doubt that Alisdair and Iain would berate her for acting so impetuously. It wasn't impetuousness, she told herself. It wasn't that she didn't understand the risks. She just couldn't help herself. She had to have answers. The answers she needed, she told herself, were confined strictly to the business of Dunbar's and Sandy's secretiveness. Lord Munro. She would call him Lord Munro, in her mind and to his face. She had resolved that from the moment she'd seen him walk out with Barbara. After all, the name was a childhood whim, an action of a little girl who no longer was her, who had given the thought to a Sandy that really didn't exist any more either. She only needed to look at him to know that. He was fat, he dressed like a fop.

So it was the need for answers and the secretiveness that made her lie on the bed and wait for Glenna and Barbara to fall asleep. It was a small enough victory that Barbara was here in this bed and not in Munro's. He obviously didn't find her that alluring. It had been her first thought, rather than thinking that she wouldn't have to worry about encountering Barbara later.

It was also that need which moved Morag to rise once they

were asleep and draw her long robe over her nightrail, slide into a pair of soft kid slippers and slip into the hall. She made her way along the short corridor and down the stairs, thankful for the torches and moonlight that lit the way. Her hands were clammy and her heartbeat skittered along, but she moved determinedly. She slipped out into the inner close, pulling her robe close against the cool night air. She'd decided to cut through the inner close to save time and also lessen the chance that someone might see her. A hazy memory nudged at her of Sandy, no Munro, leading her across the inner close in the moonlight. Calling her "poppet". His tone, his manner, so tender, so caring. She blinked against the tears that threatened to come. Why hadn't he said to her from the first who he was? Why keep it secret? Did he think her a child? Was that the reason for the tenderness, the caring, and his use of his old name for her? He'd hinted as much earlier. But she wasn't a child. She would tell him that for a start. She focused on the anger that rose at the thought.

That anger carried her all the way to his chamber and prompted her to knock on his door a little more loudly than she intended. A few moments passed before the door was flung open and he stood before her, clearly annoyed. When he saw Morag, all manner of emotions, from horror, concern and something else flickered in his eyes. He grabbed her and pulled her inside.

"What are ye doing here?" he hissed. "And dressed only in your nightwear? Are ye mad?"

She shrugged her arm from his grasp and drew herself up, her chin lifting. "I came tae see ye."

He snorted. "Well that much is obvious. What I want tae know is why did ye come tae see me?"

"I want answers," she said stiffly, trying to keep her anger fuelled. "And your curt manner isna going tae help things."

"Do ye no ken that if someone saw ye come tae my chamber, your reputation is ruined?"

"Like Lady Barbara's reputation is ruined?" she asked in a tone heavy with sarcasm.

"What's Lady Barbara tae do with it?"

"As if ye dinna ken."

He gave her a lowering glance. "Nay, I dinna ken."

She snorted. "Ye can hardly be ignorant of all the gossip that's circulating about ye and Lady Barbara."

He frowned. "Of course I ken. That was the whole point. Tae draw suspicion from ye so that whelp Rory wouldna ruin your own reputation. And now you've chosen tae jeopardise all that work I've done by sauntering tae my chamber as bold as brass, ye silly goose."

She scowled at him. "I didna saunter. I was careful. I even cut through the inner close. Just as ye did that night with me." She looked down at her hands. "Why did ye really no tell me that ye ken who I was when I first met ye?" she asked. "I'm nae child. I ken that time has passed."

She raised her eyes to his, to carefully gauge his reaction. But it was difficult, for he turned his head and ran his fingers through his hair. She saw his fingers were bare of rings and realised that all his jewels and finery had been removed and he wore a plain jerkin that hung loose, his shirt large and billowing around his full waist. The hose was dark and unremarkable. A bird stripped of its plumage. She smiled at the thought, because he looked as magnificent as any rare plumed bird she could imagine. So tall, so fair. Even with the scars that she could now see covered the back of his fingers as he removed them from his hair.

He gave her a composed look. "Och, ye were but a wee lassie. We're hardly the same as we were then. Ye didna remember me, anyway, and so it was better that way."

"But I would have remembered ye if ye'd said. Of course I would."

"Well it's best for ye if no one realises there is a connection between us. For the sake of your reputation, at the very least."

"Is it so embarrassing then, for ye tae acknowledge our previous acquaintance?"

He gave a frustrated sigh. "Ye're deliberately misunderstanding me. It's for your sake that I didna say anything. My own reputation has nae need of guarding. I'm confined tae the devil by many already."

"And copied by the rest," she said tartly. "Dinna gammon me, my lord. Ye dinna care tae even have a friendship, now? Is it Lady Barbara that takes your fancy, since ye've told the world that ye've bedded her? Ye dinna seem reluctant tae spend time in her company this evening."

"Ye're determined tae see what isna there, though I told ye that I did it for your sake. And ye have nae room tae speak. Ye were cavorting with that young lad who just arrived at court."

She gave him an incredulous look and then burst out laughing. "The fair young lad? Ye mean Alisdair?"

He shrugged with an air of studied nonchalance. "I dinna ken his name. I wasna introduced."

"Well if ye hadn't gone off for a little taste of Lady Barbara I would have introduced ye tae the newly arrived fair young lad, *my brother*, Alisdair MacGregor."

"I thought Iain was your brother," Munro said dumbly.

"He's my older brother and Alisdair is my younger brother."

"Younger brother?" he said slowly. He looked away, biting his lip. A moment later laughter slipped out, became louder and continued for a few moments before he stopped.

"Who's the goose now?" she asked, her mouth fixed smugly.

He sighed. "Aye, well, we'll move on from that conversation. Ye said ye wanted answers. Answers tae what, exactly?"

"Well, ye did explain Lady Barbara. That was one of the questions I had."

He gave her an amused look. "Aye, as ye say, that's been answered."

She arched a brow. "Ye were protecting me," she said flatly.

"And for that verra same reason ye dinna acknowledge me when we first met."

He nodded. "Just so."

"And I suppose it was tae protect me that ye're so secretive."

He frowned. "Secretive?"

"Aye. How is it ye found out about my meeting with John Dunbar? How is it ye tracked me tae Lord Erskine's apartment?" Her eyes narrowed. "Ye seem to ken so much about what goes on."

"It was hardly difficult," he said.

He turned and walked over to the window and looked out into the darkness, his back to her. She moved closer to him, wanting to see his expression, but also drawn by something else she refused to acknowledge.

"Ye were hardly discreet, Morag, no matter that ye thought ye were. And neither was that cub, Dunbar. He fawned over ye like ye were royalty."

She flushed. "He dinna fawn. Granted, he paid me attention. But was it so hard tae believe that someone might do that without any ulterior motive?"

"Nay, it isna hard tae believe at all." He swung around. His face was carefully composed, his expression neutral. "Quite the contrary. But ye are young and inexperienced and it was obvious that he found ye convenient prey for his plans."

"And just how is it ye found out about his plans?" she said, her voice heavy with sarcasm. He'd wounded her pride, she knew, but it pained her more than that. Was she really such a child to him?

"I dinna ken his plans, not really, only suspected. His family's politics are mixed, but he is known to have Protestant sympathies. It wasna until ye explained what he wanted ye tae do, that I understood fully."

"Well, I'm glad I could help," she said, real bitterness creeping into her voice.

"Aye, well, ye came tae nae harm in the end and we can be thankful for that."

"Because ye only want tae protect me, since I am such a young and inexperienced lass."

"Aye. I promised your brother I would, and so I have."

She stared at him, the rage surging up with a roar. "My brother asked ye tae look out for me?"

He frowned at her. "Is that so verra bad? Your brother cares for ye."

Her humiliation and anger deepened. There was no reason at all for his care of her, only instructions from her brother, a some-time friend. "My brother is an interfering, pompous goat. How dare he ask ye? I suppose it took ye a while tae recall exactly who he was asking tae protect? I mean I could hardly have found a firm place in your memory, since as ye say, I was only a wee lassie when we met last."

He gave her a bewildered look. "Nay, it was nae task tae recall ye. I kent who he meant from the first mention of your name. He wrote when it was arranged that ye should come tae court. I was happy tae oblige him." He looked her up and down. "And ye canna say it wasna warranted. Ye've managed to get yourself in a few scrapes already. First the Campbell lad and then John Dunbar."

"Well, I'm happy tae relieve ye of the necessity tae continue to watch over me." She drew herself up and gave him her most formidable look. "Consider your duty completed."

He nodded, appearing to be unperturbed by her tone or her expression. "I agree."

She looked at him cautiously. "Ye agree?"

"Aye. I think it's best that Alisdair accompany ye back tae Glen Strae."

"Ye may think what ye like, but I have nae plans tae do that. I told Alisdair the same."

A small smile spread across his face. "I take it ye argued about it?"

"Oh, he argued alright. I just told him flatly I wouldna leave and there was nae more tae say about it." She gave him a haughty look. "And I'll tell ye nae different."

"I have nae doubt of that." He moved closer to her and clutched her arms firmly. "This is nae game," he said softly. "The danger is real. John Dunbar's plan is real and he means it tae be completed. If ye remove yourself from the court, he can nae longer use ye for it. Do ye no see that?"

She looked up into his eyes, fully aware of his hands on her arms. Her anger seeped away to be replaced by a yearning, a desire so strong that it made her breath quicken. His eyes held hers and she couldn't say anything, aware only of his scent that was his alone, the feel of his hands burning through the thin layers of her gown and robe and how the space between them could be closed with only a slight movement forward. He lifted a hand and brushed it against her cheek and she leaned into it, her body moving forward. She thought of his kiss, made in haste to protect her, but creating a memory that lingered even now on her lips. She opened her mouth slightly as if it was taking place here and now. She put her hand over his where it still rested on her cheek and turned it over. With her eyes locked on his she placed a kiss on his palm and inhaled the smell of leather that lingered on them from the gloves he had worn. She saw the scar on his wrist and allowed her lips to travel down to kiss it.

He moved his hand away and cupped her head, a slight groan escaping him. He bent down and brushed his lips along hers and she sighed in response. He deepened the kiss, opening her mouth, his tongue probing gently. It lasted only a moment and he broke away, turning to the window.

"I must beg your pardon, Morag. I forgot myself. It's the worst possible behaviour and I am appalled that I took advantage of ye in every possible way. There is nae excuse."

"But ye dinna take advantage!" she said, and moved to put a hand on his shoulder but he shrugged it off, still facing away.

"I did. Ye are a young innocent lass and I am a man of experience. Allow me tae be the judge of what's proper."

She looked at his back in confusion. "Sandy, ye have nothing tae fault in your behaviour. I wanted tae kiss ye, indeed I was the one who kissed your hand. Is a kiss so verra wrong?"

He laughed. "Consider, mademoiselle," he said, switching to French. "You're in my room, late at night, unchaperoned, clothed only in your nightshift and robe. That's hardly the height of propriety and would easily get you an unredeemable reputation and banishment from court. Add that to a kiss that could have easily led to much more and the scandal would have tarnished your family for years to come."

"You think I care for that?" Morag asked, her voice rising. She felt at once bereft and angry, struggling to understand his change in mood.

He turned and frowned at her. "No, but I do." He strode forward and took her arm. "I must see you safely back to your room. And tomorrow, I'll speak to Alisdair about taking you home."

"You can speak to him all you want," she said sullenly. "But you won't get me to go back home."

CHAPTER 21

$\mathcal{M}$orag awoke feeling weary and bedraggled. She hadn't fallen asleep until just before dawn and it was as though she had walked the hills and glens all night. She'd left Sandy too confused and miserable to think much of her journey back through the courtyard and up the stairs to her own corridor and door, though she knew she was lucky to have passed undetected. It wasn't until she entered the chamber and began to remove her robe and slippers that she felt the pair of eyes watching her from the bed. She'd turned and looked and saw Barbara, her stare unblinking.

"Unquiet stomach," Morag said softly and hoped that would be an end of it.

Barbara said nothing, just continued to stare at Morag, who gave a weak smile and crawled into bed, thankful that it was Glenna she lay next to and not Barbara – who would surely know that with a body as cold as hers was now, it wasn't due to spending a long time in the guarderobe. Especially when any sane person would have used the covered pot in the wooden cupboard, put there after her last late night acquaintance with the guarderobe.

When she settled down to sleep her mind continued to work, sifting through the encounters and fragments of conversations, while Barbara lay so near her, her own wakefulness subtly evident through the breathing that was far too shallow for one asleep.

It wasn't until Bridie came with food and to help her dress that she found some semblance of composure. A drink of small beer and a chunk of bread with some cheese settled her stomach and a wet cloth to her face refreshed her to a degree. Until she patted her face dry and she was reminded of Sandy's hand on her cheek, the soft brush of his lips against hers and she felt her face redden. She almost put the cool cloth to her face once again, to calm it. She rubbed her face a little, to give some excuse for its reddened condition and thought of Sandy's fingers, the rough scars there and on his wrist. She halted rubbing, the cloth poised on her cheek. The scars, she knew the feel of those scars. The memory was faint, but remarkable and recent. She withdrew the cloth slowly, suddenly understanding Sandy's secretiveness.

"You're looking verra pale today," said Bridie. "Are ye well?"

"She dinna get much sleep last night, did ye, Morag?" said Barbara in an insinuating tone.

"Nay, I did not." Morag felt herself redden further. She stole a glance at Barbara and saw the fleeting malicious look levelled at her.

"Och, ye poor wee cratur," said Bridie. "Are ye sickening again?"

"Perhaps ye should fetch Mistress Cunningham, Bridie," said Barbara, her expression speculative. "That's the second time in only a few days that she's been ill and forced to spend time in the guarderobe. It might be serious. And we wouldna want the Dowager Queen tae be subjected tae anything that might make her ill as well."

"Oh, Morag," said Glenna putting a hand on. "Is it the same

trouble or is it something else? Shall we ask Mistress Cunningham for a physician?"

"Oh, I think it might be the same trouble," said Barbara. "Though I'm dinna think the physician would be able to help."

Morag refrained from throwing Barbara a dark look. She took a deep breath and lifted her chin. "I'm fine, really. It's no anything that another cup of small beer and some air wouldna cure. A poor night is all. I'm certain it was that I had just a bit too much marzipan yesterday."

"Och, it was verra good, but it does nae good tae favour it too much," said Glenna.

"Some things that are very tempting and look tasty are better left alone," said Barbara.

"Are ye speaking from experience?" said Morag, unable to resist at least a little barb to counter Barbara's provoking words.

"Dinna take on too much today," said Glenna. "Let me know if ye feel verra ill and I'll tell Mistress Cunningham, so ye can avoid any heavy duties today."

Morag gave Glenna a reassuring smile. "I'll be fine, really I will. And besides, my brother is here and I canna leave him tae his own devices. Who can tell what he would get up tae?" She'd said the last words on a light note, hoping to shift the attention away from her own state.

Glenna laughed. "Is he that devilish, or is this court too much of a field of stumbling blocks?"

"I'm nae so sure I'd call him devilish," said Morag. "But he can be stubborn in his pursuit of an objective, and he has his own way of finding peculiar kinds of trouble in which tae enmesh himself. So if ye combine that with what assuredly is a court filled with what ye describe as stumbling blocks and I would call traps, there is much tae be attentive tae where my brother is concerned."

Glenna laughed again. "He sounds like a character indeed."

"Aye he is. A troublesome thorn when he wants tae be."

"I have yet tae meet this troublesome thorn of yours," said Barbara her eyes filled with curiosity. "Will I like him?"

Morag gave her a bland look. "He can please most people when he wants tae. Unless he finds them wanting in some way."

Barbara gave a sly smile. "I dinna think he would find me wanting."

"He doesna seem tae your taste," said Glenna. "Ye would class him a pup as ye seem tae like older men. Like your latest, Lord Munro."

"Aye. Now there's a man," said Barbara. "And I must say he tasted verra well indeed."

"And will ye be tasting him again?" said Glenna, her eyes dancing. "Tell us."

"Yes," said Morag, her tone flat. "Tell us."

"It might be that we have a tryst again soon," said Barbara.

Morag studied her to see if there was truth to her words, but gave up. Barbara was sly and so often full of things true and untrue she couldn't discern either at this moment. All she knew is she wanted to trip her on the stairs, push her from the window so she fell on the stones below, or at the very least slap off the smug smile that framed her face at this very moment. Instead, she turned and signalled Bridie to finish dressing her.

"Ye can meet my brother soon," she said to Barbara. "I'll be seeing him first thing."

SHE FOUND Alisdair with the other courtiers in the Dowager Queen's outer chamber, where matters serious and frivolous provided hours of banter, side glances and laughter. A small group of women huddled around a lute player who strummed with some affectation, his bright doublet slashed with cuttes too numerous to count. Morag didn't often find herself here, among the throng of courtiers, for the Dowager Queen's ladies in waiting were too often confined to her inner apartments where the ill and aging Dowager Queen kept a quiet life unless matters of state called her to the dais here to sit on her throne.

Today the Dowager Queen felt well enough to venture into the throne room and Morag was glad for it, if only that it provided a distraction from other matters that she was best served to put from her mind. She scanned the room for her brother, but couldn't locate him until she felt a tap on her shoulder. She turned around and there he was. She gave him a generous smile. He grinned back at her.

"Sister, can it be from that smile you are actually glad to see me?" he inquired in very correct French.

"How could I not be?" she said. "You are the dearest of my younger brothers."

"As you are my dearest and best sister," he said dryly.

She gave him a playful tap on the arm. "I am here for you now, am I not? To see that you come to no harm in this den of vipers, as I'm sure your tutor wouldn't hesitate to call it."

Alisdair raised his brow. "I doubt that you would know what my tutor would say in any situation, as you generally disregarded anything he said."

"Ah, but it doesn't mean I didn't hear it. I just disregarded it."

He laughed. "As you say."

Barbara and Glenna approached and they all exchanged brief bows and curtsies while Morag introduced Barbara.

"And is this the brother we've heard so much about?" said Barbara. She gave him a coquettish smile. "The devilish one?"

Alisdair snorted. "I fear you've mistaken me for my brother."

"I think not," said Barbara. "But perhaps you might explain that you are not devilish, for your looks, your manner, they all hint at something just a little bit devilish."

Glenna looked at Alisdair with dismay. "I don't think your

sister meant it in any way but kindly and with humour. As one might to a younger sibling."

Alisdair levelled a brief smile at Glenna. "Of course," he said stiffly.

"Oh, and now I think I see something of the devilishness," said Barbara with a tinkling laugh. "So polite, so formal, but all the banter and easy humour just vanished with a snap." She waved her hand and leaned towards him. "Perhaps I might be able to coax back your good humour."

A smile played on Alisdair's lips, though his face reddened slightly. "Perhaps."

"Oh don't pay any attention to her teasing," said Morag. She was embarrassed that he should behave so badly to Glenna and had had just about enough of Barbara's flirting. She'd been amused at first, but Alisdair seemed taken with her which annoyed Morag.

Alisdair looked at Morag and grinned. "I don't mind it all. I've enjoyed it. But if your friends will excuse us for a few moments I would lief speak with you."

She glanced at Barbara and Glenna. "We won't be long, I'm sure."

Alisdair nodded at Barbara and Glenna and guided Morag to a far corner where they could be alone.

"Is there anything amiss?" she asked, lapsing into Gaelic. "Have you heard something since we last spoke?"

He gave her a surprised look. "I haven't. Have you any reason to suspect there would be?"

She shook her head. "It's just that I couldn't think what you may want to speak to me about in private if it wasn't about any serious news."

He frowned at her. "I wanted to speak with you in private because I didn't want to embarrass you in front of your friends."

"Embarrass me?" she said stiffening. "What would you have to say that would embarrass me?"

"I mean I don't want to have to argue with you and scold you in front of others."

She could feel her temper rising. "Well there isn't any need to argue with me or scold me, so let us forget this and go back to the others."

He put a hand on her arm, restraining her. "We have a matter unsettled and I intend to settle it now. I haven't the time to fritter away here."

"If you mean the matter of my return to Glen Strae, then you can rest assured that the matter is settled." She pulled her arm from his hand and walked away.

Morag threaded her way through the gathered people towards the lute player. Her brother wouldn't dare make a scene in front of him. Glenna caught her arm and Morag stopped.

"Did something happen? You look shaken," said Glenna.

Morag forced a smile. "It's nothing, really. My brother takes it upon himself to be the laird and pronounces that my conduct is such that I must leave court and return to Glen Strae."

Glenna's face fell. "No, but you cannot! I would miss you so."

Morag looked over at her friend and her face softened. "Would you? I know I would miss you."

Glenna squeezed her hand. "I would indeed. You have been a true friend to me and I count that as special and rare in my life."

In the distance she noticed Sandy enter and she struggled with herself not to try and catch his eye. But she need not have troubled herself, for a moment later his own gaze alighted on someone else in the other direction and he began to head towards them. It wasn't until he arrived at Barbara's side that she realised who it was. Morag watched, her mouth slightly parted, as he bowed and lifted Barbara's hand for a playful kiss. Barbara looked up at him, her eyes widening, no doubt, with deliberate intention, as was the not so subtle thrusting of her voluptuous breasts. What a hoor, those paps will fall out of her dress if she leans over any further, thought Morag, watching the two flirt, until Glenna brought her back to the conversation with a tug on her arm.

"What has got you scowling with such intensity?" she asked.

"Och," she said lapsing into Scots. "'Tis only thon hoor over there displaying her goods tae Sandy as if they were a tray of sweetmeats."

Glenna arched her brow. "Sandy, is it?"

Morag reddened and forced a laugh. "Och, it isna any great mystery. I met him as a child when he visited my family one summer. It's something I only recently recalled. He was called Sandy then. It was a lapse only."

Glenna raised her brow gave a slow smile. "Of course. A lapse only. And your temper over Barbara behaving in her usual manner hasna anything tae do with that lapse, has it?"

"Nay," she said sharply. "Of course not. I just find her irritating, especially now that she primps and poses about since winning that wager."

Glenna glanced over at Barbara. "Well she says she won the wager, and Lord Munro hasna done anything tae gainsay her, but he hasna confirmed it with words."

Morag frowned. "Aye, well," she said after a panicked moment. "But he does pay her great attention."

"Aye he does. But maybe it serves his purpose tae allow all tae think she has won. It would stop the constant speculation and wagers."

Morag studied Sandy. He was meticulous in his attention. Just the right amount of flirtation, just the right amount physical contact, but no more. His face held the appropriate interest, but did it hold the fire she'd seen in his eyes last night? But then he brushed his hand along Barbara's collarbone and lifted the necklace she wore and Morag saw Barbara shudder slightly. The shudder was not feigned, it was real and spontaneous.

"Perhaps it began that way, but I think it may now be more," said Morag, striving to keep bitterness from her voice.

She should never have gone to his room last night, that much was clear. She should have stayed in her bed, for it did her no good to watch him woo Barbara after rejecting her. To watch as the spark began to kindle between them. She forced herself to turn away so she wouldn't torture herself any longer.

Glenna placed a hand on her arm. "It's only play for her, Morag. There isna anything behind it, I'm sure."

Play. Perhaps now, but that didn't mean it might become something more. Morag pasted a smile on her face "It's nae concern of mine, but I thank ye for your words."

"Lady Glenna," said a stern voice. "May I have a moment of your time?"

The pair turned to see Mistress Cunningham standing before them, her face serious and unreadable.

Morag started to excuse herself but Glenna put her hand out to stay her. "Do you mind if Lady Morag remains here?"

Mistress Cunningham gave Morag a cursory glance. "Perhaps it might be for the best, in view of the situation."

Glenna gave her a puzzled look. "Is there something amiss?"

Mistress Cunningham wasted no time in getting to the point. "Word has just reached Lady Erskine. Your mother isn't well. In fact it is feared she hasn't long left, and your father requests that you return home at once."

All colour fell from Glenna's face and she reached to grip Morag's hand hard. "My mother?" she said faintly.

"I'm sorry, child," said Mistress Cunningham. "The arrangements are nearly complete. There will be a small escort to accompany you and your brother back to Glenorchy. You'll leave this afternoon, so you had best go now and oversee the packing of your things."

With only a nod and no word of comfort she departed, leaving Glenna and Morag to stare after her. After a moment Morag turned to her friend and squeezed her hand.

"I'm so sorry, Glenna. I know how much you care for your mother."

Tears filled Glenna's eyes. She bit her lip and nodded. "She has been unwell a long while now, so it shouldn't come as a surprise."

"I'm sure it's no less of a shock, for all that you knew you must be prepared at some point. It's when the moment arrives, you realise that no amount of preparation can offset the shock."

Glenna studied her face a moment. "Yes, of course. You understand. You lost your mother as a young child."

"It was hard. Growing up for the most part without my mother to guide me. But you've known your mother longer and so the pain might be sharper. I've lived with mine for a long time."

Glenna nodded and gave a small smile. "Will you help me pack?"

"Of course. We are dear friends. And that's what dear friends do."

She took Glenna's hand and drew it through her arm. Together they made their way to the door to the chamber. Just before they reached the door, Sandy intercepted them and took Glenna's hand.

"Lady Glenna, I just heard the sad news. May I give you my sincere condolences for such awful tidings. Your lady mother by all accounts is a woman of great worth and high understanding."

Glenna smiled weakly up at him. "Thank you."

"And I'm sure my brother Iain would echo them," said Morag.

Sandy regarded her, his expression appreciative. "Yes, he would."

Glenna lowered her head and Sandy offered her his handkerchief that hung from his sleeve.

"Keep this. I'm sure you will find it useful in the days to come."

She took it, gave him her thanks and moved away, Morag accompanying her. Morag glanced over her shoulder as she exited the room and saw that Sandy stood there, still regarding them both, his face filled with compassion. The look stayed with her, much as she might try and banish it, for she knew it would do her no good to have anything more positive to add to the growing store of thoughts and memories that concerned Alexander Munro.

CHAPTER 22

*M*orag made her way up the stairs, heading to the Dowager Queen's chambers. She had just watched Glenna and her brother depart, the small escort of soldiers surrounding them. She'd given Glenna a warm embrace, but couldn't manage more than a cold nod to Rory. He'd ignored her completely, toying with his reins impatiently while she uttered some final words of condolence to Glenna and extracted a promise that she would write to her.

Now she found it difficult to conjure any kind of interest or excitement in the afternoon ahead, spent quietly in the Dowager Queen's apartment, sewing awkward stitches under Mistress Cunningham's beady eye, or reading some prosy sermons aloud. Perhaps she might convince them to allow her to sing a little song. Though Glenna wouldn't be able to accompany her on the lute, Morag speculated she might be able to adequately accompany herself. She would make herself be confident.

She started to hum a potential selection when someone pulled her into the window alcove. Startled, she stared into John Dunbar's eyes and flushed. He kissed her on the lips, a quick, impatient peck that left her even more unsettled.

"My sweet," he said, cupping her chin. "Have you managed it yet?"

She took a deep breath and frowned, her mind whirring with possible answers. "No," she said finally. She forced frustration into her voice. "The guards. They were up and down the corridor all night. I think they must suspect something."

Anger flashed in his eyes, but it was gone before she could really register it. "I'm sure they suspect nothing. I would have heard if they did." He took her hand and rubbed the palm with his thumb. "You must take courage, sweeting. You have a perfectly good reason for entering the room. And you must act quickly. Lord Erskine will return soon and our chance will be lost." He kissed her again, this time slower, his tongue running along her bottom lip. Morag fought the revulsion that suddenly seized her. "You do want your revenge, don't you?"

"Of course I do," she said. She removed her hand. "Though Rory has now left court, so some of my wish has been filled."

He snorted. "He may have left, but it wasn't in disgrace and that's what you wanted. What we both want," he added. "Come, you will try again. Tonight. Promise me?" He drew her into an embrace, one hand cradling her head, pulling her to meet his lips, his other hand rubbing her back.

She endured the kiss, trying to seem responsive, and she was grateful that he didn't even notice its lukewarm level as his mouth travelled down along her jaw line and down her neck. What had ever possessed her to think his attentions were even the remotest bit pleasing?

"I promise to try," she said, drawing away a little. She looked into his eyes. "Really. I'll do my best."

He took her hand and kissed it, turning it over. She was beginning to find this attention from him more than tiresome. She withdrew her hand slowly.

"Have you heard that Lord Erskine might return sooner than planned?" she asked.

He stilled, his attention sharpened. "No, why? What have you heard?"

She shrugged. "Nothing. I just wondered if you might. In view of the worsening situation with the 'Beggars' Summons'. Honestly, they sit around and talk, talk, talk. And then the Queen herself. Still in France under the French King's thumb. What is Scotland becoming? A pawn of France?" She eyed him carefully.

"Aye," he said lapsing morosely into Scots. "We forget we are Scots first, I think sometimes. Mary is hardly a Queen. She's young and ruled by her Guise relatives. Meanwhile, we must cobble our own future as best we may – for we get nae help in that quarter. Unless it serves the French."

"Aye," she said. "Ye have the right of it, Lord John. We'd be better off ruled by Scots men who have our interests at heart."

He smiled down at her and laid a hand on her cheek. "Ye've the heart of the matter, there, sweeting. And perhaps we might see a change. Sooner rather than later."

"What do ye mean?" she asked in an innocent manner.

He placed a finger over her lips. "Wheest. 'Tis nought to worry a braw lassie like ye."

She pasted a smile on her face. "Nay, I ken that ye are a man that has many important connections and I'll no trouble ye for an explanation, because I trust ye and I'm certain that ye will act for the best."

He returned her smile and leaned down, kissing her once more. She parted her lips slightly, pretending to welcome his tongue and he embraced her tightly, his breath becoming a little ragged. Two could play at this, she thought.

SHE SLIPPED into the garden and breathed a sigh of relief when she saw no one was about. The weather was dull and threatened rain, but it wasn't cold at least. She needed the small respite to collect herself before she faced the dreary prospect of the Dowager Queen's apartments. She'd reasoned that few if any would miss her for a little while more, thinking she was still bidding Glenna farewell.

Though she'd felt brave and defiant when she'd been with John Dunbar, deceiving him into believing she was still in league with him and weaving herself deeper, now she felt shaken from the encounter, her nerves and anxiety at what she had dared catching up to her. Would he share some of his secrets with her, enlist her to help with something more serious, something that even endangered the Queen herself? But what was she supposed to be doing anyway but stealing some sort of document in the casket that no doubt served that exact purpose?

In the cold light of reflection, she realised that Sandy might be right. She was in over her head and the play was dangerous. She really wasn't a card woman of experience. But what to do? Would she leave it to Sandy to manage after all?

"Morag."

As if summoned by the very thought of him, the sound of her name on his lips brought a surge of joy. She turned and smiled.

"Sandy," she said simply.

She watched him approach, the pale light carving shadows along the hollows of his cheeks, casting his hair as a colour more red than gold. His silver doublet seemed muted, less vibrant than his usual exuberant colours, and combined with his dark slops and hose, made his outfit seem especially subdued. His girth was no less wide, a state belied by his muscular legs and arms and broad chest. She smiled sardonically, seeing now for the first time the incongruity of the ungainly belly he insisted on sporting. She remembered the one time he hadn't sported the large stomach, or the rings.

He strode towards her, his gait showing no trace of mincing or any other kind of charade that would mark him as foppish.

She arched a brow, showing some of her wry humour at the situation. This might be one game she could play with some skill.

"Were you looking for me, my lord?" she said pleasantly. "You've found a moment to spare from your conqueress?"

He stopped in front of her, a puzzled look on his face. "Conqueress?"

"Lady Barbara."

"Lady Barbara?"

"Come now, don't pretend witlessness with me. Lady Barbara, the woman who won the wager. She's certainly ensuring all and sundry know that she is the winner. With every wile and artifice she has."

Sandy laughed. "Come now. No need to tease. You and I both know the truth of that, if anyone does."

"Ah, but do I know the truth? There are many truths of you, Sandy. How many know them all?"

He frowned at her. "And what exactly do you mean by that? You know that I'm speaking the truth about Barbara. And why it appears differently."

"Perhaps. But you aren't always forthcoming. In fact, I could say you are full of secrets."

He gripped her arm. "Out with it. Tell me what your meaning is. Clearly this isn't about Lady Barbara, is it?"

She took his arm and pulled back the glove that covered his hand, to bare his wrist. She leaned down and kissed the scar there.

"Perhaps it is rather what you should tell me." She kissed the scar again.

"My scar?" he said in a dismissive tone. "What is that to you? It's nothing. I acquired it years ago in a sword fight."

"I'm not disputing that. Nor the scars on your fingers," she said taking his hand and squeezing it. "I'm sure it was all honourably won and I don't doubt that the person who gave them to you paid a heavier price."

He shrugged and studied her carefully. "As I said, it was years ago."

"And it was a short while ago that a man with such scars as these helped me back into the castle after relieving me of a horse that was to be conveyed to one of my clansmen," she said softly in Gaelic. "The man was the *Droch Spiorad*."

She watched his face carefully, but he gave nothing away. Not even the slightest hint of alarm.

"*Droch Spiorad?*" he said. He shook his head. "Are you saying you think I am the Dark Ghost they speak of at court?" He gave a snort. "I'm afraid you're mistaken."

She tilted her head. "I think not, Sandy. But we'll leave it for now. I mean to do nothing about it, if that's what concerns you." She took up his hand. "I knew you hadn't changed," she said softly. "You're still the brave golden knight."

He carefully withdrew his hand from hers. "I'm nothing of the sort. You can dispel that image from your head immediately, for you shall quickly be sorely disappointed. I game, I dance, I play music, but I am no brave golden knight."

She shrugged. "I didn't say you weren't a courtier as well. And I know you gamble on many things. And you're very shrewd about it."

"I haven't sought you out to speak in riddles with you," he said. He placed a hand heavily on her shoulder. "Morag, I have to leave court for a short while, but I want you to promise me that you won't take matters into your own hand with John Dunbar."

"Where are you going?"

He shook his head. "It's of small matter where I'm going, but rest assured it won't be for long. And when I get back I will deal with John Dunbar, so you won't have to worry about it."

"He is pressing me still, you know."

His brows drew together. "Is he? Well I'll ensure he doesn't, then. Just promise me you'll leave it to me."

"But if it's nothing, why won't you tell me where you're going?"

He gave a frustrated sound. "I'm merely off to a hunting lodge near Dundee. I have to attend a friend there for some matters."

She gave him a dark look. "Dundee? That's a journey for just 'some matters'. Do you really mean matters for the Dowager Queen?"

"No. Personal matters. I have relatives there."

"You, a Highland Munro, have relatives in Dundee?"

"Yes. Is that such a stretch of the truth?"

She gave him a disbelieving look. "Of course it is. You can't expect me to believe that."

"Well, it doesn't matter what you believe. It doesn't change the outcome."

She studied him again, taking in his calm countenance, the tiny quirk to the corner of his mouth that showed a lurking humour. Perhaps he was telling the truth. But some instinct told her it was a lie and he was on the Dowager Queen's business. And that could mean nothing but danger, she was sure of it. Her stomach dropped.

She placed a hand on his cheek, suddenly fighting tears. "Dear, sweet Sandy," she said in a hoarse whisper. "You will take care, won't you?" She leaned up and pulled his head towards hers, their lips meeting. She kissed him fiercely, full of the passion that rose up inside her, afraid that it might be the last chance she would get to kiss him like this.

She slid her arms around his neck and pressed her body up against his, not caring who might see her, only aware that she must make the most of this moment. And for a moment Sandy gave way, clutching her tighter, falling into the kiss, his tongue meeting hers. She moaned softly, the desire rising inside her like a tide.

He moved her deeper into the shadow of the hedge, away from the prying eyes, his lips still on hers. She ran her hands through his hair, loving the texture of his curls on her fingers. He broke away and began kissing her cheek and along to her ear, nibbling a bit on the edge and then down along her neck. Her breath became heavy and ragged, the heat rising inside her.

"Oh, Sandy," she murmured, her voice heavy with desire.

"Morag," he whispered in a gravelly voice. "Promise me."

"Anything," she said, gasping.

"You will say nothing to John Dunbar."

"I'll say nothing to John Dunbar."

He kissed the top of her head.

"That's my poppet," he said. "I'll ensure he'll be kept busy tonight and you'll have no need to worry then. Tomorrow, I've arranged with your brother to take you back to Glen Strae."

She stilled, her ardour doused instantly. Had she heard correctly? "You did what?"

He pulled away a little. "I arranged for you to return to Glen Strae tomorrow. It's for your safety. John Dunbar is dangerous, and since I won't be at court for a time, I would feel better knowing you were safely at home."

She stared at him, speechless with disbelief, until the anger took over. She stepped back from him, afraid she might start hitting him and not stop. "You had no right to make arrangements for my return to Glen Strae with my brother," she said in a dark tone.

He closed the distance and put his arms around her but she shrugged him off. "But Morag, I don't mean it to insult you. It's for your safety."

"Well you can forget your arrangements. The fact that you didn't ask my permission before you made any kind of arrangement is most definitely an insult. And that you should presume that I would leave court because you deem it so, is even more galling. Besides, it's not for you to make the decision whether I leave or stay, it's for Lady Erskine."

He remained unruffled. "I know that. And so does your

brother. He's going to ask permission from her as soon as he is able to see her."

She straightened and looked up at him. "Well it seems that I have to waylay my brother quickly, before he finds Lady Erskine." She nodded to him. "I bid you farewell, Lord Munro. And wish you all speed and luck in settling your 'personal matters' to your satisfaction in Dundee."

She turned on her heel and moved away quickly, leaving a stony faced Sandy in her wake. She wouldn't let him get the best of her in this. She would stay at court, if only to ensure that John Dunbar did no further ill. She forced the thought of Sandy's purpose in Dundee out of her mind. She had to focus on finding her brother and convincing him that Sandy was mistaken in the wisdom of sending her back to Glen Strae.

CHAPTER 23

"I won't go, so you can save your breath and say nothing. I care nothing for what Lord Munro may have said, for he knows little of the situation and even less of me."

She held her brother's eyes, forcing herself to remain calm, to keep her words even. It was a struggle, a war that she'd waged in the time since she'd left Sandy and found her brother. It had taken a while, but that was good in a way, because it allowed her time to cool down and to create arguments that might convince Alisdair. On the other hand, she could only hope that he hadn't made any arrangements for their departure – and if he had, well, he would just have to unmake them.

Alisdair stared at her in bemusement. "Why so irate, sister? Has something happened to cause you to fume like a child in a tantrum?"

She opened her mouth to bite out a sharp retort but closed it quickly. It would do her no good to rise to his baiting. He knew better than anyone else, save Iain, how to raise her ire with a few brief well-chosen words and she knew that's what he was doing now, in order to gain the upper hand. She took a deep breath.

"I am not in a tantrum," she said, her words carefully spoken.

"I am just galled that Lord Munro had the presumption to think he knows what is best for me and make arrangements under that mistaken belief."

"He told you then," said Alisdair, a grin breaking out on his face. "I have to say that the man is really growing on me. I find that I like him well, no matter that his appearance may have made me think otherwise."

She pressed her lips together. Lord preserve her from these laddies and their mutual admiration of one another. "I care not what you think of Munro, nor the man himself. He has no right to have voiced his opinion to you about me."

Alisdair raised his brows. "But Morag, just yesterday you were claiming him as a childhood friend of yours and Iain's. Your praise was high and it was you who urged me to treat him as such."

She glanced at him and looked away, her face reddening visibly. "That may be so, but I have since come to realise I was mistaken. He has changed and is no longer as trustworthy as he once might have been. Besides, I was only five at the time and sorely lacking in judgement."

"And you feel that you have more judgement now?"

She frowned at him. "Of course. I'm nineteen. I'm experienced in assessing people and when they can be trusted." She pushed aside the thought of John Dunbar and the extent to which she had believed and trusted in him, only to be proven a fool for it.

"Well I'm afraid I must differ with you on that. Your conduct, at least what I have heard tell of it, belies that. And whatever you may now think of Lord Munro, I agree with him. Which should come as no surprise to you, Morag, since I said the same yesterday. And I think Iain would agree as well. I must escort you back to Glen Strae."

"But there's no need. Nothing has changed since yesterday.

I'm innocent of faulty behaviour. Anything that happened is not to be laid at my door, but Rory Campbell's," she added darkly.

"I don't deny that Rory Campbell had a significant part to play with that incident over the horse, but it's more than that and you know it. You have flirted shamelessly with someone named John Dunbar and from what I hear, you may have had a tryst with one other person at least. Though I have yet to discover who it might be. And the names of any others, if there are others."

She stared at him, panicked for a moment that he might be on the verge of discovering about herself and Sandy, that Rory Campbell and his companions had seen her in his embrace. But then she remembered the dark apartments, where in that first week of her arrival she'd gone with Glenna and Barbara and drunk too much.

"Nothing happened in any of those cases," she said, forcing all the indignation she could muster in her words. "And if you were told differently, then that person is a liar."

"It matters not whether it is true or false," said Alisdair calmly. "It's how it appears to others and what others say that is the issue."

"Well that I cannot control, however I might want to."

"But you put yourself in a position to be talked about."

She snorted, then decided to try another tactic. "But if I leave now, it only gives credence to the rumours. It would be better if I remain here, wait for their attention to shift to someone else, which it most certainly will. In fact, I'm sure they are now more taken with Lady Barbara's exploits with your friend Sandy than they are with me."

He laughed and shook his head. "You do realise that Lord Munro wished you to leave for your safety, not because of the rumours that have been circulating about you? This rebel cause, centring around the 'Beggars' Summons', is becoming dangerous and he would see you away from it, as would I."

"He exaggerates, Alisdair. He sees danger where there is none."

"There is danger, and well you know it." Alisdair sighed. "Though you're my older sister, I won't be deterred from my duty, but I will say this. We can put it off for a few days and I'll make my explanations to the Dowager Queen herself that our brother's wife is in need of her sister and companion in time for the birth of her first child. Which is only the truth."

She sighed, unable to argue with such a statement. "Very well, a few days grace and then I will go with you. If the Dowager Queen gives her permission."

He smiled at her and grasped her arm. "Come now, let us restore each other to our good graces and enjoy the last remaining days we have at court."

She nodded, suddenly tired by the effort she'd made to remain here. And why had she fought so hard? What was here for her? Glenna was gone, the only real friend she had here. Sandy and she were no longer on good terms, even she did remain here until his return, and John Dunbar was a threat, albeit she was reluctant to admit it to herself.

"There you are, my sweet."

Morag nearly jumped when he spoke into her ear. Her strategy to avoid both him and her brother seemed to have failed. John Dunbar was standing right next to her, after unearthing her from her huddling among Lady Barbara and her newly acquired entourage of admirers and hangers on and now she could see her brother in the distance making his way towards her through the groups of people gathered in the Dowager Queen's chamber. John Dunbar drew her away with little effort, her attachment to the group so negligible that no one noticed she was leaving.

"An urgent word," he murmured.

He pulled her to a quiet corner, so that she faced him and no one else. He smiled and wore a pleasant expression, but there was something in his eyes that made Morag nervous.

"I'm afraid I haven't been able to do anything more about which we spoke," said Morag.

He laughed, but she could hear the false note in it.

"That is less important than what I have to speak to you about."

Morag felt the knot in her stomach tighten. "What is it?"

He lowered his voice even further. "Matters that we spoke about are coming to a head."

She gave him a puzzled look. "Matters?"

He laughed again, clearly giving a show of light hearted banter. "The unrest."

She stared at him thoughtfully. "I see. You mean it's getting worse?"

He nodded, his smile growing wider. "Events are moving towards a hopeful conclusion. But it's not certain and it's time to enlist some help to ensure the outcome we wish for."

She nodded slowly, trying to make sense of what he was telling her. The 'Beggars' Summons' deadline was soon and the resistance to it was growing. Was there going to be some show of force?

"Enlist help?"

He nodded. "From outside sources. Those with connections, authority."

She wasn't certain what he meant by that. "I see. Is it so certain there will be trouble?"

"Oh it's certain. I've just had confirmation. And it's important that we support it as much as possible."

He took her hand and kissed it. "I need your help with that, though."

"My help?" she said, alarmed.

He turned her hand and kissed the palm, a smile on his face.

"It's perfect. No one will be the wiser. I understand that you are returning to your home. Well, your journey home will bring you in touch with a person I wish you to pass on certain letters to that I have prepared."

"You want me to pass on letters?" she whispered. She could hardly think. His request had stunned her.

"Don't worry. It's a simple thing, but one that will help a cause you've got close to your heart."

"But I thought getting the casket was of greatest importance to that end?"

He sighed. "It is. But this is more pressing. If we wait a moment later, it could be too late."

"This hopeful conclusion will occur that soon?"

He nodded. "A matter of a day or so."

That was uncomfortably close. An uprising. Did the Dowager Queen know of this, she wondered, panicked. Were they all in danger?

"Where is this happening?" she managed to say.

He paused a moment, considering. "Dundee," he said finally, in a soft voice.

All thoughts but one fled her mind as she stared at him, frozen. Eventually, she took a deep breath.

"Tell me what you want me to do," she eventually heard herself say.

~

SHE STOOD there after John Dunbar had given her instructions and left, still trying to absorb all that he'd told her, but all she could focus on was Sandy and the knowledge that he rode to certain danger. She licked her lips slowly, forcing her mind to work, but it was impossible.

"Were you just trying to taunt me with your obvious false statement that your behaviour is always beyond reproach, or do you really have such different standards of conduct than the rest of us? Or perhaps it's just that the conduct here is so reprehensible and you've been here long enough that you think that the behaviour I just witnessed was acceptable?"

She frowned at Alisdair. "Must you be such a prig, Alisdair? It really is very tiring."

"A prig, is it? I don't think Iain would consider it priggish to ensure your reputation remains intact."

She gave a small snort. "My reputation is hardly in danger from that conversation."

"That certainly isn't how it appeared."

"Alisdair, it was a bit of harmless flirting. All courtiers do it. It's expected, even."

He looked at her doubtfully. "It seemed more than flirting."

She paused a moment then spoke, going with the impulse. "You're right. It wasn't flirting. It was actually something very serious."

"Serious? You mean that man wants to bed you?"

She laughed, feeling a slight edge of hysteria. "Brother, your mind is the morally reprehensible element here. No, far from it." She lowered her voice. "It's to do with Sandy. He's in danger."

Alisdair's brow drew together. "Back to Sandy, now, is it? What's changed from a short while ago when Lord Munro knew nothing about you?"

She gave an impatient wave. "That was different. This is important. He's gone to Dundee. He told me some pretence about seeing a friend for personal matters or some such activity, but I know for a fact that there is to be an uprising there in a few days."

"And what's that to do with him?" he eyed her suspiciously. "Don't tell me he's involved in it? Does the Dowager Queen know about it? The Council?"

"Of course Sandy isn't involved in the uprising. I don't know if the Dowager Queen or anyone in the Council knows about it.

If anything, he's riding there to find out what's happening. We must go after him, don't you see? Warn him."

"Who is we?" he said. His expression was growing thundery. "You're going nowhere but back home to Glen Strae where you'll be safe." He raised his brows. "I hope you've packed and are ready to go?"

"No," she said sharply. "I'm going to ride to Dundee. I can't even think of travelling home while I know that Sandy could be riding unsuspecting towards a dangerous mob."

"Then tell Lady Erskine. She'll ensure the Council and the Dowager Queen are informed and take action. They should be told immediately, in any case."

She looked at Alisdair and tried to suppress her frustration. She knew his reasoning made sense, and it was the best action to take, if not for the fact that Morag knew who Sandy was and that his identity and whatever he was tasked with in Dundee might be known only to the Dowager Queen and maybe one or two others. That any kind of interference might spoil what he'd intended to do. She dithered, trying to decide what action to take for the best.

"If we tell them about the uprising they will want to know how it is that I know," she said finally. "I can't risk that, for they may think that I'm involved in some way."

He gave her a sceptical look. "And are you? Just how is it you came by that information?"

She bit her lip. "I overheard it."

He raised his brow. "How?"

She sighed. "Look it's nothing. I was helping out Sandy. He… sometimes overhears things during his gaming and entertaining and in this case that's what happened to me. I was at one of these entertainments and I couldn't help but hear it discussed."

"At an entertainment? And when was that? Because you had no concern for Munro's safety earlier today."

"Yes, I mean no. The fact is that I heard it and then just now someone said something to me that made me understand the meaning of the conversation at the entertainment." She cursed herself inwardly, knowing she'd made a mess of the explanation in her anxiety to convince Alisdair of the need to act immediately.

"Alisdair, can we just leave the detailed discussion until later? We have to go now. The longer we delay, the harder it will be to catch up to Sandy."

"Morag, this is madness and you well know it," he said slipping into Gaelic. He cursed.

"Don't call me a stubborn pig," she said tartly.

"I will if you act like one."

"For once in your life, Alisdair, will you act like the Highlander you are? Grab up your sword and let us be off?"

"If I were to 'act the Highlander', as you put it, I wouldn't do it with you in tow."

"Oh, you know I fight just as well as you. Better, in fact."

He uttered another Gaelic curse. "I don't know anything of the sort."

"You know that I have been reiving for years and that's why I was sent here. So stop your babbling and let's set off. We can get Bridie, load our bags and leave her at Dundoon, with Mungo and Liam. She's a good rider when it's needed so she'll not slow us down before then."

He sighed loudly. "You seem intent on this, then."

"Yes. I'm intent. If you take leave of the Dowager Queen for us both, I'll find Bridie. We'll get the baggage and join you outside."

He nodded and left her. She watched him anxiously, hoping that he wasn't just bluffing and would refuse to go anywhere but on to Glen Strae once they reached Dundoon. After he'd disappeared from sight she took a deep breath. She still had to get those letters and the name of the contact. She scanned the room, hoping that John Dunbar hadn't left. He'd said he would give them to her tonight. If he couldn't do it now, then she could do nothing about it. That was one scheme she would have to abandon.

~

"My lady. So soon we meet again. I am a fortunate man."

John Dunbar bowed over Morag's hand, a puzzled look on his face. She'd managed to unearth him outside, in the inner close talking with some other courtiers. She'd cast her eyes over them before joining him, but they were only vaguely familiar to her and she couldn't tell if they were part of his little band of spies or just innocent acquaintances.

"My lord, I am sorry to trouble you so soon," she said demurely. "But I fear I must take my leave of court immediately and since you were so kind in your attentions, I wanted to be sure to bid you farewell."

He held her hand tightly, the surprise flashing across his face. "So soon? Sad news indeed."

He turned the other men. "If you will excuse us, I must pay all the courtesies necessary to Lady Morag and to ensure they are conveyed to her family as well."

He bowed to them and escorted Morag away from the group until they were out of earshot. "This isn't what we planned. What has happened?"

She sighed. "My brother has decided we must leave right away. He's determined to get away before nightfall. I had hoped to stall him, but he's refused. Will you be able to get the letters to me now?"

He stood silently slapping the glove he'd been holding against his hand. "If it can be managed, I'll have the letters secreted in your baggage. The contact will be in Dundoon, staying at the inn." He gave her a description of the man and told her the phrase she must utter first, to signal that she was the envoy carrying the letters. He had her repeat it and then nodded when she'd done that to his satisfaction.

"So, I must bid you farewell, now, my sweet," he said lightly. He kissed her hand as Morag muttered a response. With a smile he gave a quick bow and left her. She watched his retreating figure for a moment before she turned and hurried off to her chamber. She must catch Bridie before her baggage was packed. She needed to retrieve some clothes before the baggage was removed from her chamber and loaded on the horses.

Morag was glad to be taking action. She just hoped it wasn't too late. Dundee was three days' ride if the weather and roads were good. Sandy already had nearly a day's start on them. Could she convince Alisdair to ride at least some part of the night? It wouldn't be easy, and most likely she would fail, but she would do her best. Sandy was all that mattered. She bit her lip. For all his protests about his suitability for her hand, she knew there was no one more fitting than he was. She just needed to show him. Somehow.

CHAPTER 24

*M*orag made her way across the outer close, a sack clutched in her hand. She'd explained to Bridie her intentions to ride out after Sandy with as little detail as possible. After much effort at persuasion, Bridie had convinced her to change into a riding dress rather than her intended choice of trews, shirt and doublet. Those she now had in the sack and was going to tie them around the pommel of her saddle so she had easy access to them. She would change quickly once they reached Dundoon. Her sack also contained her ballock dagger, not quite as good as her sword, but better than just the *sgian dhu* strapped to her calf. For now she would have to rely on that and Alisdair's swordsmanship should they need it before they reached the town.

She made her way around the small group of men clustered together unloading a few carts filled with vats. She could see Alisdair with the horses just beyond, as well as the servants loading her small kist and other baggage on the spare pony. For a moment she spared a pang for Thunder, who would have carried her swiftly to her destiny. Her old mare would just have to do.

A servant stood beside her mare, fiddling with the ties of a sack that was strapped to the horse. She couldn't make out what he was doing exactly, but she had a good idea. Bridie caught up with her at that moment and tugged at her sack.

"Shall I strap that tae your horse for ye?" she asked.

Morag tightened her grip on the sack and forced a smile. "Nay, I'll do it. I can secure it better from atop the horse."

It was a lie and they both knew it, but Bridie just shrugged and started to move ahead of her. Morag held her back on impulse, determined to give the man at her horse as much time as necessary. She glanced at Alisdair, his gaze catching sight of her and then moving towards her horse.

She raised her hand to Alisdair to attract his attention. "On second thought," she said to Bridie, "can ye take the sack tae Alisdair and ask him if he'll carry it for me? He'll have more room than I will with all my skirts."

Bridie laughed. "I can of course."

By the time Morag arrived at her mare and greeted her brother, the man was gone and the bag safely secured. Alisdair moved over towards her and laid a hand on the bag tied to her mare.

"That man seemed intent on securing that sack to your mare," he said in Gaelic. "Is there anything important in it?"

He started to open it and Morag resisted the urge to tug his hand away.

She shook her head and tried to remain calm. "It's only a few personal items that I might need quickly on the way. Women's troubles."

His hand stilled and he flushed. "Oh. Well. You would of course want that by your side."

He turned away and moved to the pack pony to check the baggage there. Morag stifled a giggle. There were occasions when having monthly courses, curse that they were, could prove useful. They were rare though.

"Women's troubles?" said Bridie softly at her elbow.

Morag shrugged. Bridie knew it instantly for the lie it was, since she dressed Morag every day and dealt with any rags that her monthly courses required.

"He's too nosey by half," said Morag she said in a low voice. "There is no cause for him to know all about my personal things or what I choose to carry by my side."

Bridie giggled. "Oh I know how nosey brothers can be."

Bridie cleared her face as Alisdair came back over to them. "Shall I give you both a boost up?" he asked.

"Thanks," said Morag. "Do Bridie first. I'll just check the halter on my horse a moment."

Bridie moved off with Alisdair to her saddled pony. With the two of them engaged, Morag felt the sack that was tied to her mount. She could feel some cloth and something heavy, but she also thought she could detect the crackle of paper. There was no time to untie the sack. She could now only assume the letters were there. And hope that no one else would be curious enough to discover them.

MORAG STILLED the foot she'd been tapping. Her impatience was hard to contain, and even easier to see, dressed as she was in her trews and doublet. Alisdair was busy giving Liam last minute instructions before the two of them set off. Bridie was safely installed in the small inn where Liam was staying, the baggage unloaded and placed in Bridie's room that she was sharing with another maidservant traveling with a household. Morag and Alisdair could be away for up to six days or more, if things didn't go smoothly. But Morag hoped that there wouldn't be any problems. She was counting on it.

Morag glanced out the window onto the street below. People walked by, some with a sense of urgency, others more leisurely, the drab colours and threadbare state of some of them marking them for either servants or farmworkers. The bright flashes of colour of a few trews and shawls that sprinkled the tradesmen or their wives made up the other passers-by. The crowd was thinning from earlier, as the evening hours approached. Morag was grateful that the light had held so far.

Suddenly, a man stopped under her window and glanced up at her. Startled, she pulled back. It was best she didn't let anyone see her without her bonnet and with her braid down. She edged forward, hoping that the man had gone, but he still stood there and his eyes locked on hers. She pulled back again. Why was he staring still? She recalled the description John Dunbar had given her of the contact for the letters. John had said that he would find her, rather than risk her trying to seek him. Was this the man? At this range it was hard to tell. But did it matter? She would be away soon and he would be left behind, still trying to seek her out. Would she dare to confirm it? Perhaps there was an innocent reason for the man to stare up at her window.

"Are you ready now, sister?" her brother asked in Gaelic.

Morag whipped around to face Alisdair and stared blankly at him. "I am. But I might just need to see to myself a moment. Just to be sure. I'll meet you at the horses."

Alisdair glanced meaningfully across to Liam, who returned an innocent look. "Fine, we'll leave you to it, then."

The two left and Morag allowed a small bit of relief to wash over her, before speaking to Bridie.

"Don't look out but there's a man below staring up at the window. He's intent on harming our chances to help Sandy. I need you to go down and distract him so I can leave here without him seeing. But you must not allow him up to this room. Will you do that?"

Bridie grinned. "Of course. And if he's handsome enough I might even give him a promise."

Morag shook her head. "Don't promise him a thing. He'll only have you caught to do his bidding."

Bridie shrugged. "Of course." She took Morag's hand and squeezed it. "Safe journey, mistress."

"Thanks. I hope so." Morag squeezed back.

She watched Bridie leave, then snatched up her ballock dagger and bonnet, placing the bonnet on her head, tucking her braid inside it. She looked at the sack. On impulse, she caught it up. It would be safer with her, she decided. That man might decide to search the room if she didn't show soon enough. A few moments later she risked another glance out of the window and saw Bridie was busy with the man, her arm through his so that she turned him away, her other hand pointing down the road.

Morag smiled. Perfect. She strode to the door and opened it. She was as ready as she could ever be. She only hoped that any further problems that might arise on the journey could be solved so successfully.

MORAG SQUINTED UP AHEAD and could make out the faint light of dawn over the horizon. They'd ridden all night, but had stayed on the road, not wanting to risk injuring the horses on cross country scrambles. She was tired and sore, but still determined to carry on. They'd stopped a few times to rest and water the horses, which gave her time to ease her limbs and muscles, but it didn't quell the sense of urgency that drove her on. As if detecting it, Alisdair had said little and pressed on, never questioning the wisdom behind the urgency. That had surprised her and stirred a deep well of gratitude towards him.

"We should stop now," he said. "Find some water and rest the horses. There's enough light to find our way."

They led their horses off the track towards a stream they could hear trickling. Morag eased her tired limbs and took a moment to close her eyes. Around her, from across the stream the sounds of waking birds and other forest creatures came alive to join the soothing flow of the water. She took a deep breath, willing the sounds to relax her, to help her let go of the anxiety that had gripped her since she'd talked to John Dunbar.

When the horses had drunk their fill, the two ambled back to the track, Alisdair leading.

After a few moments he broke the silence. "If we don't meet up with him soon, we'll have to take a longer break at the next village or town to get something to eat and to rest the horses more, or see if we can get fresh ones. Failing that, we'll find a farmhouse."

"I suppose you're right," said Morag, reluctance in her tone.

"If we don't do that, one or both of the horses may fall lame, or worse. And we're no good to ourselves riding on without a thing in our bellies."

"I heard what you said, and I agreed," Morag said tartly. "We'll stop at the next opportunity."

They mounted their horses and rode on a short ways until Morag halted.

"What?" said Alisdair impatiently. He brought his horse up and turned it to face her.

"Shhh. I think I hear something. Hoof beats."

She slowly reached for her ballock dagger at her side and drew it out. Alisdair turned the horse forward.

"We should get off the road," he said.

"Nay, there's no time. And no real cover nearby."

"It could be a group of hunters, or an innocent party. Put the ballock dagger away."

The horses and their riders came into view. Soldiers. Six of them.

"Put the ballock dagger away, Morag," said Alisdair firmly. "We can brazen it out. After all, we're no real threat. Let me do the talking."

Morag frowned as the soldiers' markings became clearer. "English soldiers," said Morag darkly.

"You're right," said Alisdair, darkly. He straightened and drew his sword.

He urged his horse onward. Morag followed, snorting inwardly at Alisdair's sudden aggressiveness. But she couldn't fault it. Best to be on the offensive. Go at them charging, rather than wait to be slaughtered without a question asked. Such action was almost guaranteed from English soldiers, who had no right or reason to be this side of the border. Was the new English Queen exploring some possible invasion? Taking advantage of the uprising?

Anger rose up inside Morag and as she rode towards the small band of six solders she slipped the small targe that she'd tied to her saddle back at Dundoon. When she reached the soldiers she let loose a war cry, Alisdair echoing her call. She swung her sword against the first rider. Filled with rage, she fought madly, shoving and thrusting her way through the group and smiling when her sword bit home. She fought on, swinging, disregarding the tiredness that slowly crept on her and her sword slowed only slightly. Then, without immediately understanding what had happened, something sliced her side. A sword, she thought briefly. She fought on and ignored the pain, adrenaline carrying her forward, until suddenly her vision blurred and dizziness seized her. In the distance she could hear her brother's roar of anger and someone else shout.

She turned and struggled to clear her vision, fighting against the dizziness. She made out a blond head and a sword flashing in the rising sun. Sandy. She blinked again, uncertain if it was a hallucination. Was he here? Was the sword about to fall on him? She opened her mouth in warning, but her vision clouded over and she was falling until everything went dark.

"Morag, *mo cridhe*," said a voice in Gaelic

A searing pain seized Morag and she moaned. She tried to press her hand to her side to help her manage the pain, but someone stopped her.

"Don't touch it, *a stor*, I've only just bandaged it. You don't want to make it worse."

Morag's heart caught at the sound of the familiar voice. Was it a dream? She forced her eyes open, waited for her sight to clear, until she could see the beloved features in front of her.

"You're alive," she whispered. She smiled and another stab of pain seized her.

"Shhh, don't stir. Don't even try to say a word. You must rest. You've been sorely wounded and I wouldn't have you make it worse."

Sandy patted her arm and gave her a reassuring smile.

She shook her head. She knew she must speak. There was no help for it. She had to tell him. Warn him about the danger. She licked her lips.

"Sandy, you must hark at what I'm to tell you," she said in a hoarse voice. "It's important."

"Shhh. I'm sure it will keep, *a stor*."

She shook her head. "It canna wait. John Dunbar. You were right. He's supporting the uprising. They are planning something in Dundee."

He placed a finger on her lips. "I know *a cailin*. Didn't you realise that's why I was going there? You seemed to, no matter what I said to counter it. In any case I saw the English soldiers and decided to follow them to find out what they were up to." He frowned. "Scouting around to see if the uprising will take hold, I'll be bound. But they won't be reporting back to their mistress."

"They're all dead?" she asked.

"Thanks to you and your brother. I came along and only tidied up what you'd both had done."

She started to lift her head to take in her surroundings but he pressed her back down.

"Where are we? Where's Alisdair?"

"Don't worry about that. We're safe now in a little copse a ways off the track. Alisdair has gone to find a cart from a farmhouse I'd seen, so we can take you back there until you're well enough tae travel."

"I'll be grand," she said. "Just give me a wee while and I should be able to mount my horse."

"You won't be doing anything of the sort," said Sandy. "You're badly injured, you wee dolt. And what were you doing haring off on such a thing? You could have been killed."

His brow was creased with concern and his eyes were filled with worry. She smiled at him, drinking in his face, his concern. Her heart swelled.

"I wanted to warn you of the danger. I know the risks, but I'm good with the sword. You saw yourself."

"And my heart nearly failed at the sight of it. When that great Sassenach lummox sliced you in the side with his sword I wanted to cut off his bollocks and disembowel him in one strike."

She giggled. "I'm sure you would have, if that were at all possible."

"Hmmph, well, he'll not be lifting his sword in this country or any other country again."

"Well I can't say I'm unhappy about that," she said and smiled.

He studied her. "You can't go haring in to battle like that again, *a stor*. Promise me you won't, for my heart canna take it."

"It's a hard promise to make," she said softly. "All I can say is that I will try to do as you ask."

He sighed and smiled slightly. "I suppose that's the best I can hope for. I would have ye safe. As I'm certain would your brothers and your father." He raised her hand and kissed it. "Now rest. It may be a while longer before Alisdair makes it back."

Morag closed her eyes, suddenly tired, the kiss lingering on her hand, content enough for now.

CHAPTER 25

*I*t was the sound of voices that brought her back to consciousness. She opened her eyes and saw Alisdair, his brow furrowed. His tone was argumentative.

"It's too risky," he said.

"And you would propose we wait here?" said Sandy in a reasonable voice. "For what? Until a cart could happen along? And where would it take her?"

"We can wait for the farmer's return. The woman said he would only be gone a day or two."

"But that's too long, don't see that? We must get her to a place where I can tend her wound properly."

"But she's not fit to ride, and ye can't be sure that she wouldn't come to harm riding with one of us."

"We have no choice, lad."

Sandy's tone was firm, authoritative. And perhaps it was that tone, or his air of quiet assurance, but Alisdair conceded with a nod and began to gather up their things. Sandy, noticing Morag, gave her a smile and came over and knelt beside her.

"Ah, you're awake *a stor*," he said softly. "Do ye feel up to a ride? It's not very far, I promise."

"I am," she said, her voice barely a whisper.

"You're a braw lassie," he said and kissed her on the forehead.

He rose from her side and with Alisdair began to saddle the horses. Her brother gave her dubious looks, until finally, when he could contain himself no longer, he went over to her.

"Are you certain, Morag? You don't want to stop here until we can fetch a wagon?"

She mustered a reassuring smile and shook her head. "We can't stop here. I'll be fine. I'm just a wee bit tired and hungry. Once we're at the farmhouse and I have something to eat I'll be right as rain."

He sighed and nodded. "Well, if you're certain." He moved back over to the horses with a sidelong glance at Sandy, who just grinned at him and shook his head.

When all the preparations were complete, Sandy mounted and held out his arms. "Lift her up carefully tae me."

Alisdair gave him a stubborn look. "I'll carry her on my horse. You can dismount and hand her to me. She's my sister."

Sandy heaved a sigh and gave him a severe look. "Alisdair, I won't argue with you. Just do as I say and hand her up to me. Carefully."

Whether it was his look or his tone, Alisdair ceased his efforts and silently moved over to Morag. With painstaking care he gathered her up and handed her to Sandy. Morag winced as a sharp pain shot through her side, but she managed to suppress any sound. Sandy's arms came around her and he pulled her up against him, tucking her wounded side out so that he wouldn't jostle it with his body. He wrapped his cloak around her, pulling it under her chin as though she were a babe.

"Are you comfortable?" he asked, smiling down at her.

She nodded and nestled into him a little more. If not for her wound, she would revel more in this opportunity to get this close to Sandy, enjoy the feel of his arms around her. She could sense his breath stirring her hair. Even through his jerkin she could feel his firmly muscled chest and stomach and then a thought struck her. She giggled.

"What's so amusing?" he asked.

"I was just thinking what it would be like tae be here on the horse with you and your big fat belly in the way."

He snorted lightly. "Well, a few days with you and any man would lose his belly and his mind."

She laughed but then looked up into his face, suddenly serious. "Have you lost your mind, then?"

He laughed. "You have any doubt? You've led me on a right merry dance,"

He clicked his tongue and urged his horse on. Alisdair went behind them, leading Morag's horse. They travelled slowly, allowing for Morag's injury and the need to limit the jostling as much as possible.

Eventually, they reached the farmhouse. It was generous to call it such, with its one room and barely a byre leaning against it, though a small stone shed just behind that probably housed the horse and cart that were somewhere with the farmer. At the sound of their approach the farmer's wife had emerged from the house, a youth close behind. He was presumably her oldest son, by the look of him. He moved forward and greeted the three of them as they pulled up in front of the house. His accent broad and local, Morag had to struggle to understand his words of welcome. Sandy answered him, seemingly understanding his strangled speech with ease.

With the greetings exchanged and arrangements made, they began to dismount. There had been no small amount of argument about who was to take the farmhouse or the shed, until the farmer's son finally conceded that Sandy's group would be fine in the shed. Alisdair had shot Sandy enough black looks to leave no doubt that he'd sided with the farmer's son over where the best place for them to stay and tend Morag. But Sandy had prevailed.

Sandy handed Morag down to Alisdair, before dismounting

himself. Morag insisted she was well enough to walk the short distance to the shed. She batted both Sandy's and Alisdair's hands away when they tried to assist her and she walked gingerly towards her destination, her determination evident in every step she took. When she arrived there Sandy was at her side, directing Alisdair in curt tones on the proper placement of a blanket and other items the farmer's wife had hurriedly gathered for their comfort.

When Morag had been safely arranged on a blanket topped pallet of straw and the farmer's wife gone to fetch them some food, Alisdair rounded on Sandy.

"Why did you insist on this stinking shed? The farmhouse is bad enough, but this!" He waved his arm around in disdain.

Sandy straightened and eyed Alisdair with exaggerated patience. "Oh, young pup. Will you not lower your hackles? It's best for all that we stay here. If anyone should come looking for us it would be easier to hide if we're here – and besides, the farmer's bairns would be less likely to betray us by accident or remember what we look like."

Alisdair's angry face eased a bit and eventually he nodded. "Oh, very well. I suppose you know what you're doing."

Sandy smiled sardonically. "That's very kind of you."

"Oh, Alisdair," said Morag impatiently. "Just let Sandy manage things. He's had a lifetime's worth of experience compared to you."

"I'm only trying to look after you," said Alisdair hotly.

Morag softened. "You are. I'm sorry I spoke so."

Alisdair nodded and looked away. "I'll just go see to the horses, if you want to tend the wound."

He left the shed and Morag could hear the sound of his boots on the stone slabs outside the shed. She looked up at Sandy, who was crouched a small distance away, sorting through the bandages and the herbal compound the farmer's wife had given him and was now laid out on a cloth. She watched him, the light shining on his face, carving the planes of his cheeks, his jawline in relief, and her heart ached. She could see the tiredness etched on his face, but it did nothing to dispel his handsome features. As if feeling her eyes on him, he looked up at that moment and caught her gaze.

"Is your wound paining you?"

She shook her head, feeling herself flushing.

Sandy finished his preparations and came to kneel beside her. With deft, sensitive movements he unlaced her leather jerkin and lifted the blood stained shirt just enough to reveal her bandaged side. Blood stained the bandage, but it wasn't soaked and it didn't appear fresh. Carefully, he pulled the bandage away and examined it. His head blocked her view so she couldn't quite see its condition.

"It looks clean. I might give it a stitch or two to be certain it closes."

His tone was neutral, so Morag couldn't tell if he just didn't want to alarm her, or if it was really as he'd said.

She let out a little breath. "Whatever you think for the best."

He looked up and gave her a reassuring smile. Without further comment he began his ministrations. When it came time for the stitching, she was surprised when he pulled out a small needle and thread from his own things. Seeing her surprise, he gave her a wry smile.

"It's good to be prepared wherever I go."

She forced a smile and nodded. She knew exactly what he was implying with that statement. He was often engaged in dangerous work, so much so that the risk of injury was part of every journey, every action. She looked away towards the stone wall, as much for the pain it caused her at that thought as for the anticipation of the pain of the sewing of her skin.

He reached among his things and pulled out a small flagon and offered it to her.

"Drink this," he said in a firm voice. "It will help with the pain."

She eyed the flagon warily and took a sip. Her mouth and throat felt afire as she swallowed the potent drink.

He took up the needle and began his work. She tried to distract herself with thoughts of Alisdair. What was taking him so long? Was there some trouble that had kept him? He'd only had to remove their baggage. The farmer's son had offered to rub the horses down in trade for conceding the shed instead of the house for their use. And then she remembered. The bag.

"Sandy," she said in an urgent tone. She turned to look at him and winced under the large stab of pain that assaulted her. "Oww," she said involuntarily pulling away.

"Keep still and don't talk," said Sandy a little tersely, "and it won't hurt as much."

"But I must tell you. It's important. You have to retrieve the bag that was tied to my saddle. It's important you do it before Alisdair looks inside."

He stopped his sewing and looked up at her. "Why?"

"There's no time to explain. Just do as I ask, please," she added in a pleading tone.

"Tell me now, if you want me to fetch the sack."

She gave an impatient sigh. "Fine. The sack contains letters John Dunbar asked me to deliver to some contact in Dundoon."

Anger flashed across his face. "John Dunbar? You were doing the bidding of John Dunbar?" His voice had taken on a deadly quality.

"Well I'm not doing his bidding, of course. I just said I would. So he wouldn't get someone else to do it."

"And just what is contained in those letters?" he said, his eyes narrowed.

"I didn't have the time to look, but he inferred they concerned enlisting the English to help with the uprising."

"And what were you proposing to do with the letters, and

what were you going to say to John Dunbar when he asks you if you'd delivered them?"

"I was going to get rid of them somehow. I just haven't had the time yet," she said hotly. "As for John Dunbar..."she gave a shrug. "I was going to say that I had delivered them."

He snorted. "And that was your plan?" He shook his head. "Who was your contact?"

She took a deep breath and thought a moment, eventually telling him and the phrase to give him.

"And was he expecting you specifically?"

She shook her head. "I think so. He said the man would seek me out."

Sandy gave her thoughtful look. "He did, did he? Well there's no help for it."

He looked down at her side and finished off the stitches with a few swift movements that had her wincing and suppressing cries of pain. With a few swift moves he'd put the herbal paste on top of the wound and placed a fresh bandage on it. He secured it with a strip of linen, wrapping it around Morag's waist, pulling her forward so he could run it around the back of her. Though the movement was careful, it held little affection. It was all Morag could do not to cry. She steeled herself against the feelings.

"I'm sorry if my actions displeased you, that my efforts to ensure your safety caused you such trouble. But you needn't worry. I will take care of it. You must tend to your own affairs. I have no doubt you must report back. Don't let me trouble you further. Go. Alisdair will see me safely back to Dundoon."

He finished securing the bandage, pulled down her shirt and tied her jerkin, tugging it into place with a firm pull. Only then did he look up at her and speak.

"You'll not go back to the castle. It's too dangerous. You'll go on to Dundoon as you told Alisdair you would, collect Bridie and your ghillies."

She stared at him, her emotions a mixture of anger, annoyance and other things that she didn't want to examine.

"It's not for you to say what I will or won't do," she said with icy coolness. "As I said, you may go on your way and leave me to my brother."

Alisdair entered, a tray of food in his hand, her sack slung over his shoulder. "What's this about leaving?" He set the tray on the floor and swung the sack from his shoulder. "I brought in your sack. I thought you might need it...to tend to your... women's troubles," he said looking at Morag. "The lad is bringing the rest of our things."

He started to hand the sack over to Morag but Sandy intercepted it.

"I'll take that," he said. He looked at Alisdair. "I've stitched her up and tended the wound. There's a fresh bandage on it which should last until ye get tae Dundoon, where Bridie can tend it. In the meantime, see that's she's fed and well rested before ye resume your journey. Maybe a day or so."

Alisdair gave him a puzzled look. "Why are you taking the sack? You haven't any women's troubles. What would you be needing it for?"

Sandy glanced at Morag a sardonic look on his face. "Not the kind you mean, lad. But get your sister to explain her mistake."

"You're not going with us?"

He shook his head. "Change of plan. I have things I must see to." He glanced at Morag again. "Make sure that she doesn't get in to any more scrapes, will you?"

Alisdair snorted. "As if I can prevent her."

Sandy gave him a wry smile and nodded. "How well I know that. Do the best you can." He gave Alisdair a curt bow, taking his leave as if the circumstances were some ordinary call at a house. He turned to Morag, an amused look on his face. "My lady Morag. Do your best to stay out of trouble."

Morag blinked, hardly believing that he could leave her in this manner. "Where are you going?" she dared to ask.

"As you say, I have to report back. They'll be waiting for me." He gave her a sweeping bow. "Farewell."

She started to speak, but something held her back. Was it pride? Was it the light tone of his voice or the amusement in his expression? She just nodded dumbly and watched him go.

~

"THERE IS NO USE ARGUING. I'm going to Stirling and that's the end of it. You may do what you like."

"But you promised me you'd go on after we found Sandy and warned him," said Alisdair. "That's done and you're wounded. Why on earth would you go back to Stirling?"

They'd been arguing all morning while she slowly gathered up her ballock dagger and tidied her clothes. He'd followed her out to the horses, where the farmer's son greeted them. He'd contradicted her request that the son help her saddle the horses. She was too stiff and sore to do it herself, but she was certain that once on the horse, she would be well enough to make the journey back to Stirling. They could stop at Dundoon, where she could change and collect Bridie. From there it was on to the castle. She knew the journey would take a few days, but it was better than waiting here. She had to get to the castle, she had to know if Sandy had gone back there to report. Her instinct told her differently.

"Things have changed," she said. "I have to go to the castle, now. I need to know that Sandy returned." Fortunately, in the confusion of Sandy's departure, Alisdair had forgotten to question her about the sack's contents. He had little idea about how serious things might be. What Sandy might have been compelled to do.

"But your wound! You canna show up at the castle wounded. How would ye explain it?"

She shrugged. "No one will know. Bridie will help."

He gave her a sceptical look. "I can't change your mind?"

She gave him a serious look and shook her head. "I'm determined to go. You can come along, or go your own way."

He looked at her angrily. "As if I'd do that." He gave a heavy sigh. "Very well. But do you promise me that once you discover if Sandy has returned, you'll go to Glen Strae as you promised you would before?"

She studied him and saw the worry in his face, his eyes suddenly looking older than his seventeen years. She softened. "I will my dear brother. I will."

CHAPTER 26

She eyed the castle as they approached, looking for some sign of Sandy's presence, though she knew it was a ridiculous notion that he might be visible. Her side ached from the long journey, but she refrained from touching the bandage. She knew full well that Alisdair would berate her at the very least for pressing on instead of halting in Dundoon for a few nights as he'd wanted. As it was, both he and Bridie kept casting worried glances at her.

They'd reached Dundoon to find Bridie fretting and bickering with Liam. At the sight of Morag and Alisdair, Bridie had fussed so much Morag was forced to speak to her. The fussing had revived as soon as Bridie saw Morag's wound. It was some while before they had a moment's privacy and Morag could quiz Bridie about the suspicious man and Sandy. The conversation had resulted in little, except that the man had disappeared after a day or so, though not without pestering Bridie a few times. As for Sandy, she'd seen no trace of him.

Morag didn't know whether to be relieved or worried at the news. The next few hours though, would provide clarity on that score. She hoped Sandy would be here, in the castle, safely ensconced in a game of cards, or some such amusement, his belly in place and his beard and hair oiled. She'd even allow Barbara's arms around him, if that's what it took.

The party rode through the gates and on to the outer close. Morag looked across at Alisdair whose face was set. She hoped he would keep to the tale they'd agreed upon for the reason they were returning. He'd wanted to say it was because they were concerned about the uprising, but she'd disagreed. Such a tale would lead to close questioning and she didn't think they would stand up to close questioning. One of them was bound to say something contradictory. Alisdair scoffed at that and said they would probably only question him. She argued that it was best to say something simple. Something like she'd left a piece of jewellery behind and it was very dear to her. He'd snorted at that, but eventually had conceded.

But now, as some of the courtiers came into sight, she wondered at the wisdom of something so simple. Perhaps it was too simple? She straightened and decided she would convey it with bravado. That alone would convince them.

After a few less than curious glances the courtiers turned to their own affairs and Morag and her small group rode by into the inner close. Once they'd dismounted and handed over their horses with instructions for their baggage to the stablemen, the group headed into the castle. She tried to calm her nerves as the steward met them at the door. His face marked surprise, but he said nothing as Alisdair gave him a curt nod and inquired if their previous accommodations were still free. It was barely a moment's pause before he nodded. No explanations needed for the steward. That was for Lord and Lady Erskine and Mistress Cunningham.

The steward ushered them through the corridors and summoned a groomsman to show Alisdair to his room and a maidservant for Morag. Bridie left to see to the safe disposal of their things and to arrange for bowls of water and soap to refresh themselves after the journey.

Morag managed to reach her room without encountering Mistress Cunningham, but she knew it was only a matter of time before the woman would descend upon her. In the meantime, she could at least relieve one pressing worry.

"Do ye ken if my Lord Munro has returned?" she asked the maidservant.

The maidservant looked at her shyly and shook her head. "I dinna ken, my lady. I havena heard. Some riders came in this day before ye. Perhaps he was among them?"

"Perhaps," said Morag lightly.

Rationalisations streamed through her mind. There were many reasons why this maidservant wouldn't know if Sandy was in the castle and for some reason she held on to them, even though in her heart of hearts she knew he wasn't here.

She reached the room and the maidservant left her there to stare out of the window, wondering what she would do. How long could she wait here for Sandy to return? Alisdair would object and she would need to find reasons for him to agree to stay. She refused to consider the possibility that Sandy wouldn't return.

The door opened with considerable energy and Barbara came tumbling in, nearly breathless, Jean close behind.

"I heard you'd returned," she said in French, her voice bubbly and full of interest.

Morag nodded, too startled to say anything as she struggled to gather her wits.

"I suppose you were worried about the uprising," said Jean. She plopped herself on the bed and picked at the coverlet.

Barbara made a scornful sound. "Of course she was." She turned back to Morag, her eyes widening. "It's gathering momentum. They're saying it may even reach us here."

"In the castle?" asked Jean, a touch of hysteria in her voice.

Barbara shrugged. "You never know. These peasants are ruthless. They're mad. And that awful devil Knox is stirring them up to do terrible deeds."

"But surely the Dowager Queen will do something to stop them," said Morag. She made an effort to keep her tone even and calm. She only hoped that Barbara was indulging in her usual fits of dramatics.

"I'm sure she will," said Jean in an uncertain tone.

"Maybe," said Barbara. "We'll see. I did hear she was trying to get her uncle to send over some troops. Perhaps they'll get here in time."

"I'm sure some of our own troops will be here if they're needed," said Morag. "And Lord Erskine will have doubtless have it all arranged."

"And there is the Dowager Queen's own guard," said Jean.

"Yes," said Morag. "I'm sure it will be fine."

"Maybe," said Barbara. "Did you see any evidence of it on your journey? Is that why you returned?"

Morag looked at her, considering if she should change her story. "Well, we did encounter some rumours that had Alisdair concerned," she said, hedging. She sighed. "But I left a piece of jewellery behind, and since it was something to which I was very much attached, we decided it might be just as well to return."

Barbara gave her an odd look. "A piece of jewellery? But where did you leave it? Not here in this chamber, surely."

"Uh, no," said Morag. "No, it was somewhere else. I realised I must have dropped it when I couldn't find it among my things." She forced herself to halt the rambling explanations that were tumbling out of her.

Barbara's eyes suddenly gleamed with delight. "It's that John Dunbar, isn't it. You left it in his chamber and you're afraid it will be discovered. Morag, you devil."

"Oh, Morag!" said Jean. "Tell us all. Were you indeed with him?"

"I, uh, no," said Morag, reddening despite herself. "Not exactly. Well, we…we did have an encounter and I think he may have dislodged a brooch I was wearing. One that was my mother's."

Had that really just come out of her mouth? What more could she have said that would cause her even more embarrassment. What would Alisdair say if he came to hear of this?

"An 'encounter', was it?" said Barbara in a wicked tone. "Just exactly what happened in this encounter?"

"Did you kiss?" said Jean, her eyes sparkling curiously. "What was it like? Did it go further?"

Morag looked from one to the other helplessly. "No, well, he kissed me, yes. But it wasn't like that."

"Oh I wager it was. I saw him ogling you a few times. He seemed very amorous." She made a few leering gestures and Jean broke into peals of laughter.

"He was perhaps overly attentive on occasion, but I assure you nothing too outrageous happened." She looked at Barbara. "Besides, you have far more experience in such things than I. You have a bigger tale to tell about Lord Munro for example."

Barbara's face closed down and she shrugged. "Ah, but that would be telling. And I promised not to."

"He made you promise not to tell anyone?" Morag asked.

She knew better than to believe anything Barbara said about anything, and especially about this particular area, but she couldn't help herself.

"Of course. He said the more mysterious we made it, the more people were to imagine it as something far beyond any dream. That such an approach would benefit us both."

Morag gave her a curious look. It had a ring of truth to it. "Has he spoken of it recently? Has he bedded you since?"

Part of her wished the answer was affirmative, if only to have some relief from the worry. But the other part of her hoped fervently that she would say no. Perhaps an answer that contained a "no, but he's been at court" would be the best of both worlds.

"Well, how could we bed since he hasn't returned from hunting, or whatever it was that prompted him to leave."

"Not too taken with your company, then," said Morag.

She could have stabbed her tongue for letting such words fall out. But Barbara just laughed, clearly glad to have aroused some jealousy.

"Ooh, don't you worry, little Morag," said Barbara. "Your handsome courtier John Dunbar is still here. He was only asking for you a little while ago, after he heard that you'd returned. I told him I would let you know when I saw you next."

Morag stilled at her words, all thoughts fled from her mind. It took a few moments before she was able to force a smile and proffer her thanks for the message. Bridie entered a little while later and that broke up the group, Barbara and Jean to leave and see what other mischief they could stir elsewhere and Morag to allow Bridie's ministrations to her wound. It seemed as though the ministrations took much less time than they should, because all too soon she was leaving the chamber and on her way to the Dowager Queen's apartments. She only hoped that the Dowager Queen had decided not to hold court in her receiving chamber, but limit it only to her ladies-in-waiting in the more private chambers. She really didn't want to encounter John Dunbar.

HER STRATEGY HAD MADE sense at the time. Go along the outside walkway to the Prince's Tower to the Dowager Queen's apartments. That way she would avoid most people and any chance encounter. Once inside the rooms, she would be in public view and there was little John Dunbar could do to her then.

She had mounted the stairs up to the walkway carefully, listening for any tell-tale footsteps. Once she'd reached the walkway she breathed a little easier, she made her way along the path until a hand grabbed her arm and spun her around. John Dunbar.

She opened her mouth to exclaim but nothing came out.

"My sweet little spy," said Dunbar. "And just where have you been?"

She blinked. "What do you mean?"

"I mean, where are the letters I gave you? What did you do with them?"

She edged back a little, but he closed the distance on them. "I…nothing. I gave them to him as you asked."

He raised his brow. "Did you now? And he said nothing to you in return?"

She stared in his cold eyes and managed to shake her head. "No. Should he have?"

He pushed her up against the stone wall, his arm across her neck. The force of his movement evoked a searing pain across her side where the wound was and she struggled to suppress a cry and the urge to double over.

"Oh yes, he should have said something. If you really gave him the letters. He was to give you a phrase to repeat back to me, if the exchange had gone through. Which it clearly did not. I've heard nothing back from him, or anyone else, to even suggest otherwise."

She stared at him, fear rising inside her. She had no doubt that his intentions were anything but merciful for her betrayal.

"I'm sorry," she said, flinging wildly about for an explanation. "I didn't want to tell you that I let you down. You see he couldn't get me alone to pass the letters to him. My brother wouldn't leave my side." She made the last phrase end in a wail.

He looked at her sceptically. "If that were so, where are the letters now?"

"In my chamber. I'll get them for you if you like."

He shook his head. "You're going nowhere, my sweet." He

263

lifted a curl that had escaped from her snood. "No, I think the time of trifling with you has ended. You know too much and I'm afraid, my little honey pot, I can't trust you any longer."

Morag's eyes widened. She had no doubt about his intentions, she just couldn't believe he would try to kill her here and now. But the eyes and face darkened with murderous intent. She struggled against his grip, but he tightened it, his arm across her throat pressing harder. On sudden impulse she brought up a knee as hard as she could through her bulky skirts and aimed for his groin, pushing aside the wave of nausea and pain from her wound. The effect on her assailant wasn't as painful as she could have hoped for, but he did release his grip long enough that she could stagger away. He grabbed her arm, pulling her back to him, but she still had time to reach under her skirt, her breath coming in pants. She fought the wave of dizziness. She couldn't black out now.

With a deft movement she withdrew the *sgian dhu* from its strap at her calf and brandished it. It wasn't much, but it was better than nothing. All the training from Davey, Rob, and even on a rare occasion Iain, came flooding back to her. She blinked, forcing herself to concentrate amid the screaming pain.

The two of them circled, John still grasping her arm, but staying well out of range otherwise. They continued around, each eyeing the other carefully, looking for the best opportunity to win advantage. And then Morag saw it. The flicker in his expression, the tell-tale sign he was going to make his move and Morag prepared.

It all happened fast, his move, her retaliation and the quick jut and trip that she planned before planting the knife under his ribcage and pushing upwards as hard as she could. She heard the grunt of surprise and the breath expelling quickly before he slumped to the ground.

She stared down at him, too stunned to do anything. She hadn't thought about killing him, exactly. She'd just gone through her usual defensive moves that seemed to have taken on a life of their own until she had taken a life. This life.

It was by no means the first life she'd taken, but all in all there hadn't been many and none so well born, so well connected as John Dunbar. The others had been accidents, taken in the heat of battle during some small clan reiving or clash. What was she to do? Closing her eyes, she pressed her hand to her side, giving into the excruciating pain that took hold for a moment. But that was all she had – a moment. She looked quickly around her, fighting the panic that threatened to overtake her. Should she try and hide the body? How would she even manage that?

After a few moment's consideration she withdrew her *sgian dhu*, wiped it on Dunbar's clothes and replaced it at her calf. With a deep breath she dragged the body into the shadows of the castle walls, breathing heavily, the rush of strength from the fight starting to leave her body. At least no one looking out of the windows would see the body from above. She leaned down and tried to clear her vision and wiped her brow. She was sweating in earnest now. Soon her body would give in and betray her if she wasn't careful. Her first need was to check her wound. There was no more she could do for now here. Anything else would have to wait until she could get Alisdair to help her move the body later, when it was dark. She must pray that no one else would discover it in the meantime.

CHAPTER 27

$\mathcal{C}$olour drained from Alisdair's face as he stared at Morag. "You convinced me, against my better judgement, I hasten to add, to return here to Stirling Castle. I at least thought, if nothing else, we would be safe. But no sooner had you stepped inside the castle and you bring us to this calamitous pass?"

His voice had risen a little at the end of his tirade, filled with suppressed fury. Morag glanced around the chamber, hoping no one had overheard their exchange. As soon as she'd dragged Dunbar's body to the wall, she'd retraced her steps and taken the usual way to the Dowager Queen's chambers. Luckily, she'd seen no one until she'd arrived at the floor of the apartments. Once inside she had sought out Alisdair, who'd only just arrived. She had by-passed meaningful looks and implicit summons from Mistress Cunningham to get to Alisdair's side as soon as possible. She'd decided that Barbara and Jean could do the honours of explaining her return to Mistress Cunningham, if they hadn't already.

Alisdair had noted her alarm and had immediately demanded an explanation. The resulting lecture wasn't unexpected but was hardly helpful.

"Keep your voice down, Alisdair," she said. "I tell you it wasn't my fault. I didn't know he was going to accost me."

"But I don't understand. Why did he accost you?"

She sighed wondering what she could safely tell him. Perhaps it was best he knew everything. "Because he was a spy," she said softly. "And he thought I was helping him. When he discovered I betrayed him, he tried to kill me. Only I got to him first." She tried not to sound smug at her last words. She'd often told Alisdair she could protect herself and now he wouldn't doubt it. A moment later she gave herself a mental reprimand. This was hardly the time for bragging or pride. She'd made a real mess of things, if truth be told.

Alisdair had been studying her in horror. "A spy?" The incredulous tone to his words made her raise her brow. "Are you sure?"

"Of course I'm sure," she snapped. "Would I have risked killing him otherwise?"

Anger flashed in his eyes. "I don't know. I'm finding I know less about you than I thought. Except that it's clear you still get involved in hare brained schemes."

She made an exasperated noise. "Look, Alisdair. I promise I will explain all later. For now, I must ask your help. We have to hide the body somewhere when it gets dark and hope in the meantime that no one discovers it."

He shook his head. "I'll help you, of course. But regardless of whatever else you say, we're leaving here first thing in the morning."

"No," she said sharply, before she could even think. "No, you said we would find out if Sandy was here before we left."

He gestured around the room. "And do you see him here?"

She bit her lip. "No, but—"

"But nothing. No arguments. We're leaving first thing in the morning. Bridie already knows this, so there should be no delay."

She frowned at him. She would say nothing for now, not while she still needed his help.

~

"Did you ask John Dunbar about your piece of jewellery?" asked Barbara.

The innuendo in her tone left Morag in no doubt that she was asking more than if she'd had a discussion about a piece of jewellery.

"No," said Morag in the best breezy tone she could manage. "I haven't seen him yet. Tomorrow I'll search the garden when it's daylight, since that's where it might have dropped."

Barbara arched a brow. "The garden, eh? Perhaps he can help you search...the garden."

Morag sighed. Apparently there was only one thing on Barbara's mind.

They were in their chamber, the evening finished. The Dowager Queen had retired early, worries about the uprising clearly compounding her illness, to leave her tired and depressed. Morag had used that opportunity to excuse herself and return to her chambers. Barbara had followed suit not long after, bored and restless.

"Is there no entertainment you could go to tonight?" Morag asked hopefully.

"No, everyone is either plotting and planning about the uprising, or they are too dispirited to want to bother."

"Oh, what a shame," said Morag.

Barbara shrugged. "It was all getting rather dull, anyway. Anne has left, as have Lords Robert and James. And Lord Munro hasn't returned so...."

She left the sentence hanging but Morag knew full well what she was suggesting. No entertainment in bed either.

Barbara sat on the bed and twiddled a strand of her hair. She puckered her lips and looked over at Morag, as if deciding something. "Perhaps I'll go see what Thomas Maxwell is up to."

Morag looked at her. "Thomas Maxwell?"

Barbara shrugged and yawned. "Why not? He might be worthy of a little entertainment."

Morag gave a small laugh, picturing the stocky, good humoured man. "He might."

Barbara rose off the bed and left with a quick word of farewell. Morag noted she hadn't been asked along, but she wasn't sorry at all. She had other things to do.

She left the chamber, closing the door soundlessly. Carefully, she made her way down the stairs and headed towards the stairs to the walkway. There was no moon tonight, for which Morag was extremely grateful. Someone grabbed her arm and she gave a startled cry. She turned to see her brother at her side, his court clothes changed to darker ones.

"Leave this to me," he said quietly.

"No, it's fine, I'll help you," she said. "You'll need me at least to look out for anyone coming along."

"I don't need your help," he said. "I have someone with me. Return to your chamber. The less you're involved, the better. If someone should discover us, any story I make up is better coming from me than you."

She paused, realising the truth of his words. With a sigh she nodded and turned. It was then she noticed Liam standing a little distance off. Alisdair must have fetched him after he spoke with her. She looked at her brother with a bit more respect at that moment.

"Thank you Alisdair," she said softly. "I'll not forget this."

"See that you don't," he said gruffly. "And the least you can do in return is be ready to leave first thing in the morning."

She nodded, her mind and heart too full to say more. He was right. It was the least she could do.

∼

BACK IN HER chamber she opened her kist and dug inside it. After a few moments she unearthed paper, quill and ink and set it on the small table. She moved the candle closer and settled herself on the stool that was beside it and composed her thoughts. What could she say to Sandy? She had no guarantee that she could even get the letter to him, but she must try. She must find a way to mend whatever needed mending and let him know how she really felt. How else would he know? How else would she know if he felt the same, if even just a little? It was a risk she had to take. Otherwise she would be returning to Glen Strae and would probably never see him again. She couldn't face that. The hope, the possibility that he might come to her there, was the best she could manage, so she had to try. It was better than nothing.

AT THE FIRST sight of the castle it was at once difficult to believe she had ever left it and yet it seemed a lifetime ago when she'd last been here. A small cloud of mist hung in the distant mountains, and the air was filled with the scent of gorse and the promise of summer.

She stopped a moment to admire the view and unbidden tears gathered at the corners of her eyes. She didn't know whether to be thrilled or completely downcast. She'd achieved what she'd wanted when she'd departed. To return unwed and unchastised, ready to pick up her life exactly where she'd left it. What a silly young cub she'd been.

She blinked the tears away and urged her horse further. She knew she wanted only one thing, but it was all in the hands of fate now. There was nothing she could do but hope. It rankled that she could do nothing more.

Alisdair came up beside her, pointing. "Look at yonder ridge. Isn't that Iain there?"

Morag squinted into the distance at the familiar figure. "It is indeed. I suppose someone saw us and let him know?"

Alisdair snorted. "Of course. No one can move about without the whole glen knowing the whole of it."

The group urged their horses on, Liam following closely behind. They'd made steady progress on the way home and only once had they seen any signs of unrest. Morag had been glad of that, for she didn't think her side could bear any more battles for a while yet. It was healing well, albeit it slowly enough with their constant journeying, but at least she hadn't suffered from any fever or other signs of festering. Still, she could feel it when she broke into a short gallop to close the distance between her and Iain.

When they met, Morag was relieved to see the joy on Iain's face. Nothing untoward had happened at least, as she cast her mind through various possibilities. No further killings, her father safe and well – and Abby. Suddenly she thought of her sister-in-law.

"How's Abby?" she asked at once.

She examined his face carefully in the briefest of moments before he answered. If it was possible, his face lit up even more.

"She's well and delivered of a fine and healthy daughter not two days since."

"Oh, Iain, I am so happy and pleased. Congratulations!"

She dismounted from her horse and went over to her brother. He leaned down and accepted her kiss on the cheek and the squeeze on his hand.

Alisdair, just arriving with Bridie and Liam, gave them a puzzled look that broke into a grin. "Abby?"

"A daughter," said Iain. "Fine and healthy, the pair of them."

"And the babe already has you eating out of her hand, I'll wager," said Morag with a laugh.

"If she's only half as wilful as you are, I will have to guard against that," said Iain as he accepted Alisdair's clap on the back.

Alisdair laughed. "You'll have your work cut out for you, then. If you only knew what mischief this one has gotten up to, you would escape immediately and head to the shielings forever more."

Morag gave Alisdair a dark look. "Don't listen to him Iain. He's exaggerating."

Alisdair snorted. "If only it were true."

Sobering, Iain looked from one to another. "Well, that tale will keep for now. Abby's anxious to see you and show you the bairn."

"And Father, he is well?" asked Morag.

"The same," said Iain. "You know well what he's like. Never complains and insists on overseeing everything himself, though you know that his old wounds are causing him great difficulty."

"Aye, I know. Never complains, but always in poor temper," muttered Morag.

Alisdair gave her a sidelong glance but said nothing.

"Come," said Iain. "There's a welcome for you all back at the castle."

MORAG WATCHED Abby nurse her daughter and was surprised to find that among the joy she felt for her sister-in-law, there was a little envy to see her so settled and secure in her marriage with Iain. There was no doubt that he doted on both Abby and his new daughter and the love they shared was as strong as ever. Would she ever have that?

"Have ye a name yet?" asked Morag.

"Aye, well," said Abby, her Scots nearly as thick as Iain's. "There's still some discussion about that. I wanted tae name her after your mother and Arbella, but he wants something fierce like Maeve, the warrior queen, or some Pictish Queen whose name I canna remember."

Morag burst out laughing. "Och, I fear that Iain is having a wheeze. You ken how he likes tae tease, and I've nae doubt this is what he's doing."

Abby frowned and then giggled. "Aye, maybe so. Perhaps I shall let him have his way, say with the name of the Pictish Queen and see what he does."

"Nay, nay. Both names. Let him swallow that. I'd say he would be begging mercy in a trice if ye mention it tae Father as well."

Abby's eyes twinkled. "Och, ye're the devil itself, Morag. It would be worth it tae see the look on Iain's face with his father hearing that."

The two of them burst into laughter again and the baby stirred and stopped suckling for a brief moment, her new born eyes startled wide.

Morag sighed. "She's a bonny wee thing, Abby. Ye're fortunate," she said, unable to help the wistful note in her voice.

Abby looked up at her, concern in her face. "What happened at court?" she asked in a soft voice. "I ken that ye told Iain the basics."

"With much unhelpful input from Alisdair," said Morag darkly.

Abby gave a wry smile. "Aye, but ye ken well that I can see past all of that." She hesitated. "There's more, isn't there. Things that ye didna tell Iain and Alisdair has nae idea about."

Morag looked at her, tears suddenly flooding her eyes. She wiped them away and bit her lip. "Aye, there's more."

Abby waited a moment before speaking. "And there's a man involved?"

Morag nodded.

Abby smiled encouragingly. "This man wouldna by any chance be the Alexander Munro that Alisdair mentioned? The foppish courtier that suddenly seemed very capable when ye met him on the road?"

"He isna a fop," she said in a low voice. "It was a disguise."

Abby studied her and sighed. "Dinna tell me. He's a spy." She frowned down at her daughter. "It's a dangerous life, ye ken."

"Aye," she said stonily.

"And a life that isna fit for marriage, a family."

"Aye."

"And does he return your feelings?'

Morag looked across the room and out the window. "I dinna ken."

"I see."

"Aye, exactly."

"And how did ye leave it with him?"

Morag sniffed. "We quarrelled. He wanted me tae return tae Glen Strae at once and I didna want him tae take matters in tae his own hands." She put her face in her hands. "Och, Abby it all went so wrong. I was worried, ye ken. I didna want him tae endanger himself."

"I'm sure he could see that, Morag. Just as it's plain that he was worrit for your safety."

Morag lifted her head. "Aye, maybe. But it wasna anything more than that."

"How do ye ken that for certain?"

Morag shrugged. "He would have said. He was sending me away. It was his last chance tae tell me before sending me off home for good."

"And there had been nae indication of any feelings towards ye before that?"

She cast her mind back to all the incidents of their encounter, something she'd been doing in detail for the past few days since her arrival here. She looked over at Abby.

"Any stolen kiss? Any affectionate words or gestures?"

Morag blushed, thinking of his kisses and even now she could conjure up how they made her feel.

"He called me 'a stor' and 'mo cridhe' when I was wounded," she said shyly.

Abby studied her carefully. "Was it only endearments that he gave tae ye?"

She shook her head. "Nay," she whispered.

Abby nodded. "There, ye see? I'd say there's a good chance he does feel something toward ye."

Morag snorted. "Aye, something perhaps. But nae anything of note. Nothing that would convince him tae give up spying, I'll wager."

"Does he ken how ye feel at all, do ye think?"

Morag toyed with the edge of her sleeve. "I wrote him a letter and told him before I left Stirling. I dinna ken if he's read it, and if he has, what he thinks of its contents."

"So, ye must then have some patience. Ye'll see in time."

"Patience. I dinna ken if I can bear the waiting, Abby."

"Ye'll have tae. There's nae other choice."

Morag frowned and nodded. What more was there to say? Even if he did have feelings for her, Sandy had to decide if his duty to the Dowager Queen was more important than anything he might want to have with Morag, that's if he even was still alive. But she would know if was dead, she was sure of it. She thought again of the words he'd said about being too experienced and confined to the devil. He had actually chosen already. Chosen and warned her that she wasn't part of his path, his duty.

She put her head once more in her hands, the pain that shot through her heart too severe to allow a breath. After a few moments she forced herself to inhale, to get her heart to beat again. She would get through this. What other choice had she?

CHAPTER 28

Morag jiggled the baby on her knee, careful to support her properly and an excited chortle escaped. She put the child on her lap and buried her face in Arbella's belly and made bubbling noises. An answering squeal made Morag smile.

"Morag!" said Abby, just entering. "I've only just settled her."

"Och, it canna do any harm. Arbella loves it, do ye no my wee thistle?"

Abby shook her head and sighed. "Morag, ye're as restless as a bull and have been for weeks. For months, if truth be told. Ever since ye arrived. Will ye go now and ride out? Rob was only asking after ye the other day, said Davey hasna seen hide nor hair of ye hardly. And ye two used tae be thick as thieves."

Morag frowned. She'd been avoiding Davey, she knew. A sense of guilt? That and the fact she had no idea what to say to him. She wasn't the young naïve girl any longer, the one that pledged a troth so lightly and willingly. But she knew she had to face him sometime. To let him know that things were different now. She was different. And that any binding between them was never real, only a fantasy a young girl imagined.

She steeled herself, stood up and handed Arbella over to Abby. "Ye're right. I should go out. I'll take a ride over tae see Davey. As ye said, it's long overdue."

SHE FOUND him at his croft, his ruddy auburn hair visible from a distance as he emerged through the door, his mother right behind him, peering out. She smiled at the sweet face that broke into a grin and strode forth.

"Mistress Morag. My lady!" he said in Gaelic.

He met her at the small gate and swung it open, grabbing the reins. She widened her smile and he flushed. Even now, he acted more the servant than her equal. How could she have imagined that he would regard her any differently? Though his admiration shone in his eyes, it was for something out of his reach, but nonetheless attractive.

She reached down and touched his hand. "Davey. It is good to see you. I'm sorry I was so long in coming. With the new babe… well I just got caught up in it all."

He waved a hand. "You've no need to give apologies to me. I understand that you're busy and would see me when you could."

She nodded and gave a sad smile. He was too good really. With his hand to steady her horse, she dismounted quickly and gave him a quick hug and turned to greet his mother.

"Margaret, you're keeping well?"

"I am, mistress. Won't you come in for a jug of ale and a bite tae eat?"

"I would if I could, and thank you well for it, but I must return soon. I just needed a quick word with Davey, if you don't mind."

The spare woman nodded. "Of course. I'll leave you be and go back to my spinning. This new crop of wool looks to be fine and soft and will make some lovely looking cloth."

"At your fair hands, I have no doubt it will," said Morag warmly.

The woman withdrew, the door remaining open to provide some much needed light, whatever task she undertook. It was only out of politeness' sake that she'd mentioned spinning, for Morag could see the chair and spinning wheel there outside the back of the house where she would have the best light.

Morag tied her pony to the gate and turned to Davey. "Shall we take a walk up the track?"

He smiled and nodded. She could see that he was a little nervous, uncertain what she had come to talk to him about. Well she wouldn't keep him in suspense for long. When they were only a few steps on the track, she spoke.

"I'm sure you can imagine what I've come to talk to you about."

He reddened again and looked away. "N-no. Well, I don't know exactly."

She took a deep breath and stopped drawing him to face her. "You realise that I was a young, foolhardy lass when I left here last spring. My head was stuffed with silly notions and imaginary brave deeds."

Davey scoffed. "Oh, you were brave and bonny, fearsome in a fight and the best to have onside during any battle."

She gave a short laugh. "It's kind of you to say so, but however good I was at a fight, I was too often picking them, and you know that."

"You were defending the clan's honour."

"I was doing what I imagined upheld the clan's honour, which more often than not caused more trouble and little, if any, honour."

"But I heard how you took that horse from Rory Campbell. It was grand and glorious!"

"It was silly and thoughtless, for all it did was provoke him into actions that had terrible consequences for an innocent clan member and brought shame on the clan."

He frowned and considered her words. "Maybe, but you can't lay it all at your own door. It was the Campbell mongrel who ordered the deed. Didn't even do it himself, the coward."

She placed a hand on his arm. "You don't need to defend me. I know my part in it all too well. And I have been reminded of it." Sandy's words echoed in her mind, though she tried to thrust them aside.

He looked down at her hand and she removed it. "Davey, what I'm trying to say is that I'm no longer the girl who left here." She licked her lips. "The girl who pledged her troth to you and made you do it in return. I release you from it Davey. You're free to go and woo any of the many women who I'm certain would be glad for your attentions."

He regarded her solemnly. "Mistress, you must never think that I didn't find it an honour that you would ask me, but don't for a moment think I would have held you to it. I wouldn't have dreamt of it. I knew full well that you weren't really in a mind for anything but to keep a bond here in Glen Strae. One that could ease your way at court among all those fine people until you found your place. And I had no doubt you would. Find your place there. For you're the bonniest thing ever to grace this glen."

He stopped there, his speech ended. His face reddened once again, the ruddy colouring betraying all the emotions that filled him. Morag looked at him, seeing for the first time not her young playmate, but a man. A man who was maybe wiser than she'd been, and maybe even now as well.

"You're a brave man, Davey. And a kind one too, to have put up with my antics all these years. I won't ever forget you, no matter what." She leaned up and kissed him on the cheek.

"You talk as if you'll never see me again," he said puzzled. "You're not leaving, are you?"

She gave a wry smile. "I'm not. You're right. You'll see me. I'm going nowhere." She began to retrace her steps. "I have to go back now, Davey. You will take care now, won't you?"

He nodded gently. "Of course. And you do the same. I'll see you in a few days' time when the harvesting begins."

She nodded and continued on. When she reached her pony, she released the simple knot that held the reins to the gate and mounted. With a wave she rode off, back towards Glen Strae and another day at the castle. He was right, the hay would be harvested soon. It would be Lughnasadh before she knew it and the sheep and cattle come down from the shielings. The seasons would turn once again. And so her life would be from now on. Counting the seasons. She'd waited long enough. It was past time and she knew he wasn't coming. She'd known it all along, really, and each day that had passed after the first month had only served to taunt her with the certainty of it.

She sighed and picked her way along the rugged track, careful of the rabbit holes that sometimes sprung up out of nowhere. Iain would hate it if she brought home one of his ponies lame. And she had resolved she would cause no further trouble. She'd done enough of that to last a lifetime.

Thanks to Alisdair's quick actions and cunning, nothing seemed to have come of John Dunbar's death. No one had connected her to his killing, and from what she could understand from Iain's discreet inquiries, Dunbar's death had been ascribed to those responsible for the uprising. She was grateful to Iain for discovering the outcome and for the fact that he had asked no question of her, and had added only a brief statement that he'd also heard that Sandy had returned to Stirling Castle safely. He'd also mentioned in a studied nonchalant manner that though Sandy was a good man, his current work made his life not his own. The same thing Abby had said more, or less.

The uprising had led to the sacking of many religious houses, the mob stirred by Knox's sermons in Perth and Dundee. In response, the Dowager Queen's forces had marched on Perth, but were forced to withdraw and negotiate after another reformed contingent had arrived. The arrival of the French mercenaries in Perth had caused the earls of Argyll and Munro, along with his father Châtelherault, both Protestants, to abandon the Dowager Queen in anger and join the Lords of the Congregation. By July, Edinburgh had fallen to the Protestants and the Dowager Queen had retreated to Dunbar. Eventually, in late July, just after the death of the French king and the accession of his son with Mary Stuart his Queen consort, a truce was signed which promised religious tolerance.

Morag had known Iain was glad that she was well away from court and all the events there. But most especially glad that she was away from Sandy. She'd scoffed at him for a hypocrite when he'd raised the issue about Sandy's suitability. But he'd only replied that his past experience of that former life had made him more qualified to pass judgement and protect her. It was obvious then that Abby had conferred with him, though she couldn't blame Abby for that. She knew her sister-in-law had her best interests at heart. And Morag had tried to put Sandy out of her mind. Every day, she tried. She only hoped that someday she wouldn't have to make such an effort.

She rounded the bend and descended the small ridge, her focus on the path before her. When the track levelled off she raised her head for sight of the familiar view that always filled her with joy and love for her home. Glen Strae stretched below her, a long and twisting valley that rose high to the tufted bog and moorlands, then suddenly changed character with the force of the burn that thundered down from Fionn Lairig, The White Pass, as waterfalls and cataracts from the melting snow and spring rains.

Something caught her eye in the glen. She could make out a rider following the road up to the castle. Curious, she urged her pony downwards. If she cut across the moorlands, she could meet the rider before he arrived at the castle and greet him. It would satisfy her curiosity as well as ensure his presence was welcome. She patted the *sgian dhu* at her calf. Though she'd promised herself there would be no more reiving, no more battles with her ballock and targe, dressed in Iain's old clothes, she wouldn't go abroad without some kind of protection, no matter how feeble. It made her feel better, if nothing else.

Once off the track and on the field, she moved into a gallop, covering the distance the best she could with the pony. He was sturdy and well used to the rough terrain, but his speed wasn't going to match any good horse.

She left the field and was onto the next one, avoiding a few stumpy trees. She could make out the rider's shape, now, his tall bearing, the broad shoulders with a length of tartan wrapped around them. It wasn't a tartan she recognised immediately, but she was too distant to get a clear view of the muted colours. But then the sun peered out enough and glinted off the bright bonnet that topped his head and the gold hair that curled beneath it. Her heart stuttered. She blinked again. She must be imagining things.

She urged her pony on faster, but the beast had no more speed to give and she was reduced to the gait that seemed to take forever to bring her closer to the mounted rider. She daren't shout or catch his attention in case she was wrong. In case this was all a dream, or a trick of the light.

The rider looked up, hearing her approach from the distance. He halted his horse, stared at her and then all at once kicked his horse into action and began riding towards her, a gallop that was far and away faster than her pony could ever manage. And as he approached her, the smile on her face grew until she was laughing and the tears in her eyes began to stream down her face.

He reached her and was down from his horse before she could bring her pony to a halt. The reins dropped from his hand and he grabbed her from her pony and swung her down.

"Morag, *a stor*!"

"Sandy! Sandy, Sandy," she cried, her hands on his shoulders. "You've come," she said in Gaelic.

He set her down and gathered her into his arms and kissed her passionately, his lips parting hers, probing her. She sunk into it, savouring his taste, his touch and felt her response. After a moment he withdrew a little and stared into her eyes and wiped the tears from her face with his thumb.

"Why the tears, my poppet?"

She shook her head, shyly. "Joy? I-I thought you weren't coming. That your duties to the Dowager Queen would keep you away. And that I'd given you so much trouble in the end you realised it was best to keep well away from me."

He shook his head and smiled. "How could you ever think I didn't care for you? Didn't I nearly lose my wits trying to protect you?" he said in a teasing tone.

"Perhaps, but you protected me only because you'd promised Iain and I had entangled you in my mess to such a degree."

"Nonsense," he said and kissed her on the nose. "What else could I do? I'm besotted with you, surely you must know that."

"When I first arrived at the castle?" she asked. Could he really mean it?

"Nay, ye goose, as a little devilish maid of five years."

She laughed and slapped his chest. "Ye're teasing me now."

He kissed her once again, pressing deeply, his tongue parting her lips, exploring her. His arms tightened around her, his hand moving towards her hair where he weaved his fingers in the locks that had loosened in her mad gallop.

"You were a captivating little bairn," he said when he finally ended the kiss. "But when I saw you first at the castle, so brave and bonny in your old-fashioned gown, trying to look so poised and self-possessed, I was unable to help myself, not matter how much I tried to prevent it."

She kissed him back, her joy uncontainable. This time his lips found her neck, his hands reaching inside her light cloak to her breasts, covered only by a light shift and a thin kirtle. She ran her hands along his back, to do a bit of exploring herself, wishing that his leather jerkin wasn't so thick so she could feel his muscled back and chest. She knew that she would give herself to him there and then if given half a chance. She reached down towards his breeks and heard his answering moan. He pulled away, his lids heavy, his mouth swollen with kissing.

"I'll be taking you here in the gorse bush if I don't stop now."

"I have no objection," she said breathlessly.

He shook his head. "I'll no have you that way. It'll be done as you deserve, properly, in a bed and with your kin's blessing."

She looked at him hopefully. "You've come to get their blessing?"

"Of course. What else did you think I was here for?"

She shook her head. "I didn't stop to think. I was just so glad to see you. I couldn't care less what your purpose is, only that I know that I will go with you on whatever terms are offered. I don't care what Iain says that you have your duty first to the Dowager Queen. I understand that, and I will take what little time you may have to give me."

"I would never have you on those terms."

"But Sandy, I don't care. If that's the only way I'm to have you then, so be it."

He placed a hand on her face. "Didn't you hear me, *a stor*? I will have you only with the blessing of your kin."

"But they won't approve because you must serve the Dowager Queen. Don't mind them, though. I'll go with you, regardless of what they say. I'll tell them we are handfasted. And it would be true." She gave him a coquettish look. "Didn't you agree to be handfasted to me when I was a bairn?"

He laughed and shook his head. "What am I to do with you?"

"Take me to bed, of course," she said. "As soon as possible. I believe there is a wager to be won."

He snorted. "A wager is it?"

"Well, you didn't actually bed Barbara, did you?"

He curled his lip. "You know I didn't."

"And you bedded no other since the wagers were set?"

He shook his head. "Even if I wanted to, it was too risky to bed anyone in the castle. Not with my disguise."

She giggled. "Oh. Of course. Trust you to make it into a sport." She patted his stomach. "Well the belly is gone now, but I'm still determined to win the wager." She leaned up and began to kiss him again, one hand sliding into his hair to thread her fingers through the locks and tighten her hold. She pressed her body along his and felt his response. He succumbed to her advances, his soft groans sounding against her ear as he kissed her neck once again, sucking and biting playfully, until eventually he pulled away.

"Come, we must stop now."

She gave him a pleading look. "We could go somewhere more private. There's a copse just in yonder field."

He kissed her lightly and shook his head. "We'll go on to the castle. I can't have you arrive with half your clothes out of place and gorse flowers in your hair."

"It will be simpler if we go to the copse," she said. "I might not be able to see you alone so easily once we reach the castle. Especially if they think you'll be wanting their blessing for us to be together."

"I hope they will have no objections, *a stor*," he said. "For I have every intention of asking for your hand in marriage. To have the contracts drawn up as soon as possible."

"But I told ye that they won't give it," she said, her tone worried. "We must make a plan now, before we arrive."

"Have no worries, *mo cridhe*. All will be well. My duty to the Dowager Queen is complete and I have been released from her services. And with her blessing when I told her the reason."

Her eyes widened she struggled to take in his words. "Truly?"

He grinned at her. "Aye. Truly."

She threw herself on him and hugged him with all the joy that coursed through her body. "Oh, Sandy! I love you!"

He put his arms around her and returned her embrace. "And I love you, *a stor*. As I said, besotted from the first look at you in the castle yard."

She pulled back from him. "And I adored you when I saw you as a young maid, like the god you were. Like the god you are."

He snorted. "Hardly that."

She grinned and placed a hand on his chest and his groin. "A warrior of godlike proportions."

"Well, as to that, you've yet to see what my proportions are, but hopefully it won't be long until that time comes." He grabbed her hand. "Come now. Back on your pony and we'll go meet with your family. Time's a wasting."

She smiled and with a joy she never thought would come to pass, she mounted her pony and once Sandy was safely mounted followed him back to the castle, the first step on her new and exciting life with him.

EPILOGUE

*M*orag felt the strong clasp of his hand and arm encasing hers as she looked into his eyes. They were filled with as much joy and love as she felt and she bit her lip, trying not to smile and laugh at what was supposed to be a solemn moment. The priest stood before them intoning the blessing, her father by his side, ready to speak the words of binding that would unite her to Sandy.

A sudden squeal sounded and Morag turned her head to see Abby among the large gathered group shushing Arbella who, at a bouncing six months old, wriggled in her mother's arms. Iain grinned at Morag, a look of pride on his face. "A Highland cry of approval," he mouthed. Alisdair nudged him, his face full of mock disapproval that softened when he looked over at Arbella. He'd surprised Morag by becoming a doting uncle and playing and teasing Arbella at every opportunity. Probably glad he wasn't the youngest for a change, thought Morag.

She was glad he was home, though. He'd been surprisingly kind when she'd first arrived back at Glen Strae after leaving Stirling. It had been as if they had both realised the other wasn't as young as they had always seemed in their mind. And now, after a brief sojourn back in Edinburgh Alisdair had returned, finished with his studies and helping Iain and his father. Even in the months since court Alisdair had filled out even more, becoming almost the blond version of his brother with all his work around the land, and even more surprising, practice with the sword. The events at Stirling seemed to have produced another side to her brother. He still had his priggish and bookish moments though. She recalled when he corrected Sandy over some point of literature and then attempted to best him with the sword a while later. Sandy had merely looked amused both times.

As if sensing her thoughts, Sandy gave her arm a playful squeeze and she grinned at him. She couldn't wait until the words of the contract were spoken and they could get down to the celebration. She glanced at her father, who was glaring at the priest himself. The priest, oblivious, droned on. She looked back at Sandy and he crossed his eyes. She suppressed a giggle. Instead she moved forward slightly and stepped on his toe, her skirts covering the offending move. Her shoes were sturdy enough, she would change to dancing slippers later, but she knew they would make little impact on Sandy's thick leather boots. Still, his eyes widened at her touch and a wicked gleam came into his eyes. She would pay for this later. She raised her brows and cocked her head slightly in reply. His mouth twitched so slightly, the beard making it nearly impossible to see.

No longer oiled and combed within an inch of its life, the beard was nearly as fair as Sandy's hair, which gleamed from the light of the window behind them. He looked so alarmingly handsome today in his black and silver doublet and slops, a length of tartan pinned crossways across his chest and shoulder. No handkerchief in sight. Every inch the Highlander he was.

Members of his clan were here, come to witness the contract and enjoy the celebration. His sister, Elisabeth, was among them, his only sibling and close relative now that both his parents were dead. Elisabeth was older than Sandy and several times a mother, but she had greeted Morag warmly when they met yesterday for the first time. She would get to know his sister more when they travelled back to his lands, for Elisabeth had married into a Ross clan nearby to the Munro lands, far north of here.

The priest finally finished his blessing after an impatient and rather loud huff from her father. The blessing finished, her father spoke the words of contract. He only re-iterated a summary of what had been formally agreed and spoken of the day before, with Sandy and her father signing and the rest of the family members from both sides as witnesses.

With the formalities completed, her father invited all to feast with them and gave the clan cry. The gathered group answered the cry several times. Then Sandy shouted his own cry in reply and they all shouted it in response. The feast had begun.

MORAG STOOD IN THE STARLIGHT, gazing up at the sky and wiped her brow. It was crisp and cool in the clear Autumn night. There was no moon but the stars were bright and behind her the torches blazed in the great hall. She breathed deeply, hot from the dancing. Sandy had lifted her high and swung her hard and she had matched his steps with energy and joy. But now she needed a moment to cool down and savour the day and the night to come. She didn't know if she could be able to contain all the happiness that filled her at this moment. It seemed to want to burst from her like a fountain. She finally had her Sandy. Honourably and with the blessing of all whom she loved. How could they not like Sandy, though?

She'd been more nervous about his family and what they would think of her past exploits. Sandy's uncle, Duncan Munro, who had escorted Elisabeth and represented the Munro clan as the nearest kin to Sandy had merely laughed when Iain had teased her about her exploits in front of him. "He'll finally have met his match, then," was the only comment Duncan had when he finished laughing. Elisabeth had only smiled, shaken her head and said "what was one more bairn to look after anyway?" That had gotten a smart remark from Sandy, to which Elisabeth had only tutted. It had reminded Morag of her own relationship to her brothers. The interaction had caused Iain to roar with laughter, as if to prove the point.

"Are you tired, quean?" asked Iain in Gaelic, coming up behind her.

She turned and smiled at him. "Not at all. Just hot. I came to cool down a bit. The autumn air is fresh but it's a clear night and not to be missed."

Iain chuckled. "I think you'll be missing most of it the way Sandy's been looking at you all night. Like he wants to gobble you up on the spot."

She slapped his arm and laughed. "Ah and you yourself are always looking that way at Abby, so don't making as if you're the innocent."

Iain grinned at her. "I wouldn't dare. I have a child that now belies any innocence in the matter."

"And a child more beautiful you couldn't ask for," said Morag, picturing Arbella earlier stuffing her face with marchpane. "I will miss her."

"I know you will," said Iain softly. "But you'll come often to visit. You are her favourite aunt, after all."

She elbowed him in the ribs. "I'm her only aunt."

"But still favourite." He put his arms around her and drew her in for a hug. "Don't worry little sister. No one could ever forget you, nor ever want to."

She squeezed him back. "I'll just have to make sure of that."

He pulled back and studied her, a twinkle in his eyes. "Do the Munros realise what they're taking on?"

"A wonderful wise and beautiful woman," said Sandy from behind them. He stepped forward and put a hand on Iain's shoulder. "And they count themselves lucky to have secured her for the clan."

Morag broke away from Iain and went to Sandy, who put his arm around her waist, kissing the top of her head.

"I guess you know what you're getting into," said Iain, laughing. "I've warned you enough and you have enough experience yourself. It's the rest of the Munros I was wondering about."

She slapped his arm again. "Enough. I know how I've behaved in the past and it's done. I'm a reformed woman." She looked up at Sandy. "Truly."

He kissed her nose. "You know it's you I love, reformed or not."

Iain lay a hand on Sandy's shoulder. "I know you'll keep her safe, whether she is reformed or not. And that's the main thing. I couldn't have wished for a better husband for my sister. My only sister." He gave him a meaningful look. "My treasured sister."

Sandy looked at Iain, his eyes twinkling again. "Never fear, brother. Your threat is understood." He paused, his expression serious. "And unnecessary."

Iain nodded, the brief tension in his face and grip on Sandy's shoulder easing. "I know you will." He straightened and nodded to the both of them. "I'll leave you both, now. I'm sure you're eager to go to your marriage bed and are in need of some time to yourselves for a taste of things to come."

Morag found herself blushing at his words as he came up and gave her a big kiss and hug along with a few murmured endearments before he left. But her blushes and thoughts were soon swept away when Sandy took her fully in his arms and began to raise a different sort of blush from her.

After a long and lingering kiss, he raised his head from hers. "I know you'll miss your family and I want you to know that I will do everything I can to ensure you get to visit them as much as possible. And they know they're always welcome to visit us."

She smiled at him. "I know. I'm happy to go with you, as I've always said, wherever it is you need to go. But I will miss them. And I'll miss watching Arbella grow and change. But it can't be helped."

He squeezed her gently. "Hopefully it won't be long before we have bairns to watch grow and change."

She smiled shyly at him. "I'd like that."

He leaned down and kissed her again, this time taking it slowly, exploring her lips thoroughly, their tongues meeting. She sighed into it, feeling herself respond, her body coming alive as his hands wandered along her body and aroused her more. He pulled back.

"Shall we go and make a start on our family now?" he asked, his eyes dark with desire. "We'll slip away up to our chamber."

"You don't think they'll notice?"

He shook his head. "I count on you to know how to slip past them, for aren't you practised at sneaking out of the castle? This is only a matter of sneaking into it. Surely that's easy enough."

"Well I have much incentive, my lord," she said batting her eyes. "So how could I fail?"

"How could you indeed?" he said. He took her hand. "Lead on, *mo cridhe*."

She laughed and started forward, eager to get to their marriage bed and start their life.

If you have enjoyed this book please post a review. It helps so much towards getting the book noticed.

Review link for Goodreads: If you enjoyed the book it would be so helpful and much appreciated if you could review it:

https://www.goodreads.com/book/show/55575656-high land-lioness?from_search=true&from_srp=true&qid=ZY5lzx peB7&rank=1

Reviews for other outlets: https://books2read.com/u/ 4DWvKD

Read the excerpt of *The Hostage of Glenorchy* at the end of this book, volume 1 of the Highland Ballad Series which features Abby.

To read volumes 1-3 (Abby's story):

The boxed set:

https://books2read.com/u/3nWRWR

The Hostage of Glenorchy

https://books2read.com/u/3n05P4

The Mists of Glenstrae

https://books2read.com/u/49xorM

The Braes of Huntly

https://books2read.com/u/49xorM

HISTORICAL NOTE

During the time of this novel, Scotland was in tumult. King James V had died when Mary Queen of Scots, his daughter, was days old and, as his only living child, Mary became Queen. Her uncle, the Earl of Arran (later the Duc de Châtelherault) was appointed Regent, much to the dismay of Mary's mother, Mary of Guise. The Earl of Arran was weak and a poor enough soldier. The Scottish lords and chiefs, used to years of exercising their authority, argued among themselves, vied for greater power and manipulated Arran while Scotland's borders were constantly overrun by soldiers of King Henry VIII. Mary of Guise decided the best course of action to counter this issue was for Scotland to form an alliance through a marriage of her daughter to the heir to the French throne. Many Scots were against such an alliance, fearing that the French would annex Scotland. When Mary was five, a treaty agreeing to the marriage was signed and Mary went to live in France, at the French court. The lords, the Earl of Arran, the French and Mary of Guise continued to plot, quarrel and vie for power in the following years.

The Guise family were based in the French province of Lorraine and were very powerful. Mary/Marie of Guise married

King James V of Scotland. Her father was the Duke of Guise and her uncle the Duke of Lorraine. Marie's daughter, Mary, became Queen of Scotland as a newborn, after her father's death on the battlefield. At this time Marie of Guise's father had died and her brother assumed the title of Duke of Guise and together with her other brother, the Cardinal of Lorraine, were highly influential at the French court. On the death of her husband Marie of Guise became the Dowager Queen and her powerful family negotiated for Marie's daughter Mary to be raised in the French court with a view to Mary becoming the bride of the heir to the French throne

The Dowager Queen's influence and power grew and she employed a policy directing various regional lords to settle dispute in their areas, rather than interfere personally. That directed blame away from the crown, but it wasn't always successful. After some careful planning she became the Regent for Mary and took the reins of government.

As more of the Lords converted to the new faith the Dowager Queen tried to follow a path of toleration, permitting both Protestant and Catholic services to continue side by side. Her goal was not religious uniformity but to keep her daughter Mary recognised as Queen and in control of the country. Neither side was content and both sides wanted more. The Catholics wanted a crack down on heresy and the Protestants wanted an over-throw of the ancient religion and an end to the alliance with France. In 1558 the Protestant Lords formed themselves into a group called the Lords of the Congregation. James Stewart, James V illegitimate son, (later the Earl of Moray) didn't immediately join the group. With Mary Tudor on the English throne there was no external power to promote their cause, but with her death and Elizabeth's ascension to the throne in November 1558 there was hope of support. John Knox was invited to return to Scot-land at their invitation in November 1558.

In January 1559 Protestants pinned to the doors of the Scottish friaries copies of a document known as 'The Beggars' Summons,' warning the friars that they must give up all their property to the poor and infirm not later than Whitsunday Term (end of May).

On 2 May John Knox arrived in Scotland after years of exile. The Dowager Queen knew as the day of the summons approached she had to take action. She could not allow her authority to be challenged any further. She changed her previous policy of toleration and moved against the Protestant preachers, planning to have them outlawed and exiled. Their supporters flocked to their side, intending to accompany them to Stirling. This was the last thing she wanted so she sent John Erskine of Dun to persuade them to stay where they were. She then had the preachers outlawed in their absence.

Knox meanwhile began a series of inflammatory sermons. He went first to Dundee and then moved on to Perth. There, on 11 May he preached a sermon that roused his congregation to violent action, smashing the interior of the church and then moving on to the town's friaries, destroying looting and driving out its occupants.

The Dowager Queen (Regent) summoned Châtelherault despite the fact that the Duke's previous Protestant sympathies were well known and it was rumoured he was going to declare himself for the Lords of the Congregation. She managed to convince him to go with her to meet the rebels that were now amassing in Perth as an army. Taking her Scots and French soldiers she travelled there, despite feeling extremely unwell, and discovered that the opposing force was too large. She was forced to negotiate and an uneasy agreement was reached on 29 May. It lasted only a little while and soon Protestant sympathisers were once again ransacking friaries and cloisters. The soldiers of the Lords of Congregation began to march and entered Edinburgh in July, where the Dowager Queen had been staying, eventually seizing authority there. The Dowager Queen fled. An eventual uneasy peace was reached in August after Henry II in France died and Mary Queen of Scots' became Queen of France when her husband, Francis, ascended to the throne and French aide was promised to the Dowager Queen. This broke down as Protestant resentment of the French soldiers grew. Châtelherault accepted leadership of the Lords of the Congregation and led a force against the Dowager Queen that was later supported with an English force sent by Elizabeth I following the Berwick Treaty between the Lords and Elizabeth. Eventually in June 1560 the Dowager Queen died at Edinburgh Castle while she was still trying to fortify the castle.

The rivalry between the MacGregors and the Campbells is based on fact. Originally the MacGregor holdings stretched from Glenorchy in Argyll to Perthshire. They claimed descent from Grogar, a son of Alpin and they had the motto, 'Royal is my name.' But their lands bordered the Campbells who in the late 15th century used every possible legal and illegal means and various representations to the king to encroach on larger and larger tracts.

ACKNOWLEDGMENTS

As usual I owe a great debt of thanks to my alpha team of readers, especially Jean, Jane and Babs. I am especially indebted to musician and Gaelic speaker Niall Gordon who helped me out with some particularly wonderful words. Any mistakes are my own and from my faulty understanding. Also I want to thank my fantastic editor, Sandra and my wonderful cover designer, Jane Dixon-Smith whose wonderful creative genius have gone a long way to help make my books a success.

I also want to thank my wonderful readers whose support down the years have help make my writing such a wonderful experience.

AUTHOR'S NOTE

Originally from Philadelphia, Kristin Gleeson lives in Ireland, in the West Cork Gaeltacht, where she teaches art classes, plays harp, sings in a choir and runs two book clubs for the village library. She holds a Masters in Library Science and a Ph.D. in history and for a time was an administrator of a large archives, library and museum in America. She also served as a public librarian in America and in Ireland.

Kristin Gleeson has also published *The Celtic Knot Series* and *The Renaissance Sojourner Series*. A free e novelette prequel, *A Trick of Fate* is available free online. In addition to her novels a biography on a First Nations Canadian woman, *Anahareo, A Wilderness Spirit*, is also available.

If you have enjoyed this book please post a review. It helps so much towards getting the book noticed.

If you go to the author website and join the mailing list to receive news of forthcoming releases, special offers and events you'll receive an e novelette *A Treasure Beyond Worth* a **FREE prequel novelette** and its ebook novel *Along the Far Shores*

www.krisgleeson.com

Music is a big part of Kristin's life and many of the books have music connected to them. Listen to the music while you read- go to www.krisgleeson/music and download the files. Keep checking back as more pieces will be added to the library in the course of time.

THE HOSTAGE OF GLENORCHY
BOOK ONE OF THE HIGHLAND BALLAD SERIES

KRISTIN GLEESON

AN TIG BEAG PRESS

CHAPTER 1

The day had started out for Abby as an ordinary day, one that seemed bothered only by donning yet again the dreary grey underdress and brown kirtle with the squirrel collar that was the legacy of her widowhood. Even the press of the stomacher against her chest, which created little mounds where she'd hardly any, had failed to elicit a smile and pull her from her lethargy.

Things began to go awry when the noon hour had passed and her father still hadn't emerged from his bedchamber into their little sitting room, where she now sat staring at the closed door. Her temper flared as it hadn't since she'd left the royal court two months before.

Still up to his old tricks, she thought. No thought for his reputation at all. She banged on the bedchamber door and paused a moment to listen for sounds of stirring inside. She'd no idea if there was anyone in there with him, but at this point she didn't care. He'd only an hour before he was meant to play for the Scots Queen and one hour was hardly time enough, if he wasn't sober.

She banged again. Hearing nothing, she threw the door open impatiently and scanned the room. The large wooden shutters were closed against the light and the oak wood panelling made the room even darker. Still, she could see the bed hangings were pulled back and the bed clothes were a mess. One of the sheets was bundled up in a ball and the silk brocade coverlet was in a heap on the floor. There was no sign of her father. *Merde.*

She went over to the coverlet, picked it up, and laid it on the bed to give herself something to keep her hands busy while she thought about what to do. It was useless to curse him, really. She'd learned that long ago. Since her mother had left all those years before, her father had rather play tunes on some woman's quim than on the lute that had brought him fame. She gave a sour smile at the thought of her father hearing that remark.

The covers straightened, she looked around. There, just tossed in the corner was his lute. She picked it up and ran her hand along its smooth belly. It was so much nicer than the one she had. It was older, and the wood more seasoned, which was what gave it its rich, full sound, and all eight courses of strings rang out beautifully. She sighed and moved to the small chest at the end of the bed and sat down, unable to resist the opportunity to play it.

She ran her fingers over the strings and picked out a simple piece on it and followed it by another, more complex one, that her father had composed and she loved. When she'd finished, she sat there for a few moments, the lute in her lap. Where was he? Warming the bed of one of the Scots Queen's ladies? Surely he'd had all of them by now. Perhaps he'd started with Queen Catherine's ladies. Well, whoever it was, knowing would do nothing to help the situation now.

She looked down at the lute and plucked a string absentmindedly. Perhaps she could play in her father's stead. If she took her place in the minstrel's gallery before anyone arrived, no one would be the wiser. She could play almost as well as her father could. It was just a private meal for the Scots Queen and ladies and a few guests from Scotland. It was for that reason that Queen

Mary had specifically asked for her father to play. As a Scot he knew the pieces from home and many of his compositions were created in the distinct Scottish style.

She gave herself no more time to think of reasons against the idea, because she knew there were too many. Quickly, she placed the lute in the leather bag and snatched up a bundle of music her father had left on the floor. She was along the corridor and stepping lightly down the stairs before she came across the small and pasty-skinned Madame de Parois, Queen Mary's governess. Except for a few stray strands, an expensive gold net encased her wiry hair and it flashed in the light, almost as a warning. Another accessory no doubt wrangled out of the young queen.

"Where are you going in such haste, Madame de Villier?" Madame Parois asked. Her prim mouth was drawn in a thin line.

"To meet my father," she said. "He's due to play for Queen Marie shortly and he asked me to bring his lute and music for him." There was little the old crow could find to argue with in those words.

Madame Parois nodded and let her pass. "Your father mustn't be late. The Queen would be displeased."

Abby curtseyed quickly. "Of course not, Madame. If I am not detained, I should be there with time to spare." She sped off before the governess could say another word.

She slipped inside the room and climbed the stairs to the minstrel's gallery, thankful that no one else had disturbed her journey to this room. Below her, the large table that ran the length of the room was laid with silver plateware, ready for the feast. Thick and expensive woven aras hung on all the walls, adding warmth as well as beauty. A moment later, one of the servants entered and brought in a second pair of candlesticks. She ducked down low on the stairs, thankful that the wood that panelled the staircase hid her from view.

The servant vanished after a few moments and she was able to make her way up the rest of the staircase to the safety of the gallery. Here the carved screens would keep her relatively hidden from view. It would have been impossible to play in her father's place without them.

She placed the lute and the music pieces on a chair and positioned a wooden music stand in front of one of the chairs that lined the small gallery. She sat down and breathed a sigh of relief. Carefully, she withdrew the lute from its leather bag and leaned it against the wall so she could organise the music on the stand.

Below her, the door opened once again. Thinking it a servant, she continued to shuffle the music in front of her until the voices caught her attention. She froze.

"We maun be quick. They will arrive soon." The voice spoke low, but she could tell it was female. She leaned forward. It was one of Queen Mary's ladies speaking English with a man she didn't recognise. Foreign, by the look of him.

"The plans have changed. Abduction was ruled out. It must be poison."

"Poison! No," she whispered loudly. "I will not agree to that. They will not agree to that. I am no traitor. Besides, it was tried it before and failed."

He took her arm and squeezed it hard. "It is not for you to decide."

Nom de Dieu, what had she got herself into? Abby pulled back from the grill. Her sudden action knocked the music stand, and the sheets that had been neatly aligned a moment before spilled from it the floor. The stand followed suit, but Abby managed to catch it before it hit the floor. Still, the noise was made and the two figures looked up to the gallery.

"What was that?" said the man. "I heard a noise."

"I'm sure it's nothing."

Abby crouched in her place, not moving a muscle. There was nowhere to go. No convenient door from the gallery directly to a corridor. There was only the stairs down to the room below. Moments passed, but it seemed forever.

"Perhaps you're right," said the man, but there was doubt in his voice. "We'll speak more about this later."

The two left, but it was ages before Abby could hardly allow herself to exhale. She remained crouched down by the stand, until a good while later the door opened again and more servants entered, on this occasion with the steward leading them. It was time to begin playing.

SHE DIDN'T KNOW how she managed to play all those hours as the meal dragged to a close. The second pavane went badly and she could only be thankful that everyone was seated and dancing was impossible. It wouldn't reflect well on her father, but she didn't care. She just wanted to make it to the end and return to the safety of her father's apartment as soon as possible.

When all the guests had departed, she quickly packed up the lute and rolled up the precious sheets of music and made her way down the stairs. At the bottom she glanced around, half afraid someone might be there and recognise her. But this time luck was with her, if you could call it that after all she'd been through, and she manage to escape out of the room and down the corridors to the stairs that would take her to the next level, where her father's rooms were situated.

Once inside her father's chambers, she heaved a sigh of relief. Her knees started to shake. She knew it was the reaction from the scare she'd had and she looked around the room for the flask of wine her father usually kept handy to help calm her nerves. It was missing. She stared at the closed door of his bed chamber. A huge tide of fury rose swiftly within her.

She marched over to the door, flung it open and saw her father propped on the bed next to one of Queen Catherine's ladies, his head buried in her bare breasts and his hand pushed up her skirts, plying away between bare thighs. His doublet lay tossed on the chest, his shoes scattered beside it. She could see the wine stains on his fine linen shirt. His honey-coloured hair was like a halo around his head.

"You whoreson!" she said in English.

He looked up at her and his blue eyes regarded her languidly. "And that would make you a whore's son's daughter," he responded, in the same language, though there was still a hint of the Scottish burr in his deep rich voice.

The woman gave a titter that served only to make Abby angrier. She switched to French. "I've just come from playing your tunes on your lute to save your skin. Don't ask me why."

"Then I won't, of course," he said.

"Oh, but your music so beautiful, Calum," the lady said. Abby couldn't remember her name, except that she was one of the Queen's dangerous inner circle.

"Well, my father certainly knows your tune," she said.

She swept in, grabbed the flask and the empty goblet beside it and left, slamming the door behind her. She marched to her own little room, closed the door, sat down on the bed, and started pouring. It was a while later before the tap came. Had she been expecting it? Of course she had. She felt dizzy with the amount and speed of the drink she'd taken.

"Abby, are you in there?" Only he called her 'Abby.' He'd shortened it from her full name, 'Gabrielle,' when she was young. After her mother left.

"Of course I am," she said, her words slurred.

"Will you let me in?"

"It's not locked. Not that that would stop you. I've heard you can spirit yourself into any woman's room." She gave a shaky laugh.

Her father entered and came to sit beside her on the bed. He reeked of wine and sex, but then her own breath probably could knock over a horse.

He took her hand and folded it in his. "What's wrong, Poppet? This isn't like you." He scanned her face. "Are you breeding?"

She snorted. "All your years at court, and experience with women, and you can't find a less coarse way of asking such a question?"

He gave her a grin. "Ah, come now, *mo cridh*, you know I am at heart a stinking Scots barbarian."

She couldn't help herself, she laughed at the reference most Frenchman made when out of earshot of the Scots Queen. The laugh made her hiccup. She tried to take a deep breath to clear them, but to no avail. Her father rubbed her back and her hiccups turned suddenly to tears, all the day's events suddenly overtaking her.

"Whatever it is, it will be all right. I promise you."

He took her in his arms and she allowed herself a few minutes to cry before she pulled away and grabbed for a square of linen to wipe her eyes.

"If only you were right, Dada," she said, using the long forgotten pet name.

"Och, dinna fash yourself, sweeting. Tell me what it is. If it's a babe, we can look after it here, nae matter what the de Villiers say." His accent had come back broad and heavy, a sure sign he was under stress.

She looked up at him puzzled.

"Or if ye prefer the de Villiers can have the babe and we'll say nae more about it once it's gone."

"I'm not pregnant," she said in a firm voice. That problem was a separate matter entirely and she didn't want to discuss it now, especially not with her father.

"Then what is it?"

She took a deep breath. "I overheard something today. When I was up in the gallery, preparing to play."

"Whatever you heard, Abby, I swear on my mother's life it's not true," he said hastily.

She frowned at him. "It had nothing to do with you. It was about the Queen. At least I think it was."

"Och, there's always talk about the Queen. It's best to pay nae mind to it and keep your mouth closed. Which Queen?"

"Your Queen. Our Queen," she corrected herself. Who was her Queen? Her mother was French, but her mother was missing. She lived in the French royal court, but in Queen Mary's service. "It wasn't gossip, Father. It was serious. A man, a Scottish man, and one of Queen Mary's ladies, talked briefly about abduction and poison."

"Tell me exactly what they said." His tone was severe, all joking manner vanished.

With care she described the scene and relayed the words exactly as she could. After she'd finished her father sat for a while, saying nothing.

"Do you think I'm right?" she asked.

"What is it ye think?"

"That it concerns Queen Mary."

He patted her hand. "I'm sure ye were mistaken. Either in the content of the words or their meaning. Ye maun put it out of your head. Ye're much too young tae be worrying about such things like treason and poison. I'm sure it was nae more than idle chat about something innocent."

"I know I didn't mistake what I saw and heard." She could hear the stubborn tone in her voice. The wine had fuzzed her mind so she couldn't find an argument to convince him. "I'm a widow, Father. I am old enough to know what I saw."

"Ye're only eighteen, and still my daughter, and I say ye'll forget about it." His tone was playful but she could still hear the edge in his voice. He leaned over and tickled her. "And ye're still young enough that I can tickle ye until you cry for mercy."

She straightened, and with all the dignity she could muster, spoke. "I am most certainly too old to be tickled." She hiccupped and giggled. He laughed and she joined in, not certain why. The two shared the laughter until he stopped and he spoke again, his handsome face serious once more.

"Since you keep reminding me you are a widow and eighteen, I've been meaning to tell you that I've arranged for you to go to Scotland for a while."

"Scotland? But why Scotland, why now?"

"I think it's time you lived among Scots. Learn first-hand about the Scots blood that runs in you."

"Are you coming?"

"You know I have to remain here. I'm the Queen's Scots musician. Her lute player, her touchstone of music from her homeland."

"I don't understand."

"I want you to feel that Scotland is your homeland, that it's part of you."

"But it is part of me. Aren't we speaking Scots English? And I can play the Scots music just as well as you."

"Aye, ye can play the music fine enough, but ye've nothing of the language," he said, allowing his Scots burr free reign. He looked her in the eyes. "Now listen here to me. There will most likely come a time when Queen Mary will return to Scotland and we'll go with her. I want you to be well acquainted with Scottish custom and the language when that time comes. It could be important."

She saw the earnestness in his eyes and the soundness of his arguments. She sighed. "Alright. I'll go. When?"

"As soon as possible."

"What?"

"Ye'll go to the Laird of Glenorchy at Kilchurn Castle. I'll give ye a letter for the steward arranging it all. The laird's wife is not a well woman and needs a companion. It's perfect. I'll arrange to have someone take ye there. Ye'll leave tonight."

"Tonight? That's so soon. I can't possibly be ready by then."

"Get one of the servants to help. Margaret, she'll do it."

She rose and rolled her eyes at Margaret's name. "I think I can manage without one of your doxies."

He slapped her backside. "Nae more of that language. I raised ye better than that."

She smiled but raised a warning finger. "I'll do what you say, but you have to let me take one of the lutes with me."

He pulled a face. "Fine. You can take the mandora. Its cherry wood makes for a sweet sound."

She frowned, but refused to pout. It was the lute on which she'd learned, but it wasn't as nice as the one she'd played this afternoon. Still, she would take what she could get.

She dreaded this journey and the destination. There was little she could say about her Scots side. Her father hadn't been very forthcoming and she knew only that he was a Gordon and had no family left. There were plenty of Gordons about, she knew, but her father claimed no relationship to any of them. So who was this Laird of Glenorchy? She'd never heard her father mention him before and had no idea who his wife was or what she was like. And she had little faith in her father's reassurances about the conversation she'd overheard.

A companion to a sickly woman. The idea held little appeal for her, she had to confess, though there was a chance that she might find opportunities to play for the woman. Perhaps she could convince the laird to let her play with the musicians, if he had them in his household.

The more she considered it, the less she liked the idea of being a companion to a sour old woman. It was bad enough here at times with all the petty squabbling over Queen Mary's discarded clothes and trinkets. She'd served some of these ladies just before she got married and was loath to repeat the experience. It was one benefit of widowhood. At least until her father picked another husband for her. So far, she'd managed to avoid that, but it would come soon. Perhaps he had someone in mind in Scotland, and this was what her visit was about. Or was it worse?

Was the conversation she'd overheard as sinister as she suspected it was? She considered it again, reviewing all the words and then her father's reaction and that he had made her leave in the dead of night. All her uneasiness returned.

Later that evening, her father entered the room. The clothes she'd decided to take were neatly folded on the bed, ready to go into the chest she'd emptied. Warm clothes, mostly, for she'd heard how cold it could get in Scotland.

"Here, as you requested," her father said. He handed the lute to her. Stains from the oils of her hand had darkened the neck at the top, just before its bend. It had served her well all these years, and her skill had improved to near perfection. At least that's what her father had told her many times. She was a master in her own right.

He pulled out a folded and sealed parchment from his doublet. "I've written the letter for the steward. Ye're to give it to him when you arrive. He's directed to ask the master of music to vouch for ye as a companion for the laird's wife."

"The master of music?"

"Aye. Cormag Kerr. I knew him years ago."

"And he'll remember you."

"Aye. I have nae doubts on that."

She believed him. There were few who met her father who wouldn't recall his startling eyes and handsome face. Though her hair was more red gold than his, she had his height and slim build, but she wouldn't count herself striking like he was.

She thanked her father, took the lute and the letter from him. She placed the lute on the bed and stared at it for a long time, plans slowly taking shape in her mind. It was clear she needed to be away, safely. Perhaps she wouldn't be forced into becoming a lady's companion after all.

CHAPTER 2

"*I* was told tae meet a lassie," the man said in a broad Scots burr.

She adopted her deepest voice and infused it with as much authority as she could muster. "You were misinformed."

She could just make him out in the starlight and saw that though he was shorter than she was by a half a hand, he was much broader. Tucked inside heavy boots, he wore plaid *trews*, the loose hose of the Scots. A pungent smelling fur skin was draped across his shoulders, atop the shirt and plaid that wrapped his body, suggesting something primitive. She thought of the French remarks about Scots barbarians and wondered if it was closer to the truth than she had realised.

He gave a muffled "hrrumph" and pointed to the small box at her feet.

"And ye'll be takin' that as weel?"

She nodded, not trusting herself to speak if she didn't have to. A breeze stirred at the back of her neck and refused to allow any regrets for the long thick hair that used to cover it. The hair was shorn and there was no use lamenting.

She drew her father's fur lined cloak around her and made a

move to climb up into the cart. It was no use expecting help in that way, she reminded herself. The oversized boots made her passage to the seat more difficult than it would have normally, and for a moment she teetered. She caught her balance and felt the cloth that bound her breasts move. She shifted uncomfortably.

"Too much farewell drinking, laddie?"

"Aye," she said and tried to growl. "I'm not feeling very well."

"Well, lean forward a bit, and ye'll soon feel right enough." He thumped her on the back. "Ye'll get your drinkin' heid, laddie, wait and see. Ye just need more practice."

She replied with an unintelligible sound and put her head on her knees. She rode like that for some time, until the light started to appear and the cart halted. Looking up, she could see that they'd pulled into a little copse.

He jumped down from the cart. "First things first," he said with a grin. He walked over to a bush, parted the folds of his plaid and lifted up his shirt, showing his bare thighs and rump. Dick in hand, he gave a contented sigh as a long stream of urine sprayed forth. She sat there fascinated for a moment. He caught her glance.

"Have ye nae need for a piss? I'd ha' thought after all that drinkin' it would be pourin' out ye."

She paled. "I did that before I met up with you."

He nodded and said no more. It was a momentary respite. Soon, though, she would have to come up with a way to relieve herself that wouldn't cause suspicion.

He pulled out a bundle and unwrapped some bread and cheese. Reaching behind in the cart bed, he picked up a leather drinking bag. He broke off a chunk of bread and cheese, handed them to Abby, and then began to munch his own portion, crumbs falling onto his thick, dark beard. She followed suit, glad that his conversation was not governed by court etiquette.

The silence hung over them and in the end she decided to break it. "What's your name?"

"They call me Angus Dubh. Black Angus."

"Angus." She paused. "I'm Gabriel." She tried out the new version of her name for the first time, pronouncing it in the English way. It sounded strange.

"Like the angel?"

"*Oui.*"

"Ye'd be better off changing that 'oui' to an 'aye' where ye're goin', angel or no."

She knew he was right. The French response was automatic. Her tendency to slip into it reminded her that she must be on guard at all times, and not just for the language, either.

He pointed to the back. "We'll stay here for the time. Best get what sleep ye can."

She climbed into the back and tried to cushion herself against the hard boards with the cloak. She pulled her father's good silk bonnet further down over her head to fold in the soft curls that ended just below her ear. She hadn't been able to cut it as close as the fashion here dictated, but looking at her companion's long ragged hair, she concluded it hardly mattered.

"Budge over, laddie," Angus said. "Ye're tae skinny to take up all the room."

She moved over as much as she could so that her face ended up pressed against the side of the cart. The trunk was at her head, forcing her to bend her knees to her chest.

"Are ye lonesome, lad?"

"What? No."

"Then why do ye look like ye're about to make love tae the wood on that side o' the cart?"

"I just wanted to make enough room for you, that's all," she said.

"I'm nae as big as yon tree. I've plenty room now."

She eased herself over a small bit and released her breath

carefully as Angus shuffled himself into position and pulled his animal skin tight around him. A minute later she could hear loud snores coming from beside her.

She reached inside her doublet and checked once again that the letter her father had written was there. The changes she'd made had been hasty, but she had managed to scrape off the ink that stated the important words and change them for the ones suited to her plans. The rest would take care of itself, she hoped.

SHE SPEWED ONCE MORE into the pot. Her stomach was churning and though she was certain it contained nothing more, there was no convincing her body. She retched again, but there was no result. Her eyes were watering and her nose was running. She was a sight.

Angus stood patiently by the stool where she sat, a wet cloth in his hand.

A rumbling lower down told Abby that her body was trying going to try and empty its other end, at short notice. She glanced desperately at Angus and wondered how she was going to manage to open her bowels in his presence.

"Please," she muttered hoarsely, "I need to use the pot."

He gave her a queer look. "I'd say ye're doing a handsome job of using the pot already."

She reddened. "Not in that manner. I mean..." she glanced downwards.

Angus's face cleared. "Och, ye mean ye need to take a shit and ye want me tae go. Why didn't ye say so?"

He gave chuckle and left the cabin. Abby jumped off the stool, tore at her clothes and planted herself on the pot. She gave no thought at that moment to what Angus might make of her request. It was only later, after he'd returned, that she tried to think of a reason for her actions. Her stomach was still unsettled, but she felt more at ease than she had since they'd left Calais port the night before.

"I appreciate all your kindness, Angus," she said. "I'm sorry I'm so much trouble. You must excuse my fastidiousness before in asking you to leave. I-I just wasn't well."

"Wheesst," he said. "I'd nae expect anything different from a *Francach.*

That was her answer. She was a *Francach.* Too fussy to relieve herself in front of anyone else. Her excuse to protect her privacy so that she could conceal her identity was as easy as that.

THE HORSES PICKED their way along the rutted track, splashing mud from the spring rains high enough to reach the soles of her boots. The rain had ceased an hour ago and a watery sun hung in the sky, making the wet trees glisten. She could see her breath every time she exhaled. It was hard to believe that it was May here, the air was so cold and damp. In addition to her chilled bones, her backside was bruised and sore and her toes were numb. She yearned for a warm fire.

They had landed on the Scottish coast and hired three horses with the money Angus had acquired from the sale of the cart and horse back in Calais, strapping her trunk to the back of the third horse. The cart would be impossible on the tracks where they were heading. She'd seen the truth of that in the days they'd spent travelling to Stirling, then further west on to Tarbet, where they made their way along the top end of Loch Fyne. The sight of the loch had taken her breath away, with its mountains rising tall around it and the wisp of mist that hung over it. It was an image she took with her in the damp days that followed that took them Cladich and nearer to Loch Awe and Kilchurn Castle.

They'd only spent one night a hostelry and that was at Stirling. Every other night had been out in the open after lighting a small fire and cooking whatever Angus managed to catch, or failing that, what he'd brought from Stirling. But they were near Kilchurn now, or so Angus told her.

Beside her, Angus whistled, clearly glad that his task of delivering her safely was nearly over. His journey would continue after that, and take him further into the highlands. She found herself strangely wishing that he would stay with her. At least for a few days, until she could be certain that everything would work out as she'd hoped.

"Well, angel, laddie," he said now as they rounded a bend in the track. "We're coming up to Kilchurn Castle." He pointed over to the left. "Bonny enough there by the loch, eh?"

She looked in the direction he pointed and saw a large lake before her. In the distance on the far shore stood a castle with a tall stone tower several storeys high and a one-storey south wing. Even from this distance she could see the stone work was stained from decades of exposure to the elements and God knew what else. Behind it rose a majestic mountain, its peak still bearing traces of snow. The loch and the mountains were beautiful, but she eyed the castle cautiously. The castle was imposing, considering it was in a remote Scottish area, but there was little of the splendour of the French royal residences she was used to. She sighed. This was where she would be living, at least until her father permitted her to return to Paris. Or made other arrangements.

Her unease lessened. Its remoteness gave her the assurance that it was less likely she would be found, despite lack of promised comfort.

The track opened up and she could feel the penetrating cold of the mist coming off of the lake. *Loch*, she corrected herself. As they came closer to the castle, people milled in the track, bearded men wrapped and belted in lengths of plaid draped over their shoulders or wrapped around their bodies, while others had skins that had seen better days pinned across their chests. Their legs were bare and leather shoes or wooden clogs enclosed their feet. A few other men, either soldiers or a better class of farmer, wore leather jerkins over roughly woven tunics or plaid *trews*. The women wore plaid or plain tunics woven in the same fashion that reached to their ankles. It was a motley group and they all looked up, their eyes red and rheumy, when the horses passed by.

Abby tried not to stare. It wasn't a pleasant sight to see these people in such a ragged condition, and it gave her no confidence about her new home, or the sophistication of the Master of Glenorchy. Angus's vague destination seemed more promising than this place, at the moment.

The three horses proceeded through the castle gates, passing by the tower, into the yard. The castle wing stretched on one side of the tower and overlooked the castle yard with its stables, a pen containing a small number of hunting dogs, a weaving shed, smith, and other outbuildings one side and the loch the other. A curtain wall surrounded the rest of the yard.

A small group of people was gathered around a platform in front of the stables where a man was tied to a large wooden pole. Another man, clad only in plaid *trews* and leather boots, wielded a whip against the man with force.

Angus halted some yards from the scene, but it was close enough that Abby could see the man tied to the pole was bleeding from great weals that covered his back. She winced each time she heard the whip strike him.

"Why are they whipping that man?"

Angus shrugged. "Could be any number of things. Poaching, theft."

"But the man's fainted with the pain. Surely he's had enough."

Angus looked over at her, puzzled. "It could be worse, *Francach*. Some masters'll cut off a hand, or kill man for poaching on his land. This Master's nae so bad, I'm thinkin'."

She studied the group. A woman wept silently near the platform, a young boy clinging to her skirts. The others gathered there watched silently, their faces grim. She could detect anger in a few pairs of eyes.

A young man detached himself from the group and made his way over to them. He was tall and broad shouldered and his hair hung in short dark curls around his face. She could just see the glint of an earring at one lobe. A man of some note, then, despite the denial his clothes made. He wore a soiled leather jerkin, torn in places, and roughly woven plaid belted around his waist. A ratty fur was draped around his shoulders and tucked at the waist. On his feet were wooden clogs.

He nodded to Angus. "Are ye lookin' for someone?"

"I've come to deliver yon laddie to the laird. Or rather the steward."

The young man looked at Abby and it was then she saw the sea blue eyes, fringed in lashes that any woman would envy. There was speculation in them now as he looked her up and down like she was some kind of horse for sale.

"I'm here to see the Master of Music, Cormag Kerr," she said.

The man looked back over at Angus, his brow lifted. "A *Francach*?"

"Aye, though he claims tae have Scottish connections."

"Is that so?" He tilted his head, scanning her from head to foot. "I suppose 'tis possible, given his colouring. But he's nae a brawny lad, tha's certain."

"Maybe, given time, there might be somethin' tae him," said Angus.

It had gone on long enough. "Could you please tell me where I might find Master Kerr?" she asked.

"Ye'll find Master Kerr in wi' the mistress, I'm thinking. But it's Hamish Douglas, the steward, ye'll want tae speak tae first. He'll be in the room off the kitchen." The man pointed to the small door on the south wing of the castle.

Abby nodded her thanks and turned to Angus. "Would you

mind waiting here while I check with the steward and get someone to carry my chest inside?"

"Aye, laddie, I'll wait."

She slipped off her horse, gingerly and made her way to the door, conscious of her spattered, sagging hose and the ill-fitting boots. The feather of her bonnet hung limply down along her brow and she reached up to shove it back into place. She was hardly presentable, but there was nothing she could do about that.

Once inside, she was confronted with a large room filled with smoke, heat and the strong odour of roasted meat. A large trestle table filled a good portion of the room, and around it three women worked, kneading bread dough and chopping vegetables, while two lads turned the spit containing a couple of pigs over a large fire. The fat dripped off the pigs and splashed into the fire with a sizzle. The sight and the smell of them made her stomach grumble loudly. One of the women looked up at her.

"Can I help ye, laddie?" Her face was flushed pink with the effort of kneading and her golden hair hung in a soft frizz about her face. She was comely enough for her years and her smile was warm and welcoming.

"I'm looking for the steward, Mister Douglas," Abby said.

She nodded towards the side of the room to a door. "He's in there, doin' the accounts. Hae a wee knock afore ye open it, mind. He isna fond a bein' disturbed when he's doing the countin'."

"Thank you," Abby said. She made her way over to the door, conscious again that all eyes were on her. She pulled the fur cloak a little tighter around her.

When she reached the door she gave a small knock. There was no answer. She tried again, this time louder. The door swung open wide, and a wiry figure of medium height confronted her, his grey eyes full of annoyance.

"What?" He stared at her, eyes glaring. He wore a linen shirt and a clean leather jerkin over brown *trews*, a sober enough dress for a serious man.

She sketched an awkward bow, determined to be courteous. "I've come from Paris, to join the musicians, on the recommendation of Calum Gordon, Queen Mary's lutenist. Master Kerr can vouch for me." She handed him the letter. She'd rehearsed this scene many times in her head, but she hadn't bargained for such a hostile reception. She forced a smile and tried to put in a bit of the "devil may care" look her father always used so successfully.

His annoyance turned to a scowl. "A musician, you say?" He gave that indefinable "hrrumph" she was coming to know. He took the letter she held out. "Wait here," he said and vanished inside the room and closed the door.

She stared at the door for a few moments before a voice behind her called out.

"Ye may as well sit and have a bite to eat, laddie. Ye look half starved."

She turned gratefully and saw the woman who'd spoken to her earlier gesture to a bench at the table. Abby took the seat indicated. The woman gathered up a wooden plate, a small hunk of bread, and a bowl of something indeterminate and placed it in front of Abby.

"Get some parritch in ye, now." She beamed at Abby and watched while she made a tentative gesture towards the bowl with the horn spoon. "Go on now, dinna be shy. It'll stick to your sides and ye'll find yourself more able for Himself, there in the room."

Abby forced the spoon into the mixture and drove it into her mouth. It was gooey and oversalted, but other than that, it wasn't half as bad as she thought it would be.

"How are ye called?" asked the woman. "I canna verra well call ye 'laddie,' there's too many of them around already." She glanced over at the lads by the fire, their two faces as red as their hair. One of them poked the other and got a shove in return. She could see now they were twins. She refrained from crossing herself at such an unlucky sign.

"Well? Do ye no know your own name?"

"Oh, it's Gabriel. Gabriel de Villier."

"A *Francach*. I thought as much by your accent."

"My—my mother was Scots." She caught herself in time, realizing if she said it was her father that was Scottish it would raise more questions.

"Was she now? And what was her name, if ye don't mind me asking."

"Gordon," Abby said, hoping that would cause no further questions.

"Gordon. Ah, I ken that name, all right." She glanced to the other woman beside her. "Well, ye're welcome here, Gabriel Gordon de Villier. I am Mistress Ferguson and this is Cáit and Aileen, my helpers. Over yonder are Dougal and Alex."

The door opened at that moment and Mister Douglas stepped out. He barked some orders in Gaelic and one of the twins got up and went off through the other door into the wider reaches of the castle. The steward's eyes lit on Abby and he motioned her forward, the letter still in his hand. She excused herself from Mistress Ferguson, braced herself and made her way over to steward.

The steward's expression had eased only a fraction, but it was enough for Abby to take heart.

"I've read the letter. I've sent Dougal to ask Master Kerr to join us here. We'll see then whether he'll vouch for you and your lute playing."

She nodded and tried to keep the smile on her lips. She could only hope that her father was right and Master Kerr would remember him.

～

Printed in Great Britain
by Amazon